Never WAGER WITH A *Wallflower*

OTHER BOOKS BY VIRGINIA HEATH

THE MERRIWELL SISTERS

Never Rescue a Rogue

Never Fall for Your Fiancée

The Discerning Gentleman's Guide

Redeeming the Reclusive Earl

Miss Bradshaw's Bought Betrothal

The Scoundrel's Bartered Bride

Her Enemy at the Altar

His Mistletoe Wager

That Despicable Rogue

THE WILD WARRINERS SERIES

A Warriner to Protect Her

A Warriner to Rescue Her

A Warriner to Tempt Her

A Warriner to Seduce Her

THE KING'S ELITE SERIES

The Mysterious Lord Millcroft

The Uncompromising Lord Flint

The Disgraceful Lord Gray

The Determined Lord Hadleigh

THE TALK OF THE BEAU MONDE

The Viscount's Unconventional Lady

The Marquess Next Door

How Not to Chaperon a Lady

A VERY VILLAGE SCANDAL

The Earl's Inconvenient Houseguest

His Maddening Matchmaker

Never WAGER WITH A *Wallflower*

MERRIWELL SISTERS BOOK 3

Virginia Heath

ST. MARTIN'S GRIFFIN
NEW YORK

This is a work of fiction. All of the characters, organizations, and events portrayed in this novel are either products of the author's imagination or are used fictitiously.

First published in the United States by St. Martin's Griffin, an imprint of St. Martin's Publishing Group

www.stmartins.com

Library of Congress Cataloging-in-Publication Data

Names: Heath, Virginia, 1968– author.
Title: Never wager with a wallflower / Virginia Heath.
Description: First Edition. | New York : St. Martin's Griffin, 2023. | Series: The Merriwell Sisters ; book 3
Identifiers: LCCN 2023016839 | ISBN 9781250787804 (trade paperback) | ISBN 9781250787811 (ebook)
Subjects: LCGFT: Romance fiction. | Novels.
Classification: LCC PR6108.E1753 N53 2022 | DDC 823/.92—dc23/eng/20230413
LC record available at https://lccn.loc.gov/2023016839

Our books may be purchased in bulk for promotional, educational, or business use. Please contact your local bookseller or the Macmillan Corporate and Premium Sales Department at 1-800-221-7945, extension 5442, or by email at MacmillanSpecialMarkets@macmillan.com.

First Edition: 2023

10 9 8 7 6 5 4 3 2 1

To my son Alex, who frequently makes me laugh, often
drives me to distraction, but, like every perfect hero,
never fails to do the right thing in the end.
I am so proud of the man you have become.

Never

WAGER WITH A

Wallflower

Dear diary,

Now that womanhood beckons, it is time to set aside all my childish daydreams and put some serious thought into the sort of man I want as my future husband. I would prefer a handsome one, of course, but I am not so shallow that such a triviality is the be-all and end-all. So long as he is kind, loves children (because I plan on having at least six), and is guided by the strong morals necessary to raise them right, I am prepared to overlook a plain face.

I have decided, however, that certain criteria are not negotiable. First and foremost, he must love books. Second, he must love me more than any book, no matter how marvelous the story. Finally, and in saying this I mean no disrespect to my dear papa—wherever he may be—I will not entertain a man who drinks to excess or wastes his evenings in the vile pursuit of gambling . . .

—from the diary of Miss Venus Merriwell, aged 14

Chapter One

November 1830 . . .

"Do we have an accord, Mr. Sinclair?"

As Lord Mallory was still talking to his back, Galahad wandered over to the farthest window to inspect the flaking wall and allow the silence to stretch a little bit longer. It was a tactic his grandpa had taught him back home in New York to encourage others to nervously fill the void and bare their hand.

His companion didn't disappoint.

"It would be prudent to shake on it today, Mr. Sinclair, as I doubt these impressive buildings will take long to sell on the open market."

Gal rapped the most precarious-looking crack on the wall with his knuckles and, as he had hoped, a huge chunk of plaster slipped and shattered on the floor by his feet. For good measure, he kicked the rotting piece of baseboard he had selected on purpose beneath the leaking window frame, and it instantly splintered into dust, too.

That was when he shook his head.

He didn't speak. Didn't need to. Because his wily grandpa also taught him that sometimes no words worked far better than all the clever words in the world. He didn't need to turn around to know that despite the cold, the seller was sweating as he awaited his verdict. So profusely he could almost hear it leaking from the man's pores.

"I could drop another five hundred, Mr. Sinclair, but that is my absolute limit." Which miraculously put him at the absolute top end of Gal's. "You'll be getting a steal for that price. An absolute steal. I doubt you'll find anything any cheaper in Covent Garden."

It might well be pushing the limits of his pocket, but a "steal" didn't even begin to describe it.

Three adjacent four-story town houses in the beating heart of London's pleasure capital, for just shy of six thousand pounds, was the deal of the century! Neglected empty husks they might be, but the shells were as sound as sound could be. He'd been hunting for a year for a property like this, and everything he'd seen had been smaller, twice the price, and nowhere near as well situated as this trio of matching beauties.

He had never been one for dancing, but while his expression remained blandly unconvinced, inside he was twirling pirouettes while his mind was already adjusting his original plans and drawing up new ones. Because as his canny grandpa also often said, plans, like dreams, should never be set in stone but rather allowed to shift with the tide, so a wise man kept them adaptable. Especially when the opportunity exceeded all his expectations. And boy, this did!

Three buildings! All in a row!

Five minutes in and his whirring mind knew already that he had to knock them all into one grand space. A unique theme for every floor. Music, singers, dancing girls, and a bar that never ran dry on the bottom level to attract all the fun lovers as they tumbled out of the nearby theaters. Gaming tables on the second and third floors. Affordable and raucous on two for the occasional gambler or those with limited budgets out for a good time. Higher stakes, more exclusive and intimate on three so that those serious about their wagering wouldn't have to waste time with the hobbyists. That floor would be the holy grail. Swanky and luxurious and by invitation only. Served by a separate guarded but gilded staircase that rose majestically from the lobby for all to see—but for only the chosen few to climb. Something to aspire to, because the British loved nothing more than to feel superior to their fellow men.

Or women.

He intended to buck the usual trend and throw his doors open to anyone with a purse stuffed with jangling coins. Gal didn't care who his future customers were so long as they spent their money. Never mind that putting the cat among the pigeons in the stuffy, and often suffocating, confines of English society like that also warmed the egalitarian American half of his blood.

He'd snag the entire attic for his own office and apartment because he was all done with temporary lodgings. After more than a decade of roaming, he wanted his own place. His own walls to do with as he pleased. His own décor and furniture. That sense of hearth and home, which had been missing for too long. Even the Albany, where his aristocratic cousin had somehow managed to finesse him a suite of well-appointed rooms, had too many rules and caveats for Gal's liking. And it was too constricting. Too . . . English.

Mallory's feet shuffled, his obvious impatience marking him as desperate. "I must warn you—I do have other interested parties."

Gal quashed the urge to roll his eyes and give this hapless lord a friendly lecture on the dark art of negotiation, because they both knew he was currently the only ready buyer. Mallory's widowed and childless aunt hadn't been dead more than a few days, and because she had passed miles away in her seaside house in Brighton, the news of her death hadn't yet reached the capital's newspapers, so nothing had been advertised. Never mind that British politeness dictated that any potential rival would feel duty bound *not* to inquire about the future of her extensive and lucrative property portfolio until she was safely ensconced underground.

Thankfully, not hailing from these parts had always been more beneficial than a hindrance, so he wasn't similarly afflicted, and, as the Brits were so fond of saying, the early bird always caught the worm. That's why he had taken it upon himself to call on her only nephew himself bright and early this morning, fresh from his own long and hasty journey back from Brighton last night, to be the first to offer his condolences. Then he'd hinted he might be in the market for some property in Covent Garden if Lord Mallory happened to be in the market to sell off some of his fresh inheritance. Cash, of course, because cash was always king no matter what a man's rank or nationality, and he had it on good authority that Mallory was strapped for it.

Many suspected the reckless young lord might not have two ha'pennies to rub together, a quaint English colloquialism that he loved and used often, but he knew it without a shadow of a doubt. Mallory was up to his eyeballs in debt and trouble, and with some nasty characters, too. The sort who owned the most debauched hells in the capital, which catered to the most base and hedonistic clientele. The sort who beat you to a pulp first then asked questions after. Absolutely not Gal's sort of business at all, but as gambling was his stock-in-trade, he kept his ear to the ground for just such an eventuality. Another one of his grandpa's invaluable tenets. A good businessman had to go find his own opportunities first, then make damn sure he seized them at the opportune moment before somebody else did if he wanted to get ahead.

Moments certainly didn't come more opportune than this, and for once he could not see any catch when there was always at least one. Always some fly in the ointment to spoil complete perfection and force you to grind your teeth.

"Double that and I'll shake on the deal this second." Galahad turned smiling and held out his hand even though he knew he was pushing his luck. He'd always intended to buy one big building, not three, and renovating this vast space on what was left of his budget would take some serious juggling. But fortune favored the brave, or so the old proverb claimed, and when opportunity knocked on your front door, only a fool didn't fling it open in welcome, so Gal would make this work.

No matter what it took.

Mallory blinked, then swallowed, so he knew he had won before the fellow lunged for his hand. "All right!" The relief on his face was palpable as he cranked his arm like a pump handle as if he hoped water might miraculously shoot from Gal's ears. "On the proviso that the funds will be transferred with all haste, as we discussed on the way over, Mr. Sinclair."

That the money-hungry lord had dragged Gal to Covent Garden almost as soon as he had called at the fellow's house was his first mistake; discussing the swift exchange of any fee so hot on its heels was his second, because any idiot surely knew that when you appeared too eager to sell, you lost all the power in a negotiation. That rookie mistake had turned a speculative visit by way of a rumor into something so tangible and real he could smell it, while also giving Gal all the best cards.

Which made this the perfect moment to play his ace.

"You can have it all tomorrow if your solicitor draws the papers up quick." He winked at the man, who was now practically salivating at the seductive thought of a lifeline of unexpected cash so soon. "In my experience, it is staggering how rapidly something can happen if you offer to pay a man double his usual fee." Not to mention that an expedited sale worked in Galahad's favor, too, when the truth was three adjacent four-story town houses in the beating heart of Covent Garden were also rarer than hen's teeth. The last thing he wanted was some other entrepreneurial type swooping in and stealing this sweet opportunity away after he had waited so long for it.

"Greasin' the wheels also gives me less time to come to my senses and change my mind about buyin' this rickety ruin so far away from home." Experience had taught him to over-exaggerate his accent at moments like these to highlight the sense of otherness that naturally made people wary, making sure he used enough charm to soften some of the intentional sting in his words. So he laughed as he slapped Mallory on the back, ensuring his expression showed enough ambiguous insincerity to sow the seeds of doubt that he might very well change his unfathomable foreign mind if the solicitor dallied and take his huge bundle of cash elsewhere.

With perfect timing, which he had to stifle the urge to cheer at, another precarious piece of plaster chose that exact moment to crash to the floor beside its twin, causing Mallory's eyes to widen.

"I shall pay him triple, Mr. Sinclair—and will begin the rapidest of processes this very morning." Eager to get going and get those papers drawn before the rest of the walls collapsed and his shady associates murdered him, Mallory pulled up the collar of his coat and strode toward the door. Once outside, he used an enormous rusty key to lock the building, then pocketed it before he shook Gal's hand again. "I shan't keep you, Mr. Sinclair, as I'm sure a busy man like yourself has better things to do this dour Tuesday morning than freezing to death." He gestured to the icy street and the filthy piles of slush clogging the gutters. "It's cold enough to freeze your knackers off."

Mallory scurried off to his carriage without offering him a ride back to Mayfair, no doubt already mentally divvying his windfall among his many creditors, leaving Gal standing on the steps of what he hoped would one day soon be London's biggest and brightest gaming club.

Cold enough to freeze your knackers off.

Another quirky new British saying to add to his ever-increasing lexicon of conversational oddities. Four years on since he'd crossed the Atlantic and still half the things that came out of his new countrymen's mouths both baffled and amused him. So many he collected them like curios to ponder when the mood struck, or practice when the moment called for it. People liked people like them, after all, and sometimes it paid to blend in as much as it often paid to stand out.

Besides, for better or for worse, London was home now. There was nothing left for him across the ocean except memories, and he had brought all of those with him—the good and the bad. The family business was gone. The family house he had spent his childhood in was long gone, too, and the only blood tie he had left was to his cousin Giles who was born and bred here. That had been as good a reason as any to put down roots in this strange land when he'd had nowhere and nobody else to anchor him to a place, and he still didn't regret it even if he was certain he would never fully fit in here.

But such was life and his, all things considered, was currently very good indeed.

He had enough money saved in the bank for this venture, he had a head full of plans he'd tinkered with for a decade, and now, apparently, he finally owned the property to carry them all out in. Best of all, there wasn't a single fly to be seen anywhere to sully his ointment.

Grinning, he wandered down to the street to survey his new empire properly and metaphorically patted himself on the back as he did so. It might well clear him out of every cent of his hard-earned savings, but this was an excellent location on the busy thoroughfare of Long Acre, blessed with more passing trade than he had ever envisioned. The first of his three identical new buildings on the end of the row of terraced town houses sat on the corner of Mercer Street, which would be the ideal place to have the entrance because the comings and goings of his boisterous clientele would affect none of his neighbors.

It was close enough to the Rookery of St. Giles to be disreputable without being dangerous, and near enough to Drury Lane to draw the respectable theater crowd, who did not know it yet but would be his bread and butter.

He measured out the entire breadth then length of his three properties using strides that were as close to a yard as he could get them, then did a pleasing calculation in his head confirming that he had twice as much floor space as he had originally envisioned. Which meant this place had the potential to earn him twice as much money as he had hoped, allowing him to swiftly refill the hole in his bank balance. So all in all it was perfect.

More than perfect.

Utterly perfect in fact.

After four solid years of relentless work near the bottom of the ladder he was going to climb up the damn thing, and he intended to do it in style. If there was a drawback to his purchase, or an annoying little catch somewhere beyond the enormous cost, he certainly couldn't see it.

He spun a slow circle on the boundary of the third and final house, noticing that it sat beside a fourth that occupied another corner, so he took a moment to contemplate that, too.

Although clearly occupied, this identical building wasn't in a better state than the three of his. The window frames were rotted in places where they hadn't seen a lick of paint in years. Like asymmetrical freckles on a face, many of the rectangular leaded panes within them were boarded where the glass was missing. Those mismatched splats of wood announced to the world that the owner had to count his pennies. The misaligned front door had seen better days, as had its dull brass work and dirty façade. A quick scan of the roof showed tiles to be missing and broken pots on the chimney. The more he looked, the more he saw there was an air of dilapidation about it hinting that the owner was really struggling with the place.

That made the cogs of his resourceful mind turn some more. There was another potential opportunity here—he could smell it. Not now, perhaps, as he didn't have the ready funds for another building yet—but in a year or two, when his coffers were replenished, this would be another sound investment to make an offer on. To own the whole block would be magnificent. The possibilities . . .

A carriage pulled up alongside, distracting him from his thoughts. One he recognized only too well. The door opened and a certain someone emerged, clutching one of the ever-present books she carried and the smallest, silliest little reticule he had ever seen. A bag that would barely hold a few coins, let alone anything useful, and which was completely at odds with her practical, no-nonsense character.

Just one glance his way was enough to make her simultaneously purse her plump lips and look down her nose as she inclined her head in disapproving greeting, hugging the book to her middle like a shield. "Galahad Sinclair. What on earth are you doing in Covent Garden this early in the day? Or should I not ask because *this* is Covent Garden and you are . . . well . . . *you*?" Never had one insignificant three-letter word been filled with such unsavory implication.

She was always testy with him. Always had been in the entire four years he had known her. For all that time, he had walked on eggshells around her. Never quite feeling comfortable in her presence despite her sister being married to his cousin Giles and their colliding infrequently as a result. They had never taken to each other. Always tacitly avoided much in the way of interaction. Even when they had both been made godparents to little Giselle—Giles and Diana's cute-as-a-button daughter—they had maintained a wary six feet of distance while standing at the christening font.

He blamed the way they had met, which to be fair to the both of them had been the most unconventional meeting of two people possible. One minute he had been snooping around his cousin's moonlit grounds waving a lamp, pretending to be the dumbest intruder who ever walked God's earth. The next flat on his back in the mud after being floored by a raving banshee in a nightgown screaming blue murder in the loyal defense of her family.

He didn't mind admitting she had scared the bejesus out of him that night. Still left him unsettled, truth be told, although hell would have to freeze over before he ever admitted that aloud, so he doffed his hat with the lazy smile that was guaranteed to vex her.

"Why, if it isn't the celestial Miss Venus."

Instantly she bristled, because she hated her name. Gal sympathized, because he had been saddled with a dreadful one himself. Yet while everyone else called her Vee, he couldn't bring himself to. Only part of that was because he rather enjoyed the way her big blue eyes shimmered with indignation behind the lenses of her spectacles each time he used it. The rest was because he couldn't help thinking the improper name suited her.

She certainly had the dangerous curves of a Venus. The riot of copper-gold curls, which she worked tirelessly but futilely to tame, were reminiscent of all those shameless Renaissance Venuses who cavorted naked in oil paints and hung in fancy galleries. Or like that enormous, saucy seven-foot bare-breasted Roman statue of Venus they had in the British Museum. The one that made all the ladies blush at her brazenness, because the seductive look in her marble eyes declared that she was in the midst of getting undressed for something sinful. Meanwhile, all the visiting men ogled that giant Venus in masculine appreciation. All seduced by the look in the earthy statue's eyes and wondering, as they gazed at the garments hanging from her generous hips, what an unbridled night tangled between the sheets with the official goddess of love might be like. These were all improper and carnal ideas, which the prim Miss Venus Merriwell undoubtedly hated more than her unfortunate name, because they undoubtedly gave those same gentlemen ideas about her, too.

She was unaware that her eyeglasses and demure clothes only added to her allure. Because most hot-blooded men, Gal included, couldn't help wondering what lay beneath them. Especially as her lush figure filled those plain garments so well. "What are you reading this time?" He tilted to read the title even though he had already done so.

"*Much Ado About Nothing.* It's my favorite book—well, it's technically a play really—because it has absolutely everything a good story needs. Great characters, intrigue, skulduggery, comedy, and romance." Her eyes sparkled as she stroked the well-thumbed volume like an old friend. "My sister Minerva and her husband, Hugh, had the entire works of Shakespeare leather-bound for me for my twenty-first birthday." A day he had been present for, albeit reluctantly, so he remembered her squeal of delight when she had opened their gift. "But this volume is special. I fell in love with it at fourteen and I've re-read it at least once every year since."

"Shakespeare?" Sometimes he knew exactly what levers to pull to irritate her. "Never heard of him. Is he new?"

"If you consider two hundred years old *new.*" Her expression told him she thought him an idiot. She had always thought him an idiot. Not that he had ever really tried to convince her otherwise, as it worked so well in repelling her. "Surely you have heard of the Bard in America? Shakespeare is the father of English literature. His plays are constantly performed in the theaters. *Hamlet* is running in Drury Lane as we speak." When he blinked back vacantly, her voice rose an octave, and the curls poking out of her bonnet bounced as she waved her free hand about. "He also wrote *A Midsummer Night's Dream* and *Henry the Fifth* as well as over a hundred famed sonnets. You *must* know Shakespeare."

Gal frowned as if he hadn't the faintest clue. "Sounds too fancy for my tastes. A fella who writes sonnets sounds a bit too dry and . . . boring to interest me." That comment made her big blue eyes shimmer with so much indignation, Gal had to stifle a smile. "But I'm always happy to learn something new, so tell me what your dull ol' book is about."

"I take it, by your unsubtle change of subject and distinct lack of answer to my original question before the concept of Shakespeare confused you, that it's true?" She gave him one of her withering schoolmistress's looks as if he had indeed been a bad boy. "You *are* here in Covent Garden this morning because you've gambled yet another night away and haven't yet been to bed."

As it was a definitive statement rather than a question, he decided not to disabuse her of her predictable outrage, because it was always predictable whenever he was concerned. For all her charitable deeds, and her habit of trying to see the good in everyone else, she had never once given him the benefit of the doubt. Never mind that he had turned out to be more hero than villain all those years ago when she had pinned him to the ground enraged. He had been on a covert, but intensely personal, mission to thwart his odious father from stealing Giles's dukedom.

And there was no point correcting her that he didn't gamble any night away, his customers did, while he worked his fingers to the bone to make sure they all had a good time. Why would he attempt to when Venus was so wedded to her initial, visceral loathing of him that she could never see past it? And it went without saying that that suited him right down to the ground, because everything about the tart vixen appealed to him too much and he really didn't need that sort of distraction in his life.

So instead he shrugged, deliberately vague about how he came to be here so that her pretty eyes narrowed his way again.

"I'm merely taking a walk before I hit the mattress. Stretching my legs and getting some fresh air after a stuffy night spent indoors. And by fresh I mean frigid, as it's cold enough to freeze your kn . . ." Perhaps not a turn of phrase suitable for such a prim and proper young lady's ears? "Certainly colder than I've seen it in years."

"We are due more apparently." She offered him a begrudging half smile, because the weather was always the safest topic of any here in England. In his humble opinion, the whole country was as unhealthily obsessed with it as they were with drinking their awful tea. "Imminent and heavy. So it is probably advisable to stay inside and batten down the hatches while the storm clouds above do their worst." She pointed to the ominous violet-gray clouds that hung heavily over the city like a shroud. "Especially if we have another blizzard like we did on Thursday."

"Which begs the obvious question, Miss Venus—" She almost succeeded in covering the wince at the second mention of her hated name in as many minutes, but he couldn't suppress all of his amusement at that. "—seeing as you *always* go to bed at a respectable hour, what business brings you to the bowels of Covent Garden this chilly blizzard-loomin' morning?"

She beamed. "Why, the orphanage, of course. Snow or no snow, I still have a full day of lessons ahead, and I couldn't let my students down."

He knew that she spent most of her days teaching the forgotten and motherless children of the slums. It was impossible to avoid that knowledge when her entire family, and even his flippant cousin Giles, viewed her as some sort of saint who walked on water.

"I didn't realize that was *here*."

Please let it not be right here!

She laughed and that made her fine eyes sparkle. "I know you spend most of your time in your den of iniquity at the docks nowadays, but where else do you expect the Covent Garden Asylum for Orphans to be, Galahad, if not here—in *Covent Garden*?" She wafted her gloved hand toward the misaligned front door he had only just been contemplating and the small, dull brass plate.

He squinted at the tiny words engraved on it in abject horror before he blinked back, stunned. "*This* is your famous orphanage?" They were neighbors!

Neighbors!

"*This?*"

"It is indeed." She bristled at his obvious disgust and set her jaw, reading the cause of it entirely wrong. "And irrespective of what you might think of its shabby exterior, Galahad Sinclair—" She looked him up and down as if the very sight of him offended her. "—*we* are rightly proud of what goes on inside."

And just like that, there was a big, fat, unwelcome fly flapping in his ointment.

Chapter Two

I still cannot decide whether I want to live in a quaint thatched cottage or a castle. I suppose that all depends on whether I marry a farmer or a prince. I have no objection to a farmer, of course, as the world needs food, but think it would be more romantic to wait for a prince . . .

—from the diary of Miss Venus Merriwell, aged 14

"Good morning, Reverend . . . Mrs. Witherspoon." Vee stripped off her gloves and stuffed them in the pockets of her coat before she hung it on the hook behind the back-office door. She forced a cheery smile at the two occupants, even though five minutes with Galahad Sinclair had thoroughly spoiled her good mood.

That cocky, golden-haired, green-eyed devil never failed to rub her the wrong way no matter how many times she promised herself that she wouldn't allow his barbed but well-aimed *Miss Venuses* to get under her skin. The handsome wretch always managed to make her feel both stupid and self-conscious. As if he saw her, everything she stood for and everything she said or did, as one big joke. And a pitiable, humorless joke to boot, which really galled because she had an excellent sense of humor. Usually. It just went into hiding around him.

"Ah—you are back!" The jolly-faced and white-haired Reverend Smythe was sitting behind his desk sipping his morning tea as he opened his correspondence, while the small, rotund, but indomitable matron who kept the orphanage running like clockwork bustled around him fussing. "We thought you'd be snowed in at Hampshire for weeks with this dreadful weather, didn't we, Mrs. Witherspoon? We had a full twelve inches here on Thursday. It took an hour to shovel a path to the doorway."

"We had closer to a foot and a half in Fareham that day, but thankfully nothing since. Hence the main roads were quickly cleared, and I was able to travel home only five days later than I originally planned." She sat opposite the reverend as a steaming hot cup of tea appeared before her.

"Aside from a week's worth of lessons and the shoveling of all that snow, what else have I missed?" She knew already a lot would have happened in the ten days she had spent in Hampshire with her sister, because thanks to the forty children who called this home, this place was always a swirling vortex of activity. It was one of the reasons she loved working here. You never quite knew what to expect from one day to the next. Whether that be a minor triumph or a major calamity, there was never a dull moment.

"The pump outside froze, so we've been having the devil of a job getting water." True to form, Mrs. Witherspoon began to list them while ticking them off on her fingers. "But we did get a nice, unexpected donation from the Guild of Tailors and a promise to take on two more apprentices next year as soon as we have some reliable boys turn twelve."

Vee huffed. "Only two?" Placing the older children with decent masters to learn a trade was getting harder and harder.

Plenty of the unscrupulous ones wanted orphans, of course, to exploit and work into the ground, which was precisely why she thoroughly vetted them before she allowed anyone access to theirs. It was the sworn mission of the Covent Garden Asylum for Orphans to give the unfortunate children within its walls a decent future—and certainly one that was better than their past—so she owed them all her utmost diligence.

If they fell back into the vicious circle of poverty and hopelessness from whence they came, it would be near impossible for them to ever climb back out.

That Vee knew from bitter personal experience.

But while she had dropped almost to the bottom of that bleak pit of despair, at least she had always had Minerva and Diana, her older sisters, beside her. Most of the children here had no one.

"Only two this time, but some Quakers have bought out the big silk merchants on Half Moon Street and the reverend seems to think they are open to taking on a couple more, and your modiste needs another junior seamstress after one of hers ran off to join a traveling theater troupe. It was always her dream to be on the stage, apparently, never mind that she'd be earning more still stitching Madame Devy's fine gowns than prancing about in a gaudy costume." Shaking her head in disbelief that anyone would want to do such a thing, Mrs. Witherspoon clasped her hands beneath her enormous bosom like a disapproving opera singer.

"There's also been a ridiculous bill from our idiot butcher, which I am in the midst of querying. Can you believe he is charging us for three entire ribs of beef the fool is adamant he supplied when I certainly never ordered any?" She tutted and her hands went to her generous hips this time. "As if a charitable institution such as ours would waste our precious money on ribs when even the price of brisket is extortionate at this time of year!"

She rolled her eyes heavenward as if praying for strength. "The Claypole twins almost set fire to the boys' dormitory again because *somebody* left his matches and his pipe lying about." Mrs. Witherspoon gestured toward the reverend with a withering look. "And thanks to the weight of all the snow, the roof is leaking again, badly, so that's yet another thing that needs fixing."

"Oh dear." The leaking roof was a constant source of woe and a significant drain on their overstretched funds.

"Oh dear indeed, as I've had four tradesmen look at it and they've all said the same thing—it's reached the point where it's more patch than slate and the whole thing needs replacing. The quotes to do that are eye-watering—but what choice do we have? We've put it off for two years already and if we leave it much longer and the rafters rot, all those tradesmen to a man stated there is a grave danger of the whole thing collapsing. So there goes the donation from the Guild of Tailors and the yearly yuletide stipend from Mrs. Leyton-Brown."

The three of them sighed in unison at that blow despite it being long expected, because as far as money was concerned, their beloved orphanage was an exceedingly leaky boat. No sooner did it come in than it flowed out again. Often without any pause on its journey into somebody else's hands.

"We also had a new admission last Wednesday. A little boy that the good reverend found on the street—and by found, I should clarify that the scamp tried to pick his pocket outside the Theatre Royal, so he thought it best to bring the child back here. Even though he swore he wouldn't collect any fresh waifs and strays until we wave goodbye to some, and even though he knows that we are stuffed to the rafters." The reverend got another look. "As it is, the poor lad is having to sleep on a makeshift pallet on the floor of the nursery."

"Which is infinitely better than the freezing pavement I found him shoeless on."

Mrs. Witherspoon adopted her aggrieved opera singer stance again, but without much conviction. "That may be, Reverend, but we cannot save everyone . . . as much as we might want to."

"It's been quiet then." Vee and the vicar exchanged a smile because, despite owning one of the biggest and kindest hearts on the planet, their whirling dervish of a matron did like to moan. "And there I was expecting to come back to utter chaos."

"We need a miracle, that's what we need." The matron wasn't ready to stop moaning. "Preferably one that is coin shaped."

"Something will come up to save us," said the reverend with his customary optimism. "Something always does."

"On the subject of something coming, your new books arrived first thing this morning." The matron slid a large parcel toward her across the floor. "Sixty pristine reading books alongside this *private* letter from His Lordship addressed to you." She produced it from her apron pocket. "I haven't sent an acknowledgment for the books as I thought you'd want to thank Lord Dorchester yourself for his continued generosity toward our orphans' educations—and his *obvious* interest in the way that *you* teach them." The comment was loaded with innuendo, as Mrs. Witherspoon was convinced the man had taken a fancy to her. As Vee cracked open the seal of the letter, hoping to see some private sentiments that indeed confirmed the theory, the older woman made no secret of the fact that she was trying to read it over her shoulder. "Will you be seeing him in person anytime soon?"

Vee scanned the depressingly impersonal and succinct missive quickly before folding it again in irritation despite Lord Dorchester's continued generosity. How like him to explain why he had selected the books he had, and why he had purposefully ignored several of her suggestions because novels were nothing more than "silly fictional flights of fancy that hold no great educational value to improve impressionable young minds."

Not that he had ever taught a young mind anything himself, of course. And never mind that her four years of teaching experience had taught her that those exciting "flights of fancy" also gave those impressionable children a love of reading that encouraged them to want to continue doing it outside of lesson time.

The love of reading went hand in hand with a love of learning, fueled it and nurtured it. Whereas dry texts only snuffed out that flame. No matter how many times, or how logically, she made that argument, it always fell on deaf ears with her serious, mature lord who always knew better. This was a flaw in his character that was becoming increasingly difficult to overlook, no matter how much prudence dictated that she tried.

If his curt dismissal of her learned opinion wasn't irritation enough, his "private" letter made no inquiries about her at all! He hadn't even bothered asking why she had missed attending his mother's reading salon this week after the snow delayed her in Hampshire, when she had never missed it in the three months she had been attending. It did not bode well that he hadn't even noticed her absence. Or cared for her much at all.

If at all.

He was certainly both deaf and blind to every single hint she had dropped these past three months that they could be more than two people who shared a love of books and academia.

Because, his tendency to ignore her opinions aside, in many ways she was increasingly convinced that they might be perfect for each other. Especially now that she had given up on all her foolish notions of a passionate love match. Passion might well have gone hand in hand with love in her sisters' marriages, but it had caused nothing but misery for Vee, who seemed to have no trouble stoking a gentleman's passions while leaving his heart untouched.

Besides, her poor heart had only just stitched itself back together after it had been thoroughly broken by the treacherous Lord Argyll last season, and she was in no hurry to repeat that dreadful mistake.

Ever.

Thankfully, she had, however, learned from it. She was all done with romance and all the insincere but dangerous nonsense that came with it. Romance was for dreamers and fools, and she was no longer either. That was why she had decided that the future father of her children, and head of the happy family home she had always longed for, would be as far removed in every way as possible from the handsome but ultimately unworthy young gentleman who had turned her head and scrambled her wits.

Despite the fifteen-year difference in their ages, Lord Dorchester and she were both bookish scholars at heart with a thirst for knowledge and a shared philanthropic desire to improve the lives of the less fortunate through education. That was a surer foundation for a marriage than romance, and a stronger one.

Yes—he was a tad too serious and uncompromising, and that sometimes came off as arrogant or dismissive. And yes, he could also be a bit judgmental and patronizing when he lectured those around him on what was right and what was wrong. But there was no denying he had a moral compass that pointed resolutely north exactly as hers did; that he had a reputation as an upright and upstanding gentleman, was free from scandal as well as solvent, and was mature enough to be guided by the thoughts in his head rather than the appendage that resided in his breeches.

Surely that had to count for something?

She had certainly never met another living soul with whom she could discuss Homer's *Iliad* or history or philosophy with such informed passion. And unlike the insufferable Galahad just now, if Lord Dorchester was passionate about anything, it was Shakespeare. Almost as much as she was. That had to count for something, too, despite her preference for the Bard's comedies and his for the "more worthy" tragedies. Dorchester could also converse extensively on everything from the Byzantine empire to botany, and from agriculture to astronomy, and could lecture knowledgeably on them all for hours.

Hours and hours.

Sometimes without pausing for breath.

But that was another minor flaw she was choosing to ignore in favor of all the things she admired about him. He was the most learned man she had ever encountered, for goodness' sake, and Vee loved to learn. So that was another point in his favor, albeit an unromantic one.

Not that she cared about romance any longer.

After four demoralizing seasons searching for the man of her dreams, all she had encountered were nightmares.

Vee had had offers. Plenty of them over the years—but unfortunately, they had all been improper and from the sort of gentlemen who were only ever interested in the carnal and not the spiritual, in the mythical goddess of love from the gutters they were convinced she had to be rather than the reality of the bluestocking she undoubtedly was to her core.

If anything, the fact that she possessed a mind at all was irrelevant, because she was only ever seen as attractive by the sort of man who had no interest in it whatsoever. Nor any interest in forever for that matter. Like the Judas Lord Argyll who had played her like a fiddle when it suited him and promptly forgotten her when a better, blue-blooded opportunity had presented itself.

She was twenty-two, for pity's sake! Quite sick and tired of being judged by her stupid name and the much-too-generous figure fate had saddled her with. Sick and tired too of the silly, shallow, and selfish men who couldn't see past her larger-than-average bosom.

Whereas Lord Dorchester wasn't that sort of man at all.

Being closer to forty than he was thirty, he appreciated her mind most of all, she was convinced of it. He also seemed oblivious to her bountiful physical endowments. He had never ogled her or made inappropriate suggestions regarding her improper name or talked to her cleavage or tried to seduce her into bed. He certainly showed her more respect than that vexatious young Yankee who considered her one big humorless, prudish joke!

Lord Dorchester never made jokes.

Vee sincerely doubted he was capable but refused to hold that against him, either, because instead, they discussed politics and science and books. Or at least he discussed them while she listened. And while he wasn't charming in the slightest, when one looked at him in the right light, parts of him were aesthetically pleasing.

If she ignored his unchecked dandruff, which never seemed to be brushed from his ill-fitting coats.

Or the slight, stooping shoulders it dusted.

Or his unattractive tendency to sniff all the time as if his nostrils were blocked.

Or his small and unsettlingly smooth hands, which always felt clammy.

But those were also minor flaws in the grand scheme of things, and with her new pragmatic approach to her future happiness, she was working hard to appreciate the man beneath. In the apparently vain hope that he would appreciate the intelligent woman beneath the ghastly name and voluptuous figure. Or at least *see* her as a woman at all.

An irony that wasn't lost on her after she had spent the last four years being ogled by men who saw only her flagrant womanhood.

"I believe he is due to attend the Rokeby Ball on Friday, so I shall be sure to send the orphanage's regards for his continued benevolence." Knowing him, he would likely forget to ask her to dance as he had at the last three balls they had conversed at until she had unsubtly prompted him. Not that Lord Dorchester ever asked anyone else to dance, either—but still. His continued indifference was most unflattering when she was trying so hard to appeal to him specifically with her daring new gowns. "Unless I see him beforehand, of course, in which case . . ."

"Oh dear," the Reverend Smythe interrupted with a grave expression on his face as he stared at the missive in his hand. "Oh dear, oh dear. Poor Mrs. Leyton-Brown."

"Has she taken a further turn for the worse?" The matron sank into the chair beside Vee. The ailing Mrs. Leyton-Brown had always been one of the orphanage's most generous benefactors.

Not only had her annual stipend kept the wolves from the door, but she had also been one of their most relentless fundraisers in society, holding benefit after benefit in their honor, until ill health had forced her to spend more and more of her time at her house in Brighton. She had even donated this building to them when the reverend had wanted to create a different sort of orphanage, simply because she believed in his vision.

"Hasn't the poor dear suffered enough?"

To add to her many health burdens, Mrs. Leyton-Brown had suffered a stroke six months ago, which had left her bedbound.

"Her suffering is at an end now, Mrs. Witherspoon." The Reverend Smythe passed the letter across the desk so both ladies could read it. "She apparently died peacefully in her sleep last week. This is from her solicitor in Brighton who is the executor of her estate. He has invited me to call at his office at my convenience to sign the particulars of the generous bequest left to us by Mrs. Leyton-Brown in her last will and testament."

"What a selfless and generous soul she was." Vee did not want to sound mercenary, but in their current predicament, the orphanage needed all the generous bequests it could get its hands on. "Do we know how much?"

"Let's hope Mrs. Leyton-Brown left us enough to fix the roof." Mrs. Witherspoon winced with guilt as she said this. "God rest her."

The Reverend Smythe patted the older woman's hand with a bittersweet smile on his face. "Oh, I am sure it will, Mrs. Witherspoon, and then some. I've never mentioned it, because it felt disrespectful to do so to a benefactor who has already done so much for us, but when I visited her in Brighton in September, Mrs. Leyton-Brown faithfully assured me that not only was she leaving our little orphanage a sum of four figures in her will—"

"*Four* figures!" The good they could do with a thousand pounds took Vee's breath away.

"God bless her!" Mrs. Witherspoon clutched her bosom in excitement. "We can finally fix the roof."

"We can indeed." The reverend's smile transformed into a grin. "We might also be able to do something about our distinct lack of space, because—" His wily old eyes shone as he paused for dramatic effect. "—she also promised to leave us the building next door!"

Chapter Three

I am trying not to think ill of Papa for missing my birthday—again. Even if it is for the third year in a row. I am convinced there must be a very good reason for his continued absence and silence. I am also trying not to think ill of Diana, who said his lack of presence in our lives was surely present enough . . .

—from the diary of Miss Venus Merriwell, aged 15

The Rokebys' ballroom was too damn crowded, not to mention unbearably hot and stuffy despite the fresh dusting of snow outside. Such an unholy crush, Gal was sorely tempted to turn around at the door and head back outside into the cold where he could at least breathe. He didn't, because these necessary forays into society were for business, not pleasure, and were more necessary now than they had ever been. The majority of the well-dressed bodies filling this place were potential future customers he had been subtly ingratiating himself with for years, but he needed to start seriously wooing them if he was going to get them—and their heavy purses—through his doors when he opened them in the spring.

For the sake of family and professional harmony, he also needed to build some bridges between himself and the prickly Miss Venus now that fate had decided they were going to be neighbors. There would be no avoiding her once he signed the papers, and the last thing he needed was to be cast as the villain of the piece again because she was the family saint and he had always been more sinner. A gambling club coexisting peaceably next to an orphanage was destined to be a difficult enough sell, without the added complication of their fraught relationship. So he had given the matter a great deal of thought to find a way around it. Enough that he had already come up with a plan to ensure things went smoothly.

First, he would make a concerted effort to turn the permanently frosty atmosphere between them more cordial before he bared his hand: to unruffle her perennially ruffled feathers where he was concerned and declare a truce. That unfortunately would require him to get to know her better, which he had always avoided like the plague although he couldn't quite explain why, even to himself, and to temper his overwhelming inclination to rile her a little at every given opportunity. Instead, while he anxiously waited for the contracts and while he interviewed tradesmen to do the extensive renovations needed once he took possession, she'd be treated to the Galahad who lived up to his noble and courtly name. The charming, diplomatic, and gallant Galahad he usually had no problem being for every other woman who walked on this earth, but whom he had never quite managed to muster for her.

Second, when everything was signed and sealed, and when they were on a friendlier footing, he would tell her of his purchase while buttering her up further with an offer she couldn't refuse—a nice, healthy annual donation to the Covent Garden Asylum for Orphans. A calculated bribe that benefited the orphanage and made his club a more attractive neighbor.

And third, in a few more months—fingers crossed—if the untrustworthy Mallory didn't renege on the deal before the papers were signed and his lifelong ambition was finally up and running and ready to rake in the coin, Gal would do everything in his power to go back to avoiding her again wherever possible.

For some inexplicable reason, he was looking forward to that part of his new plan most of all.

He stared at the crush again, sucked in a fortifying lungful of air, then huffed it out before he pasted an approachable expression on his face.

Once more unto the breach.

"Good evening . . ."

"Nice to see you again . . ."

"It's been too long . . ."

Gal took a full fifteen minutes to thoroughly charm every member of the great and the good he passed before he spied Giles at his usual spot beside the refreshment table engaging in his favorite pastime—eating. Although where the irreverent Duke of Harpenden put all the food he consumed was a mystery because there wasn't an ounce of spare flesh on his impressive frame.

Giles maneuvered his loaded dessert plate to his other hand before he shook Gal's. "Why the bloody hell did Lady Rokeby invite so many people when this room is hardly big enough to swing a cat and is hotter than blasted Hades?"

"It beats me—yet here we all are anyway. At least I'm here to finesse a few future customers. What's your excuse?"

"Diana." Giles gestured toward the seemingly empty alcove with his plate as he dropped his voice so only Gal could hear. "She's working."

"Still?" That beggared belief when the *ton*'s most unconventional duchess was due to give birth to their second child in less than two months. "I thought she would have taken some time off from *The Tribune* by now." His voice was hushed, as only the most trusted few in the family circle knew that Diana was the Sentinel—unmasker of criminals and ne'er-do-wells as London's most feared newspaper columnist.

"So did I, old chap." His cousin shrugged in a what's-a-man-supposed-to-do way. "But the harridan is a law unto herself and completely unstoppable. She's been chasing some swindler for months and is convinced she's almost got him, so I've been tasked with putting on a sociable show for the Rokebys while she does some subtle eavesdropping on her prey." A bite-sized strawberry tart disappeared into his mouth. "How goes your quest to buy a building?"

"I might have a lead on something interesting." As much as he trusted Giles and had happily shared all his lofty plans with him over the years, Gal wasn't one for confiding in anyone. He preferred to hold his cards close to his chest until it was safe to bear them. The best-laid plans, like life, could always change with the flip of a card, as he well knew from bitter experience, so he would hold these until the ink was dry on all the legalities and the debauched Mallory had handed over the keys. "Certainly more interesting than anything else I've seen up till now, so we shall see." He tapped his nose, which was about as much confiding as he was prepared to risk until the deal was all done and dusted. "I have a good feeling about this one."

"It must be good as I've never heard you be quite so gushing about bricks and mortar, old chap." His cousin sighed in delight as he popped a second strawberry tart into his mouth. "If you've finally found a suitable building, you really do need to give some serious thought to a suitable name for your fancy den of iniquity. I'm still convinced it should be called Sinclair's—just to infuriate all our illustrious ancestors and have them spinning in their ostentatious graves. It's simple, it's neat, and it already has the word *sin* incorporated into it. If ever there was a name *syn*onymous with improper behavior, it is surely ours. We've been rotten for centuries."

"But Sinclair's makes it sound so . . . British." Gal had been mulling the name ever since he had decided to make this alien city home. Especially as he had a feeling his original choice and the name of his grandpa's place—The Four Leafed Clover—wouldn't work here. It made it sound like a common tavern, when it would be anything but.

"When in Rome, Galahad. It's worked for White's and Brookes's so there is really no need to start from scratch."

"Maybe . . . but I want to sound different. Be different."

"I am right. You know I am right and once you come to your senses and acknowledge that, I shall be able to say that I told you so. Sinclair's has an understated elegance to it as well as a dash of ancient and aristocratic gravitas that will draw in the hordes who aspire to that. When you are the cousin to a scandalous duke, it would be foolish not to capitalize on the association."

"Why is everything here about class and station?"

Giles shrugged as he eyed the refreshment table with interest. "Because it is, old chap, and that is that. We British are a pompous lot." He groaned as he gestured left with a brief lift of his eyebrow. "And talking of pompous . . ."

Heading directly toward them was Venus. Hanging on the arm of the dull Lord Dorchester again while the rest of her family trailed behind them.

She hung on his arm a lot of late, he had noticed, although he was damned if he could fathom why beyond the fact that the irritating minx had a knack for setting her cap at the worst sort of man. She'd picked some duds over the years—libertines, dandies, fortune-hunters, flatterers, dyed-in-the-wool fornicators, and failures—but she was really scraping the barrel this time.

In Gal's humble opinion, Dorchester was the dictionary definition of what the Brits called a prig. A puritanical, vacillating, know-it-all fuddy-duddy who acted older than his already extensive years and wiser than Socrates, and was too puffed up with his own importance to notice his shortcomings. What the hell did she see in him? When he was almost old enough to be her father.

More important, why did he care?

"Hello, Giles." She beamed at his cousin before she kissed his cheek, and once the kissing was done offered Gal a frosty approximation of a smile that didn't touch her eyes.

Clearly she was still riled about the way he had handled their impromptu meeting in Covent Garden and still of the opinion that he had disapproved of the state of her beloved orphanage. He would probably need to apologize for that. Even though she hadn't given him a second to clarify before she had stomped up the steps and slammed the door behind her. "Galahad."

"Well, don't you look delicious, Vee!" His cousin's gaze swept down her cornflower-blue gown in appreciation. "Madame Devy has outdone herself this season!" Gal couldn't deny that Giles had a point. The new hourglass fashions with their nipped waists suited her down to the ground—so much more so than the Empire-line styles she had worn when he had first known her. She had been wearing some pretty dresses all season, but none as grown-up as this enticing confection that seemed to be magically held up by just her plump breasts and some discreet boning, and hung off her shoulders, exposing acres of perfect skin. "If I wasn't a happily married man, and your sister wasn't quite so terrifying, I swear you would draw my manly eyes and turn my head."

Gal's eyes were certainly drawn to the pert and creamy two inches of cleavage currently on display, which he was certain he had never seen before because he knew, without a shadow of a doubt, he would have remembered it.

"Your Grace." Lord Dorchester suddenly blocked his splendid view by bowing to Giles. "It is always an honor to see you." He acknowledged Gal as he always did his apparent inferiors—with a curt and dismissive nod. But because Gal had the audacity to be a foreign inferior, and one from a former treasonous colony to boot, Dorchester's beaked nose wrinkled slightly as if his imported stench offended him.

Thankfully, he was spared the chore of making any small talk with the windbag because Venus's self-appointed adoptive parents, the Peabodys—the meddlesome, aristocratic Olivia and her acerbic, Boston-born-and-bred second husband, Jeremiah—were close behind. Gal adored them both but had always shared the closest affinity with Jeremiah. No doubt because they were both fish out of water in this strange land and shared a mutual sense of bemusement at some of the unique quirks of the British.

With relief, he strode toward them and was enveloped in one of the petite Olivia's bone-crushing hugs. "How is my favorite reprobate?" She held him out at arm's length in the way his mother used to do to check if his outfit and hair passed muster. "And why haven't we seen you in over a month? When I've sent you countless invitations?"

"I've been working. In Brighton."

"In the scandalous but secret little gaming hell that you've opened there?" Olivia tapped her nose, fishing. "What's it called again?" They both knew that he had never told anyone.

"A man has to earn a living, and who am I to stop people losing their hard-earned money at my tables if they are determined to lose it?"

Although naturally reluctant to disclose much about himself, Gal was always the cagiest about what he did in Brighton. Not because he was up to no good there, because he genuinely wasn't, but because what happened there was private. It was intensely personal and, therefore, not up for discussion like all of the other intensely personal aspects of his life. If people thought he had opened a second hell, he wasn't going to correct them. Especially as it was a believable assumption to make after the resounding success of The Den at the London docks.

After years of hard work, he was proud that his Brighton venture was finally turning a small profit rather than leaking money like water. However, it was the spit-and-sawdust Den that had quadrupled the size of the nest egg his grandpa had left him. That alone had paid for his new premises in Covent Garden and would also fund their refurbishment, so he was rightly proud to own it no matter how scandalous others might think it.

Olivia adjusted the knot of his cravat, smiling. "I have always had a soft spot for an entrepreneur. Especially one who rolls up his sleeves and isn't afraid to get his hands dirty."

"If only everyone here in Mayfair thought the same." He quirked an eyebrow in the direction of Venus's boring lord, annoyed that the idiot had made him feel petulant when he usually rose above such nonsense.

Jeremiah rolled his eyes. "Take no heed of Dorchester. I've been here off and on for a quarter of a century, and he still looks at me as if I'm something nasty stuck to his shoe." He echoed Gal's thoughts exactly as he glared at the pair. "I haven't the faintest idea what Vee sees in the uppity fool."

"Me either." Olivia made no effort to hide her disapproval as she gazed in the couple's direction. "I have said as much repeatedly, but apparently, I do not know him like she knows him, and she admires his *great mind*."

"Not half as much as he admires it." Another bull's-eye from his fellow countryman. "I've never met a man who liked the sound of his own voice quite so much."

"He sure likes to look down his nose, too." It was a nose Gal's fists itched to punch tonight, which was odd when he wasn't a violent man unless the situation called for it, preferring diplomacy over fisticuffs—even in the docks. "I know that's a common trait here in Mayfair, but somehow when he does it, it raises the hackles more."

Jeremiah nodded his agreement. "That's because everything about him grates. Even his lauded philanthropy leaves a bad taste in the mouth, as I'm convinced all his sermonizing about his benevolence is more self-aggrandizing than genuinely generous. As if he wants to be seen to be doing good because he craves superiority more than he wants to help." Which was an insightful and more succinct summation of the man's character than Gal could have managed.

"I've also told her that one should never trust a man with thin lips." Gal always adored Olivia's warped logic, and as per usual she felt no need to substantiate her outrageous comment with any evidence. "But as she is apparently two and twenty, and increasingly headstrong in her dotage, my sage motherly advice is ignored nowadays more often than it is heeded."

Jeremiah rolled his eyes at the subject of their conversation in obvious loathing. "Thin those lips may be—but still they are not." With reluctance, Gal looked and saw Venus hanging on Dorchester's every word like a devoted puppy. "From the second Vee insisted he join us, he hasn't stopped yapping. And my goodness, doesn't he have an opinion on everything! In the ten minutes it took us to battle our way over here, he covered everything from taxation to taxidermy and the cause of cold weather to the benefits of colonization. But of course, we couldn't scurry off like every other sensible person we encountered—I tried but was restrained." He glared at his wife.

"I wasn't going to be the only chaperone left alone with him, you wretch!"

"I'll bet they have to gag him to shut him up in the House of Lords." Jeremiah clearly needed to vent about the experience some more. "He's such a *learned expert* on everything, it's a wonder Parliament haven't surrendered and handed over the reins of this nation to him! Because Lord only knows nobody else has more opinions on how to run a country!"

"It was an exceedingly long ten minutes." Olivia patted her husband's arm in sympathy as she smiled at Gal. "But I fear Vee will need more than being bored to death before she realizes her droning viscount is a dead loss who isn't any more interested in her intellect than any of the previous men of her acquaintance have been. Even though we all know that he is much too old for her and that she is trying to settle for something she doesn't really want."

Of their own accord, Gal's eyes wandered to her again before he wrenched them back with a shake of his head. "You can't make a silk purse out of a sow's ear, and she can do better." So much better. "Look at all the fellas gazing at her and pretending not to."

There was something about Venus that made even the happily married men shoot her a covetous glance. An allure that went beyond the lovely face, the enticing figure, and the graceful way she carried herself. Enough of one that even Gal, who really didn't ever want to notice her, still found his eyes wandering her way whenever she was near.

"Exactly," said Olivia, giving him an odd, calculating look. "But if she will not hear it from me, perhaps she will listen to someone from her own generation." There was a worrying glint in her gaze now.

"Maybe you should talk to her about it, Galahad? Find a subtle way to point out all that is wrong with him. Make her see Dorchester in the same unforgiving, bright light that we all do."

If he'd have taken a sip of his drink, he'd have spat it out in shock. "Me?"

"Why not? There's only a few years between you and you are not one of her immediate nagging family, so it might come better from you than anyone."

"I think that's better coming from one of her sisters."

"Diana has tried, Galahad, but their personalities have always clashed so her words are hitting a brick wall. And Minerva is of the opinion that Vee is a grown woman who needs to come to her own conclusions rather than be nagged into them, as that would only entrench the problem. She is convinced that the more time Vee spends with Dorchester, the more he will repel her naturally in his own inimitable way. Whereas I am worried that if we leave it unchecked, the worst will happen and he'll make her his viscountess. Especially as poor Vee is worried about being left on the shelf and has always had the tendency to make allowances for unworthy males. She spent years giving her feckless father the benefit of the doubt after he abandoned her. While both her sisters rightly despised him for leaving them in poverty, Vee still held out hope that the wretch might return changed."

"People don't change." Gal's mother had believed his own feckless father's lies on that score and had lived to rue the day. Twice. That second abandonment had been catastrophic—for both his mother and him.

"Of course they don't!" Olivia dropped her voice to a hushed whisper. "But after that vile Lord Argyll pursued her tirelessly last year, flirted outrageously until he convinced her that he loved her, and suddenly lost interest when greener grass beckoned, she has become rather jaded and disillusioned about men. Disproportionately so in my humble opinion, as that libertine Argyll was always a dud, too, but I suppose he did break her heart and hearts take a while to mend."

Gal had loathed the socially and politically ambitious Argyll more than he disliked Dorchester, and all that mutual flirting had made his blood boil, hence he'd made a concerted effort to avoid the pair of them by avoiding most of last season. When he'd learned the predator had ruthlessly transferred his affections from Venus to an influential government minister's daughter, he had been relieved but not surprised. But he suddenly hated the scoundrel more now that Olivia claimed he had broken her heart. "She had a lucky escape with that one." Argyll had never been able to keep his pecker in his pants, and his recent advantageous marriage hadn't curtailed that.

"We all agree—but Argyll was the straw that broke the camel's back and the reason she took herself to the wallflower chairs. Although I cannot say that I blame her for removing herself from the fray for a while. I suppose that passionless, dead loss Dorchester seems like a refreshing change from all the seducers who see her as naught but a juicy fruit that is ripe for the picking."

Gal glanced her way again and took in the still subtly staring males all around her and was suddenly fuming at the rest of his sex because he knew exactly what they were thinking, and none of it was proper. Knowing the arrogance of some of them, they wouldn't have been able to keep those lustful thoughts to themselves, either, and even if they had, Venus was no fool. She would know exactly what they were all thinking, so was it any wonder she had become jaded if she had been bombarded with all that every time she dared to wear a nice dress?

It also explained why her gowns normally erred more on the side of prim than not. Those sensible garments had nothing to do with her character and everything to do with theirs. That Dorchester was oblivious to her physical charms no doubt accounted for some of the reason he appealed to her so. For all his jumped-up pompousness, at least she would feel safe around him.

But that certainly wasn't anything to do with Gal.

"I'm erring on the side of Minerva here. Better to allow whatever is going on to run its course. Miss Venus is as smart as a whip. She'll work it out." He sincerely hoped that she would and that that would be the end of it.

Instantly that hope was dashed, because Olivia wasn't anywhere near done with him. "You know Vee is selling herself short." In case he tried to escape, she threaded her arm through his, tight. "She has it in her stubborn head that because she is a bookish sort, only a bookish sort will do, when we all know that opposites attract, and she misguidedly thinks that they have fundamental things in common—as if those flimsy things are suddenly the be-all and end-all. She is on the cusp of making a hideous and irrevocable mistake. We cannot allow her to marry him. The family needs your help in that, Galahad . . ." She stared up beseeching and he knew he was being played by a master. Lady Olivia Peabody was a force to be reckoned with at the best of times, but when she put her mind to something, she used both fair means and foul and put her shoulder behind it. "Help *us* to help *her* see sense."

He shook his head as he extricated himself from her grasp and raised his palms before she resorted to outright blackmail. "As much as I concur with all your concerns regarding her beau, Olivia, I am not the man for that job. She suffers me for Giles's sake and nothing more. Besides, Miss Venus and I have never had the sort of relationship where my advice about anything would even be tolerated, let alone welcomed."

"More's the pity as you've always had a sound head on those distracting broad shoulders."

She looked him up and down this time like a piece of prime horseflesh up for purchase. "Do I at least have your promise that you will hint at your disapproval if the opportunity presents itself?"

"Of course." Because hinting that she was an idiot for fancying herself shackled to that dullard Dorchester for all eternity would be the perfect way to pour oil on those troubled waters! The best way to build some bridges between them before he opened his rowdy homage to vice right on the pious Saint Venus's doorstep! "I'll make some subtle hints of my disapproval *if* the opportunity presents itself." So subtle it would take the world's biggest magnifying glass for her to notice them.

"Good," said Olivia, dragging him toward her charge with surprising strength that belied her diminutive stature. "Let us create an opportunity. Ask her to dance. Because she rarely dances nowadays, and a crowded dance floor is always an excellent place to discuss delicate matters."

Chapter Four

I measured myself again this morning and am sad to report that my dratted bosoms still refuse to stop growing . . .

—from the diary of Miss Venus Merriwell, aged 15

"The current problems on the Continent all rest squarely on the shoulders of bad governance." Lord Dorchester had been joined by his favorite cronies and was now waxing lyrical about the spate of revolutions that had occurred this year across the Channel. It was one of his favorite current topics, so Vee felt petty for being so fed up with it. "France still isn't fully over Napoleon despite their sensible readoption of the monarchy because . . ."

"Sorry to interrupt." Olivia caught her elbow, relieving her of the chore of listening, only for her to turn and come face-to-face with Galahad, who typically looked more handsome in his perfectly tailored evening clothes than any man had a right to. The cut of his coat drew her eyes to the vexing wretch's broad shoulders and almost caused her to stare at them in appreciation—which vexed her further. "But I have a dashing young man here eager to steal a spot on your dance card."

He didn't look the least bit eager. To be frank, he looked as horrified by the suggestion as she was. "Oh . . . um . . ." She was instantly flustered because they had categorically never danced together before. Never sat beside each other at a dinner table or coffee table, for that matter. Or even loitered within ten feet of each other anywhere. They certainly hadn't ever managed a conversation longer than a few minutes in all the years she had known him. Had never even touched since the night she had attacked him—not that she could recall at any rate—so the prospect of three whole minutes making polite small talk during the enforced intimacy of a dance was unsettling. Especially as she was still smarting at his mocking the state of the orphanage the other day with his much-too-dismissive eyes.

"I am not sure I have any left." Beyond the nineteen remaining out of the twenty listed.

"Nonsense!" Olivia snatched the card from her wrist before Vee could stop her, then to her further horror opened it where he could see all the glaring empty spaces still left upon it—because she had only granted the one. "Which do you fancy, Galahad?"

"That one." He jabbed at the country dance directly beneath the imminent waltz for which she had penciled in Lord Dorchester. Remembering his manners, he inclined his head and smiled politely. "If that suits you, Miss Venus."

"Of course." She bobbed an insincere curtsy, making sure her wayward eyes never ventured anywhere near his shoulders on the way up or down. "I shall look forward to it." About as much as she looked forward to losing all her teeth to old age and being forced to eat nothing but mashed food till she died.

"Splendid!" Olivia beamed at them both. "I shall leave you bright young things to your conversation." She shot Galahad a pointed glare. "And your dance." With that parting salvo, and with a wicked glint in her calculating blue eyes, Olivia bolted, leaving them standing together awkwardly.

"You really don't have to dance with me." He threw her that lifeline the moment their tormentor was out of earshot. "Although I think it might be good for both of us if you did."

"Why on earth would you think that?"

"Because . . ." He huffed out a sigh that made him look boyish and somehow more appealing. "I reckon it's time we buried the hatchet, Miss Venus."

"And why would we want to do that?" It seemed daft to pretend she had no idea what he was talking about when there had always been not so much a rift between them as a gaping impasse.

"Because your sister is married to my cousin. Because we collide all the time as a result. And because I've never been entirely sure exactly what we've been at war over. Have you?" He had her there. Aside from the unequivocal fact that he—and his dratted shoulders and twinkling green eyes—unsettled her for some reason. "Besides, it occurs to me that all the animosity we seem to harbor for each other is from the past, and a version of the past that wasn't entirely accurate back then, yet it still taints the now even though it shouldn't." There was no hint of his usual mockery as he held out his hand. "Truce?"

She stared at the offending limb for several seconds before she shook it, then immediately regretted it because his touch sent her pulse berserk. "Truce."

They yanked their hands away simultaneously as if they had both been bitten. His to hide behind his back and hers to fiddle in discomfort in full view. The flesh on her fingers felt suddenly more alive than it ever had before.

"On the tail of that truce, I should also like to apologize for any unintentional offense I caused you the other day. It wasn't the state of the orphanage that horrified me, Miss Venus—" As always and despite their new peace treaty, the way he insisted on using her full name made her bristle. "—so much as the fact that we have known each other for four years and yet, to my eternal shame, I had no clue where it was. It was remiss of me not to have asked before, or to have shown much interest in your worthy endeavors, when it is a cause close to your heart and the necessary work that you do there is beyond admirable."

Vee blinked, waiting for the veiled insult, and when none came blinked some more. "Thank you for clarifying."

He shrugged, looking more boyish and handsome and annoyingly sincere. "I would have clarified at the time, only you stomped off before I could." To her shame, she had stomped. He had a knack for making her stomp. "So how many little rascals do you have in that place?"

"Forty." She remembered the reverend's pickpocket. "Forty-one to be precise, as of last week. Boys and girls who run the gamut in ages from five to twelve years."

He whistled his surprise. "That's a lot. More than enough to keep you busy then. All characters, I'm guessing, because you have to grow a big one to survive on the streets alone." An insightful comment Vee would have questioned had Lord Dorchester not clicked his fingers by her ear.

"What is the name of the new king of France, Miss Vee? The one who replaced Charles the Tenth?" He clicked his fingers again and she suppressed the urge to frown at his rude summons, noticing that Galahad didn't. His expression at the curt interruption was positively thunderous.

"Er . . . Louis Philippe, the Duke of Orléans, I believe."

"Yes indeed." Lord Dorchester didn't even bother thanking her as he continued his lecture. "Charles was ultimately usurped by the court of public opinion in much the same way as our despotic King Richard the Third—because his shoddy behavior had lost the goodwill of his subjects."

"Or so Shakespeare would have us believe." That surprising comment came from a still-frowning Galahad. "And ol' Henry had to find a way to justify him killing the king and stealing the crown from the head it rightfully belonged on."

"Shakespeare was a chronicler of *our* past, Mr. Sinclair." Lord Dorchester said this in the most patronizing fashion, as if speaking to a child who couldn't possibly understand it. "He had no reason to warp the facts of what happened more than a hundred years before he wrote about it."

"Didn't he?" Galahad's dark-gold brows kissed in consternation. "He wrote plays for the elite, didn't he? Relied on the patronage of the aristocracy to pay his bills and knew if he didn't write something pleasin' for ol' Henry's granddaughter, the sittin' queen, he'd likely have his head separated from his shoulders with a blunt blade."

For some reason he was drawling certain words to sound more of a stranger to these shores than not, which was a bold move when discussing the intricacies of English history with a peer of the realm whose family was intrinsically part of it. "That strikes me as incentive enough to do some tweakin'." His mischievous green gaze locked with hers and managed to send a ripple of awareness everywhere. "What say you, Miss Venus?" He was daring her to disagree with Dorchester.

"Well, I think . . ." She thought Galahad had made a valid, if surprising, point and one she completely concurred with, but for a moment she considered lying to please her lord. But as that was disingenuous and because Lord Dorchester was always saying that debate was healthy, she told the truth. "Shakespeare isn't the most reliable source to glean accurate historical facts from. I've always taken his royal plays as fiction more to entertain than to educate, as that would have been their intended purpose back in his day and . . ." As Lord Dorchester's less vibrant green eyes were shooting her daggers, she smiled as her voice trailed off. "Well, frankly, you know I have always preferred his comedies."

"Which have no educational value whatsoever." Dorchester rewarded her traitorous opinion by turning his back to continue his discussion about the new French king as if she hadn't spoken at all, effectively excluding her and Galahad from the rest of the conversation.

"I prefer the comedies, too." It was Galahad who came to her rescue by pretending the slight hadn't happened. "Give me a Falstaff over a Hamlet any day of the week."

"I thought you'd never heard of Shakespeare."

Galahad shrugged, a contrite smile playing with the corners of his mouth. "Maybe one or two of his plays made it all the way to the savage, uncivilized shores of New York. And maybe I went to see a couple—including that one that you put so much stock in that you re-read it every year. I rooted for Beatrice and Benedick throughout, by the way. I liked her grit and his wit."

"That does surprise me." Or more, he had. "I can only assume you feigned ignorance to irritate me."

"Guilty as charged." His smile this time was disarming. "I might have read them all."

"All?" Something strange happened in the vicinity of her heart. Something strange and most disconcerting. She decided there and then that she much preferred Galahad when she had thought he couldn't read, because that had made him easier to dislike.

He nodded. "Even all one hundred and fifty-four of his *famed sonnets*." He shrugged unrepentant, grinning, displaying a perfectly straight set of pearly white teeth. "Although I have to admit I do find some of his comedies a bit far-fetched. All those women posing as men and the men not noticing makes me wonder what those Tudor women looked like." He pulled a face. "They must have been very *homely* ladies indeed."

"Homely?" By the amusement dancing in his eyes that word must mean something quite different to him than it did to her.

"It means ugly in my version of your language, Miss Venus." He nudged her playfully with his elbow as he winked, which was rather . . . charming. "More attractive on the inside than on the out."

"Ah . . . well . . ." What a gentle way of insulting someone. "I suppose those plays made more sense in Shakespeare's time because all the female parts were played by males. Women weren't allowed to tread the boards until the end of the next century."

"I did not know that." He chuckled at the ridiculousness of it. A deep, silky sound that did odd things to her insides. "Another one of life's great mysteries solved. Though now you mention it, it suddenly all makes such perfect sense I should have figured it out before. No wonder those men never noticed all those incognito ladies were ladies—when clearly they all wore beards."

She would have told him more about how Shakespeare put his plays on, but the first bars of the waltz had begun so Galahad had stepped aside. He swept his arm in Dorchester's direction. "They are playing your tune."

"Apparently so." When her lord failed to turn around to claim her, she tapped him on the shoulder. "I believe this dance is yours, my lord."

"But we are in the middle of a riveting discussion." Dorchester seemed put out by her interruption. "You do not mind if we pass this time, do you?"

Vee smiled tightly, put out by his continued indifference, and humiliated to have been dismissed so curtly in front of Galahad. "Of course not." He had turned back to his friends before she even uttered the second word.

"You should mind." Galahad appeared furious on her behalf and was glaring at Dorchester's back. "That is no way to treat a lady."

"It really doesn't matter."

"That's as good as saying that you don't matter, Miss Venus." His stormy emerald gaze flicked to hers. "If he asked you to dance, he should honor it. Especially if he nabbed the honor of the first waltz."

Technically, it had been Vee who had done the asking. Not outright in an overt would-you-dance-the-waltz-with-me way, but more in the casual, rhetorical, should-I-save-a-space-for-you-tonight kind of way that had forced Lord Dorchester to nod. Probably on sufferance. It had been she who penciled his name beside the first waltz. Her contriteness at that must have showed on her face as Galahad gaped open-mouthed in despair. "Unless he didn't—and you forced his hand."

"Lord Dorchester isn't a huge fan of dancing. He is a scholar at heart." Good heavens, this was awkward. "Like me. To be frank, I really couldn't care less if I ever danced at these affairs or not." She feigned boredom to cover her embarrassment. "I much prefer the conversation, especially if it leads to a stimulating debate."

He glanced back at Dorchester, who was still holding court and hadn't paused for breath, or even noticed that he was rudely ignoring her. "Where I come from a conversation is a two-way affair, Miss Venus, and a debate is an exchange of ideas and opinions, not one participant dominating and drowning out everyone else with his pontificating."

"He simply feels very strongly about the current political climate in Europe, that is all. He isn't usually so—"

"Lecturing? Domineering? High and mighty? Selfish? Downright thoughtless?"

Urgh! She hated that Galahad's criticism echoed all of her own in this precise moment. "I can see how you would think that, but he isn't the least bit like that once you get to know him as well as I do. Lord Dorchester—"

"*Lord* Dorchester? Surely if you know him so well, he wouldn't be a lord to you?" She wanted to kick him in his irritating shins for his galling perceptiveness. "Or are you, like me, too beneath him to use his Christian name? Or worse, he thinks himself so superior to everybody else, only his mother gets to call him *Marmaduke*." He said the name with an impeccable and clipped aristocratic English accent, making it sound foppish and daft. "And I thought our names were bad."

"None of us can help our names, Galahad."

"We can't, but we can all help the way we behave and treat others."

She was furious at both men now. Galahad for being his usual annoying self and Dorchester for forcing her to defend the indefensible. "It's clear that you do not like him." Yet another name to add to an ever-growing list of people who didn't. Including hers at this precise moment. "But . . ."

He groaned aloud. "*But?* What the hell do you see in him, Miss Venus?"

"Lord Dorchester is a proper gentleman of quality—unlike some I could mention!"

"I'm not sure that the daughter of a forger is in any position to criticize my pedigree."

Maybe she would kick him in both shins. Or higher. "By quality, I meant that he knows how to behave!"

"*That* is quality behavior?" Galahad frowned as if she had taken leave of her senses. "He's rude and obnoxious, thinks he knows everything, and refuses to be corrected. Looks down his nose at everyone *and* he's a narcissist. I've never met a man who considers himself so undeservedly superior to everyone else in a room."

"He is very different in private than he is . . ."

"Why are you so blind to his flaws when the rest of us have already worked out that your droning viscount is a dead loss?" A question that Olivia had asked her almost verbatim in the carriage tonight, as well as yesterday and the day before when she had lectured her on the importance of the frisson and urged Vee to hold off picking a mate until she truly felt it.

"Olivia put you up to this, didn't she?" Vee wafted her hand in the direction of her meddling relation, who was watching them with interest while pretending not to. "You didn't really want to bury the hatchet at all, did you? You were dragged over here expressly to find a way to enlighten me regarding your disapproval of Dorchester."

He went to deny it then huffed. "Yes . . . and no." He winced. "Yes, I cannot deny that Olivia is worried about your attachment to him when she does not see any evidence that your regard is reciprocated, but no, that isn't why I came over. While I do think that windbag is a pompous ass—" He jerked his thumb in Dorchester's direction. "—I also think that whoever you've pinned your colors to is none of my business, and I told Olivia so. But I *did* come over here to bury the hatchet."

"In my back, apparently."

She knew it had been too good to be true. She and he attempting cordiality and sociability when they had never been able to manage it before. Not that this failed attempt had lasted long thanks to his thinly disguised ulterior motive.

"But at least you can report this inconsequential slight back to Olivia. It will add weight to her argument that he is wrong for me in every possible way, and you'll both get to gloat about my continued poor judgment regarding the male of the species while you congratulate yourselves that you told me so." All of a sudden she wanted to go home. Wanted to run out of this stupid ballroom and have a good cry at her own continued stupidity wherever men were concerned. Because they were right. She knew they were right. Every sign from the universe screamed that she was barking up the wrong tree—yet again—out of desperation. Instead of admitting that aloud and surrendering to the truth of it, she folded her arms and summoned what remained of her battered pride. "You've had your fun, so go away, Galahad."

"Miss Venus, I . . ."

"I said go."

With a sigh, he did exactly that, but he hadn't gone six feet before he marched back to grab her hand. "Let's dance."

He tugged her but she dug her heels in. "I'd rather not. Contrary to what you might think, I am a wallflower by choice and rarely have any trouble finding dance partners." That at least was the truth. There had been several men ogling her all evening who never failed to ask to take a turn with her across the dance floor before they suggested she might want to take a very different sort of turn with them somewhere private afterward. "I certainly do not need one out of pity."

He glanced heavenward for strength. "If you want that idiot, you aren't going to get anywhere with him until he *sees* you." Which, irritatingly, she had also worked out for herself. "And that idiot isn't going to *see* you when you've turned yourself into his lapdog, always there and loyally waiting for him to throw you a few scraps—so let's dance. Let's give him the opportunity to see you like all the sensible men in this ballroom do—as a beautiful, intelligent, and desirable woman he would be damn lucky to converse with, let alone hold in his arms."

He yanked her to follow again, and, a little stunned at his unexpected compliment, she did.

At the edge of the floor, he stopped dead and held his palm out flat. "Take off those eyeglasses."

"If I do that, I won't be able to see your smug face!" With his hand still outstretched, he rolled his eyes in a manner that made Vee instantly seethe. "Which now that you mention it might not be a bad thing."

She slapped them into his palm, and he pocketed them, then held it out again for her to take. The second she did, he pulled her into his arms. They were strong arms. The square shoulders beneath her fingers were as unmistakably sturdy as they looked, too. He was broader than Dorchester and taller, overwhelming in his maleness and youthful vigor, and the big hand that engulfed hers wasn't the slightest bit clammy. Or too smooth to have seen an honest day's work. The slightly roughened texture told her in no uncertain terms that Galahad's hands did more than waft in the air while he pontificated. He also, and much to her consternation, smelled and felt divine, and the intensity of his gaze gave hers no option but to lose herself in it.

"I'll give you fair warning that for the next few minutes I am going to hold you too close, and you are going to act every inch a woman who is enjoying it." Although against her wishes her wayward body was enjoying it already, so she sincerely doubted much acting would be required.

"Under no circumstances are you to look his way, understand? Even when I twirl you right past him." She nodded again, and his serious expression softened to one of amusement. "You also might want to have a go at smiling, Miss Venus, rather than glaring like you want to murder me. No matter how much you currently do. Give that fool something to be jealous about and I guarantee he'll come running to you for a change."

Begrudgingly, she did, and he chuckled. The silky rumble still had the same devastating impact on her nerve endings, only this time it was amplified because she could also feel it in the most improper and distracting manner against her ribs. Because the wretch was already holding her so scandalously close her bosom lay flush against his chest.

And they liked it there.

"Now, that wasn't so hard, was it?"

Vee decided not to dignify that with a response.

To vex her further, Galahad proved to be an expert at waltzing who maneuvered her effortlessly and gracefully around the floor. Probably because the waltz was one of the few dances he'd ever deigned to dance on the rare occasions when he attended society affairs, and he usually danced them with whichever attractive lady he happened to be linked to by the gossip columns. He had a penchant for young widows, or the most daring and flirtatious single ladies with the most dubious reputations who liked to have a good time.

Just like him.

"We're coming up on Marmaduke now." That murmur, so close to her ear, raised distracting goose bumps on her flesh. "So eyes front and center, missy, and let's put on a show . . . talk to me."

As if hypnotized, she smiled up at his face. It startled her that not all of that smile was a sham. "What do you want to talk about?"

He pulled her closer still, his hand slipping from her waist downward until it rested intimately in the small of her back, scandalously waking all of the nerve endings that resided below her waist. "What do you like about teaching those orphans?"

She forced herself to focus on the question and not the odd effect he was having on her body. "It is good to give something back to those less fortunate."

"Too predictable and rehearsed an answer." He rolled his eyes again without malice, forcing her to notice how striking they were. The unusual green irises were ringed by a deeper green and flecked with amber. The lashes that flanked them were a darker brown, which surprised her when the hair on his head didn't have a single strand of dark brown in it. It ran the gamut between pale gold and burnished bronze instead, with no two strands the same. Exactly like his eyebrows. "I'm interested in all the other less pious reasons you do it, Saint Venus. The real things that have you going back there day after day when you are already guaranteed a spot in heaven after so many years of charitable benevolence. What's in it for you?"

"I enjoy the work." Good gracious, but she was off kilter. Locked in the sublime cage of his arms, she felt as if she were simultaneously floating and falling. "The sense of accomplishment and purpose. I have never been very good doing nothing."

"That big ol' brain of yours likes to keep busy."

"It does . . ." Had he just complimented her intelligence for a second time? He must have, because like a dolt she was already floating some more. "I enjoy the challenge of finding ways to rob Peter to pay Paul, or of solving the many problems that the orphanage throws up. For example, this week, after the roof sprang another leak and was finally condemned by every tradesman we asked to patch it, I'm in the throes of haggling a decent price to replace it." They were all still eye-watering, though, so she sincerely hoped Mrs. Leyton-Brown had been as generous as the reverend had claimed . . . else they would continue to be rained on indoors in perpetuity.

"I also adore the children, so most of the time it honestly doesn't feel like work. Frankly, it is impossible not to adore them. As you already said, some of them are real characters, and that ensures that I constantly have to think on my feet. Every day throws up a different challenge." Like this current challenge. *Who knew dancing with Galahad would be so . . . intoxicating?*

"And that clever mind of yours must love a challenge." To her chagrin, alongside all the nods to her intelligence, she realized that she also adored his accent and the sultry timbre of his voice. Certain syllables even gave her goose bumps.

"We have these twins—" She paused, fearing that she was too overwhelmed to realize that he was only being polite and wasn't really interested in what she had to say, but his expression was every bit as interested as he had claimed to be. She could see that as clear as crystal in his expressive eyes. "—Tommy and Sydney Claypole. Two absolute tearaways who seem to thrive on causing trouble. Not the awful, malicious, and dangerous sort of trouble. More relentless and purposeful mischief, because I suspect they like to make all the other children laugh. Today they decided to torment all the little girls with spiders. Not one or two, because that would be too pedestrian a prank for the Claypoles—but an entire trinket box full. They must have been collecting them for weeks to get quite so many, and they released them in the girls' dormitory first thing."

Those emerald eyes twinkled with mirth. "I am sure much screaming ensued."

"It is a miracle none of our neighbors called the police as it turns out twenty girls can make quite the cacophony." Vee chuckled herself at the memory. "Although to be fair to the girls, the matron and the reverend did their own share of screaming as neither are fond of spiders, so it was left to me to bring order to the chaos."

"Which you did with . . . ?"

"A sturdy broom, some vigorous sweeping, and some very stern words to the Claypoles after I managed to clear away their contraband collection of arachnids." Words the two rapscallions had listened to with bowed heads that did not disguise the proud smiles on their freckled faces at their achievement. "Not that I believe for one second they will change their ways as they so faithfully promised, as they seem to enjoy a good carpeting for their misdemeanors almost as much as they enjoy the pranks they pull."

"I suppose being told off makes them feel like they have parents. That they aren't all alone in the world and that they belong somewhere." Another insightful comment that surprised her. "And going out of their way to do something naughty guarantees them some regular and private time with somebody like you—someone who cares enough about them to remind them of the error of their ways. We all want to be appreciated for something, after all."

"You might be right. I hadn't considered that." Her smile for him now was entirely genuine, and that felt . . . odd. But strangely pleasant. Like discovering that your taste buds have changed overnight and you suddenly enjoy the flavor of something you rebelled against before. "Anyway, they are twelve and should have left us for an apprenticeship somewhere, but every single one we put them up for, even the ones where we have ensured they will stay together, they manage to sabotage it in some way before they have even started."

"How long have they been with you?"

"Ever since we opened. Before that, they had spent a year living rough on the streets."

"That explains the sabotage." His expression was more wistful than amused. As if he understood rather than sympathized. "The orphanage is their home, and they are scared to leave it in case they go backward. The streets are awful for anyone—but especially hard for the young who are easily exploited. They chew you up and spit out the bones. I would have done the same given half the chance."

Something in the way he said that made her wonder. "Did you ever live on the streets, Galahad?" Because she got the distinct feeling, somehow, that he might have.

"I've lived everywhere, Miss Venus."

Then, perhaps because he wanted to distract her from that, and because he kept asking all the right questions, she found herself opening up to him in a way she never had before. Telling him all about the twins and the scrapes they had embroiled themselves in, and before she knew it the dance was done. More bizarre, she was disappointed that their little interlude was over as he led her by the hand from the floor. Yet she was buoyed and exhilarated by it at the same time.

Over the course of those few short minutes, she had gone from feeling unseen and inconsequential to interesting and vibrant. Seen for who she was for a change, both inside and out.

"I am ready for our dance now." She hadn't even noticed Dorchester waiting impatiently for her at the edge of the floor until he spoke. He held out his hand to claim her and Galahad held hers tighter—not that she had been tempted to let his go—but instead of bristling at the reminder to have more respect for herself where her lord was concerned, it only served to strengthen her resolve not to allow him to take her for granted.

"Thank you for the honor of that dance, Miss Venus." Her unlikely ally smiled politely as he stealthily returned her spectacles to her empty palm, but the conspiratorial look in his striking eyes reminded her that he knew he was responsible for her lord's sudden bout of interest. "I enjoyed it immensely." He lifted her hand and placed a lingering kiss on her fingers. All for show, of course, yet she still felt it everywhere. "I'm already lookin' forward to the next."

Galahad released her with a convincingly heated look and melted back into the crowd, and because she couldn't seem to take her eyes off him, she watched him go. She was thrown more off kilter by that waltz than she had been by any other before.

Or, more bizarre, by any dance partner.

"Our dance, madam?" Dorchester's tone was clipped as he waggled his hand again in outraged reminder, but at least he refrained from clicking his fingers. She could tell from the tightness of his jaw that that apparent concession took all his willpower and clearly went against the grain.

Which she supposed spoke volumes about his character.

"Would you mind if we passed for now?" If that sentence surprised her, it completely flummoxed him. "Only I have just spied someone that I desperately want to talk to."

She took a leaf out of Galahad's book and made a lazy, smiling exit, leaving her lackluster and lackadaisical dead loss of a viscount gaping at her retreating back.

Chapter Five

I borrowed Much Ado About Nothing from the lending library and am now hopelessly in love with it. I wept happy tears when Beatrice realized she was in love with Benedick as I was rooting for them all along, but when he confessed "I do love nothing in the world so well as you," I swear my heart melted. I have since revised my criteria for my own future husband to include the necessity of him having the most beautiful way with words . . .

—from the diary of Miss Venus Merriwell, aged 15

Gal had been in two minds about accepting Olivia's invitation to dinner. He usually pleaded work for all such big "family" occasions wherever possible—which was always true and could just as easily be tonight—but hadn't because of Venus.

After Lord Mallory had called upon him this morning, confident the deeds of the three buildings in Covent Garden would likely be signed over in mid-December, the clock on his anonymity was ticking. He needed to ensure that she was more friend than enemy before all the renovations started after Christmas.

So here he was. Sitting around the Earl of Fareham's boisterous

Berkeley Square dining table with all of them, wishing he was anywhere else.

That wasn't because he disliked anyone here. Far from it in fact. He usually dined with Giles and Diana every month if they all happened to be in town at the same time. Similarly, he occasionally collided with Jeremiah or Hugh at White's and happily spent an hour with them. He also saw them all at the few society affairs he attended, where he made sure to spend at least half an hour catching up. He felt out of place at these big but intimate family gatherings, yet desperately wanted to fit in at the same time.

Having a family connection again, no matter how precious, felt alien still. Growing up, it had been just him, his ma, and Grandpa until Gal had turned twelve. Then, when fate stole that solid, reassuring male presence in his life away, it was him and his ma. By the time he turned fourteen, fate had ensured it was only him, and had forced him to find comfort in his own company ever since. So being included in a noisy, teasing, competitive, and growing family that already numbered ten without him was unsettling.

Added to that, because this wasn't work and he didn't have to pretend to be the accommodating life and soul or have his hardheaded businessman's façade to hide behind, he was never quite sure how to behave or which version of himself to play for the crowd. He knew, deep down, the only person these fine people wanted him to be was himself, but as he had kept that private for so long, out of necessity and self-preservation, lowering those defenses made Gal uncomfortable. They were only halfway through the dessert and already his sociable mask felt tight. He had shrunk into himself and was counting the minutes until he could make a polite excuse to leave.

A situation that was hardly going to improve diplomatic relations between himself and Venus as fast as he needed to. Despite the slight thaw at the ball last week, they had barely exchanged more than a "good evening" so far—and that wasn't going to be enough to get her on his side and keep her there. For once, he had to stay and socialize till the bitter end and not escape to the solitude of the night the second the final plates were cleared as he wanted to. More tonight than he usually did.

He blamed that on their waltz.

His eyes drifted to Venus, who sat laughing beside his cousin, and he wanted to kick himself some more for not capitalizing on his small victory with her at that awful ball sooner. Thanks to that waltz, something had shifted that night, and it wasn't only all the latent animosity between them.

Something strange but overwhelming had moved within him, leaving him disconcerted, and he irrationally blamed her for that entirely. He was even a little bit furious at her, truth be told, as somewhere between the first moment she had taken his hand on that dance floor and the last second before he had reluctantly released it, she had apparently bewitched him.

She had certainly woken some inconvenient feelings inside him that were best left snoring.

Desire had been one of them, although that unwelcome reaction was the least of Gal's worries and the most easily explained. A man would have to be made of granite not to be stirred holding that delicious armful of overt femininity so close. Miss Venus was an attractive woman with a figure tailor-made for seduction, so was it any wonder his body had been thoroughly seduced by hers? But desire was a transient and fickle thing, and one that could be easily transferred or indulged if he found another willing and less dangerous woman than his cousin's venerated and pious sister-in-law to slake it on.

Unfortunately, his inappropriate and untimely desire wasn't the only issue at play here, because Saint Venus had also managed to stir more than his blood during that dance. She had stirred his heart a little, too, and that had never happened before.

He'd always avoided any romantic entanglements that elicited feelings. Affectionate feelings were dangerous. Not only because they were a diversion he didn't have the time for, but because there was a paralyzing reverse side to caring if fate decided to be cruel. He might never have been *in love*, but he'd been crippled by grief twice in quick succession when someone he loved had been cruelly ripped away. That dark, vulnerable place wasn't somewhere he had any desire to visit again, especially when experience had taught him that it was when your belly was exposed that people took the most advantage. And especially when he still had an unfulfilled dream to turn into reality and the safe harbor of a fortune to amass.

An entanglement with Venus was a distraction he could not afford right now, but despite that, he recognized all the worrying symptoms of a deeper attraction than the pure and uncomplicated carnal. And, Lord help him, he had been plagued with all of them this last week. He'd certainly pondered her far too much in the last seven days than was healthy, that was for sure. Wondered where she was or what she was doing more often than he was comfortable with. Pictured her in that orphanage, where he knew she would be in her element, doing her good deeds with a pretty smile on her face.

Gal glanced back down the table where she was smiling again, and he almost groaned aloud at the pathetic way his heart leaped at the sight. He'd conjured the dazzling image of that sunny smile more times than he cared to mention this week, too. Alongside the way her big blue eyes had danced when she was animated and talking about the things that she loved. Thankfully, his dreams, at least, had involved more of the carnal than not, so he was trying not to analyze them quite so much as he was his waking thoughts, but all of them combined pointed to a troubling preoccupation with her that he couldn't seem to fight. The sort of preoccupation that fed temptation and gave a man ideas, when he was, by nature and circumstance, a lone wolf, and she wasn't the sort of woman a man like him should be contemplating a dalliance with.

Miss Venus was the settling-down sort, always had been, and he wasn't interested in that. He needed to *build* relations with her, not *have* relations with her!

And he damn well needed to remember that distinction.

As his grandpa had been so fond of saying, if a job was worth doing, it was worth doing right, and sometimes a man had to make sacrifices to reap all the rewards of his labors.

He had waited a decade to do this. Worked all the hours God sent, scrimped and saved and sacrificed all manner of things to get to this pivotal place, so come hell or high water he was going to do it properly. Do what he had been born and raised to do and make a huge success of it—no matter what his needy body or his foolishly leaping heart had to say on the matter.

"You're quiet tonight, Galahad." Minerva's observation startled him out of his reverie as he sipped the obligatory cup of tea the British began and ended every meal with. Or started every day with. Or produced at a moment's notice in honor of every visit, occasion, or crisis as if it were as essential to living as air was for breathing. "A penny for your thoughts?"

"I fear you'd be wasting a penny, Minerva, as I am occupied with work. As usual." It wasn't a lie, he supposed, seeing as Venus was the current fly in his business ointment. "I'm always pondering ways to make more profit to see me through to my dotage." Which was definitely the truth. He never wanted to be penniless again. The thought kept him awake at night—when he wasn't thinking impure thoughts about her baby sister, of course.

"You know what they say about all work and no play." There was no judgment in her tone, only concern for his welfare. "But I do understand the overwhelming urge for financial security, Gal, and respect your dogged determination to achieve it." Like him, Minerva had had to work hard for her living before she married Hugh. All three of the Merriwell sisters had. "Don't run yourself ragged trying to double your fortune overnight when Giles has proudly told us that you are already a man of some substance. Enough of one that you can afford to occasionally pat yourself on the back and smell the roses."

"I intend to do precisely that in the not-too-distant future. Just as soon as . . ."

"He gets Sinclair's up and running." Sometimes his cousin Giles had the ears of a bat. "He thinks he might have finally found a home for it."

"You've found some premises?" Minerva beamed. "That is wonderful news! Where? When? Have you made an offer yet?"

Suddenly all the eyes around the table rested on his expectant. "I'm still at the negotiating stage, so I'll keep you posted." His toes curled inside his boots at the lie, no matter how necessary it was at this delicate point in the proceedings. Even without the need to befriend Venus, the contracts might well be in the process of being drawn up, but he was too cautious to tempt fate until they were signed and the deeds safely in his pocket. Especially when this deal involved a snake like Mallory.

"His plans for the place are marvelous." Giles was beaming proudly. "I've certainly never seen anything like it. Sinclair's will be neither a gaming hell nor a gentleman's club. It's going to be part music hall, part tavern, and part pleasure palace."

"I am not sure I like the sound of the last part." Olivia's eyes had widened. "I am also not sure we should be discussing brothels over dinner."

Before Gal could correct her misinterpretation, his cousin did. "By *pleasure palace*, I meant a place for everyone to have some fun at his tables. Ladies, too. Respectable ladies, Olivia, rather than those *of the night*—so we can all visit it together once it's opened."

"I've never been a brothel keeper, Olivia." Gal decided that point needed additional clarification. "Nor have I any intentions of starting." His grandpa had been a stickler for standards and had run a clean house back in New York, and as a point of principle he had always continued that tradition. Having been at the mercy of people who had shamelessly exploited him when life had robbed him of choices, it would be a cold day in hell before he followed suit.

"In that case, I shall look forward to visiting. When does your pleasure palace open?"

"As I said—" He loathed strapping on his liar's mask as that had always been the most ill-fitting disguise in his collection. "—I haven't bought anything yet, so I'm trying not to get too excited in case there's a catch." His gaze flicked involuntarily to Venus's. "In the meantime, I'm focusing on the businesses I do have rather than the one I might."

If ever there was a moment to change the subject subtly, this was it. "In fact, Minerva caught me pondering whether or not to expand the offering we give the customers at The Den." It wouldn't hurt to vocalize something that he had been genuinely mulling. Or had been a week ago, before he stupidly danced that fateful waltz. "Replace some of the hazard tables, which cause the most trouble with cards. Something that keeps those sailors drinking my liquor longer, requires more skill than luck, and, most important of all, doesn't cause all-out war when a fella loses his shirt to another at the end of the game."

"Your sailors have more restraint than some people I could mention." Hugh motioned to Jeremiah with a flick of his eye. "Cards always cause all-out war here at Standish House. They have had to be temporarily banned—*again*—because somebody broke the card table when he knocked it over in a fit of pique last month. Not naming any names, of course." But Hugh pointed his finger at his stepfather as he pretended to cough into his fist.

The rest of the table sniggered while Jeremiah went on the defensive. "It's been four goddamn years!" He jabbed the air. "Four. *Goddamn.* Years!"

"There is no need to resort to coarse language, dear." It always amused Gal that despite all her flagrant inappropriateness in other aspects of life, Olivia could not abide salty language—no matter how innocuous.

Jeremiah's eyes narrowed at his wife's quick admonishment. "There is every need. Because it isn't possible and it's driving me mad! Mad, I tell you!" He glared at Venus with irrational hatred for a moment, which was bizarre when he clearly adored her and thought of her as a daughter. "It's not natural!"

"You had to kick that hornet's nest, didn't you, Hugh?" Diana shook her head. "Any second now he's going to be spouting steam alongside all his festering theories of skulduggery."

"Well, it certainly begs the question as to how the swindler does it." Despite Jeremiah's continued glaring, a butter-wouldn't-melt-in-her-mouth Venus forked up the last piece of her dessert unfazed by his vitriol. "I've suspected for quite some time that there is foul play involved and I flipped that table to prove it!"

"And found nothing, dear, as usual." Olivia rubbed her suddenly irate husband's back while Miss Venus grinned smugly. "No hidden aces. No mechanical devices. Not even a tiny illicit mirror with which she could monitor an opponent's hand." She went from rubbing his back to wrapping her arm around his shoulders. "You need to let it go, Jeremiah. All this pent-up fury cannot be good for a man of your age."

"I feel I am missing something here?" An understatement when Gal had no clue what the hell any of them were talking about.

"That's because you have wisely always disappeared before the evening games begin, old chap." Giles mopped his lips before tossing his napkin on the table. "And are blissfully unaware of the deal dear Vee here has to have done with the devil."

None the wiser, Gal threw up his palms bewildered, doubly intrigued by the arrival of the wicked glint behind Venus's beguiling prim spectacles. "What sort of a deal?"

"The sort where Lucifer has guaranteed that she never loses." Giles threw up his own palms as he shrugged. "No matter what the game, if it involves cards, you don't stand a chance. Poor Jeremiah has been trying to beat her at something for four years, and every single time she rinses him. It would be most entertaining if she didn't also rinse me and Hugh in the process, but we are at peace with it."

Hugh nodded in resignation. "We accept it as one of the divine, cosmic mysteries we mere mortals are never supposed to understand. Whereas poor Jeremiah hasn't. His hubris will not allow him to accept continual defeat. He is convinced of fraud and it's eating him from the inside that he cannot prove it—as you can plainly see."

"I am not a cheat, Galahad." Venus's cocky expression suited her. "Merely lucky."

Jeremiah banged the table, causing all the cutlery to rattle. "Nobody's luck holds for four years!" He was right, of course, but Gal held his tongue. The sainted Miss Venus was up to something—and he was damned if that didn't intrigue him. "If she's not a cheat, then she's a witch!" Jeremiah slapped the table again. "One of these days, I am going to prove it!"

"And this is why cards have been banned in this house," said Hugh with a grin while his stepfather seethed. "And why my grandmother's rare Italian marquetry game table has had to be repaired three times since I married her sister. Venus Merriwell is unbeatable."

"I'll wager I could beat her." Not only because he knew that a schoolteacher with a talent for parlor games was no match for a man who had grown up at the foot of a card table. But also because it gave him the perfect opportunity to spend some time with her as he needed to. That Gal would also get to hide behind the shield of a fan of cards where he was always the most comfortable was the clincher that made him throw the gauntlet down. "That is, if Miss Venus is confident enough that her luck will hold that she is brave enough to take a professional on."

All the eyes on the table swiveled from him to her expectantly.

She didn't disappoint, skewering him with her glare. "Oh, I am brave enough, Galahad, *and* trust me, whether you are a professional or not, I am still going to enjoy thrashing you."

Chapter Six

Minerva keeps warning me that reading in the small hours by one candle is going to ruin my eyesight. I have told her that that is poppycock . . .

—from the diary of Miss Venus Merriwell, aged 16

The tension was palpable as they all traipsed into the drawing room and watched Payne, the Standish butler, prepare the table. Enough that even Vee was nervous. Galahad, on the other hand, was a changed man from the quiet and almost shy gentleman who had sat with them all at dinner. Now he was suddenly all confidence and sinful swagger, and certainly all smiles as he allowed her the choice of game.

"How about whist?"

He quirked one golden brow, his green gaze amused. "An interesting choice. One that requires as many tactics as it does luck."

As that felt like a loaded statement, she smiled back blandly, trying not to notice how much the twinkle in his emerald eyes suited him. "Unless it's not to your taste, in which case we can play something *easier*?"

"Oh, I don't mind whist." He folded his big body into one of the chairs at the table, then smoothed his palms over the baize as if he had never encountered the stuff before. Vee found herself mesmerized by his hands—horrifying herself by wondering what they would feel like smoothing over her skin with the same gentle attention. "It feels strange being sat on this side of a card table again. I'm more used to watching nowadays than participating." Then he frowned at the pack of cards Jeremiah had placed in the center of the table. "Refresh my memory, as it's been a while—doesn't whist need four players?"

"It does, but as this is the clash of the Titans, I think you should both be paired with the worst card players in the family." Giles was already enjoying himself. "Then you are both handicapped and it's a proper fair fight." He grinned at his wife. "Which of you wishes to be saddled with Diana and which with the equally incompetent card player Minerva? Both will be a hindrance, but I can guarantee one will be more belligerent than the other." The final barb was directed at his wife, who curled her lip in disgust but did not argue the point.

"I'll take Minerva." Vee was no fool, and Diana had a temper on her as bad as Jeremiah's when the game did not go her way.

If that bothered Galahad, he hid it with an easygoing shrug. "Five tricks a game and the best of three rounds?"

She nodded, biting her lip at his language when any idiot knew that where whist was concerned they were called rubbers and not rounds. At least here they were. Maybe things were different on the other side of the Atlantic.

"I have hidden away all the sharp knives, my lord." Payne sighed at the room in general, shaking his head at the lot of them. "But I feel I must remind *certain* people that there are only so many times that a hundred-and-fifty-year-old table can be fixed, even by the most skilled of carpenters, before it must be consigned to the bonfire." The butler stared pointedly at Jeremiah. "I should also like to remind *everyone* that many of the servants who work here have to be up at five to light the fires and prepare the breakfast, so would request that you all refrain from the usual shouting and hollering that usually accompanies one of these uncouth card games after eleven o'clock. Furthermore . . ." At Hugh's groan, the outspoken retainer smiled. "If you require me to open a book, as I suspect you all do, for the sake of candor I am putting five shillings on Miss Vee. No offense, Mr. Sinclair, but she really is a demon."

"None taken, Payne." Galahad waved that away with another lazy smile. "I only hope you can afford to lose it."

They all took their places, Vee opposite Minerva and Diana beside her. At Galahad's insistence that it was always ladies first, she dealt the cards, which she did without preamble, before turning the last card over.

"Diamonds are trumps."

While her sisters began to sort their decks, he rifled in his waistcoat pocket for something, then waved a silver coin triumphant. "I almost forgot my lucky quarter." He winked at her as he snapped it down in front of him. "That could have been disastrous."

Vee studied it and him surreptitiously as she arranged her own cards, wondering if a man who made his living from gambling really believed in the nonsensical concept of superstition. Perhaps, judging by the state of that silver coin, he did. It was clearly a token he had kept and held for many years, as most of the indentations that had been pressed into it had been worn smooth. He also did not sort his cards into suits; instead he fanned them open to scan them and discarded them while he waited for the rest of their party to be ready and decided to make chitchat the moment the play started. The second Diana laid the two of clubs he laid down the ten. A high card that was wasted so early in the game when any other in the same suit would have done.

Clearly his skills at whist were very rusty indeed.

"Who are those expensive flowers from?"

"Lord Dorchester." The ostentatious hothouse arrangement on the mantel wasn't to her taste, but she wasn't going to admit that to him.

His smile was smug. "Ahhhh . . . our waltz worked, then, as I'm guessing he's never sent you a bouquet before?"

She most certainly was not going to admit that he was right about that, too, so she offered him a stony glare over her cards while Minerva laid the jack. One that told him in no uncertain terms she took her whist seriously and wasn't in any mood for small talk.

Olivia, however, nodded like a woodpecker. "After months of never sending a single bloom, that lot came yesterday after Vee failed for the second week in a row to attend his mother's reading salon." The traitor shot Gal a loaded look. "She was too busy, apparently, which was most unlike her when she usually finds any excuse to bury her nose in a book." She was going to murder Olivia once this game was over.

"It's a sensible tactic." Amusement danced a jig in his annoying green eyes. "Miss Venus has finally realized that absence *always* makes the heart grow fonder."

She refused to dignify that insufferable quip with an answer but punished it swiftly by playing a trump and laying the two of diamonds on Minerva's jack to take the first trick. Then she smiled sweetly as she helped herself to one of the counters that kept score.

Throughout the whole of the next three tricks, he played only slightly less clumsily, because he wouldn't stop talking. Only this time it was to ask his partner questions about her latest investigation. As Diana had more interest in that than she did whist, Vee won two of those tricks and Minerva the third. At last, he seemed bothered that Vee was trouncing him and concentrated for the first time, flicking his lucky quarter backward and forward across his fingers in silence as he occasionally frowned at the three counters sat by her elbow. He won the trick, the wretch, but only because he wasted his last decent trump card to do it. Which meant, by the end of the hand, that he had nothing left to stop her and Minerva stealing the game with the required five tricks to his one.

Because she hated dealing, Diana passed the messy deck of cards to Galahad to distribute, and he gathered the pile slowly into a neat stack. To remind him of his failings, Vee couldn't resist mirroring him by piling up her four shiny counters in a precise column, too.

"I told you I would win." After his annoying perceptiveness about the depressing Lord Dorchester situation, she was keen to put him back in his place.

"As the British like to say, one swallow doesn't make a summer, Miss Venus." His gaze flicked up from the cards and he sighed. "But I'll confess, I find no incentive to win when I play for buttons." He gestured to her counters before leaning closer across the table in challenge. "What say you we up the ante? Play for something that will get my competitive juices flowing?"

"How much do you have in mind?" As she really hadn't punished him enough for the "absence always makes the heart grow fonder" dig, she decided to be a bit reckless. "Shillings or *sovereigns*?"

He scoffed at that idea, picking up his lucky quarter again and weaving it idly through his busy fingers. "Where's the fun in you losing money?" He swept a hand to encompass the entire drawing room. "When there's no shortage of that here in Mayfair or, not to brag, in my pocket? No . . ." He shook his golden head, smiling. "I want to play for something that matters." Those emotive green eyes bored into hers. "Win something that matters to you. Something you wouldn't want to lose."

"Such as?"

He cast his eyes around the room until they settled on the open book she had left lying facedown on the arm of the sofa. "Your precious copy of *Much Ado About Nothing*." He turned back smiling in challenge, not giving her the time to refuse. "When I beat you, I want it to sting."

"In that case . . ." Vee nodded toward his hands, not needing any time to decide what to steal from him. "I want your lucky quarter." The merest twitch of his brows before he nodded told her that, like him, she had chosen something that really mattered. "Deal the cards, Galahad, and may the best woman win."

"I admire your confidence, Miss Venus. I really do." He winked as he picked up the neatened pack and cut the cards in half, weighing them briefly in each hand. "Let's hope your vanity isn't misplaced."

Rather than shuffling them like any normal person would, suddenly he was an expert because, like the coin, those cards wove through his fingers at lightning speed, flipping and twisting as if he controlled them all with naught but magic.

"I say," said Hugh, beyond impressed. "Somebody's been hiding their light under a bushel." Her brother-in-law looked her way wide-eyed. "If I were you, I'd be worried now, Vee."

She was worried, because she suspected she'd been had, but it would be a cold day in hell before she let any of them see. "I'd expect a man who owns two gambling hells to be a master of showmanship—but a fancy shuffle is little more than artful deception. Much like Galahad's feigned gentlemanly manners."

He winked again as he effortlessly dovetailed the two halves of the pack together with a flick of his thumbs. The flirty gesture unsettled her because she liked it. "Showmanship and artful deception are the most essential skills of my job and the easiest way to keep my customers happy. Never underestimate the power of seducing someone with a few cheap tricks, Miss Venus. Sometimes performing them is essential to winning them."

As he dealt them, the cards whipped and spun fast around the table and all landed practically on top of one another in front of their intended player, but again, when he fanned his, he made no attempt to sort them into suits.

Almost as if he realized that made things harder for her.

This game was more evenly matched, but despite his superior shuffling skills, and thanks to her sister's atrocious playing, his wandering concentration, and his need to chat, his skills at whist weren't anywhere near as impressive. He won the second rubber by a whisker on the last trick—more by luck than judgment—because his last low trump card was higher than hers and he laid it on the king of clubs.

Everything hinged on the last hand dealt, and her hand was magnificent. Magnificent enough that she purposefully allowed him to win the first two tricks to make him use up all his best cards because she wanted to annihilate him. She stole the third without breaking a sweat, but because spades were trumps and she still held three, including the unbeatable ace, she had to work hard not to give away the fact that she had already won.

While Diana stared at the two cards left in her hand as if praying for divine intervention, he asked Vee a question. "Have you dealt with any spider emergencies since I last saw you?"

"Thankfully no spiders. But the Claypole twins did put jam in Mrs. Witherspoon's bedroom slippers a few days after, so they are in serious trouble with her and have been sentenced to a month of the same bedtime as the little children as punishment, exactly as she had threatened." Like an idiot Diana laid her ace of hearts, leaving her holding a useless two of spades by Vee's best estimation because she had been scowling at her hand in disgust this whole game and always saved a trump till the bitter end no matter how the game went. Usually the wrong trump.

"Who is Mrs. Witherspoon again?"

"The matron of the orphanage. She lives there and tries very hard to be terrifying—but really is as soft as butter." With nothing else to beat Diana's card, Galahad had no choice but to play a trump card to win the trick.

As he studied his hand with a bland expression, he picked up his lucky quarter again and flipped it faster than before. Perhaps in panic? "If they knew the punishment in advance, why do you think that they still went out of their way to put jam in her shoe?" He snatched a card, for once more irritated than lazy, and tossed it down.

It was the queen of spades.

The significance of it made Vee's pulse race with excitement—because she knew unequivocally that that was the third-best trump card in the pack, barring her unbeatable ace and Minerva's king. The jack was long gone. And so were the eight, nine, and ten, because she had already played them. The arrogant fool didn't have anything lower, or he'd have played it.

He swallowed when Minerva played her king. "Using your theory that they like to spend time with the adults, I suspect it might have something to do with the fact that Mrs. Witherspoon always reads to the little ones at bedtime and this week's book has always been one of their favorites." She smiled at the twins' shenanigans for two reasons. First, because she adored them both despite all their mischief, and second, she was mischievous enough herself to want to toy with Galahad like a cat did a mouse before she went in for the kill.

That was why she almost laid her five of spades instead of her ace to allow Minerva to take the leveling trick. Almost—until she decided that she would much prefer to give him a sound drubbing herself than with her sister's help.

She laid the ace on Minerva's king just to spite him. "Two apiece. It seems we are level."

Except they weren't.

Diana had nothing and she was certain—given the speed at which his lucky quarter was traveling from his index finger to his little one and back again—that Galahad also suspected the last remaining trump in the pack was in Minerva's hand. Either way it guaranteed Vee the win by default.

"Have you found someone to fix that leaky roof and the money to pay for it?" As he was attempting to cover his disquiet with chatter, she let him for her own amusement.

"I am still haggling but am hopeful we at least have the money thanks to Mrs. Leyton-Brown."

His lucky quarter stilled as he frowned. "Mrs. Leyton-Brown?"

"A lovely lady and a stalwart of society until ill health forced her to leave it." Olivia's smile was wistful as she remembered her acquaintance. "She died a week or so ago. All very sad, but expected as she never recovered from her last stroke. Her illness aside, she was a ripe old age. She had to have been well over eighty despite her outrageous claims to be a good twenty years younger. You must have met her, Galahad? Or at least seen her, as she was quite the character and not easily forgotten. She had a fondness for ostrich feathers and always proudly sported the tallest plumes on her headdress at every evening function. Always dyed some vivid shade to match her dress or her hair. She was famous for dying her coiffure all the colors of the rainbow."

"While Mrs. Leyton-Brown was indeed a character, and one often gossiped about for her sartorial eccentricities . . ." Vee shot Olivia a chiding look. "She will be most remembered for her philanthropy and for being the orphanage's most generous benefactor. She gave us the building back when we started and has apparently now left us a generous bequest in her will to ensure that our good work continues."

"How generous?"

She shrugged, guiltily, because it felt wrong to speculate aloud to the sheer size of that bequest when they had not yet heard categoric proof of it from the solicitor. "All I know is that it is a timely miracle when we really needed one. As soon as the snow clears, I am accompanying the Reverend Smythe to Brighton to visit her solicitor where we shall find out exactly what that bequest entails and sign all the particulars."

"Sad though it is that the world has lost such a generous character, thank the Lord for timely roof miracles." The lucky quarter began to dance again as Galahad smiled. "If I might be so bold as to offer you a suggestion, seeing as I know that town well, when you visit Brighton, avoid staying near the Royal Pavilion as all the inns nearest there charge the earth for inedible food and shoddy accommodations. In fact, I'd avoid all the inns near that part of the seafront for that same reason. They are priced for the tourists who know no better. I heartily recommend The Mermaid. It's still by the sea but a little farther west in the direction of Hove. Decent beds to sink into, quality linens, delicious food, and far enough away from all the noise that you'll get some sleep but not so far that you can't walk into town in no time."

"Thank you. That is good to know." As the winner of the last trick, Vee finally laid her five of spades, feeling triumphant because she knew it was the highest trump left, and a second later Diana groaned as she tossed down the two, exactly as Vee had suspected.

"I hate this stupid game!"

All eyes swiveled to Galahad, who did not move a single muscle, and Minerva, who was still smiling enigmatically as if she knew something the rest of them didn't.

Olivia sucked in an audible breath. Jeremiah and Giles shuffled their chairs farther forward. Hugh stood to get a better view of the table. Even Payne leaned closer, his usual bland expression replaced with one of anticipation. The tension in the room now so palpable you could cut it with a knife.

After an age her vexing opponent sighed then kissed his quarter in defeat, ready to hand it over.

Or so she thought—until he tossed down his card.

The six of spades.

He did not wait for Minerva to toss down her useless card before he grinned. "Three to me and two to you. I guess that makes me the winner?" He glanced toward her book with only the slightest hint of triumph. "Unlike your terrible twins, I'll be reading myself a bedtime story tonight."

"Well I'll be damned!" Jeremiah punched the air. "The witch's spell has finally been broken!" For once, even Olivia was too busy gaping to admonish him for cursing.

The room erupted around them while Vee blinked at his card. It seemed inconceivable to lose on such a low card when her hand had been one of the best she had ever been dealt. She glared at Galahad with narrowed eyes, begrudgingly impressed. To his credit, he didn't crow about his victory. He winked, pocketed his lucky quarter, then stood and quietly retrieved her favorite book from where it still lay on the arm of the sofa before he headed toward the door.

"Good night, all. Thanks for the dinner and the fine company. And thank you, Miss Venus, for an excellent game."

He left amid much backslapping, waving away all offers to walk him to the door, while Jeremiah whooped with delight as he cracked open the fine whiskey he had been saving for a special occasion.

As she heard it click closed behind him, Vee knew that for the sake of her own sanity she couldn't leave it like that, so she dashed to follow.

His long legs had already taken him several yards across Berkeley Square before she skidded down the steps behind him.

"Galahad!" He turned, pausing so she could catch up. "How did you do it?"

"How did I win? Well, that's easy, Miss Venus. You're not the only person on this planet clever enough to be able to count and memorize cards, any more than you're the only one to read Shakespeare." He smiled and not the least bit smugly. To her chagrin, it was devastating. Galahad Sinclair was too attractive for his own good. Too likable as well, devil take him. "But surely a better question is, How the hell did I beat you when you had such an unbeatable hand?"

"So how did you?" She folded her arms against the cold and in case her wayward bosoms decided to proclaim exactly how attracted they were to his devastating smile. "Because we both know that *was* an unbeatable hand."

"Few hands are entirely unbeatable—but I'll concede yours came pretty close. I'll also concede that you're good, Miss Venus. Good enough that I had to throw three tricks in a row in that first hand before I could read you, like you read one of your precious books." He tapped *Much Ado*, chuckling, before he slipped it into his greatcoat pocket. "But I'm better."

"How does that cryptic response answer the question? *Your* question." She rolled her eyes. "You just taught me a lesson, I'll concede that, albeit begrudgingly. But I like to learn, Galahad, and improve, and cannot bear a conundrum that I cannot understand. So be a *quality* gentleman for once. Or take pity on me—I do not care which—and put me out of my misery, as I shall only tie myself in knots *not* knowing and won't sleep for a week trying to work it out."

He gave some serious thought to that request. "If you want my *professional* advice, I'm going to need your word that whatever I confide in you remains between us."

"Well, of course it will! If I tell them how you beat me, they will also know how I beat them, so that isn't going to happen."

"I'm going to need your word, Miss Venus. A solemn pledge to go alongside our truce."

She raised her right palm, glaring. "I *solemnly* pledge never to tell a soul what you are about to divulge." Then she held it out. "I am even prepared to shake on it like a gentleman."

He stared at her outstretched hand for a moment before he took it and shook it, and for some inexplicable reason the contact made every nerve ending she possessed fizz before he released it and shrugged.

"You hold your cards closer when you know that they are good, you act too nonchalant when things get sticky, and when they get really sticky you fiddle with your locket. In that final hand *you* allowed me to distract you. With something I knew you couldn't resist, allowing *me* to steal enough of the space in that big ol' brain of yours that you missed the real significance of that queen I played."

Her eyes narrowed as everything slotted into place quickly. "The orphanage."

"When I laid the queen, you assumed that because I had laid it it was the only trump card I had left, and because you were desperate to win every trick from me to teach *me* a lesson, you used your ace too early. Thus unwittingly leaving me still holding the six and you without a trump card high enough to beat it in the final trick."

He shrugged as he chuckled. "Don't feel bad, Miss Venus, because we all have an Achilles' heel. All I needed to do was work out where to aim my arrow to take you down. Which meant that while I was oh-so-casually distracting you with conversation, clumsily playing with that ol' quarter you couldn't keep your eyes off, you committed the cardinal sin, as would any *drawing room amateur* who doesn't know the first golden rule of gambling: You underestimated your opponent. You allowed all those latent prejudices you've always held about me to taint your thinking and you allowed your ego to sabotage yourself."

"You were acting! All the way through!"

He smiled in confirmation. It made his dratted, disarming eyes twinkle in the most alluring fashion. "You've got to admit I'm damn good at it. Good enough to convince both you and Minerva that I was going to lose that final trick to one of you." Out of nowhere his silver coin appeared in his hand and danced between his fingers before he tossed it to her. "Keep it. It might help you to keep beating Jeremiah in case he ever cools his temper long enough to get wise to your methods."

Vee caught it. The worn metal was warm from his touch, and that heat alone apparently had the power to make her stupid nerves fizz even more. "But it's your lucky quarter . . ."

"It's just a quarter, Miss Venus. I make my own luck. Always have. Always will. Luck has nothing to do with your talent for winning, either, does it?"

She shook her head, impressed at his perceptiveness and intelligence now that she was suddenly forced to view him in an entirely new light. And perhaps would have sooner if she hadn't harbored so many incorrect prejudices about him. Reminding herself that four years ago, this same man had hoodwinked both her family and his own father for weeks, perhaps months, to ensure that Giles hadn't been stripped of his dukedom. Galahad Sinclair had always possessed a remarkable talent for acting. Why had she allowed herself to forget that?

Because he vexed her.

Because he had always vexed her.

"Apparently I'm not the only one here with a big ol' brain." She mimicked his accent with a begrudging smile. "Bravo, Galahad. Well played. Enjoy *Much Ado* again."

"I will."

He turned to go but hesitated. "Seeing as we are being frank with each other, much as I enjoy how the Bard handled Beatrice and Benedick's scathing but evenly matched banter, I've always preferred *Taming of the Shrew* myself because, exactly as it happened in our game, the heroine eventually had no choice but to surrender to the cleverer hero."

She had seriously underestimated him. "I'll begrudgingly grant you clever—on this one occasion—but certainly never cleverer. I'll beat you next time, Galahad. On that you can be certain." She had to beat him. He'd unsettled her enough tonight to last a lifetime and she had no idea how to feel about it.

Galahad answered that challenge with a shrug. "I've no doubt you'll win this book back from me someday soon, so I'll take good care of it until the rematch." He tipped his hat, looking somehow more handsome than she had ever seen him. "Good night, Miss Venus. It was a pleasure reading you."

Chapter Seven

My world has ended. All my dreams are shattered. Apparently too much reading by one candle in the small hours does ruin your eyesight! No decent man is going to want to marry me now that I have to wear spectacles . . .

—from the diary of Miss Venus Merriwell, aged 16

"Clothes always maketh the man, Mr. Sinclair, and trust me, check is the pattern *du jour* this winter."

While he was ambivalent regarding the checks, and his fancy Mayfair tailor had never steered him wrong in the three years that he had been dressing him, Gal was still unconvinced by the loud purple fabric he had unrolled on the counter. However, he did not doubt that clothes did indeed maketh the man in the aristocratic circles he was working his hardest to impress. He used a less flamboyant and more reasonably priced tailor on Cheapside for his more no-nonsense attire for The Den, while Bardwell & Bardwell dressed him—alongside several dukes—for Mayfair. This was Giles's favorite tailor shop, and, like his cousin, Bardwell's specialized in sartorial panache. The sort that made a man stand out rather than blend in, which was exactly what his new business demanded, even if standing out jarred with his natural preference for blending.

"I don't think I'm a French lavender sort of fella, Mr. Bardwell."

The proprietor never called any color by its proper name. In honor of the exclusive clientele he served, common words like *blue* and *red* were frowned upon in favor of their more elaborate relations. "But I'll take those checks in the brown."

The tailor nodded, noting it in his ledger while correcting him at the same time. "The *burnt umber* is an excellent choice for a waistcoat, sir, and will complement your strong wheaten coloring." He gestured to Gal's freshly cut hair with his pencil. "Might I suggest a coat in fine-gauge wenge wool to go with it? As that combination will emphasize your impressive shoulders, too."

He couldn't help but smile at that ridiculous word. "I was with you for the umber and the wheat, Mr. Bardwell, but I'm afraid that you've completely lost me with the wenge, as I wouldn't know what that shade was if you slapped me in the face with it."

The tailor reached for a book of swatches and rifled through them until he found a dark sort of brown, which he held against the slightly reddish brown of the checks. "*Wenge*, sir. Don't they go well together? These two, paired with some tight buff breeches, will have all the ladies in Hyde Park swooning as you ride past them." He also liked to flatter his customers by commenting on their magnificent physical attributes or by claiming everything made them more attractive to the opposite sex. While such sycophantic tactics were water off a duck's back to Gal, he could imagine it worked a treat for the pompous fools like that windbag Dorchester who Miss Venus put so much stock in. "What do you say?"

Internally, he was frustrated at himself for voluntarily thinking about Venus again when he was here, four hours early and on the unfashionable side of noon, because the witch had crept into his dreams again last night to ensure he slept fitfully. He still blamed their waltz last week rather than last night's card game for his continued preoccupation with her. That damn dance had given his body ideas about the vixen it had no right having, let alone holding on to. But hold on it had, as last night's fevered but vivid dreams were testament.

Thanks to their card game, his imagination had added a new twist to its recent nocturnal torments. One involving her and him playing a game of cards using their clothes as the stakes.

His blood heated again just thinking about it.

"I say I'll give the wenge a whirl." Gal also pointed to the elaborate cornflower damask silk, which was reminiscent of the shade Venus had worn so well at the Rokeby Ball, the shade that matched her eyes, but which Mr. Bardwell insisted on calling *Bleu de France* with a matching French accent. Probably because that made it sound more exotic and justified the extortionate price he was charging. A price that had caused Gal to almost choke on his own tongue when he first heard it. "You've talked me into this, too." He decided not to wince at the additional dent one stupid waistcoat would make in his wallet. After all, he had to dress as if money were no object to attract the clientele who lived and died by those ridiculous standards into his new club when it opened.

This rash purchase was absolutely nothing to do with Venus and her eyes.

Perhaps if he told himself that often enough throughout the day, he might actually believe it by this evening when the inevitable remorse set in.

"Have I shown you the stripes that arrived last week?" Mr. Bardwell turned his back to fetch a heavy bolt of fabric from his shelves behind. "This verdigris will do wonders for your eyes. I know how much the ladies admire them . . ."

Currently, there was only one lady's admiration he was craving, damn it, and he was honest enough with himself to acknowledge that it had nothing to do with his quest to improve relations with her or his business. The relations he wanted to have with her involved them both cozied in his bed together naked watching the sun rise while he probed the inner recesses of her mind to discover exactly how that clever brain of hers thought. An expedition that he knew would take more than one night of passion, because Venus was more than a temptress. She was a fascinating dichotomy—a prim and proper card sharp with the heart of an angel, the mind of an academic, and a body made for sin.

A lethal and dangerous combination best avoided.

Annoyed that she had invaded his thoughts yet again, Gal allowed his gaze to wander to the falling snow outside the window while Mr. Bardwell did his best to blatantly sell him his entire shop. Irrespective of the early hour and the continued foul weather, Piccadilly was bustling. He couldn't help smiling as well-heeled shoppers and their servants mixed with the street hawkers on the crowded pavements, and the nose-to-tail carriages and carts moved at a snail's pace through the filthy snow.

The familiar hubbub reminded him of Broadway back home. Perhaps that street across the ocean had been rougher around the edges than this polished cousin, but the sounds, sights, and smells of this city were much the same. Even the weather felt reassuringly familiar. Winters could be as bitter along the banks of the Thames as they had been along the Hudson, and the cloying summers were just as unbearable when the hot July sun chose to be relentless. Those similarities were oddly comforting on the rare occasions Gal allowed himself to hanker for the past, echoing a distant beat he understood and could fall into step with most of the time.

". . . I think this new dove kerseymere would be an asset to your wardrobe, too, Mr. Sinclair." As Gal turned back to his tailor, he saw something else familiar out of the corner of his eye. Or perhaps in his wayward, lusty imagination. A fine, curvaceous figure and a distinctive walk that could surely only belong to one woman as she bustled past the window. "A coat in the same cut as we are doing in the wenge . . ."

With last night's carnal dream so fresh in his memory and the unwelcome impact of it still resonating in his needy body, if this was Miss Venus, then he should let her go about her business.

Chasing after her with no justification beyond the worrying compunction to simply see her smile wasn't wise when he had drunk his fill of it last night across the card table. There would be other, better opportunities to find a plausible excuse to collide with her and improve their fledgling relationship over the coming days and weeks, and Rome wasn't built in a day. It would be much better to allow the strides they had made last night to marinate, then collide with her again within the safety of a family or social situation. Because there *was* safety in numbers, and being alone again with her suddenly felt . . . dangerous.

That was a more sensible plan of action.

"Whatever you think best, Mr. Bardwell." Yet contrary to that sound plan, for some inexplicable reason his fingers had already grasped the doorknob to follow her anyway, even while his head screamed at his feet to stay put. "I shall be back presently but . . ." As his head began to scream at his mouth, too, for uttering words it shouldn't be uttering, he stood on tiptoes to follow her progress down Piccadilly. The second her sensible blue bonnet melted into the crowd, some irrational force more powerful than him convinced Gal to dash out onto the street to follow her before he even finished his sentence.

For the first few yards he thought he'd lost her, but he finally caught sight of Miss Venus crossing the road. Or at least all his senses told him that the compelling woman in blue was Venus.

It had to be her.

The unconscious sway of her bottom as she strode with purpose, contrasting with the useless, silly little reticule that swung from her gloved wrist, was surely proof enough?

As Gal hurried across the road in reckless pursuit, she paused only long enough for him to notice that she wasn't alone as she shepherded three boys into Hatchards bookshop. Like a man possessed—or bewitched—he followed, then skidded to a brief halt outside so that he might enter the building with a casual nonchalance that he hoped looked convincing.

As she was already engaged in a conversation with a shop assistant at the counter when he burst through the door, and because he had no earthly clue why he was even here when he was supposed to be elsewhere, he darted behind a long row of bookshelves. He used the excuse of perusing the titles on offer as an opportunity to compose himself because, frankly, and to his complete surprise, he was in dire need of some serious composing.

His stupid heart was racing, and more than the exertion of a short dash warranted. There was something peculiar going on in some of his other organs, too. A fluttering in his stomach hinted at excitement or anticipation, or both, and a tightness in his throat suggested he was nervous. The sort of nervous a fella got when he wanted to make a good impression on a girl he was taken with rather than the ominous-bad-feeling kind that would have been preferable at this precise moment.

All very odd and unlike him.

Clearly, the long, fitful night filled with inappropriate dreams had left him too tired to think straight if he was fancying himself fancying Venus. His lifelong dream was so close he could taste it, so now was the time to remain single-mindedly focused on his business and not . . .

"Hello, Galahad." He inwardly cringed at the sound of her voice and attempted to arrange his features into a look of surprise before he turned to greet her, only to fail thanks to the stunning smile she bestowed upon him. A smile that completely disarmed him and made him grin back like a besotted idiot. "How is it possible that I usually only see you once in a blue moon and yet here we are colliding again for the second time in less than twelve hours, and the fourth in two weeks?"

"Well, howdy." Too late he tried to act more surprised at the sight of her than he was at the disingenuous greeting that his mouth had vomited. His performance so unconvincing his toes curled inside his boots.

Howdy.

Howdy, for pity's sake! When no self-respecting Yankee who resided north of the Carolinas ever uttered such a southern colloquialism. He had grown up in a tavern in New York City, for pity's sake, not a tobacco farm in Tennessee!

"This *is* a bizarre coincidence." The lie made his stupid throat tighten some more, and caused it to do unflattering things to his voice. Really, no self-respecting grown man's vocal cords should squeak. He swallowed to lubricate them but was horrified when the squeak then turned into an irregular croak. "What brings you here?" His constricted throat burped out the words like a bullfrog.

"Why, books of course." She swept her arm around them in amusement at his patently stupid question. "Isn't that what usually draws a person into a bookshop?"

Scrambling for something more erudite to reply without sounding like either a mouse or a toad again, he scanned the shelf in front of him for some inspiration and pulled a face. "But this is the novels section, Miss Venus. Far-fetched tales of intrigue and derring-do written to entertain the lowly, educationally inferior masses rather than the weighty, learned tomes you usually read." Great. Instead of erudite—and on the magnificent back of "Howdy!"—he had plumped for insulting.

"I read as many novels as I do learned tomes, Galahad." For once she didn't bristle at one of his barbs. "But ironically, it is the entertainment of the masses that has brought me here today as I am using my pin money to treat the orphanage to some new books. Preferably novels filled with intrigue and derring-do, as I am of the firm opinion that children deserve to read for fun as well as for education." She squared her shoulders as if expecting criticism for that opinion. "Some might disagree with my teaching methods, and think novels are silly fictional flights of fancy that hold no great educational value to improve impressionable young minds, but I have always found a love of reading leads to a love of learning. That is certainly what has always fueled my thirst for knowledge, so I shall teach from those *inferior* books regardless."

"As I prefer a flight of fancy over a weighty tome any day, you'll hear no arguments from me. I'm no teacher, but it seems to me that impressionable young minds surely need opening before you can fill them."

"Exactly!"

Glad that he'd managed to say at least one sentence without either squeaking or burping, but still floundering thanks to the beautiful smile that hadn't faded, Gal gestured to the three boys who had gathered behind her, the two tallest of whom were eyeing him with proprietorial curiosity. "Who are your friends?" By the identical features, matching red hair, and gangly, almost-adolescent-but-not-quite bodies, he had already worked out that those two freckle-faced sentries were the infamous Claypole twins.

"We were about to ask you the same thing, Miss Merriwell." The twin on the left folded his arms, eyeing Gal like an enemy. "We were worried this bloke was bothering you."

"Mr. Sinclair is an old family friend so he isn't bothering me in the slightest." She smiled at the boys as she motioned them forward. "This is Tommy, and this is Sydney Claypole." She swept her hand decisively toward each as if she had no problem telling them apart, although how she could was beyond Gal when they were two ginger peas in a pod. "Who I have had the grave misfortune of teaching these past four years. And this young man is Billy Tubbs. Billy only joined the orphanage recently after the reverend found him on Drury Lane. Boys, say hello to Mr. Sinclair."

"Hello, Mr. Sinclair." It was said in impressive, parroted, and broad cockney unison, but that did little to disguise their obvious suspicions. Suspicions about a stranger's character that he well understood and respected more than they could possibly know.

To disarm them and stop them glaring as if he was a potential danger to their beloved teacher—or worse, themselves—Gal smiled at the twins. "I hear you boys have a fondness for jam and spiders."

"They have more of a fondness for mischief and mayhem *involving* jam and spiders, Mr. Sinclair." She answered for them with a roll of her eyes. "And have been seconded here today to carry all my shopping as part of their ongoing penance for both pranks."

"I suppose that's only fitting after ruining a pair of bedroom slippers this week on the back of scaring all those young ladies witless." Gal was being purposefully familiar with their antics to reinforce the fact that he was indeed an old family friend of Miss Venus's, but he allowed the twins to see he was impressed by their industry, too, to win them over. "While we're on the subject of that earlier incident, I'll confess I'm curious, boys—where on earth did you harvest so many spiders at this time of year? From what I heard, the girls' dormitory was crawling with critters."

"The cellar," said Sydney with a proud grin, thrilled that an adult was interested in him at all. "There's more spiders in there right now than you can shake a stick at." That earned him a warning glance from his brother, which he ignored. "Especially in the wintertime, as they are hiding from the cold."

"You solemnly swore to me that you found them all in the yard!" Miss Venus's cinnamon brows had furrowed, but uniquely at Tommy and not at Sydney who had unwittingly made the confession. "How on earth did you get into the cellar again when I made sure that it was double-padlocked after last time?"

Tommy glared at his brother first in an I-told-you-not-to-say-anything kind of way, then shrugged all innocence. "Somebody left it open, miss."

She eyed Tommy, who was clearly the mastermind behind the Claypoles' shenanigans, in exasperation. "Or somebody picked the lock to the key cupboard again." Her hands went to her beguiling hips. "How many times do I need to tell you, young man, that just because you *can* pick a lock doesn't mean that you *should*?"

The boy hung his head in mock shame. "I'm sorry, Miss Merriwell."

"And how many times must we discuss how unacceptable it is to lie, Tommy?" She wagged her finger in time with her chiding words. "Pranks involving spiders are atrocious. Breaking and entering is illegal. But lying is downright *despicable* and I will not tolerate it!"

The boy shuffled from foot to foot as he stared at them. "I'm sorry about that, too, Miss Merriwell."

"If you were truly sorry, Tommy, I wouldn't have to keep repeating myself about the same unfortunate behaviors, now, would I?" She stared unblinking at the lad until he withered under her glare, then shooed him away. "Go make a start on that list of books I gave you while I consider how to punish you for breaking into the cellar and *lying* to me about it!" Her curled lip left the boy in no doubt she was more aggrieved at the latter of that pair of sins. "Two of everything and pile them neatly on the counter." Her schoolmistress's finger wagged again. "Woe betide anyone who doesn't behave in the most exemplary fashion! That most especially goes for you, Tommy Claypole!"

All three boys hurried off to do her bidding, and she huffed out a sigh. "Honestly, I swear that whatever I say to that boy goes in one ear and out the other."

"Yet he still absolutely adores you." That was as plain as the freckles on the young miscreant's face. "Having seen it with my own eyes, I am more convinced than I was before that he misbehaves to get your attention."

"As much as I hate to give you any credit for anything, Galahad Sinclair, I suspect you might be right." She glanced over at the subdued boy and shook her head. "Although I haven't yet figured out how to stop it. Tommy Claypole is, and always has been, an unstoppable force of nature and a hard nut to crack."

Gal took a moment to study him, watching how the boy took charge and dispatched the other two to the task at hand like they were his own personal troops. "He's a natural-born leader, though."

"Always has been. Unfortunately, that also presents the biggest challenge—no matter how often he is punished, he still frequently leads the other children astray. Especially his brother. Sydney is his most trusted lieutenant"—she said that word in the weird British way where the *lieu* became *left*—"and would follow him to the ends of the earth and fling himself off the edge if his brother told him to."

"Maybe you're approaching the problem of Tommy all wrong, Miss Venus."

"Suddenly you are an expert on how best to deal with children?" She bristled at what she took as a criticism as she ran her finger along the books beside them until she found the one she wanted and yanked it out. Then used *The Rime of the Ancient Mariner* like a shield clutched to her distracting chest. "Have you taught many orphans in your dubious gambling career, Galahad?"

"None whatsoever." Beyond himself, that was. He'd had to learn fast when he'd been left to fend for himself. "But I do know people and how to manage them, Miss Venus, and while it's practically impossible to completely banish the flaws born or bred into them, you can always iron them flatter with the right incentive."

She peered down her nose unconvinced as she wafted a regal hand in the air. "Please, do enlighten me with your superior masculine expertise and wisdom." She really didn't want to hear it, but he was enjoying her outrage too much to completely back down. Her lovely eyes always shimmered like stars when her hackles were raised. "For what could I, with my four years of experience teaching orphans, possibly know about how to deal with them?"

"I'll admit everything I know about teaching orphans could be counted on zero fingers—" Gal held up his fist with a wiggle as proof. "—but I do know that when a prime opportunity presents itself, only a fool doesn't exploit it."

"How splendid. Riddles. Just what I needed to help me tame the untamable Claypoles." She spun toward the bookshelf again and searched for another volume. "I shall be sure to act on that sage advice as soon as I've solved the puzzle." She reached up and used the tip of her finger to attempt to prise a copy of *Ivanhoe* from the highest shelf rather than ask him to do it. "Because I do so enjoy a puzzle." She played the no-nonsense schoolmistress well—the teacher's glare punctuating the end of that tart British sarcasm was magnificent. It got more terrifying the second he dared to laugh at it and raise his palms in surrender.

"Before you send me to the corner to wear the dunce's hat, allow me to explain my theory—and it very much is a theory rather than a set-in-stone, I-know-best solution, because you are the expert here and I know absolutely nothing about teaching. However, it strikes me that if Tommy Claypole is an intelligent and natural leader who has the enviable talent of influencing others, instead of giving him a free rein to lead them where he pleases in his ongoing quest to get attention from you—" Gal effortlessly grabbed the offending book that was eluding her and passed it to her, forcing her to look at him before he let it go. "—then *exploit* both of those things. Use his talent for leadership to suit your purposes by giving him some proper responsibility. Make him *your* most trusted *left*-tenant, Miss Venus, and I guarantee he'll not only bend over backward *not* to let you down, he'll also follow *you* to the ends of the earth."

Her nose wrinkled in either disgust at him, or disgust that she hadn't considered that as a potential solution, as she grabbed a third book to add to her stack. "Much as it pains me to admit it, that is actually rather good advice. It might be worth a try seeing as everything else so far has failed."

"And so might this." He shrugged. "As previously stipulated, I might know people, but I'll concede my knowledge comes from dealing with people who can grow a beard." He took the books from her and smiled at the thick Swift novel sitting on the top of the pile. "Good Lord, I've not seen this for years. I am so glad it's in print over here, too. My mother used to read *Gulliver's Travels* to me at bedtime when I was little. Over and over again because I refused to settle if she tried to read me another." Gal couldn't resist flicking through the pages to remind himself of the imaginary islands and people, his eyes focusing on the nonsense names he had giggled over as a boy—Lilliput, Glubbdubdrib, Brobdingnag, the Yahoos. "I loved the idea of strange worlds across the sea filled with stranger people. I even considered joining the navy back then so as I could travel the world like ol' Gulliver did, but my ma was adamant no decent ship would take me on as their surgeon until I turned at least fifteen."

While he chuckled at that forgotten but pleasant memory, her expression was wistful as she stared at the cover. "You're lucky. I don't remember my mother at all, she died when I was small, but I do remember

Minerva reading this book to me in our dingy rooms in Clerkenwell when I was little, too. I have the fondest memories of being magically transported to another place for a little while . . . a much better place where poverty and hardship didn't exist and the world was filled with new adventures." As if she were embarrassed to have admitted that much, she offered him an awkward shrug. "I believe my love of books began then—and probably all thanks to that fictional ship's surgeon Gulliver."

Gal nudged her with his elbow. "Don't tell me we actually have something else in common to go alongside our talent for counting cards? And a book at that. When I was convinced you only read dry old texts like that unintelligible Shakespearean tragedy I liberated from you last night."

"*Much Ado* is a comedy and not a tragedy, Galahad, as well you know, and that sham naive act you put on no longer washes with me after last night's sound drubbing, either." Her expression was more amused than annoyed by that drubbing. "But in truth Shakespeare's story and Gulliver's are not that dissimilar." Two copies of *Robinson Crusoe* found their way onto the stack. "Both are shameless flights of fancy filled with intrigue, suspense, and feats of derring-do."

"If you say so, Miss Venus." He leaned against the bookshelf and enjoyed watching her stretch again for another volume, allowing his eyes to appreciate her momentarily in the full masculine sense while hers were looking elsewhere. His visual pleasure was short-lived, however. Not because she noticed and not because he forced himself to stop looking, but because he felt an odd whisper against his waistcoat.

The briefest graze, so light and subtle, he didn't doubt most Mayfair gentlemen wouldn't give it a passing thought, but not subtle enough for a streetwise fella like him not to notice.

Chapter Eight

It is official. The Merriwell sisters have run out of money. I am worried sick as to what will become of us if our landlord tosses us into the street as he has threatened. Please come home, Papa! We need you . . .

—*from the diary of Miss Venus Merriwell, aged 17*

"You need to be faster than that to rob me, Billy Tubbs."

Vee blinked in shock at the sight of the wrist of the orphanage's newest recruit trapped in Galahad's grasp, his gold watch dangling from the nimble young pickpocket's fingers like a noose.

Eyes wide, the rascal did the unthinkable. He used his full weight to stamp on Galahad's foot while simultaneously jamming his bony elbow into his midriff, then bolted for the door still clutching the stolen watch as if his life depended on it.

"Billy!" To save both the boy and the watch, Vee hoisted up her skirts and gave chase. "Billy, no!" She knew already that the orphanage would never see the lad again unless she could catch him. He was a panicked, frightened, distrusting, and mostly feral boy. One she really should never have brought on an outing so soon, no matter how sorry she had felt for him. "Billy! Come back!"

But the boy didn't even glance back, let alone slow.

She had barely reached Fortnum and Mason next door when

Tommy streaked past her. "We'll get him, Miss Merriwell!" Hot on his heels was Sydney, and the pair of them were quickly swallowed by the crowd of pedestrians, only their ginger heads visible as they jostled their way through.

Galahad caught up with her next, in time to witness all three boys disappear down a narrow side street, but by the time they reached it, there was no sign of any of them. Billy could have escaped down any one of the warrens of alleyways and streets ahead. As Galahad scanned them for any clues, she shook her head. "A needle in a haystack."

Where Vee would have admitted defeat and anxiously waited outside the bookshop for the Claypoles to return, kicking herself for her own stupidity at losing a poor, lost boy who might have been saved given time, Galahad spun a slow circle, deep in thought. As he tapped his chin, she watched his eyes flicker as he pondered the options, nowhere near ready to give up. After what had to be half a minute he grabbed her hand and pointed. "If the reverend found him on Drury Lane, he'll head there. That's home. He'll feel safer sticking to his usual hiding places than trusting somewhere unfamiliar." With that he dragged her along Piccadilly and then right onto Haymarket in the direction of the theaters.

They were halfway down it when a panting Billy suddenly shot out of one of the back alleys, so panicked by the charging Claypoles on his tail that he failed to notice the adults to his left until Galahad sneaked up and caught him from behind, then held him firm.

"That was a mighty stupid thing to do." He was surprisingly calm considering the scrawny, frightened child wiggling like an eel in his arms.

"I'm sure he is sorry, aren't you, Billy?" As angry as she was at the boy both for the theft and for betraying her trust so abominably, she didn't want his young life ruined because of one ill-considered mistake. "I am sure that if you give Mr. Sinclair his watch back, he won't call a constable to arrest you." In case that was exactly what Galahad had planned she stared beseeching, hoping he would take pity on the child despite his crime. "I am sure he won't. He's a *good* man." At least she was coming to suspect that he was. "You made a mistake, that is all. We all do it. But it's not the mistakes we make that matter in the end, it is what we learn from them and how we rectify them that's the most important." She reached out to rub the boy's tense arm. "We can sort this mistake out between *us*, Billy, you'll see . . . and once we do, we can get you back home to the safety of the orphanage where you belong."

To her horror, Billy lifted his foot again, shod in the new boots she had personally issued him because he had arrived barefoot, and brought it down hard. Thankfully, Galahad had anticipated it and managed to dodge the heavy sole at the last moment without losing his hold on the wriggling boy at all.

"That was another damn stupid thing to do." With Billy's panicked feet still flailing around trying to find a suitable bone to kick, Galahad hoisted him into the air, hugging the child tight to prevent his elbows, hands, and nails from doing more damage to his person than they had already.

"Let go of me!" Billy was practically purple and so petrified her heart bled for him. "Let go of me now!"

"Not a chance!" With impressive strength his captor hauled Billy to the side of the street, twisted him to face him, then pinned the still-suspended boy with his back to the wall.

"What the hell were you thinking?" Despite the harsh tone, Galahad's restraint impressed her. He had a firm grip on Billy but only enough to keep him tethered rather than hurt. "Do you honestly think the streets are a better place for you to be living than the orphanage?" He appeared more inquisitive than enraged and completely in control of the situation irrespective of how hard the child fought him. "In this freezing weather? The proceeds of my watch aren't going to keep a roof over your head or food in your belly for long, idiot, any more than they will protect you from all the low-life criminals who make their livings fleecing little boys like you—or doing worse to them. Never mind how stupid it was to have stolen the dang thing in the first place in broad daylight. In Mayfair, no less, where there's one of those new uniformed bobbies patrolling every corner? Or is it your lifelong ambition to be transported to the Antipodes for a lifetime of hard labor?" Not at all the speech Vee expected him to make when he had been robbed and assaulted in quick succession.

Instead of the hot glare of revenge, it was compassion that swirled in Galahad's stormy green stare. "You got any family expecting you somewhere, Billy? Someone depending on you? Anyone who would even be worried that you had gone missing this past week?"

Stunned by Galahad's unexpected lecture rather than the violent beating he undoubtedly assumed he had coming, the boy shook his head.

"So you're all alone in the world?" The boy nodded, his breath sawing in and out erratically but his gaze now fixed on the man's. "Got no one and nothing except the clothes on your back and my watch in your pocket?"

Billy nodded again, looking ready to burst into terrified tears at any moment if his captor so much as raised his voice. Yet instead of raising his voice, Galahad turned to an equally stunned Tommy and Sydney, who couldn't quite believe what they were seeing or hearing, either, and spoke to them in the sort of reasonable tone one would expect in a friendly debate at a duchess's tea party rather than during a citizen's arrest after a mad dash across town.

"Do you two hate living at Miss Merriwell's orphanage, too? Is it a bad place where they treat you mean and beat you?"

Both boys swallowed but Tommy managed to find his voice first. "The Reverend Smythe doesn't believe in violence. Nor does Miss Merriwell."

"If they don't whip you, how does the orphanage punish you if, for example, you unleashed a thousand creepy spiders on a roomful of unsuspecting girls?"

"We had to polish all their boots for a week."

"Were you starved that week, too, Tommy? Sent to bed with your tummy so empty the pain of it ripped you in two and kept you awake all night?" Another insightful question that once again made Vee wonder if Galahad knew firsthand what he was asking about.

As if he understood the tack this polite interrogation was taking, Tommy Claypole shook his head again but stared straight at Billy as he spoke. "I'm always in trouble, but I still get three square meals a day plus an apple at playtime even if I've lost the right to go outside and play."

"That sounds like a nice place to be living, if you ask me." Galahad stared intently at his prisoner again, willing him to see reason. "A decent place filled with decent people. I'll wager those shiny new boots you're wearing that it's a place far better than you are used to, Billy, so why on earth would you want to throw it all away? For a watch that no decent pawnbroker will touch with a barge pole in case they get charged for handling stolen goods, and none of the indecent ones would pay a street urchin like you so much as a tenth of what it's worth?"

It was a rhetorical question that Galahad expected no answer to because he smiled at the boy who was now hanging limp in his arms and clearly mortified by his own shortsighted stupidity. "It makes no sense to toss all those good things away when life has finally thrown you a chance. Given you a warm bed. Food. Safety and security. An education so you can better yourself and lovely people who care about you, for a change, like Miss Merriwell here. Who is guilty of nothing more this morning than trying to defend you, when you let her down."

Billy's bottom lip trembled as his gaze flicked to hers, ashamed.

"It's all right, Billy." Vee smiled. "We all make mistakes. I've made some corkers in my time." So many stupid errors of judgment, usually involving men, that she had run out of fingers to count them on.

"When life tosses an opportunity your way, Billy Boy, only a fool doesn't grab it." Galahad smiled at his prisoner as he used his accent again to charm and disarm. "So what say you to givin' back my ol' watch, we finish buyin' those books, you go home with Miss Merriwell so she can teach you how to read them, and we all just forget this silly misunderstanding ever happened?"

A tear rolled down the boy's cheek as he nodded; a tear that Galahad gently swiped away with his thumb before he lowered Billy to the ground. When he held out his palm and the watch was deposited in it, Galahad even ruffled the boy's hair. "I knew you weren't an idiot, kid. Knew it the first moment I laid eyes on you."

And that was apparently that.

No lingering outrage.

No grudge.

Not even any further mention of the theft, almost as if it had never happened.

Instead, they all walked back to Hatchards together, chatting amiably about this and that as if taking a leisurely Sunday stroll after church. At the shop Galahad proceeded to not only gather up all the books they had hastily discarded but also add to the huge pile with a few favorite "flights of fancy" of his own. He even insisted on paying for them all.

Back outside, he tossed Tommy a sixpence to buy the three boys something from the confectioner's and she finally had a moment alone with him to thank him for his phenomenal benevolence and admirable good grace.

"That was very decent of you." So decent it made Vee feel guilty about every ill thought she had ever had about him. "Especially when you were well within your rights to call a constable." That he hadn't had touched her. Forced her to reevaluate, yet again, the complex man that he was, now that she had been confronted with proof that, once again, she had grossly misjudged him. "A kind and generous heart clearly beats inside your chest." Unable to help herself, she pressed her fingertips against it, only to be reminded that it was indeed as impressive and solid a chest as she, and her wayward bosoms, remembered from their waltz. Despite wanting to explore the intriguing plain of it further, she snatched her palm away. "You have been very noble."

He shrugged it off, embarrassed either by the compliment or to have revealed that side of himself. "A watch can be easily replaced—

but the lifeline you and the orphanage have thrown that boy couldn't. Besides, if I'm reading young Billy right—and after last night's sound drubbing you have to concur that I am excellent at reading people"—his green eyes danced as he winked, and her pulse quickened at the sight—"it was habit that made him steal my watch, not malice." Rather than look at her, he raised his arm to flag down a passing hackney. "A habit born out of a lifetime of desperation—because he knows no better, nor expects any better from the people he encounters."

She had clearly grossly underestimated Galahad all these years and on so many levels. He was as perceptive as he was intelligent, and as compassionate as he was vexing. Because she was sorely tempted to use her errant fingertips to smooth his lapels, she fiddled with the delicate handle of her reticule instead. "The reverend rescued him when he tried to pick his pocket, too. I was in Hampshire, snowed in, at the time he arrived at the orphanage, but by all accounts he was filthy, shoeless, and dressed in rags."

"As he's a bag of bones, I'm guessing he was also starving."

"He was. He's actually put some weight on this last fortnight, so he was alarmingly malnourished. Yet despite the bed, clothes, and food, he still distrusts the orphanage." Most children did, but for the most grievously abused few—like Billy—that distrust was entrenched so deep, it took forever to dislodge. "I only brought him along today to prove that it isn't a jail and instead of reassuring him, the first chance he got, he reverted to stealing."

Galahad's shrug said he wasn't the least bit surprised. "He's grown up *needing* to be wary of the motives of everyone around him. For a boy like Billy, if something appears to be too good to be true, it usually is. Therefore, it would make sense to have some insurance put by in case he needs to make a quick escape when his instincts are proved right. You only have to look at the way he reacted when he was caught to realize he's already had the hardest of lives. If that is what he's used to, he's going to be a harder nut to crack than Tommy Claypole."

As the Claypoles had been almost wild when they had first entered the orphanage, that truth did not daunt her. "It often takes time to earn an orphan's trust."

He smiled. Not his usual easy, charming smile, but one more intimate. Utterly potent as far as her body was concerned—but insightful. As if he understood her and approved. "But I'll wager my newly repatriated watch that you're one of those rare people prepared to put in the hours to make sure that happens, Miss Venus, so I reckon Billy's going to come good in the end." He directed that killer smile at the boys as they hurried toward them, already stuffing their delighted faces with licorice.

"And clearly you're one of those rare people who believes in giving lost and abandoned little boys second chances. Why is that, Galahad?"

In lieu of answering he pretended to be outraged. "Can you keep your voice down? Sayin' things like that is goin' to ruin my ruthless and scandalous reputation." To ensure that her question remained unanswered, he loaded the books into the carriage first and then the boys. Last of all he helped her up. If he experienced the same ripple of awareness at the brief contact as she did, he hid it well. "You boys be good for Miss Venus, or you'll have me to answer to, you hear?"

Instantly Tommy Claypole grinned at that unwitting revelation while she cringed. "Your name is Venus? Venus after the planet . . ." He wiggled his ginger eyebrows suggestively. ". . . or Venus after the goddess of *love*?" As a ferocious blush bloomed on her cheeks in confirmation, he threw his freckled face back laughing as if her unfortunate name was the funniest thing in the world while Galahad winced at his unintended faux pas.

"Sorry, Miss . . . er . . . I assumed they knew."

"We didn't," said Tommy in between fits of hysterics as he rolled around the bench seat with his brother. "When anyone asks her, she always insists that her name is just Vee."

As if all his Christmases had come at once, the rapscallion gaped with his finger pointed. "Which by my reckoning makes you a *despicable* liar, too, Miss Merriwell!"

Chapter Nine

Minerva is dragging us to Hampshire on a quest for forty pounds. I think posing as a mans fiancée for money while fraternizing with him unchaperoned in the middle of nowhere is grossly improper and have told her so . . .

—from the diary of Miss Venus Merriwell, aged 17

It was odd.

Gal knew it was odd as he stared sightlessly into his barely touched whiskey glass. He had envisioned this moment, yearned, planned, and prepared for it for so many years, he had assumed tonight would be a night for celebration and excitement. An opportunity to pat himself on the back and feel proud of his achievements. Feel elated to have doggedly chased his dream and to finally have everything in the palm of his hand to make it a reality.

To finally be happy.

Content.

Satisfied.

Instead, and irrespective of the signed deeds tucked safely in his saddlebag and locked in his usual room upstairs, exactly as he had been at every significant, pivotal moment in his life thus far, he was subdued and introspective. More than a little overwhelmed by the sheer enormity of it all, truth be told, and desperately alone. So alone it swamped him. He couldn't explain why, when he had been alone for so long now that being at peace with it came as naturally as breathing.

Usually he liked it.

His work meant he was always surrounded by people, so some genuine solitude was such a luxury he rarely ever sought company elsewhere unless he had to. He supposed it would be easy to seek some here to drag him out of this dark mood. Brighton was a party town, and The Lanes and the seafront were peppered with noisier inns than this one, filled with visitors out for a good time. There was no end of people to make merry with, except he already knew he wouldn't. Celebrating his lifelong ambition with strangers seemed sadder than sitting here and staring into his glass alone and overwhelmed.

He blamed the speed of the transaction, his mad dash to Brighton, and his significantly lighter bank balance for unsettling him. Until yesterday when he had received Mallory's express, Gal hadn't expected to sign anything until the middle of December. However, thanks to Mrs. Leyton-Brown's meticulously organized affairs and the straightforward nature of the sale, it transpired that her dynamic young solicitor had no problem turning it all around in a record three weeks once his fee was trebled. Mallory must have moved mountains to get it done so fast.

But then Mallory was desperate.

Mrs. Leyton-Brown, God rest her, had thought she was doing her nephew a favor by leaving him the solid investment of an extensive property portfolio over money. After Venus had let slip that the wealthy widow had left the orphanage money, he had made some subtle inquiries and had been delighted to learn that the old woman had apparently divvied up all the substantial funds she had in the bank to her favorite charitable causes, which she assumed needed them quicker than her hedonistic nephew did. He was glad Venus's was one of them. He was gladder that Mallory was left conveniently rich in land rather than funds, so still technically in debt up to his debauched eyeballs. Without Gal's help, although he had been sorely tempted to assist, word had soon leaked out that the reckless lord had had a windfall and his creditors had lost their patience, so that meant he urgently needed Gal's money to pay them if he wanted to keep his bones unbroken.

Hence the hasty transaction, yesterday's messenger hammering on the door of the Albany at the crack of dawn and Gal's unplanned, last-minute race to Brighton after only two hours of sleep. An interminable, miserable, and freezing journey over mud, slush, snow, and ice he hadn't minded for a second because of the bright light at the end of the tunnel. A journey that had allowed him to be waiting outside the solicitor's office first thing this morning with a severely hung-over Mallory the moment the man unlocked his doors.

He had no doubt Mallory was out there somewhere celebrating, but that fool had been out celebrating last night too before he had even known Gal would arrive, when any sensible fellow knew that a game wasn't over until the last card was played and you could never be certain what that last card was until it was flipped.

Thankfully, Gal had flipped a trump.

That thought instantly made him think of Venus, and for the first time this evening he smiled. The look on her pretty face when he had beaten her at cards was a memory he treasured and had revisited often this past week. That and the way she had looked at him after he had given Billy a reprieve in Piccadilly the day after. As if she was finally seeing him for who he really was and liked what she saw.

It had felt strange showing her a glimpse of the real him.

Disconcerting, when he usually kept that private for his own protection, but also both empowering and humbling because she had let some of her guard down too. That unfamiliar sense of kinship had felt nice. Unsettling. Significant too, although he had refused to allow his mind to wander down that dark path too far.

He had seen her only the once since, when Giles and his wife had dragged him to the theater to watch some god-awful singer named Lucretia de Vere warble her way through an opera. Because the woman on the stage was some sort of acquaintance of both the Sinclair and Standish families of old, Venus had been at the performance, too. They had been in opposite boxes and so only really collided for a few minutes during the interval, but she had smiled across the theater a time or two when she sensed him watching, and with absolutely no malice at all. Which meant he was hopeful they were making some headway toward improving their relationship, and grateful she hadn't caught him watching her as frequently that evening as he had been. Especially when his eyes had drifted her way incessantly to drink in the bewitching sight of her, then for reasons best known to themselves had absorbed every detail to sear into his memory to recollect at will.

The mouthwatering coral gown.

The loose tangle of copper-gold curls piled atop her head.

The way she tried and failed not to snigger impolitely whenever Ms. de Vere's substandard voice wavered or hit a note wrong, and the way her fine eyes sparkled when she gave in to it.

The minx had gotten under his skin, and he wasn't sure whether to be mad at that or glad. He had a sneaking suspicion it might well be the latter—despite that being an unwelcome complication he really did not need at such a significant time.

More was the pity.

The door opened, causing an icy chill peppered with snow to whip around the tavern and stir the flames of the roaring fire beside him. The logs within spat and crackled in protest; a few stray sparks popped from the grate to divert his attention from the door. Yet bizarrely, before he dared to turn back around to confirm it, the ripple of awareness that drizzled down his spine like thick molasses told him that she was the one who walked through it.

Here!

As if he had conjured Venus out of nothing but pure longing.

Oblivious of his presence, after stamping her feet on the threshold to dislodge the snow that clung to her boots and while carrying yet another silly little reticule not fit for the purpose, she approached Nelly at the bar.

"I don't suppose you have two rooms available, do you?"

"You're in luck, miss, because two is all we have left." Nelly smiled as she put down the tankard she had been drying and reached for her register. "Who shall I say they are for?"

Before she could answer, Gal did. "If my mind-reading skills are what I think they are—" He put a finger to his temple as if he was seeking supernatural help as she spun around in surprise. As a firm believer in a person's first reaction being the right one, he took great pleasure in the fact that the smile she shot him was a big one. "I'd say one of those rooms is for the Reverend Smythe of the London Parish of St. Giles . . ." He unfolded from the chair to saunter toward her. ". . . and the other is for the infamous card sharp Miss Venus Merriwell."

Damn, it was good to see her.

With his current bout of melancholy, it would've been good to see any familiar face at this precise moment. But Venus's especially, and the palpable relief at seeing her, had gone some way to shaking him out of it. "I'm not sure a respectable house like this should take in such a known undesirable, Nelly. I say you take pity on the reverend on this cold, bitter night as he's a man of God but send this ne'er-do-well packing."

"I daresay any establishment that would admit a dubious scoundrel like you would also take me, Galahad Sinclair." Even the touch of condensation that had misted her spectacles couldn't disguise the teasing sparkle in her eyes, which he took as another very good sign indeed. "And for the record, your mind-reading skills are not that good, as one room is for the Reverend *and* Mrs. Smythe."

"So I missed the vicar's wife . . ." He shrugged, trying not to appear delighted that he had her company. "I take it you journeyed here to see that solicitor?" In truth, he wasn't entirely sure how he felt about that now that the initial euphoria of her unexpected arrival was wearing off.

Should he tell her that he had already been to see that same solicitor? If he did, that meant admitting he had bought the buildings beside her beloved orphanage, and he wasn't entirely sure she would be receptive to hearing that yet despite their fledgling friendship.

However, keeping her in the dark now that those premises were officially his didn't sit right, either.

The proverbial rock and a hard place, so he'd play it by ear. Be adaptable. Tell her when he gauged the time was right.

"Indeed. Tomorrow. First thing." Then she still had no clue how much the old lady had left her. "We took advantage of the break in the weather and hoped it might hold long enough for us to spend the night here and head back to town tomorrow, but as you can see . . ." She gestured toward the door she had entered and the snowflakes melting on the flagstones. "It appears there wasn't a break here in Sussex, or if there was we missed it, because it's coming down thick enough that it's settling again. I have my fingers crossed we don't find ourselves snowed in here for a week like I was in Hampshire last month." And just like that, Gal experienced the urge to cross his own fingers and hope they were both snowed in. A week stranded in this cozy inn alone with her sounded perfect.

The door slammed open again and all his hopes of it being just her and him beside a roaring fire shattered, as her traveling companions bustled in. Gal had never met the much-lauded and universally respected Reverend Smythe before, but with his purported tireless devotion to the orphanage, Gal had pictured a more robust gentleman than the white-haired one who came in sneezing while his equally mature wife fussed beside him.

"I told you that you should have worn more layers! I warned you that you would catch a chill, Ignatius!" Without any introductions, Mrs. Smythe turned to Gal shaking her head in exasperation as if they had been acquainted for years. "He has always been prone to coughs and sniffles. Even in his prime a cold would floor him. The trouble is, there's no telling him that he has long past his prime because he simply will not have it. He works far too hard, sir. All the hours the good Lord sends, so is it any wonder he goes downhill so fast?"

"I breathed in some hay dust in the stable." The reverend flapped his wife away. "Hay always makes me sneeze."

"In the summer, Ignatius, not the wintertime."

"For pity's sake, Constance, how many times do I need to tell you that I have no plans to turn up my toes anytime soon? Your incessant fussing is as unnecessary as it is unwelcomed after eight uncomfortable hours in a carriage!"

"Perhaps a mustard bath is in order?" Mrs. Smythe turned to Nelly as if she hadn't heard him. "Could I order one of those and some hot soup to be brought to our room at your earliest convenience? Only I fear my husband's condition might quickly decline into a fever if not swiftly managed."

"I do not want a mustard bath! What man in his right mind wants to smell like a condiment?"

"Now, Ignatius, see reason. You must look after your health."

"I knew I shouldn't have brought you." The reverend looked to Venus for support. "Didn't I tell you allowing her to come with us was a bad idea?"

The older woman folded her arms. "I could hardly leave Miss Vee unchaperoned!"

"With a man old enough to be her grandfather whom she has worked alongside unchaperoned every single day for several years without issue!" The vicar spread his hands before throwing them up in the air in frustration. "After half a century of marriage to me, are you really suggesting her virtue was ever in danger, Constance? For if you are, I am mortally offended by the implication."

"Of course I am not suggesting that, Ignatius! But somebody has to be mindful of her reputation *and* yours. What would happen to your orphans if you had to leave the church in disgrace?"

Venus stifled a smile as she slanted Gal a glance that told him the pair of them were always like this, before she deftly intervened. "Reverend, Mrs. Smythe, I should like to introduce you to Mr. Galahad Sinclair. He is the cousin to my brother-in-law the Duke of Harpenden."

"Ah yes! The American chap who fleeced you out of your favorite book, Vee!" The reverend beamed as if he hadn't just been in the midst of a public disagreement with his wife and stuck out his hand. "Well done, young man! I've been trying to beat her for years, all to no avail, so I am glad somebody finally bested her." For an old man, who if his wife was to be believed was on the cusp of death, he had a very robust handshake. "I do hope you made her suffer in her defeat. Nobody deserves some time in gaming purgatory more than dear Vee here does."

"That is hardly a Christian sentiment, Ignatius." Mrs. Smythe rolled her eyes before she inclined her head. "I am pleased to make your acquaintance, Mr. Sinclair. Please ignore my husband. Traveling always makes him disagreeable."

"Whereas simply breathing makes my wife disagreeable." The reverend tilted his neck to see past Gal. "Is there a Mrs. Sinclair we should also be introduced to?"

"Good grief, no!" While the denial came swiftly, Gal's stupid eyes still gazed hungrily at Venus. "I'm as free as a bird, Reverend, and happy to be so."

"Very wise, young man, for all women do is nag a man."

It was Miss Venus this time who took him to task. "All women seem to nag *you*, Reverend, which rather suggests the problem rests squarely on your shoulders as clearly there is something about your character and behavior that necessitates it."

"And my point is proved," said the reverend with a jolly smile on his face, "as now I am being nagged by the pair of them."

Nelly directed her youngest son upstairs with the luggage before striding back toward her new guests. "Will you all be wanting dinner? We've a leg of lamb roasting, or there's a pigeon pie or some beef stew that'll warm your cockles on this cold evening."

"The stew sounds perfect, doesn't it, dear?" Mrs. Smythe answered for both of them.

"I'm about to eat myself if you'd like to join me for dinner?" The invitation came out of the blue, because Gal hadn't even thought about food until now. He'd been too busy feeling miserable.

"Thank you for the offer, Mr. Sinclair, but we shall politely decline tonight." Gal's heart sank at the reverend's words. "As much as it pains me to agree with my wife, I am not as young as I used to be and I am exhausted after such a long journey, so we shall eat in our rooms then retire for the evening. But I am sure Vee will join you." Instantly his poor heart sang again. "It is much too early for her to go to bed, and no doubt the pair of you have all sorts of family gossip you wish to catch up on without the chore of making polite conversation with two curmudgeonly septuagenarians."

Put on the spot, she smiled. "That would be lovely . . . if you can spare me a little while to freshen up first?"

"Take all the time you need, Miss Venus, as I'm not going anywhere."

She followed the Smythes upstairs and Gal found himself uncharacteristically nervous as Nelly laid his favorite table by the fire for two. Only part of that involved his dilemma about when to tell her his news, but as that seemed a safer thing to focus on than the butterflies currently flapping at the intimate prospect of spending an entire meal alone with her, he decided to give the problem his full attention.

When to tell her? How to tell her? Would it be better to save it until she had met with the solicitor and they both had something to celebrate . . .

He sensed her again before he saw her, so ended up watching her descend the narrow stairs transfixed with a strange tightness in his throat. Lord, she looked beautiful tonight. Even still wearing her sensible traveling dress. Sensible it might well be, but the deep blue brought out the color of her eyes and the soft wool clung to her curves in all the right places. The snow had left her hair damp, meaning the curls she tried so hard to tame were doing their own thing and wildly, the fat corkscrews bouncing in time with her naturally undulating motion. Her cheeks were deliciously rosy, exactly as he imagined they would be when flushed from passion . . .

"Put your tongue away and stand like a gentleman." Nelly's timely whisper was accompanied by a hard nudge moments before Miss Venus arrived at the table. "Can I tempt you with some wine, miss?"

"Er . . . yes." She seemed nervous, too, as she sat opposite. "That would be nice." As Nelly went off to fetch it and he sat, she thankfully filled the silence he had no clue how to. "As this is your stomping ground and you recommended this place, what should I eat? The lamb, the pie, or the stew?"

"Always the lamb. Nelly's daughter has a way with it, and the trimmings are divine. And the treacle pudding—" He closed his eyes as if in heaven. "—is as tempting as sin incarnate." Much like her tonight. "Exactly what you need after what I suspect was an entertaining journey . . ."

Galahad was surprisingly good company throughout the excellent meal, but as they finished their desserts, Vee realized he had asked her so much about her life that she was no wiser about him than she had been before she sat down. Exactly as he had done to her last week in Piccadilly when she had queried something personal. He did that a lot, and with everyone now that she came to think upon it, not just her. Whenever a question was directed at him, he effortlessly batted it away with a brief or sometimes enigmatic answer, and before you knew it you were talking about yourself again. It felt imperative to immediately correct that.

Imperative to understand what made Galahad tick.

"When did you first discover The Mermaid?" She gestured around her to the capacious yet cozy room whose sedate patrons were made up of genteel travelers and regulars content to eat and chat the evening away. They were not at all the sort of people she would have assumed he would want to associate with. But then again, a week ago she wouldn't have thought he was the sort to understand the dire motives of a young pickpocket, either. Everything she had wanted to believe and feel about Galahad had now been flipped on its head, making her . . . unbalanced . . . but in a good way. As if she were stood on the deck of a ship, bouncing across the waves, on the cusp of an adventure. It was as unnerving as it was thrilling, making her feel young and bold and, oddly, ripe for the picking.

"Around the same time as I washed up on these shores four years ago."

As he didn't elaborate further, she decided to pry some more, convinced that there were huge swaths of his life thus far that not even his cousin Giles was privy to—but that she now desperately needed to know. "And on that first visit, did you come to Brighton for business or pleasure?"

"A little of both." He smiled at Nelly as she came to clear the plates bearing a steaming pot of tea and two cups. "Tell Mary that dinner was as delicious as usual." There it was again. That instant deflection rather than allow anyone to see behind the curtain. Artful deception again, most definitely—but why?

"Is he always this cryptic and mysterious, Nelly?" If Galahad wouldn't give her any answers, she would seek them elsewhere.

"I prefer to use the words *secretive* and *frustrating*." The older woman pulled a face as she relieved Vee of her soiled napkin.

"*Secretive* is an excellent descriptor, Nelly." Vee poured the tea. "Do you know, I have known him for four years and yet know practically nothing about him at all." She deposited his customary two sugars into his cup before sliding it across the table. "His business here in Brighton might as well be a state secret for all his family back in London know about it."

"Why doesn't that surprise me, Miss Merriwell?" Nelly wiped the crumbs from the table then stood with her hands on her hips. "For I can honestly say the same about what he does in London."

"Allow me to fill in some of your blanks, Nelly, for Galahad here owns a scandalous gaming hell in London's docks called The Den, which I can only assume is short for The Den of Iniquity as that is what I am led to believe it is."

"Does he indeed?" Galahad was glaring at her through narrowed eyes over the rim of his teacup, as uncomfortable in his own skin as she had ever seen him, but Nelly continued undeterred. "That certainly explains where all his money comes from! Gambling, Gal? Really? *You?*"

A bizarre reaction that threw up even more questions. "I was under the impression he ran a similar dubious enterprise here, Nelly."

"The Mermaid doesn't allow gambling, Miss Merriwell, and thank goodness as I couldn't be dealing with all the trouble that goes alongside it." Nelly used the napkin to swat him with. "Are you going to tell her that you own half this place or shall I?"

He huffed at his apparent business partner, annoyed. "I think you already did that, Nelly."

The older woman grinned saucily over her shoulder as she carried the plates away while Vee blinked in shock. "You own this, Galahad? This is your clandestine Brighton business? A respectable inn where gambling is *banned*?"

He sipped his tea slowly, taking his time because he was as uncomfortable that his secret was out as he was talking about himself. "You don't have to sound so surprised that it's respectable, as my place in the docks is respectable, too." He tapped the table between them to make that point. "I'll have you know that everything there is aboveboard and compliant with all the laws. I pay every person who works for me a decent wage *and* I pay all my taxes. I just happen to cater to a crowd who enjoy a controlled raucous atmosphere, like to wager, and prefer to do it in a house that doesn't cheat them in the process." He rearranged his cup back on its saucer rather than look at her. Went to change the subject, then huffed in defeat.

"Contrary to what you might think, Miss Venus, I don't keep a brothel. I don't bait bears or dogs or innocent chickens for sport and I certainly don't take a man's marker or offer him a line of credit when he runs out of coin, then intimidate him until he bankrupts himself or makes his family homeless to pay it back. I run as honest a business there as I do here."

"But it's called The Den, Galahad. A name that has certain connotations."

"Well, I could hardly call it The Basket of Kittens, now, could I? It's a bawdy club on the wharf side that needs to appeal to the sort who wander there. A man needs to earn a decent living, Miss Venus, and fluffy little kitties ain't going to cut it."

"You certainly earn enough of a decent living to be able to live at the Albany and have Hoby make your boots."

He shrugged again, struggling to hold her gaze, preferring to sip the still-scalding tea rather than let her see the truth in his eyes. "There's easy money to be had in gaming, and only a fool wouldn't want a slice of that pie. I'm an ambitious man and I'll make no apologies for that."

She found his defensiveness of his dockside club both fascinating and ironic. "Which begs the obvious question as to why you haven't tried to replicate that success here, when Brighton is famous for gambling above all else?"

"I wanted to diversify." He was fiddling with his teacup again, and something about the tense set of his jaw told her there was more to it than that. He was hiding something. Something he would rather nobody else knew.

"That makes absolutely no business sense, and you know it." She folded her arms and stared until his eyes rose to meet hers. "What is the real reason you bought into this place?"

He glanced around and, noticing Nelly pretending not to listen to them intently from the bar, sighed. "I need to stretch my legs and walk off some of that big dinner. Fancy joining me?"

"Is that an unsubtle attempt to change the subject as usual, or a subtle way of hinting that you'll miraculously answer my question in private?"

He smiled his usual cocky smile to cover the hint of vulnerability she briefly saw skitter across his much-too-handsome face. "I guess you'll have to risk taking a turn with me beneath the moonlight to find out."

Chapter Ten

I hate Hampshire! Hugh has hired some awful actress to play our mother and I am supposed to tell anyone who asks that our father froze to death while walking in the Cairngorms! Obviously, out of loyalty to our dear, long-lost papa, I have refused most vociferously to take any part in it...

—*from the diary of Miss Venus Merriwell, aged 17*

"At least the snow's slowed." Gal pointed to the fat, full moon in the oddly ethereal purple sky, stalling for time. He was still in two minds about how much of the truth to tell her as they walked side by side out of the inn and onto the seafront. He hadn't offered her his arm, because that felt too intimate, especially when the conversation seemed doomed to be more personal than he was comfortable with. Yet something told him that he should have such a conversation with her. Be more of himself for once—for her again—because . . . *And there is another dark path I'm not sure I want to venture into!* "Although the sky ahead looks pretty foreboding still." What had he been thinking even considering telling her any of his truth? When life had repeatedly taught him that if you didn't keep all your cards hidden, someone would exploit the weakness in your hand. "Maybe we will get snowed in?"

Venus being Venus, she cut him no slack. "You were going to tell me why you bought half The Mermaid."

"Was I?"

"If you're not, I shall leave you to your evening constitutional in peace." She prodded him with her finger as he pondered where to start the tale, reading his reticence entirely correctly. "And if you dare try to make your explanation sound impersonal, when it is clearly intensely *personal*, I've decided I shall instantly cancel our truce and never waste my time trying to converse with you ever again. Either we are going to become the unlikeliest of friends or we remain reluctant acquaintances. The choice is yours, Galahad."

The quaint English phrase *in for a penny, in for a pound* sprang to mind. Because knowing Venus and her big ol' brain, the moment he told her one thing, she'd ask him about everything. To his own surprise, because he very much liked the idea of them being friends, he found himself starting at the beginning.

"I'm guessing you remember my father?"

Her nose wrinkled in disgust, her tone immediately all outrage. "I doubt any of us could ever forget Gervais Sinclair! That man was an evil, vile, malicious . . ." Gal held up his palms in surrender in case she used every foul adjective in the dictionary—all of which would have been entirely appropriate.

"For what it's worth, I'm not sorry he's dead, either." Neither was he sorry that his odious sire had died in jail where he had always belonged, nor did he harbor any guilt that he had been the one to send him there. After deserting his ailing mother—twice—his malevolent father had deserved nothing less. As Venus had been there the day Gal had turned his own flesh and blood over to the authorities, there was no point going over that old ground when it was the older that had always been the most pertinent. "He abandoned my mother shortly after I was born, so I never knew him growing up. It was my grandpa who helped my mother raise me, and because she wasn't in the best of health, bless her, he did the lion's share of the parenting."

"What was wrong with your mother?"

"She was born with a lung disorder and sometimes struggled to breathe properly. Not all the time—it flared up especially in cold weather—but when it was up it made life hard for her. Running around after an exuberant little boy didn't help matters, I suppose, so Grandpa did all he could to ease her burdens." It felt peculiar speaking about it when he never had to another living soul before. Yet the memories were always there, so strong and clear and poignant they might have happened yesterday.

"He owned a tavern on the waterfront—The Four Leafed Clover. On South Street. Right on the busy banks of the East River where all the merchant ships docked." The mention of it took him right back there. That brief, halcyon time in New York when he had never had a care in the world. "It was in such a prime spot, it was a gold mine. Always crowded. From the minute the doors opened until he had to push the customers out in the small hours."

All that hubbub was still one of Gal's favorite noises. The sounds of laughter, chatter, and dice hitting the tables meant money hitting the till. But it also reminded him of the worry-free existence he had enjoyed back then, when food, shelter, and safety had been things he had taken for granted. When he had never had to look over his shoulder or be wary of another's motives or live hand to mouth: The memories of those struggles were so painfully fresh they plagued him daily. For the most part, he used them to spur him onward. Those hardships were the fuel that powered his ambition and the stone that strengthened his necessary defenses against anything threatening it. But sometimes, like tonight, all that negativity weighed him down.

"From my earliest recollections I was always beside him as he worked, learning at his knee while he entertained his customers—or his only grandson—with stories of his past. Several of them were about that place." He jerked his thumb back toward The Mermaid. "He grew up there. It belonged to his father and was the place my grandpa first learned his trade. I came to find it almost as soon as I arrived in England,

and when I saw it was in disrepair and discovered Nelly was broke and on the cusp of closing it, I felt I owed it to my ancestors, and most especially to my grandpa, to save it."

"Oh, Galahad." Venus slipped her arm through his and briefly hugged it tight. It felt wonderful. "I never realized you were a sentimentalist."

"It's not an acceptable trait in a ruthless businessman, so it's not a side of me I advertise." That he was allowing her to see this side of him was . . . unprecedented. And perhaps more than a little terrifying when exposing any of his vulnerabilities went completely against the grain.

"So Nelly is family?"

"No." He shook his head, wondering why he still felt compelled to speak when his instincts warned him that it would be more prudent to shut the hell up. "My great-granddaddy lost the business when my grandpa was still a boy, and the place changed hands many times since. I'm not sure of the exact circumstances but I know that my family fell on hard times and were left with nowhere to live. That, I suppose, was the catalyst that ultimately sent them stateside to new pastures. It was my grandpa who first opened the tavern on the waterfront because that was his dream, and he passed the dream on to me, so I guess innkeeping is in the blood. Growing up, I recall him often reminiscing about this place." Instantly his head was filled with the sounds of his grandpa's voice, warming him from inside.

"He always wore a faraway smile when he told me about his childhood and how he used to think about the other side of this ocean from his bedchamber in the attic as he planned his future. Always lamented how much he missed it despite the good life he had built for himself in America. Always planned to return here to see it one last time but . . ."

"Fate had other plans?"

Gal nodded, wishing he did not possess that awful memory more than any of the others burdening him. Wishing more that the memory still didn't cut him to the quick each time he remembered it. "He died when I was twelve. So sudden it floored me and my ma."

"Am I allowed to ask what happened?" He could tell by the pity etched in her lovely face that she wouldn't pry if he chose not to elaborate, but for some reason he wanted to, which was bizarre when it was a memory he had been avoiding ever since it had happened.

"He was shot." The bile churned in his gut as the more dreadful images he preferred to suppress assaulted him. "By a customer. Right in front of me while he was trying to break up a fight."

She stopped dead, halting him in the process, her lovely eyes swimming with tears. "Oh, Galahad—that is awful." She reached up until her gloved hand cupped his cheek tenderly in comfort. "I am so sorry."

He found himself leaning into her palm before he realized what he was doing and shrugged to cover his uncustomary display of weakness. "Not as sorry as I am."

His grandpa's murder had been the first pivotal moment of his life, and one that had changed everything catastrophically. It had been the decisive end of that halcyon era and the abrupt beginning of the end of his childhood. His first lesson that the world could be cruel and wasn't as solid or safe as he had been convinced it was. The grief had been . . . relentless. The loss unbearable. But it had also signaled the end of everything he knew.

Which, he realized with a jolt, probably accounted for his melancholic mood of earlier. His ambition—his drive to be a success—was as much about righting the wrongs of his past as it was about controlling every aspect of his future. About rebuilding his grandpa's legacy, chasing *his* dreams, and returning what had been stolen from him as well as about ensuring Gal never had to suffer any of that misery again. He couldn't bring his ma back, or his grandpa, but he could resurrect something of what had been from the ashes. His victory today was, therefore, bittersweet because the price for it had been too high.

Too damn high.

But he had felt sorry for himself enough for one night. All the self-pity in the world wouldn't bring back his family, or the life they had once had. He had known that when he came here, determined to make a fresh start away from all that pain—but it had followed him anyway. Shaped him still. "Anyway, I guess you've worked out already that I bought this place for him—because it is here that I feel the most connection to him now that I am so far away from home." A truth he was surprised to admit aloud.

She stared back at the inn, taking it all in before she sighed. "The need to feel that tangible connection to hearth and home is one of the things that makes us human, so it makes perfect sense to me that you bought it. What happened to The Four Leafed Clover?"

Rather than tell her that sorry truth, he sugared it. "Long gone. Demolished now, I believe, to make way for something new." Watching them tear down his last link to his family back in New York had been another pivotal moment. One that had left him rudderless and anchorless, because he had always planned to buy it back. To run it as his grandpa had always intended. "Hence I decided to make a go of it here when fate dragged me back to the land of *all* my ancestors—both the good ones and the rotten eggs like my undisputedly evil father."

"When did he reappear in your life?"

He wasn't ready to talk about Gervais's initial reappearance in the dark days after his grandpa had passed, or the way the bastard had tricked his mother, and him, into believing he was a "changed man" keen to make amends for abandoning them and ready to take on all the responsibilities of a husband and father.

Gal had needed a father then so very badly, he'd welcomed the man with open arms. And because his ailing mother had started to smile once more, he'd allowed himself to briefly be a boy again. Except his vulnerability, neediness, and gullibility had quickly turned around and not so much bitten him on the ass as ripped it into shreds. So Gal skipped over almost all of the single most pivotal decade of his life with the most abridged version of the truth he could. "Gervais turned up like a bad penny a few days before I turned twenty-one, keen to profit from my inheritance so he could get himself back here to swindle Giles—and so I let him. But only to stop him."

Thankfully, he had been a very different Galahad by then. The too-trusting boy was long gone and had been replaced by the cynical, battle-scarred, and wary man that he was now—but angrier. He hadn't allowed Gervais into the solicitor's office when he finally collected the mysterious locked box of belongings his grandpa had left him for the day he reached his majority, so his father never knew that the one hundred dollars that Gal had used to pay their passage to England came alongside a more valuable nest egg: the share certificates he had used to buy The Den. He spent the anger on the cathartic pursuit of seeing that Gervais got exactly what he was due, then tried to lock all of the past in a box and move on.

"If it's any consolation, at least you found Giles and turned out to be nothing like Gervais." As if she understood he wasn't ready to let her delve much deeper, she tugged his arm to continue walking despite the thickening snowflakes being tossed around in the frigid sea breeze.

"We were both cursed with awful fathers, weren't we?" She instinctively hugged his arm tighter against the cold. "At least you know what happened to yours and have been able to bolt the door on that part of your life and put it behind you." He'd wanted to. Hoped to. But knew those experiences influenced him still and likely always would. "Alfred Merriwell seems to have disappeared into the ether so I cannot turn that page—but then he always excelled in that. My sisters like to think he came to a sticky end and is buried in an unmarked pit somewhere or rotting facedown in a ditch unmourned. But I suspect he's out there lurking somewhere still, biding his time to bother us again. I hope he is."

"Why?" Her father was a forger who had abandoned his daughters to poverty then turned up again when Minerva found Hugh, only to blackmail her. "From what I hear, you are better off without him." Gal's life would have been so much better if Gervais had remained lost. Everything would be different.

Literally everything. But then he wouldn't be here, and as much as he wanted to deny the truth of it, right here, right now with her was exactly where he wanted to be.

"That is also undisputable but . . ." Myriad complex emotions played across her features. "I hate my last memory of him. I hate that I begged him to stay. That I wanted a father in my life so much that I was prepared to turn a blind eye to all his many faults and unconscionable crimes." A childish sentiment and shameful regret he well understood. "That he left anyway. He got the last word when I realize now that I had more to say. More I wish I could say. It feels like . . ."

"Unfinished business." He understood that only too well, too. It had been the bellows that had stoked his ambition for more than half of his life.

"That is exactly what it feels like. I am not a vindictive person, Galahad, and I do not want revenge as I firmly believe that the good life my sisters and I have now is revenge enough, but . . ." She sighed heavily as she stared out to sea. "For myself, to close the door on his treachery and bolt it shut, for my own foolish pride I would like my final memory of my dealings with him to be different. Not the frightened pleas of an immature girl but the damnation of a grown woman who no longer wears blinkers and who knows, through personal and professional experience, all the pain and suffering a child goes through when a parent abandons them. I want to be able to look him dead in the eye and dispassionately tell him that he and all the other feckless fathers—and mothers—out there are not only going to rot in hell but are going to languish there forgotten when their children succeed in life despite them. Unmissed. Unmourned. But most of all unforgiven."

There was nothing dispassionate about the fire burning in her lovely eyes. A heat that explained why she worked so tirelessly for those orphans. She was righting the wrongs of her own past through them. "I'd like to spit in his eye." A naughty smile toyed with the corners of her mouth. "Or perhaps shop him to the authorities like you did Gervais. Or more likely do both. I envy you that."

"So the prim, proper, and pious Miss Venus actually does want revenge?"

"Perhaps a little bit." She held her finger and thumb an inch apart, her fine eyes dancing again exactly how he liked them before she looked away. The light in them clouded slightly. "Despite all your opinions to the contrary, Galahad, I've never been the prim and pious paragon of virtue any more than you are apparently all bad."

"Was that a compliment? A concession? Are you unwell, Miss Venus? Do you need to lie down?" He leaned closer to scrutinize her face as if he had never seen it before. "Only I barely recognize you when you're not looking down your nose at me."

She offered him a begrudging smile. "Much to my chagrin, and against all my better judgment, it appears that I am finally starting to like you."

"That feeling is alarmingly mutual, Miss Venus." He smiled, meaning it, until she wrenched her hand from his elbow to yank him to face her.

"For the record, I'd like you more if you stopped calling me Miss *Venus* to vex me, you wretch."

He chuckled as he shook his head. "Not a chance. I enjoy vexing you too much to ever give it up. But as a concession to our truce, and because you are starting to like me and I am starting to like you, I'll drop the Miss—*Venus*."

Then, because her plump lips twitched in mirth while she looked down her nose in feigned disdain.

Because the snowflakes glistened in the moonlight as they attached themselves to her riot of curls.

Because fate had brought them here. Tonight. Together. And here was special.

Because her hand was still in his and his hand was in hers, and because that felt right.

Because this was exactly where he wanted to be and because he suddenly needed to, Gal tugged her closer and, before he thought better of it, softly pressed his mouth to hers.

Her fingers briefly flexed against his as she instinctively stiffened in surprise, but straightaway, like the snow that found his face, she melted against him. Sighing against his lips as she kissed him back. It wasn't a passionate kiss, yet it filled him with desire. Neither was it hurried. Instead, it was a tentative but lazy exploration as they tasted each other. Just a taste—but still charged with so much emotion and significance that it overwhelmed him.

Knocked him sideways.

Left him so out of control and off kilter, he had to loop his arms around her waist to steady himself. Pull her closer until her lush body was flush with his. Then closer still when she wrapped her arms around his neck.

Gal was dizzy, but in a good way. The sort of way in which all the blood inside his head twirled in happy circles. Beneath his ribs, his heart seemed to be shooting fireworks into his chest as it beat stronger and surer than it ever had before. He became so aware of all his nerve endings that even the gentle but erratic rise and fall of her breathing made them rejoice at the contact. Almost as if his body had been waiting for this precise moment and this precise woman to burst into life, and Lord help him, he had never felt so gloriously alive as he did right now. Like he could sprint across the top of the ocean or fly like a bird.

Who knew a simple kiss could wield so much power? Be so potent? So poignant? So all-consuming he never wanted it to end.

But end it did. At her instigation.

Her mouth stilled against his then kissed him deeply one last time. She stepped back to stare wide-eyed as she worried her bottom lip with her teeth. As if she, too, had been stunned by the intensity of what had transpired between them and couldn't make head or tail of what it meant.

"That was . . . um . . . rather . . ."

"Unexpected." Bemused himself by awe and wonder, Gal couldn't seem to take his eyes off her. "It also suddenly makes things . . . us . . . more complicated than ever." Was he ready for this? Ready to allow someone past his defenses? Ready to relinquish some control over his life to another?

"I suppose it does." Her golden brows furrowed. "Maybe we should . . . ignore it?" Her expression was more questioning than appalled. Testing the waters. Testing him. "Forget that it happened?"

"I can assure you, that isn't going to happen. That was some kiss, Venus." As much as it scared him, he didn't have the wherewithal to lie about it. "Pretty . . . spectacular in fact. For me at least."

Her slightly awkward, slightly shy smile of acknowledgment rather than horror made his guarded heart swell. "I wonder what it means?"

He found himself grinning as he shrugged, not caring for once that the path ahead wasn't clear. "I've always enjoyed a puzzle and so does that big ol' brain of yours, so between us we'll figure it out."

"I'm not sure my brain will make any sense of this puzzle tonight." A bubble of laughter escaped as she blushed, and he wanted to catch it in his fist and keep it forever. "Me and you, Galahad? Really?"

"I know . . ." While his head was horrified at this uncharacteristic and reckless foray into the uncertain and unguarded, his heart was soaring. Flying.

Bursting.

"Best to sleep on it."

She nodded, and in tacit agreement they put at least two feet of space between them as they slowly sauntered back into the inn, gazing at each other baffled the whole time and not saying a single word. Even when they paused at the foot of the stairs they were both obviously still so confused, they stared at each other for a few moments more.

With a perplexed frown and an utterly beguiling blush she shuffled from foot to foot. "I shall bid you a good night then, Galahad."

"Good night, Venus. Maybe I'll see you at breakfast? When hopefully we will have figured this all out."

"Maybe." Although she didn't look convinced.

He sympathized.

He currently did not know which way was up, either, or what the hell to do about it, or even if he should do anything beyond run, so he left her to climb the stairs alone. Partly because he didn't trust himself not to haul her into his arms again the moment they reached her bedchamber and partly because he needed time to digest his own feelings and their ramifications. If he ignored all of his reservations and fears about letting someone in when he knew it safer to keep them out, and if he put to one side how anxious and afraid being so emotionally vulnerable in front of someone else made him, *he* and *she* and *right now* wasn't exactly the best timing. Not when he had so much to do and was about to move his business right next to her beloved orphanage.

Tonight, as his first priority, rather than try to analyze what was happening in his hardened heart, he needed to find the right words to explain all those long-laid plans the very second she returned from the solicitor's tomorrow, because the wrong ones would shoot whatever this was dead in the paddock.

He also needed to rethink things. Rejig all those meticulous plans, because the best plans were always the most adaptable. Maybe factor in how to weave her into them . . .

What the hell!

As that train of thought made him dizzy again, and because the floor or perhaps the world had suddenly tilted beneath his feet, he grabbed the banister. Hard.

She turned at the thud, quizzical. "Are you all right, Galahad?"

"Never better." And bizarrely, despite the shifting floor and shifting parameters and his flimsy control over what happened next, that was true. As his grandpa had always said, when opportunity knocked on your front door, only a fool didn't fling it open in welcome. And this—she—felt like an opportunity.

Or fate.

Or both.

Either way, he already knew he wasn't strong enough to run away from it tonight. Didn't even want to.

What the hell!

"Venus, I was wondering . . ." He stopped himself before he finished that sentence, because frankly he wasn't entirely sure how he intended ending it but knew, as sure as eggs were eggs, that whatever his suddenly needy heart was proposing changed everything, and that already scared the hell out of him. Instead he scrambled. Hastily regrouped and offered her his most wolfish grin to bring things between them back onto a surer footing, one he understood. ". . . back there . . . beneath the moonlight . . ." He motioned to the door, enjoying how the flush on the apples of her cheeks instantly blossomed into a ferocious blush. ". . . I can't help wonderin' how my kissin' measured up against Dorchester's?"

Her beautiful blue eyes narrowed behind her spectacles, but with little enthusiasm.

"A *quality* gentleman like Lord Dorchester would have the good manners never to ask such a thing, Galahad Sinclair, nor would he try to hide his gross impertinence behind that false drawl you employ whenever you try—and fail—to be charming." She summoned every bit of the haughty disdain she'd always summoned when he went out of his way to rile her, but it fell widely shy of the mark. "Something my *big ol' brain* will be sure to factor in when I consider the fate of our conundrum tomorrow."

Chapter Eleven

Hugh keeps gazing at Minerva as if he adores her, and Minerva keeps gazing at him as if she adores him right back. I feel like a bad sister for being envious that she might have found the one before me . . .

—*from the diary of Miss Venus Merriwell, aged 17*

"Is there a particular reason why you are currently sporting a scowl that could curdle milk?" The reverend's terse whisper shocked her out of her reverie. "Only Mr. Pendle's clerk is now glaring at me as if I am the cause of it." He gestured to the little mouse of a man behind the most enormous desk, guarding the solicitor's office beyond, who was indeed staring at them both warily. "And at you—in case you are indeed as unhinged as you appear and decide, for whatever bizarre reason, to lash out at him in anger. Which, for the record, you look poised to do at any moment."

"Forgive me, I was woolgathering." She forced herself to smooth the wrinkle between her brows and pasted on a smile for the clerk's sake to assure him all her hinges were precisely where they should be.

Although the Reverend Smythe and the clerk were right. Vee was angry. For some inexplicable reason, she was furious at the weather.

She had floated off to bed convinced she would be trapped at The Mermaid for days thanks to the relentless snow that had plagued the country for weeks, and had woken to the grand thaw instead. Enough of a thaw that it ensured there was absolutely no excuse not to leave Brighton for London as soon as the meeting with the solicitor was concluded. Which gave her no excuse to linger in Galahad's company while they worked out what to do about that kiss.

That out-of-the-blue but totally earth-shattering kiss.

Which she was beyond keen to try again. And again. And again ad infinitum.

She caught herself about to sigh aloud as her body and soul relived it for the umpteenth time, and thus by default also confirming to the poor clerk that she had indeed taken leave of her wits, so she clamped her jaws shut.

There had been no time to talk to Galahad about it this morning. Thanks to the reverend and his wife, who had decided to breakfast early and who were already there when she arrived downstairs. Although they insisted he join them, too, when Galahad had emerged but a few minutes after her, they had not shared a single private moment together.

He had shot her a few heated looks across the table when their chaperones weren't looking, though. Heated enough that she was convinced that, like her, he had absolutely no regrets about their kiss, but uncertain enough to confirm that he had no more earthly idea what to do about it yet than she did.

Their situation—the close bond of their families—was indeed a complication. One that could potentially create awkwardness between them and their kin forever if things did not work out, as well as perhaps creating awkwardness if they did. The family would certainly all be as shocked by this wholly inconceivable development as Vee was.

Her and Galahad? Who would have thought it possible that there could be a friendship between them, let alone the elusive frisson Olivia kept going on about? And yet undeniably a thrilling frisson was now there. It had positively sizzled as they had kissed. Enough that she had been sorely tempted to encourage him to take more liberties before common sense had prevailed and she had put some much-needed distance between her suddenly wanton body and his. Then she had felt it plain as day all night as her body had relentlessly yearned for his. Felt it keenly throughout breakfast—a tangible awareness of his presence to her core, even with three feet of solid oak table between them.

Or perhaps it had always been there and that explained why he had always bothered her so? Why Galahad Sinclair had always been the annoying itch she couldn't scratch? The man who always drew her eyes. Whom she never failed to be aware of whenever he was near?

Now, there was some serious food for thought.

How on earth could a person as clever and as intuitive as she was have missed something so staggeringly obvious? Was the annoyance she had always felt wherever he was concerned not annoyance at all, but frustrated attraction manifesting itself as irritation?

Was he the Benedick to her Beatrice?

She had certainly always thought him handsome. Always, and much to her chagrin, she found his cocky charm compelling, too. If one considered constantly lamenting about why he got under her skin compelling. But he had always done that, and she had never been able to ignore it, so she supposed that spoke volumes. Love and loathing were two vastly conflicting emotions yet with more in common than not. Both caused a visceral, involuntary reaction in the body and the mind. Both also undoubtedly clouded judgment and masked the truth. She was honest enough with herself to know that she wasn't always the best judge of character, as proven by her insistence on ignoring the obvious flaws in her father, Lord Argyll, and now, she realized, the irritating and incompatible Lord Dorchester. The idea of marrying that make-do, much-too-old fool now, when Galahad had ignited something magical within her, was as preposterous as preposterous could be. Such a compromise was inconceivable and would never make her happy—no matter how much she willed it or ignored the pompous lord's many flaws. There, it stood to reason that if she was prone to ignore the bad, it was quite conceivable she could also ignore the good. That she had confused the obvious frisson of attraction between her and Galahad for disquiet? Or distrust? Were they both too wise to woo peaceably, as the Bard himself had said?

It was entirely possible.

As well as entirely thrilling.

Her and Galahad? *How marvelously unexpected but right!*

Vee was so deep in that giddy thought, she jumped as the solicitor's door opened and a surprisingly young lawyer stepped out.

"Reverend Smythe—Miss Merriwell—all the papers are now ready for you to sign."

Vee followed Mr. Pendle into the room and perched opposite his desk, hoping her suddenly wayward and inappropriate thoughts weren't written as plain on her face as they were playing havoc with her body.

"As you will realize from my letter—" Without any preamble, the lawyer steepled his fingers the second he sat. "—my client, the late Mrs. Leyton-Brown, made some provision for the Covent Garden Asylum for Orphans in her will. It is a generous provision." His brows lifted as if he was stunned by it, which boded well. "A very generous provision indeed."

"Mrs. Leyton-Brown, God rest her . . ." The reverend glanced heavenward with a sad smile on his face. ". . . was one of the kindest and most supportive souls I ever knew. Especially to our orphans. She campaigned tirelessly to help raise us money. She did that alongside being our most generous benefactor from the outset. Without her, there would be no orphanage. She even donated the roof over our heads." Which was the first thing they intended to fix as soon as they returned to it. "Her largesse has already helped so many young souls in need."

"Clearly she was desirous of saving many more." Mr. Pendle slid a sheet of paper across the desk. "For I am to transfer you that sum in its entirety, with no caveats or stipulations beyond her insistence that you be able to continue your good works for many years to come."

Vee and the reverend stared at the figure in disbelief. As his jaw had dropped, she managed to find the wherewithal to query it.

"Seven thousand pounds? Seven. *Thousand*. Pounds." They could repair their leaky roof with gold tiles instead of slate with such a staggering sum.

Mr. Pendle nodded. "Seven thousand pounds, Miss Merriwell. Almost three-quarters of the contents of her bank account."

"Good gracious." She slumped back in her chair, as overwhelmed by the news as she had been by Galahad's unexpected kiss. "She has left us such a fortune I can hardly comprehend it."

"Yet comprehend it you must." No nonsense, Mr. Pendle passed a second sheet across the table. "If you could sign at the bottom and confirm where you would like the funds deposited, I shall ensure it is all done by the end of the week." He pushed his inkwell and pen toward the Reverend Smythe, who still apparently lacked the capacity to speak, but managed to scrawl his name on the bottom of the document, at least, while he gaped.

Mr. Pendle blotted it, blew on it, and added it to a neat stack on the side of the desk before he reached out to shake his hand. "Thank you for coming so promptly, Reverend. I did wonder if I would see you before Christmas, thanks to the weather." He reached for Vee's hand next and shook that. "I do hope it holds off long enough that you can get home without issue." As that sounded like a dismissal when the solicitor had clearly forgotten something, she had no choice but to prompt him.

"Is that *everything*, Mr. Pendle?"

"Yes. Now that the ink is dry, our business is concluded." He stood, clearly eager to be rid of them, and swept his arm toward the door. "As I said, the funds should be transferred and available to you by the end of the . . ."

"I meant, is that everything from *Mrs. Leyton-Brown's bequest*, sir?"

He stared as if she had grown a second head. "Were you expecting more than seven *thousand* pounds, madam?" He shook his head as if she was the most ungrateful person he had ever met. "When most would surely agree that Mrs. Leyton-Brown has left your orphanage a king's ransom? I have certainly never seen a charitable donation of the like in any other will I have executed."

"Oh, Miss Merriwell and myself are beyond grateful to Mrs. Leyton-Brown for her phenomenal benevolence, sir! Be in no doubt about that." Finally, the reverend found his voice to save her from further censure. "But to be frank, and sorry to sound so indelicate, Mr. Pendle, while we weren't expecting anything close to the seven thousand pounds she so generously left, we *were* expecting some property."

"Property?" This was obviously news to Mr. Pendle. "I know that she owned a lot of it but still, in my experience, property usually only ever goes to family members. That aside, why on earth would you expect any property on top of all that money?"

"Because Mrs. Leyton-Brown—God rest her—" In case a thunderbolt came to smite him for his perceived ungratefulness, the Reverend Smythe glanced heavenward again in apology. "—promised as much to me herself. Only a few months ago, in fact, here in Brighton when I visited her. It was quite a specific but unprompted promise, Mr. Pendle, pertaining to the building next door to us on Long Acre. A building that has remained reassuringly vacant since the last tenants left over a year ago. A building we were rather hoping to be able to expand into as—well, not to put too fine a point on it—the orphanage is more than a little oversubscribed and we desperately need more space. The good we can do is limited by our capacity, and that was why Mrs. Leyton-Brown promised it."

The lawyer sat again, somewhat heavily, frowning so hard his thick dark eyebrows merged into one. "Did Mrs. Leyton-Brown happen, perchance, to put that promise to you in writing, Reverend? In a note or a letter or some such?"

"She did not." The Reverend Smythe shook his head, and because the solicitor looked mightily relieved by that, all Vee's hopes that they would finally be able to expand the orphanage died like Mrs. Leyton-Brown had. "It was a verbal promise, Mr. Pendle, but . . ." Both Vee and the solicitor sat forward as he frowned. "She did make that promise in front of a witness who can confirm categorically her intent. Does that help?"

The solicitor's eyes narrowed. "That would depend on the witness, and their ability to convince a court of the deceased's intentions. Overturning the tenets of a will written in sound mind is practically impossible. Almost unheard of. A court needs more than hearsay, and while I am not for one moment trying to cast aspersions on either your good character or your witness's, nor questioning either of your motives, even the words of a vicar do not constitute proof that such a promise from the deceased ever occurred."

Yet still the reverend persevered. "Even if the witness was the deceased's own nephew? Her sole heir, Lord Mallory, not only witnessed Mrs. Leyton-Brown's promise, but promised her faithfully in return that he would ensure that it was carried out."

As hope kindled afresh Vee smiled at the solicitor, only for it to melt from her face on the back of his dour expression.

"I am certain Lord Mallory will have absolutely no recollection of that exchange, Reverend—or his promise. I am sorry." Mr. Pendle picked up his pile of papers and tapped them to neaten the edges before depositing them all in the box, which he snapped decisively closed. His tight expression suggested he disapproved more of Lord Mallory than he did their claim. "If he denies it . . ."

"Which of course he won't." The reverend smiled with a faith in Lord Mallory's honesty that neither she nor the solicitor shared.

"But if he *does*—" Mr. Pendle prodded the table for extra emphasis. "—and if the deceased's wishes weren't put in writing, I am afraid, as far as the law is concerned, you really do not have a leg to stand on. It would be your word against his word—and Mrs. Leyton-Brown's will." He retrieved that document from the box near his elbow and shook it. "Which I can assure you does not leave your orphanage any property at all."

"Lord Mallory heard it with his own ears, sir, and swore a solemn oath to his aunt to comply. He will back me on this. I have no doubt about that, so there is no need for all this talk of courts and juries." Yet even the reverend's ever-hopeful smile was flatter now.

"He really won't, Reverend. Of that you can be assured. We have been through the will together several times, and when it came to the many conversations we have had about that particular building, Lord Mallory made no mention of his aunt's promise at all."

"An oversight, I am sure." The reverend smiled in sympathy. "The poor man was probably overwhelmed with grief, and it slipped his mind. Understandably."

"I can assure you that if it did, it was quite deliberate." The solicitor stood again and motioned to the door, clearly uncomfortable, and something about it made all Vee's hackles rise. He knew something. Something pertinent that they didn't. A suspicion that was confirmed by his next statement and over-friendly but awkward smile. "If I were you, I would forget the promise made by a confused and ailing old woman, forget that *particular* building and buy another. A better, bigger building in a nicer area. My client left you more than enough money to expand your orphanage elsewhere."

A moment ago, he had said that Mrs. Leyton-Brown's will was written in sound mind. Now, suddenly, she was a confused and ailing old woman.

Something was off.

"But why should we buy a building when we were promised a building, sir?" Vee was incensed by the matter-of-fact dismissal of their legitimate claim. "I am sure that I have read somewhere that a verbal contract is as binding as a written one."

"That all depends on proof, Miss Merriwell. *Categoric* proof." The solicitor's eyes shuttered in a way suggesting he knew already that they weren't likely to get that, but she pressed anyway.

"Which you could obtain from Lord Mallory along with the instruction to release the deed to us. I presume you do have the deed, Mr. Pendle." She glanced toward the shut box on his desk emblazoned with the deceased's name. "Or has that already been passed to Lord Mallory, seeing as you have met with him and discussed this *particular* building several times since his aunt's death?" If the dissolute lord had the deed, he could sell the deed.

She could not let that happen.

"I am afraid, as I am also now Lord Mallory's legal representative, client confidentiality prevents me from discussing his private legal affairs without his express permission, and I have already told you too much." He stalked toward the door and flung it open, then practically shooed them out of it. "Should you wish to pursue your unsubstantiated claim to his property further, I must insist that you take it up with him. As it really is no longer anything to do with me."

"This is all a storm in a teacup, Vee." The Reverend Smythe pretended that he wasn't the least bit fazed by what had happened in the solicitor's office as they walked back to the inn. "Mark my words. He will come good. He's a decent gentleman . . . underneath it all."

That casual phrase, *underneath it all*, only served to set more alarm bells ringing, because the *underneath* the good reverend was alluding to was Lord Mallory's shocking reputation in the gossip columns. If they were to be believed—and because her stickler-for-details sister Diana frequently wrote one of them, Vee did—then Lord Mallory was more of a libertine than he was a gentleman. Worse, she'd had the misfortune to bump into him in a deserted hallway at one infamous ball during her first season, drunk, and he had offered, in rather coarse terms as he manhandled her, to steam up her spectacles for her, so she knew without a doubt he was no gentleman, either. He had been quite offensive when she had turned down his improper offer, so she held little hope that a man with such dubious morals and selfish character would feel obligated to uphold his aunt's promise without the additional incentive of something in it for him.

Which bizarrely did give her some small hope for the building next door. Thanks to the lawyer's parting advice, she had quickly reached the conclusion that the only way the orphanage was likely to get their hands on the promised building was if they offered to buy it from the cheating scoundrel using his aunt's money. While that ironic solution left a bitter taste in the mouth, for the orphans' sake she had to be pragmatic. It might take a tidy chunk out of their unexpected seven-thousand-pound windfall, but at least thanks to the sheer size of that windfall they could still expand, fix the roof, and have enough left over to see them right for a few years. Which was more than had seemed possible a few weeks ago, so in that respect, their good fortune was still a miracle and one she would force herself to be thankful for no matter Lord Mallory's unconscionable duplicity.

"That said . . ." The reverend could not disguise his real concerns completely, no matter how hard he was trying. "I am eager to settle the confusion as quickly as possible, so I think it is prudent that we leave here within the hour. Strike while the iron is hot, as it were. That way, if we overnight in Crawley, I can call on him after luncheon tomorrow and before he goes . . ."

"Out drinking and carousing and frittering away all of his new inheritance on wine, women, and song?" Vee had Lord Mallory's full measure. "I should like to come with you when you call upon him." Where she could at least handle the negotiations for a sale when the debauched lord reneged on his promise. Unlike the good reverend, while she always tried to see the good in people, she knew firsthand that some people had little good in them and only did what benefited themselves; her ill-fated romance with the ambitious Lord Argyll was testament. If Mallory hadn't mentioned his aunt's promise to his solicitor when he had ample opportunities to do so, it did not take a genius to work out that he intended to sell that property for his own profit. "The presence of a woman might make him more agreeable." Especially when the woman who intended to be present also fully intended to turn his guts into garters if he did not bend to her will.

"I think that is prudent." The reverend huffed as they arrived outside The Mermaid. "Although if worse comes to worst, and Mr. Pendle's grave predictions come true, it is prudent to prepare ourselves for that, too. We must remember that we have managed well enough as we are up to now—but from this day forward, no matter the outcome, we shall manage so much better with seven thousand pounds at our disposal with which we can buy somewhere better. Preferably in a less insalubrious part of town. So all is not lost, and if that is the case and we do not get the building, there must be a reason." He pointed to the annoyingly clear sky above. "The Lord moves in mysterious ways, Vee, and usually for the best. Even if we do not realize it. *Everything* happens for a good reason."

"If you say so, Reverend."

"Apart from my wife's nagging, of course, for that is entirely unfounded." He sighed. "And on that subject, I shall go chivy Constance, who will not be happy to be chivied when I faithfully promised her that we would enjoy a leisurely luncheon and a stroll around the Royal Pavilion before we left."

"Mrs. Smythe is a reasonable woman and will understand that this cannot be helped." Just as Vee was trying to come to terms with the lack of snow to scandalously keep her here with Galahad. Which, if the reverend's logic was to be believed, was likely for the best also. She wasn't the world's most reliable judge of character, after all, and knew to her detriment how easily a handsome face, charming manner, and sublime kiss could make her forget all prudence.

Vee decided to arrange for the carriage to be readied for the long journey, rather than wallow in anger and self-pity. Leaving in such haste was a disappointment after last night, but as this was for the greater good and the needs of the many, the orphans had to take precedence over any fanciful new desires of her own. Like a parting kiss on the seafront or the sudden blizzard that her wayward body was praying would delay her . . .

"Hello, Venus." His silky drawl stopped her dead in her tracks.

Chapter Twelve

Minerva and Diana were right! My father is a self-centered, manipulative, lying, duplicitous, gambling, crooked scoundrel to his core! I hate him now! Hate him! Hate him with the fire of a thousand suns! But I hate myself more for wasting so many years pathetically hoping that my dear sisters were wrong. Why am I always so pathetically gullible . . .

—*from the diary of Miss Venus Merriwell, aged 17*

Gal caught her by the elbow and whisked her outside in case the blabbermouth Nelly told her he had been wearing a groove in the floorboards all morning while he awaited her return. He didn't have a speech rehearsed so much as a series of points that, frankly, petrified him, but he still felt compelled to say. He was also as nervous as hell and didn't want to stumble through them with an audience.

Because Venus was already blushing and the tips of his ears were burning, he decided it was safer all around if they just kept walking, so he offered her his arm and steeled himself for the few initial moments of awkwardness as she shyly took it.

Lord, but she looked lovely again today. Lovelier than he had ever seen her despite wearing the exact same sensible coat as she had worn when she had arrived at his inn yesterday, complete with the same silly little reticule. So gorgeous he couldn't take his eyes off her. Gal blamed the kiss that had thoroughly bewitched him. He hadn't been able to think straight since it happened.

Conscious he was staring like a starving dog at a butcher's window, he tugged her toward the seafront. "How did your meeting go?"

"*Good . . .*"

"You don't sound too convinced."

She forced a smile that did not quite meet her eyes. "It *was* good. Mrs. Leyton-Brown left the orphanage seven thousand pounds in her will."

Gal whistled, impressed. He'd had an inkling it was a tidy sum from Mallory's outrage at it but hadn't managed to dig into any specifics. "That *is* a lot of money. You could do some substantial good with that. Starting with that leaky roof—but I sense a *but*? Was there a restrictive caveat of some kind? Or has she put the money in a trust so it arrives in an annoying trickle over eternity making it as good as useless?"

"Neither. There are no caveats, thank goodness, and the full amount should be winging its way to our bank in London as we speak."

"But?"

She shrugged, troubled, but not—he was convinced—by him or by their spectacular kiss. At least no more than he was. "*But*, while the money is marvelous and seven times what we were expecting, we were hoping to expand. The orphanage urgently needs bigger premises and we had been led to believe, by Mrs. Leyton-Brown herself, that she would be leaving us a building so that we could expand immediately."

The orphanage plans on moving?

Clearly this was Gal's lucky day in more ways than one. First this fascinating and beautiful woman was still on his arm rather than recoiling in horror at her unfortunate nocturnal "mistake," and now he wouldn't need to tackle the awkward issue of his club and her orphanage coexisting as neighbors. Not in the long term anyway, so that made everything easier.

"You can buy a lot of rooms for seven thousand pounds, Venus. Probably quadruple the number you currently have and in a much better state, too, so what's the problem? In fact, with that much ready money at your disposal, you could get a seriously good deal on a decent building with a solid roof and maybe even a garden for those little rascals to play in." Once she did, he could assist in replenishing the orphanage's coffers by offering to buy the old building from them when they had found a place to move to. The archetypal win for everyone from whichever way he looked at it. For him, her, and all the orphans she adored so much. "Trust me, the lady did you a favor. Money to buy your own building is so much better than having some rickety old place in the back of beyond donated to you. You'll be in control. You get to choose exactly what you want, where you want it, and exactly what it needs to be like for those children to thrive."

"Maybe." She didn't look convinced—more daunted by the task at hand.

Thinking on his feet, Gal decided to sell her the dream before he offered to purchase. "My grandpa always told me that a good business went hand in hand with a good location, and while your orphanage isn't a business per se, those same principles apply. Covent Garden is the perfect place for a theater or a tavern . . ." *Soften the ground first.* ". . . because it's got that sort of reputation. Same as here." Gal swept his free arm toward the town in the distance. "Exactly like Brighton, Covent Garden is where people go to have a good time. That's just dandy for them, because they can find all the fun they crave in one handy place, but it isn't really the place to raise children. It's too close to all the debauchery to raise the ones, like Billy, who have been damaged by it. Wouldn't it be better to raise boys like him in fresh air and space? Away from all the crime and the poverty that makes crime appealing?"

"Well, of course it would, but . . ."

"You need to stop thinking so small, Venus! You've got seven thousand to spend!" He took her hand and spun her to face him, excited for her at all the opportunities the sum presented. "Take it from someone who has been watching the London property market closely for the last year: Anything within the bounds of the capital comes at a premium. But if you venture a little farther out, twenty minutes west of Mayfair by carriage to one of the pretty outlying towns or villages, you get so much more for your money."

Gal could tell she was picturing such a place by the wistful look in her lovely eyes. But so was he. Conjuring a place that would have been a sanctuary for him when he had been a lost boy in dire need of one. "There, I reckon you could easily get yourself a big ol' country house with grounds and still have change left over. One with outbuildings and land to spread out away from all the smoke and clutter of the city. Room to expand enough to help over a hundred orphans, and then some, without breaking a sweat. Room to build a proper school, too, and plant a cottage garden. Places to teach those children all manner of trades that give them options in their futures—options that don't involve picking pockets or living hand to mouth, far away from the streets that would gobble them up."

The way the sea breeze played with her hair as she smiled made his heart yearn. "You certainly know how to weave a pretty dream, Galahad. But I fear, as your grandpa knew only too well, that our location, although not ideal for raising children in, is good for reminding the rich to be philanthropic. They will send that philanthropy elsewhere if they cannot see us, so as much as a sprawling place in the country works in the short term and in your pretty dream, dreams alone cannot sustain us indefinitely."

"What you call a dream, Venus, I call forward planning. You've always got to look ahead and adapt to the circumstances."

"Is that what you do?"

"Always." Plans kept you going when the world beat you down. Forced you to get up in the morning. To keep fighting. Keep moving. Keep hoping. "I'm a voracious planner. What can I say? I keep one eye on the present while the other scans the horizon for something better. You need to do the same. A better home for all those orphans is a dream that you now have the means to make a reality—and you are too smart not to think of a way to make it financially sustainable."

It was on the tip of his tongue to offer to bite the bullet and buy the place—now if need be despite that being a huge gamble—but the wind caught her bonnet and pushed it backward, so he reached out to right it but found himself caressing her cheek instead. "Because dreams do come true, Venus—if you want them badly enough. I'm living proof of that." In that moment he realized, no matter how reckless and terrifying it was, he wanted her to be part of his dream, too. No matter how complicated it made things or how vulnerable it left him. Unsettled, he bent his head to kiss her again and smiled against her lips as she kissed him back without hesitation.

Yet exactly like last night, she was the first to end it. She offered him another shy smile as she took his arm again. "All right then, Mr. Property Genius, in your informed opinion and assuming I do figure out a way to make it pay for itself, exactly how much would that promised land of milk and honey cost?"

"You could easily get a place half the size of Giles's or Hugh's stately piles with a few acres for around four thousand in today's market."

"Four thousand!" Instantly she dismissed that. "Four thousand is over half of what Mrs. Leyton-Brown left us. We can't spend all that in one go. It would be irresponsible without the guaranteed means to replenish it—which we certainly do not have at present. Especially with Mrs. Leyton-Brown and her generous annual stipend now gone. We might have a lot of pennies, but they are finite so we have to count them carefully."

"*But . . .*" He nudged her with his elbow. "That would be a seriously huge house and a smaller one would be cheaper, but I'm betting you are forgetting to factor the property you already own into your calculations." He sucked in a calming breath as despite the enormous risk involved, this felt like both the right time and the right thing to do. "In the current market, and even with its leaking roof and shabby exterior, it's worth at least two and a half thousand. Because Long Acre is such a prime spot, the right idiot might even give you three if he was prepared to pay an arm and a leg, in which case you'd only be eating into a thousand of Mrs. Leyton-Brown's money if you bought huge."

Galahad would have to use everything he had left in the bank if he bought and renovated that building, too, and he would be left high and dry if his new club was slow to take off. But he had more than a sneaking feeling already that she was worth it. *They* were worth it. They were at least worth a try.

"*Sell* the orphanage?" As he could practically hear the cogs in her mind turning, he realized that was something she had never considered.

"You have to speculate to accumulate, Venus." Just as he was doing. Speculating wildly. Recklessly. But he didn't care because his hardened heart was light again, beating again, and that felt too good to ignore.

"Is that another one of your grandpa's wise old sayings?"

"Probably." Definitely. Grandpa had always been a firm believer in risk. In trusting your gut. He often reminded Gal that you couldn't fly unless you jumped first. "But he's right. He was always right." Even though this wasn't so much a jump as a leap into the unknown. A huge, foolhardy gamble—with his money, his future, and his heart at stake.

But happy to leap and take that crazy bet, he kissed her again. "Dreams, like plans, should always adapt with the circumstances, especially if the circumstances allow them to get bigger and better, and some risks are worth taking." He said that last bit more for himself than for her because he was feeling giddy and off kilter again. The ground beneath his feet was shifting as wildly as all his long-laid and meticulous plans.

"I don't suppose you know any idiots who want to buy a shabby building with a condemned roof for *an arm and a leg* in Covent Garden?" She was being flippant, likely to cover the pretty blush his latest kiss had caused, but without realizing it she had given him an opening into the necessary part of the conversation that he had been dreading.

"I do, as it happens." To celebrate that fact, he tugged her into his arms and kissed her again, feeling giddy at the huge significance of what this all meant. "Me."

Her giggle told him she didn't believe him. "Why on earth would you want to buy a shabby old orphanage with a leaking roof, Galahad?"

"Where you see a shabby old orphanage, I see the perfect venue for my new club."

"I thought you had found premises? Has that all fallen through?" Her sympathetic frown told him she genuinely cared about his future, too, and that filled him with joy.

"So that's the darndest thing, Venus—I have and I've got the deeds to 'em packed in my satchel back at the inn. And they are right next door to you!"

"What?" He had expected surprise, perhaps even some irritation, but not the icy chill that came alongside it. "*You* have *purchased* the building next door!"

Gal forced a sunny smile and squeezed her suddenly rigid hands. "All three of them, actually, so the orphanage would make the set complete." He realized straightaway he had said the wrong thing because she yanked her fingers away as if they'd been burned.

"You own them all? Mallory sold them to you? The deeds to all *three* buildings are already yours?" She practically snarled those three questions.

"Yes, yes, and yes, but . . ."

"*But!* Don't you dare *but* me, Galahad Sinclair! How is that possible when Mrs. Leyton-Brown hasn't even been dead a month?"

Perhaps only total honesty was the way forward?

She deserved that.

They deserved that.

"Because I happened to be here in Brighton when she passed, and because I keep an ear to the ground. I heard a rumor Mallory was spitting feathers that his aunt hadn't left him any cash but had instead saddled him with a hefty portfolio of properties to unload—half of which were wrecks dotted around Covent Garden. And because I had worked out years ago that the best place to put my club was Covent Garden, I followed him back to town to inquire about them. Once he'd shown them to me, I made him an offer on the spot."

Behind her spectacles, her eyes narrowed to magnified slits.

"I swear, on my life, that when Mallory and I shook on the deal I had no idea that your orphanage was next door. I didn't realize that until . . ."

"You mysteriously collided with me on the street outside it a little over three weeks ago."

As that was also the truth, Gal nodded, only to have all Four Horsemen of the Apocalypse unleashed upon him.

"You devious, slippery snake, Galahad Sinclair!" She jabbed the air between them, incensed. "You planned this whole thing just to get your wicked way! You wanted our building, too! Didn't you? That's why you spouted all that poppycock about space and kitchen gardens and dreams coming true! You wanted the set! Of course you had an ulterior motive!" She prodded his chest this time. "*Of course you did!* Because don't selfish men always?" She marched away with her arms waving, at such speed he had to jog to catch up with her. "I am such an idiot! Always such an idiot where men are concerned!"

"Venus! Wait. It wasn't like that." He caught her elbow and she glared at his fingers as if they were something unpleasant until he withdrew them. "I didn't plan this to get my hands on your orphanage. I simply bought three buildings that happened to be alongside it. I swear I had no clue about the orphanage until you pointed it out. That was why I was so stunned when we met that day outside it. You remember that, don't you?"

Her eyelids fluttered fast as she revisited that memory and for the briefest moment she appeared to waver, until the outraged schoolmistress returned with a vengeance as she folded her arms and tapped her foot. Glaring as if everything about him disappointed her now. "Maybe so—but that doesn't explain your total silence on the matter both then and since when you have had ample opportunity to say something. If you didn't have an ulterior motive, kindly explain to me why you neglected to tell me that you had bought all those buildings the day we collided outside them and why this is the first I am hearing about it?"

"Clearly that was a mistake." One Gal bitterly regretted now. "But at the time I thought . . ." Maybe honesty wasn't the best policy as, judging by her incendiary reaction, the truth would now sound damning. Because now it was damning. "I thought . . ." *Think, Galahad! Think!* "I thought . . ."

Venus snarled with venom. "You thought, quite correctly, that I wouldn't take kindly to having Sodom and Gomorrah move in next door to the orphanage. Especially when relations between us have always been so strained." She unfolded her arms to fist her hands on her hips. "So you embarked on an offensive to sweeten me up before you told me and before you tried to charm the last of 'the set' from me!"

"It wasn't quite as mercenary as you are making it sound." Although now that she said it, it sounded pretty darn mercenary to him. "I'm a businessman—and with my business head on . . ."

"What you call business, I call selfish duplicity! Either way it explains why you suddenly wanted to bury the hatchet and declare a truce at the Rokebys' when you've never cared that we hated each other before. Why you kept turning up like a bad penny when usually I never see you from one changing season to the next. Why you came to dinner and stayed to play cards when you rarely come to dinner and never stay for anything! And why you suppressed your usual obnoxiousness to make me warm to you." He found his head bowing in shame like Tommy Claypole's because what she had said was all true. He had been selfish for the sake of his business.

Initially at least. But he could see how she wouldn't believe that everything that had happened between them since hadn't been driven by his business.

"That explains why you happened to be in Hatchards, too, doesn't it? Behaving all decent and noble when it was all plainly another one of your acts. And why . . ." Her fingers shook as she pressed them to her lips, and he watched in panic as her clever mind put two and two together to make three hundred and twenty-seven. ". . . And why you kissed me."

The hurt in her eyes almost killed him. "That isn't why I kissed you, Venus. I kissed you because . . ." She pushed him so hard he landed on his butt in the slush.

"You were acting all of it, weren't you?"

"Not all." He scrambled to his feet. "To begin with, I'll admit I was putting my business first, but things changed the second we waltzed and . . ."

She backed away, her hands raised to ward off evil and her lovely eyes swimming with the tears he had put there. "God, I really am the world's worst judge of a man's character! As if you—*you*!" She spat that with such acid it burned. "Wouldn't have had an ulterior motive to be nice to me!"

Then she was off again, her incensed heels tearing up the yards between them at such speed, it took him until she reached the inn to catch her.

"Venus, please . . ." He stayed her arm but she thwacked it with her silly little reticule.

"Touch me again, Galahad Sinclair, and I swear it will be the last thing that you ever do!"

"I appreciate that this looks bad." Especially to all the lunchtime patrons in the inn and Nelly at the bar, who were all staring at the pair of them open-mouthed. "And I'll admit that initially I was trying to soften you up a bit before I told you that we were going to be neighbors. But I swear, last night when I . . ."

"Ah, there you are, Vee!" The Reverend Smythe appeared on the landing beaming. "I've been looking everywhere for you." He smiled at Galahad as he descended the stairs, oblivious to all the gaping patrons below. "The bags are loaded, and my wife has been sitting in the carriage waiting for us for the last ten minutes." Unaware of the awful, fraught atmosphere, the vicar smiled at them in turn. "But I am sure she won't mind waiting a few minutes more for you two to say your final goodbyes."

"No need." Venus gave Gal one last disgusted look before she took the vicar's arm. "We've already said them."

Chapter Thirteen

Olivia does not recommend a debutante marrying in her first season as she is convinced a young lady must consider all her options and wait for the legendary frisson before she makes the leap. However, I know exactly what I want, so when I find the right gentleman I shall leap with abandon and to hell with the consequences…

—*from the diary of Miss Venus Merriwell, aged 17*

Vee plonked her bottom into the farthest of the wallflower chairs, well out of the way of everyone, and stared inanely at the ormolu clock on Lady Brightlingsea's mantel, willing the ornate gold hands to turn faster.

With the benefit of hindsight—which she always had to suffer retroactively because she kept being a gullible fool—she knew that coming to this ball had been a huge mistake. Yet another one in yet another depressing season filled with them. A life filled with them!

Vee had allowed Olivia to cajole her into attending this dull soiree simply because she had needed some distraction from the awful aftermath of Brighton. A day and a half on and it was still too raw. It was near impossible to focus on what to do about it all when she was so emotionally battered by it. Her heart ached as if it had been kicked, which metaphorically it had. It would have been kinder if Galahad had simply wrenched it from her chest and stamped on it rather than make that poor, battered organ hope again. Left to her own devices alone at home, she knew she would have only wallowed in the twin pits of self-pity and self-hatred while alternate bucketloads of anger, disbelief, and humiliation were doused over her head as they had been all the way on the interminable journey back.

After overnighting in Crawley, they had left there at the crack of dawn this morning hoping to make good time, but thanks to more bad weather and atrocious conditions on the roads, hadn't arrived in Mayfair until an hour before dinner. A little over an hour since dinner and now she was here—stuck for the duration—and in no fit state to socialize. Mostly because she was furious at herself for her own reliable stupidity—because she now had another humiliating final memory to add to her huge collection of hideous final memories that she wished with every fiber she did not have.

Exactly how many times did she need to be bitten before her supposedly sensible head learned that her stupid heart was always wrong? And why had it fallen so wholeheartedly for Galahad that this latest disappointment crushed her soul in a way that even that weasel Argyll hadn't managed?

If there was one consolation to the dark cloud shrouding her head, it was that thanks to Galahad, she was all done with men. His had been the final nail in that coffin and she was ready to lay it to rest forever, because surely surrendering to an eternity of spinsterhood could not be as disappointing as all her failed attempts at love had been.

"I see you are still quite determined to avoid me."

She almost groaned aloud at the sound of Lord Dorchester's irritating voice behind her, rubbing more salt into her already gaping wound. What had she been thinking latching herself to this self-centered dud? When they had nothing in common and she did not harbor one jot of attraction for him? If the thought of spending five minutes in his company tonight made her feel this aggrieved, living with him would likely kill her. Further proof, not that she needed it, that spinsterhood was infinitely preferable.

However, to avoid causing a scene, Vee pasted on an approximation of a smile before she turned to face him, in no mood for any conversation at all let alone this one. "I have been busy." Busy being used, betrayed, and made a complete fool of by another dud.

Again.

"Would you honor me with the next dance?"

"No." Because it was the waltz, and that dance had been thoroughly ruined for her by Galahad. "I do not feel like dancing tonight." Or likely ever again if it involved a man in any way, shape, or form.

"A promenade around the room perhaps? Or a trip to the refreshment table for a glass of champagne?"

"Neither—thank you—I am quite content where I am." She had placed herself among the wallflowers in the vain hope of avoiding everyone, her own family included. She had no earthly idea how to tell them that she had been that gullible, trusting idiot who had allowed herself to be let down by a worthless man again when there had been so many of them over the years. "And quite content to remain here alone, my lord, so do not trouble yourself."

Ever.

Not that he ever had.

"I, too, am content to dally awhile." He sat beside her and she almost screamed in frustration. "It seems like forever since we last conversed and I feel as if I owe you an apology for the way I behaved at the Rokebys' the other week. I was neglectful of you and for that I am sorry."

She slanted him a disinterested glance, willing him to get the message that her misguided attachment to him—and romanticized hope for the entire male species—was over. "Think nothing of it. I can assure you that *I* haven't." Good heavens, what *had* she been thinking to think this self-centered oaf might somehow be more worthy than all the selfish men before him? Now that Galahad had shattered the rose-tinted lenses from her spectacles, it was as plain as the dandruff dusting Dorchester's sloping shoulders that she had been clutching at straws. Selling herself short exactly as Olivia had cautioned. A clear case of desperation over discernment, because she wanted a family of her own.

Well, no more! Now she would make do with the family she already had and be supremely grateful for them. She hardly needed to add to their number when both Minerva and Diana had already done that, and she could shower all her love on her nieces and nephews as well as she could her own child. That way, at least she could avoid the interminable and depressing effort of trying to search for a perfect man who did not exist. At least as a doting aunt she wouldn't have to suffer this pathetic specimen's nighttime passions. The thought of any intimacy with Dorchester now made her skin crawl and it was so visceral, her lip actually curled in distaste.

Seeing it, the pompous lord shuffled uncomfortably in his seat. "These past few weeks without you have made me realize how much I value our acquaintance—" He cleared his throat, his expression uncharacteristically boyish and unsure. It did not suit him. "—I also realize that I have taken it for granted and sometimes failed to give you the attention you deserved."

Sometimes! That was rich. He had given the wallpaper more attention than he had given her. If she'd had an ounce of self-respect, she would have acknowledged that from the outset. But she had been both gullible and desperate, and so had still labored to find the good that didn't exist in a succession of useless men. Her ceaseless ability to keep putting all of her eggs in entirely the wrong basket was staggering.

But no more!

"As I said, my lord, think nothing of it. I cannot stress enough how little thought I have given to it since we last conversed."

"I am relieved to hear it." Dorchester was as immune to sarcasm as he was to humility. "Only I had assumed, when I received no acknowledgment of the *two* bouquets I have sent since, that you bore a grudge." His remonstrative expression suggested he felt aggrieved by that.

"Not at all." She was, however, beyond bored of pinning her colors to the wrong masts. The grudge she now bore thanks to Galahad's all-too-recent manipulative treachery was so large, there genuinely wasn't enough jaded and embittered space in her heart to bear another one.

And speaking of jaded . . . "Thank you for the flowers." She knew full well Dorchester had only sent them because he couldn't bear to lose out to a man as lowly as Galahad. "Although you really shouldn't have bothered." She vowed there and then that if he dared to send her any more, as a newly converted but devoted spinster she would send them straight back. After she had jumped on them first!

"I am glad you were pleased to receive them, for hothouse blooms are very expensive this close to Christmas." As Vee struggled to find the right reply to that ungallant and unromantic statement, Lord Dorchester surprised her again by reaching for her hand.

Unsurprisingly, the contact had absolutely no effect on her body.

There were no tingles.

No fizzing bubbles of excitement, attraction, or awareness.

No confusing and befuddling frisson to cloud her perennially flawed judgment.

"Miss Vee, might I speak plainly?"

Her pulse quickened at that question, more in wariness than anticipation.

"If you must." The sooner he said his piece, the sooner this awkward interlude would be over, the sooner his clammy hand would release hers and she could go back to wallowing in her private, humiliating misery.

His features did something peculiar as he squared his sloping shoulders. Both actions filled her with dread. But not nearly as much dread as his words did. "I believe the time has come to *further* our acquaintance."

Honestly! It never rained, it poured. Except in her case, it just poured duds.

Ingrained politeness made her stutter rather than send him packing as any devoted and jaded spinster would. "While obviously I am . . . um . . . flattered, my lord, I . . ."

"Now, now." He wagged his finger like a pendulum, pouting in a distasteful attempt at flirting. "Now that we are to be *more* than acquaintances, I insist that you call me Marmaduke."

"*My lord*, I do not recall agreeing that we would become more than . . ." Whatever else she planned to say evaporated in an instant, because if Lord Dorchester was a passing rainstorm, what was approaching with determined fury and narrowed green eyes was thunder.

Galahad wasn't dressed for an evening soiree in Mayfair. Judging by the windswept, unshaved, scruffy look of him, which of course suited the duplicitous wretch down to the ground, he had apparently come directly from the muddy road from Brighton without bothering to change first.

Even from fifty feet away, his angry gaze latched onto hers unwavering. He was a man on a mission, and it was clear that mission involved her. Although what else there was to say, she couldn't fathom; he had done quite enough damage already. Never mind that she was nowhere near ready for another reminder of her own naive stupidity, and the only thing she had close enough to hide behind was the useless lord who was apparently now besotted with her.

Like a startled deer, she blinked at Lord Dorchester until she decided Galahad's unexpected arrival might actually be a blessing in disguise. A chance to create a new final memory of their time together. One that didn't make her hate herself.

"We need to talk."

As he wasn't the only one who could act, Vee used every drop of bravado she possessed to glare imperious. "We need do no such thing."

"We do because . . ." Galahad stared pointedly at Dorchester. "Do you mind? Isn't it obvious Venus and I need some privacy?"

As Dorchester stuttered in outrage, she smiled at him simply to vex Galahad while saving her own face. "This shan't take more than a minute . . . *Marmaduke*." Good grief, that name tasted awful on her tongue, but the use of it made him smile triumphantly while Galahad's eyes fumed at the sudden new familiarity. To make them seethe some more, she touched the pompous lord's sleeve in mock affection and tried not to grimace in disgust. "Why don't you fetch us that champagne and I shall join you presently."

"As we shall be toasting our future, it would be my pleasure." The dud smiled victoriously at Galahad, who practically snarled back and continued to snarl like a territorial cat until Lord Dorchester was out of earshot, then huffed to cover his obvious jealousy.

"Why on earth are you bothering with him again?"

Vee did not dignify that with an answer. "I believe you were about to put forward a case as to why I should deign to speak to you when I can assure you, I have nothing pleasant to say."

He winced beneath the force of her stony glare. "We need to clear the air because . . ." He ran an agitated hand through his thick sandy hair. ". . . because I hate how we left things. If I could change how I went about everything, I would. I should have told you my plans from the outset. I realize that now. But hindsight is a wonderful thing and . . . well . . . the truth is I didn't tell you for three reasons."

"Because you are a liar, a cheat, and a manipulative opportunist?"

He winced again. "Because I didn't trust Mallory not to welch on the deal, and because . . . well . . ." He raked an agitated hand through his hair. "I'm not used to trusting others with a confidence, Venus." As that admission clearly pained him, and because, devil take him, she instantly understood, she steeled her spine. Refusing to feel pity for a man who had used her for his own selfish desires.

"And the third reason?" She knew already that this was the one that would hurt her the most. "The calculated and ruthless businessman's reason?" Clearly he knew it, too, as he bowed his head rather than see how his selfish motives would wound.

"The honest truth is, I didn't want a war on my own doorstep, Venus."

Honesty!

Truth!

Huh!

He wouldn't know the meaning of either if they slapped him in the face.

"Yet conversely, now you have one." Vee refused to let him see again how much he had hurt her, how much all his flowery fibs and lying kisses had cut her to the quick. She folded her arms. "Ironically, all entirely of your making."

"I realize that, too." He made a good show of looking miserable and contrite, which she did not believe for a second. "I made a mistake, Venus. A huge one. One I bitterly regret."

"At least we have that in common."

He reacted to that barb as if he actually possessed feelings and her words wounded them. "I guess I deserved that."

"You deserve shooting, you despicable liar!"

"I didn't lie!"

"You didn't tell the truth, either, did you?"

Because she had him there, he huffed and stared at his feet some more. "I appreciate that you're mad at me, Venus. You have every right to be, and I swear to you that I will do whatever it takes to make amends." It was staggering how effortlessly he could strap on a mask of sincerity when he wanted to. "*Whatever.* It. Takes." He reached for her hands and dropped his, frowning, when her arms remained resolutely folded.

"Whatever it takes? Really?" Her bitter laugh was loaded with all the sarcasm that flimsy declaration deserved. "I'll take my building back, if you please. Or I'll buy it back. Either-or will suffice as compensation for your deceit and the humiliation I will have to carry for as long as we breathe the same air. I believe two and a half thousand was the price you quoted back in Brighton, Galahad. Or do you expect me to be the idiot to pay *over the odds* now that you hold all the cards?"

"Venus, be reasonable—" His outraged expression confirmed he wasn't actually prepared to do whatever it took after all. He stepped closer, palms spread, and she planted her feet and set her jaw to ensure she appeared unmoved by his sham sincerity even though she was dying inside.

"Reasonable! That is rich coming from you! Of all the things you have been these past three weeks, reasonable hasn't been one of them. Disingenuous is on my list. Dishonest, too. A despicable liar, most definitely." A despicable liar who had broken her heart.

"I appreciate that from your perspective, my silence could be viewed as disingenuous. But what you call disingenuous, I call cautious. It's never a wise move in business to count your chickens before they are hatched, and I *was* dealing with Mallory, remember. A man whom his own aunt didn't trust enough to leave any money to." He edged a pace forward and halted when she raised her flattened palm in disgust. "A man in debt up to his eyeballs and in such dire need of ready cash he would have happily sold those buildings out from under me if someone had offered him more in a hurry. Surely you can understand why I didn't want to bare my hand?"

"Of course I see." Only too clearly. "You took advantage of him. You knew he needed money fast and you dangled it before his aunt was even cold in her coffin."

"I took *advantage* of the situation."

"Mallory *was* the situation. If he hadn't been in debt, you'd have had to wait to place a fair offer like the rest of us had to."

Myriad complex emotions played across his features before he scrunched his eyes closed briefly and nodded. "In business, you have to strike while the iron is hot, so I guess in that respect I did take advantage of Mallory's predicament—but he was the fool that had gotten himself in that predicament in the first place. And if he hadn't sold it to me, he'd have sold it to someone else just as fast and you'd still be exactly where you're at."

"But if you hadn't been the one to buy them, I wouldn't have been taken advantage of by you, too." It took every bit of pride Vee possessed to say that without showing him how much that hurt.

He dropped his voice to a whispered growl in case there were any eavesdroppers. "I kissed you because I wanted to, not because I wanted to take advantage, damn it!"

"Because you wanted the set?" Before he answered with another lie, she raised her gloved palm. "Save your breath for someone less naive. I have your full measure now, Galahad Sinclair. I suspect I always did, until you used your calculated charm to convince me otherwise and distracted me with your practiced showmanship."

"There was no showmanship when . . ." She stayed him with her palm again, determined not to give him an opportunity to wound her further in case the tears burning behind her eyes fell before she could escape him.

"Furthermore, kindly note that until you do the decent thing and relinquish the building next door to its rightful owners, there is nothing you can do or say that will convince me otherwise."

"This is my dream you're asking me to compromise, Venus. I've waited years to open my club. Worked my fingers to the bone getting the money together, put in ridiculous, relentless hours both day and night in the docks scrimping and saving to ensure I had enough. Then spent the last twelve months hunting for the perfect place to put it. It's everything to me, and those buildings are perfect. To expect me to sell one of them to you just because some old lady welched on a promise she made to the orphanage isn't fair. If she'd really wanted you to have it, she'd have written it in her will. Be angry at her, not me."

"Mrs. Leyton-Brown didn't welch, Lord Mallory did."

"What?" His head snapped back as if it had been slapped.

"She gave him the instruction to do it a month before she died when she was so sick she could no longer leave her bed, and he faithfully promised to honor her dying wish to donate that building to us. Promised it in front of the Reverend Smythe and his wife, then went and sold it within hours of her dying breath to you instead! Knowing full well he was ignoring her express wishes."

He swallowed. "I did not know that." And because he was the consummate actor, he even managed to say that as if it were the gospel truth. "If I had, I probably wouldn't have bought it."

Probably!

That single word said it all.

She wanted to laugh in both of his two faces at that outright lie, except this was all too tragic and painful to be funny. "But now you do know it, Galahad." She glared in challenge, willing him to be the man she had believed he was. Still hoped he was, much to her complete disgust. "So what are you going to do about it?"

"What can I do, short of shoot myself in the foot?" He waved his arms as he paced as if she was the one being unreasonable. "I bought it in good faith. I'm invested, Venus. I've spent almost every cent I had saved. I've engaged tradesmen to start work and I had to pay them half up front weeks ago and . . ."

"All things you should have had the decency to tell me weeks ago, too."

He winced as if he realized he was digging himself a bigger hole. "I had no idea about her last wishes, I swear it. You have to believe that."

She mimicked the oh-so-charming accent he employed whenever he wanted to get his own way. "Why, I don't believe a single *drawled* syllable that comes out of your *lyin'* mouth, Galahad Sinclair."

He had the nerve to growl. "I'm trying to make things right between us, Venus!"

"If you truly want to make things right, then you would do the decent thing and honor her last request."

"Now, hang on a goddamn minute . . ."

"I take it that is a firm no, Galahad, despite the fact that it should very much be a yes. Because of course it is a no, when a man like you—a man who by his own admission isn't foolish enough *not* to seize any opportunity that presents itself—has never possessed a single shred of honor."

"Of course it's a firm no!" His temper snapped. Likely because he had finally run out of charming lies to justify his duplicity. "But not because I have no honor. It's because I damn well do, and you know it!"

"What? The honor-among-thieves sort of honor? The so-long-as-you're-all-right sort of honor?"

"It was my honor that brought me to this stupid country in the first place!"

"Do not dare try to claim you came to England to save Giles when you came here expressly to get revenge on your lying, duplicitous father. The apple certainly didn't fall far from that tree, did it?"

He fought for calm, then tried again. "I am not entirely in the wrong here." Although his pained expression said otherwise. "Yes—with hindsight I shouldn't have kept the purchase from you, and there's no denying I damn well should have mentioned it before I kissed you, but that snake Mallory is the villain of the piece here, not me. And while I don't disagree that *he* should have honored his aunt's dying wishes, he didn't, and expecting me to pay for that retroactively is unfair."

"From where I am standing, Mallory isn't the only snake, and what is unfair is me being lied to and shamelessly used so that you got to win."

"I didn't use you." He didn't deny the lying, though. "What happened between us back in Brighton was . . ."

Before he came up with another flowery lie, she said, "A convenient opportunity to get your own way, which only a fool wouldn't seize? It was you, wasn't it, who said that one should never underestimate the power of seducing someone with a few cheap tricks?" The threatening tears gathered and Vee ruthlessly pushed them away, refusing to give him the satisfaction of seeing how much his callousness had wounded. "That unkind and wholly unethical manipulation aside, morally the building next door belongs to the orphans and until you do right by them, I suggest we go back to the way things used to be between us. Back to when we avoided each other like the plague and only spoke when polite company made it impossible not to."

"What about that kiss? That momentous, significant kiss? You expect me to ignore what it meant? What it *could* mean for us?"

"Us?" From somewhere deep inside Vee found the strength to laugh as if he had taken leave of his wits. "Oh, bless you for thinking that there was ever any chance of an *us*, Galahad." She let the amusement morph into disgust. "But for me it was just a kiss. Not my first. Not my last. And certainly not *my* most momentous." Vee held his gaze steady as she gestured to the edge of the dance floor where Lord Dorchester hovered clutching two glasses of champagne and shooting Galahad daggers. "Now, if you'll excuse me, Marmaduke is waiting."

"I know you're mad as all hell at me, but don't use this silly misunderstanding as a reason to run back to that pompous ass."

She wasn't running back, she was running away, but it would be a cold day in hell before she allowed Galahad to see it. So instead, she let every bit of her fresh loathing of him show.

"As my nonexistent grandpa *never* used to say, better a pompous arse than a lying one. Especially when the pompous arse is a much better kisser." With that excellent final memory to replace the awful one from Brighton, she sailed away.

Chapter Fourteen

When wronged, Olivia says that it is better to forgive and forget and move on with your life. Therefore, I have decided to put aside my devastation at my father's cruel betrayal because I am going to be a bridesmaid and Minerva is going to be a countess and all three of us will be moving from the slum of Clerkenwell to the grandeur of Mayfair. However, I do not yet have it in me to forgive, and because I have the memory of an elephant, I know already that I shall <u>never</u> forget . . .

—from the diary of Miss Venus Merriwell, aged 17

"I confess, I am intrigued to see what he does with the place." The Reverend Smythe had taken Galahad's treachery and the sale of next door on the chin. "His plans looked very grand and ambitious. Our tired building will appear the poor cousin once it is all complete."

The traitor himself had been at great pains to share those plans when he had called upon the orphanage last week. Forewarned, Vee had made herself scarce, but the practiced charmer had worked his magic on the reverend and Mrs. Witherspoon, who were now thoroughly seduced by him, too.

"All the fancy plasterwork and wallpaper in the world cannot disguise the hedonistic nature of his business. A wolf in sheep's clothing is still a wolf after all, and a gaming hell is not an appropriate neighbor for the impressionable young minds in this orphanage." Seeing as hell apparently truly did not have more fury than a woman scorned, it was a bitter and twisted response, but no less than the cheating wretch deserved. Besides, it was better to be angry at him than weep inconsolably, and she had already wasted more tears on him this past fortnight than he deserved. She was sick to the back teeth of turning into a crumpled wreck every time she closed her bedchamber door, especially when all the tears in the world would not wound a callous, calculated chancer like him one jot.

"This is Covent Garden." The reverend waved her concerns away. "Sin and sinners thrive here, and a gambling club pales in comparison with some of the depravity our children can spy daily out of their bedchamber windows the second the sun goes down. In many ways, I am hopeful that all the fancy carriages and customers that head next door will force some of those unfortunate fallen women and their lustful customers elsewhere."

Like a convert to the cause, Mrs. Witherspoon nodded. "Some nights you cannot move for lightskirts outside, and some of them are quite shameless where they ply their trade. A few have even started to hand out flyers detailing prices and the like." She shot the reverend a veiled look as if Vee was so innocent she was oblivious to it all. "They make shocking reading."

"I did grow up in Clerkenwell." Vee sent them both a pointed stare of her own. "I also have two perfectly working eyes despite my spectacles, so I see the same as you. But what goes on outside is by the by." They were comparing apples with oranges. The unfortunate women who had no other choice and the snake who could have put his dratted club anywhere else. If he'd wanted to. Or if he had truly meant all that he had said before he seduced her. "The morality of some of the street vendors here aside, our children have enough temptation on this doorstep without the lure of the gaming tables. Glamorizing them, as Mr. Sinclair seems intent on doing, will send the dangerous message that there are riches to be made in gambling all your hard-earned wages away."

"We shall caution our charges to be mindful against such unreliable endeavors in the same way that we warn about the dangers of drink or the consequences of crime, and they shall still walk out of these doors rounded and prepared. You'll see. There are always lessons to be learned here on Long Acre." The reverend sipped his morning tea. "Resisting temptation and remaining tolerant and forgiving of human foibles are valuable skills that shall make our children more resilient, for the world is an ever-movable feast."

"But how can you be so tolerant and forgiving of *him* when he stole next door from us?" It wasn't enough that Vee now hated him. She wanted everyone to hate him with her. Perhaps that was naught but a petty revenge, but it might make her feel a little bit better than the Galahad-imposed utter misery that kept her awake at night.

This time it was the Reverend Smythe who shot the matron a pointed look. "It wasn't meant to be, Vee, so you must stop torturing yourself with it. He sat down with me and explained everything, and I am satisfied that he is as much a victim of Lord Mallory's greed and duplicity as we are. Mr. Sinclair meant no malice to us when he purchased next door, and he broke no laws."

Meant no malice indeed! He had known what he was doing. He had been too good at kissing not to know how to use it as a lethal weapon!

"Lord Mallory, however, shall receive his comeuppance for reneging on his aunt's promise when he arrives at the pearly gates." Mrs. Witherspoon was standing like a pious opera singer again, fingers interlocked beneath her ample bosom and lips pinched in indignation.

"And so, no doubt, shall Mr. Sinclair, as he is about as innocent in all this as one of our local lightskirts." Not that anyone else saw Galahad's true colors except Vee. Even her own family believed the sorry yarn of contrition he had spun them, accepting that he had bought next door in good faith while agreeing that it would have been prudent to have apprised her of the fact long before she found out. They did not understand why she refused to accept his apology and move on.

But then Galahad had neglected to apprise them of the sting in the sorry tale, so nobody apart from her was aware of the lengths he had gone to to seduce her for his own selfish gain. While she was relieved at that, because having *him* know how willingly she had succumbed to his talented lips was humiliation enough, Vee was also furious at him for perpetuating his reasonable and innocent façade despite all the pain his lies had caused her. So furious she hadn't dared touch her beloved copy of *Much Ado*, which still sat on her nightstand where Minerva had left it after he had called two weeks ago to return it. How could she when he had touched it?

She had avoided him ever since their last unfortunate collision, and rather tellingly, he had avoided her, too. Probably because she had served her purpose, or was no longer fit for purpose, and just like Lord Argyll he had blithely moved on. "I wouldn't be at all surprised if he was the one who encouraged Lord Mallory to renege. After all, he had everything to gain, didn't he?" She tossed her thumb in the direction of next door.

"After speaking with him, I have absolutely no reason to believe that." Clearly Galahad had such a talented mouth, he could bewitch everyone. "There is bound to be a reason why Mr. Sinclair got the building instead of us, Vee. The Lord always moves in mysterious ways, after all, and in him we must trust even if his methods do not make immediate sense. It is ultimately by his design that we lost next door. However, what we lost in property we more than made up for in funds. Who'd have thought we'd be left seven thousand?" He chuckled as he toasted first Mrs. Witherspoon and then the heavens with his teacup. "Not I."

"For my tuppence worth—" Mrs. Witherspoon was too accepting of Galahad's treachery as well. "—You can't really miss what you've never had, and I rather like Mr. Sinclair's suggestion of relocating to somewhere nicer one day. It will be better for the children in the long run to be away from all of the temptations of Covent Garden, and with all that money in the bank, and his offer to buy this place if ever we decide to sell it, it is an unforeseen but intriguing option. It would be lovely to have a garden . . ."

It was all well and good that the matron was parroting *his* words, and that pretty dream, despite Galahad instigating it; his treachery aside, it was the *one day* Vee now took the most issue with. "But how does that help us now, when we are bursting at the seams? Finding such a place and readying it could take several years, and that is a conservative estimate when the three of us are spread too thin already and there are so many children out there who still need saving. That is without all the additional funds we would have to raise to be able to run a larger place ad infinitum. Seven thousand only stretches so far, and at least here in Covent Garden we are seen and those with money feel obliged to donate some to our cause. In the countryside we shall be out of sight and out of mind. We might well end up having to close when Mrs. Leyton-Brown's bequest runs out. Have you considered that?" Running an orphanage was an expensive endeavor that relied on the benevolence of others, and for that, they had to be seen to be believed. After pondering it incessantly during the purgatory of her Galahad-imposed insomnia, she knew without a shred of doubt that there was no other way to fund it.

"Something will come up to help us continue to thrive," said the reverend, believing it. "Something always does. Not a month ago we were worrying about how to scrape enough together to fix the roof, remember, and now, thanks to a timely miracle, that is no longer a concern. And thanks to Mr. Sinclair's superior negotiating skills and urgent need to repair his own leaking roofs, it is being done alongside his as a priority at a third of the cost we were originally quoted. Already, Vee, our new neighbor has proved himself to be more of a benefit to us than the curse you fear."

And that was galling, too. How typical of the wretch to use their misfortune as a bribe to beat her with!

She wandered to the window and gazed out, fuming that it had been less than three weeks since Galahad had stabbed her in the back in Brighton and already there was a group of tradesmen unloading their tools on the street. The speed at which he had been able to organize workmen was further proof that he had planned everything well in advance.

He was a "voracious planner," after all. One adept at "adapting to the circumstances"—even if those circumstances lent themselves to a sham seduction!

How dare he, in one breath, claim he hadn't seduced her for the sake of his new club, then begin his renovations the next? Tradesmen, good ones, took their own sweet time getting to your job unless you paid them a premium. Which—knowing Galahad's single-minded determination to get his new den of iniquity up and running as soon as possible—he had. By the smart look of Evans & Sons' fancy painted carts and plentiful workforce, he had engaged the sort of trades that had been so far out of the orphanage's league, it was galling.

It was all galling.

Mallory's flagrant dishonesty and greed.

Galahad's manipulative, convincing, and self-serving lies.

His shameless seduction to soften her up.

Her pathetic response to his charming façade and practiced kisses.

Her eagerness to drop the battlements around her heart and let him ride roughshod all over it on the back of one of those kisses.

That disgusted her most of all because her being such a gullible idiot was history repeating itself.

"Miss Merriwell." Tommy Claypole poked his head around the door. "The classroom is all set up for this morning's lessons." It was galling too that Galahad's advice about using the boy's focus toward good rather than evil had paid dividends. The moment she had given him extra responsibility, and by default some extra attention, Tommy had proved himself to be a most reliable lieutenant.

"Do you want me to find a hackney to take us to Ackermann's?"

Today, because she had faithfully promised the children that this afternoon's schooling would be entirely given over to drawing, his mission was to help her spend some of Mrs. Leyton-Brown's bequest on art materials. Paints, chalks, and decent paper were a luxury the orphanage could rarely afford, and all the children were so excited at the prospect, it had been palpable when she had informed them of it before she had left last night.

"I'll flag one down while you put your coat on, Tommy." It was, it would seem, a timely outing seeing as this morning, thanks to the impending arrival of their new roof, Galahad was being hailed as a saint. "That is if you still do not mind covering my lessons this morning, Reverend?"

Still beaming at the orphanage's apparent good fortune, the overly trusting vicar waved her away. "Why on earth would I mind teaching the fascinating subject of mathematics? Especially as I shall be spared the chore of teaching it to the disruptive young Mr. Claypole here?"

Tommy grinned unoffended, as delighted to be missing a lesson on subtraction as he was to be the one chosen to accompany her to the shops. "I'll go chivy everyone from the breakfast room for their dull day of learning before I fetch my coat." Off he went, and the reverend smiled, impressed.

"You finally have that young ruffian eating out of your hand."

"For now I do—but you know Tommy."

Annoyed that she had allowed the tradesmen to unsettle her when she was doing her best not to think about Galahad or his business at all now that he was dead to her, Vee yanked her coat from the peg. She was still buttoning it against the cold when she stepped outside, but was too busy spying on the workmen to notice that their paymaster had also arrived.

"Hello, Venus."

Because standing like a startled deer or dashing inside like a frightened one were not options as far as her severely wounded pride was concerned, Vee turned stony-faced so that she could acknowledge him with a frown. Without pausing, she marched onward, doing her best impression of a woman too busy searching for a hackney to give him the time of day. "Galahad."

"You look . . . well."

She responded to that with a curt nod toward his hired help as a second Evans & Sons cart trundled behind the first. This one was stacked high with roof tiles made of shiny black slate.

Drat him.

"I see you wasted no time marking your territory and making *our* place your own. But I suppose it was all booked and planned well in advance, as you are such an opportunistic *forward planner.*"

He sighed as if worn down by all her cynicism. "I'd explain the suddenness of Mr. Evans's arrival, but will save us both the effort of telling you that his previous job canceled at the last minute as I know the truth would only fall on deaf ears if it came from me."

"That is most thoughtful of you, as I am not in the mood for more lies." Because fate was on her side, a hackney appeared, and she hailed it. When the driver slowed beside her, she told him the destination then offered Galahad her most insincere and clipped dismissal. "I shall bid you a good day." So good she hoped his buildings were riddled with woodworm and dry rot.

"I'm guessing there's no chance of attempting civility, despite us being neighbors and therefore stuck with each other for the foreseeable future."

"We tried civility. It failed." Thankfully, Vee heard Tommy behind and turned to her charge as a means of escape. "Get in the carriage, Tommy."

"'Ello, Mr. Sinclair." Tommy doffed his cap instead. "What brings you 'ere?"

Galahad pointed to his buildings. "These. All three are now mine." His eyes bored into hers as he said this, entirely unrepentant now.

The boy smiled, and before he asked the stream of questions she knew he would ask if she didn't step in, she said, "Into the carriage, please, young man. We are in a hurry and need to be there and back in an hour as I have a class at eleven." As the boy hoisted himself in, Galahad held out his hand to help her. She ignored it. The absolute last thing she needed right now was a reminder of the effect his touch had on her stupid, wayward flesh. "Move over, Tommy."

As he shuffled farther inside, she sat on the bench, but before she could slam the door closed, Galahad rested his arm on it. "Can I expect the same frosty antagonism at Giles's dinner next week? Or will we manage to behave as adults around others?" She suppressed the urge to slam the door shut on his fingers because she had forgotten about *that* dinner. The one that Galahad attended, where they always had to bemoan the fact that he could never leave town with them in the coming days for Christmas.

Thank goodness!

"I believe I have already stipulated the parameters of our relationship going forward."

"Ah yes. Avoidance wherever possible but feigned politeness in company." Galahad's suddenly unreadable eyes flicked to Tommy, who sensed trouble and wasn't entirely sure quite where to look. "I take it that rule doesn't count if we happen to collide here in Covent Garden?"

"Here very much comes under the category marked avoidance." And she would avoid him like a dose of the pox now that he had started turning up.

"Good to know." His bland mask slipped long enough for her to see his anger, but like the consummate actor he was he covered it quickly with a smile for the boy beside her who was trying his best to blend into the upholstery. "You have a good day now, Tommy." With that parting shot, he slammed the door shut himself and rapped the side of the carriage to let the driver know that they were done.

The hackney lurched forward, and Tommy waited all of five seconds before his questions started. "I thought you were friends with

Mr. Sinclair. Old family friends." He eyed her with curiosity. "Have the pair of you had a tiff?"

She considered lying, but there seemed little point when there had never been any flies on Tommy Claypole. "We have not had a tiff. A tiff is something easily sorted."

"A disagreement?"

"I am afraid it is a bit more than a disagreement." More a gaping, unbreachable chasm. "And quite impossible to fix."

"Which of you is in the wrong?"

That he even asked that stupid question offended, and she let her expression show it. "Him. Obviously. And entirely." As even the residual lingering scent of Galahad's spicy cologne and the unfortunate effect it had on her wanton nostrils infuriated her, Vee cracked the window to dispel it despite the late-autumn chill. "For clarity's sake, and because you witnessed that unpleasant altercation, Mr. Sinclair dishonestly obtained the three buildings adjacent to ours."

"He stole them from someone?"

In a manner of speaking. "He bought them. Legally apparently, although in this instance the law is an ass." As was he.

"I see." Although by his baffled expression, Tommy clearly didn't. "And why don't you want Mr. Sinclair owning the buildings?"

"Because he intends to turn them into a den of iniquity. A bawdy, drunken house of gaming and debauchery exactly like his shady place in the docks. He does not care how his unsavory business impacts our orphanage, so in a few months, once the doubtless distasteful renovations he is having done are complete, we are doomed to then endure Sodom and Gomorrah next door forever."

"Can't you stop him? Reason with him?" Tommy's freckled face scrunched into a frown. "Mr. Sinclair seemed reasonable after Billy stole his watch."

Likely only because it served as another way to pull the wool over her eyes about his true character and intentions. "I have tried to reason with him, Tommy—but it turns out Mr. Sinclair only cares about himself." In case her despondency at that irrefutable fact showed, Vee stared out the window. "If you don't mind, I would rather not discuss it any further as I fear reminders of his treachery only make my blood boil." And made her eyes leak tears the scoundrel did not deserve.

"Did he stab you in the back, miss?"

Out of the mouths of babes! But Vee could hardly go into all the sordid details with a twelve-year-old no matter how accurate his assessment. "Do you remember when I taught you the history of ancient Rome?" Tommy nodded. "Well, if I am Julius Caesar in this scenario, he is most definitely Brutus."

Tommy took all that in. After an age, he reached across the benches to squeeze her hand. "Rest assured, miss, if Mr. Sinclair did you wrong, then he's my sworn enemy now, too. And my bruvver's."

She squeezed his back. "You are a good boy, Tommy."

At least someone else understood the truth.

Chapter Fifteen

Although I shall always disapprove of reckless gambling, Jeremiah has convinced me that there is no harm in a friendly family game of cards and is going to teach me how to play whist tonight...

—from the diary of Miss Venus Merriwell, aged 17

"All I know is somebody was in here again last night after we finished, Mr. Sinclair." Mr. Evans was still red in the face despite all Gal's placating. "This time, that someone put all the tools outside in the yard for the damp to rust them." Which was a change from the day before when all the tools had apparently played a midnight game of hide-and-seek, and it had taken Mr. Evans and his boys a good hour to find them all before they could start work the next morning.

As there had been no sign of forced entry on either occasion, or after any of the annoying little pranks that had been played over the last week, Gal had a sneaking suspicion he knew exactly who the culprit was. He was prepared to lay good money on him being twelve, freckled, and totally devoted to Venus.

"It's sabotage, is what it is, Mr. Sinclair. Sabotage! Although I have no idea what me and my boys have done to deserve it." Mr. Evans and his boys had done nothing. Gal, on the other hand, was big enough to admit he had probably earned this stint in purgatory.

He should have told her sooner that he had bought this place, and he should have confessed they were going to be neighbors before he had succumbed to the foolish temptation to kiss her. And he certainly shouldn't have even kissed her in the first place.

He realized that now.

Venus Merriwell's intoxicating kisses were as dangerous and destructive as a siren's song. Dangerous enough that they were capable of bewitching him, of overriding his reason and diverting him from the road he needed to take. For a while, thanks to her and the effect her hypnotic lips had had on him, he had lost all control of his life. All control of what he was and where he was going, and had handed it all to her, and that was madness.

Utter madness when he knew to his cost that the second you ceased to hold the reins of your life, someone else drove you headfirst into a wall. Or a dead end. Or a trap. Or off a cliff.

Therefore, she, and most especially her lips, was best avoided unless he wanted to watch all his hard-won, longed-for plans and dreams get smashed to smithereens on the perilous rocks of her pious and unreasonable whimsy.

Sell his building to her! Pay for Mallory's mistakes! Wave goodbye to everything he had worked damn hard for!

Scrimped for. Saved for.

Dreamed of every goddamn day since the day he'd lost everything.

Not today!

Yet there was no denying Gal had been so entranced by the power she held over him, so sold on the alluring prospect of her that he'd almost made the biggest mistake of his adult life. Thank the Lord fate had stepped in to save him before any real damage had been done. He'd made a fool of himself, that was all, and some dented pride was a small price to pay for his lucky escape.

As he had all his life, he would take that mistake and learn from it.

Yes, on the spectrum of kisses, that one had been stupendous, but that was exactly why Saint Venus Merriwell was best suffered at a distance going forward. In that respect, her fresh hatred of him was a bonus. Something to be celebrated, not lamented. He was furious at himself for losing control in Brighton, for succumbing to and then displaying weakness, and so livid at his own continued stupidity directly after at that ball that he could barely stand to look at himself in the mirror.

What the hell had he been thinking to go chasing after her like that, and then throwing out the baby with the bathwater on the back of one ill-considered kiss? When he knew any decision made in the irrational heat of the moment was always the wrong one.

Thanks to a mad moment of passion and a stupid ache in his heart, he had practically begged, when he had never ever stooped that low for anyone else before.

As if he had the time for a romance? With someone so determined to be a wife, for pity's sake?

A trouble and strife.

A ball and chain.

When the last place he needed to be right now was caught in the goddamn parson's trap!

With his rational head now screwed firmly back on his shoulders, Gal knew that he was too damn sensible for any of that distracting nonsense. He had likely only been seduced into the thought of it back in Brighton because she had caught him at a bad time. He had been overwhelmed, panicked, and melancholy, lost in the past and uncharacteristically lonely that night, too, so obviously her feminine softness had appealed. When you combined that with the intimacy of the moonlight, and the intimacy of the conversation and his blatant attraction to the alluring minx, it was hardly surprising that Venus had called to his soul. Toss in that kiss—that phenomenal kiss—was it any wonder he had been so thoroughly seduced?

However, thanks to some distance, and the timely reminder that no good ever came out of letting someone in, he was over it.

Over her.

Or soon would be.

On that he was resolute.

He had seen her only three times since Brighton. The first had been at that ball where she'd used the idiot Dorchester as a weapon. The second had been a week ago when she had stormed off in a hackney with a face like thunder. The last time he had seen her was yesterday, when she had briefly glanced out of the orphanage window, spotted him, scowled in repulsion, then yanked the drapes closed, so he figured he was destined to languish in purgatory for a while longer despite him directing his workmen to charitably fix her roof first.

So be it.

"We've had to waste another hour this morning oiling every tool against rust." Mr. Evans held up a saw as if it were a crucial piece of evidence in court. "It's not on, Mr. Sinclair, and it's certainly not fair to either me or my boys to waste countless hours on sabotage when we already have more than enough to do and a short window to do it all in."

"It isn't fair, Mr. Evans, and I shall sort it." Although how he was supposed to do that when Tommy's commander in chief Venus the Unreasonable wouldn't speak to him, he had no clue. "I shall find the culprit and I shall stop him."

"Until the bleeder is found and stopped, you need to employ a watchman after hours, as this state of affairs cannot continue!" Mr. Evans waved the saw in the air like a broadsword. "Time is money, Mr. Sinclair, and my time is limited. When I moved this job forward, I moved them all forward, and I told my next client I would be finished here by the end of March. The Duke of Harlow is too important a customer to upset. If it comes to it, I've no choice but to go to where my bread is buttered, even if that does leave this place unfinished."

"I understand that, too." The clock was ticking and in more ways than one. As Mr. Evans's reputation for fine work preceded him, and because Gal really couldn't afford the delay, either, when—thanks to three renovations instead of the planned-for two—his funds were depleting faster than he could replenish them. He had to do whatever it took to keep the man on the job and the job moving in a timely manner.

This new club had to open in the spring. It *had* to or Gal would have no savings left at the rate he was going through them.

"I'll stay here myself tonight to guard everything, Mr. Evans, and every night until I employ someone. You have my word." Which wasn't the most ideal or comfortable solution, but it was the best he had at this precise moment.

He scanned the dusty shell of the building where he was now going to have to bunk in resignation. Parts of the connecting walls between the three buildings were either sporting holes or fully demolished already, replaced by jacks and lintels. That meant that the drafts from every warped, cracked, or ill-fitting window whistled around the cavernous space. With the temperature outside more than cold enough to freeze the knackers off a brass monkey, and this winter's perpetual snow falling again with a vengeance, those drafts were bitter. Ladders, tools, and building materials were piled everywhere. Where there wasn't the necessary chaos of a full-scale renovation, there was rubble from the works, yet despite the evidence of a week of fevered activity, the decrepit stench of years of neglect still overpowered the fresher scent of sawdust.

All a long way from the luxury of his cozy suite of rooms at the Albany.

His ridiculously expensive suite at the Albany, too, so maybe this was actually a blessing in disguise as far as his pocket was concerned. With his funds already stretched almost to their limit, the savings on his rent would come in handy.

He'd slept in worse places in his life, he supposed, and the Claypoles' nocturnal shenanigans needed to be nipped in the bud before they did real harm and left his precious club floundering unfinished.

Having won his battle, Mr. Evans was magnanimous and thanked him for his understanding. He even sent one of his boys to the nearby shops to fetch Gal some dinner, candles, a newspaper, and firewood for the long night ahead.

The only fireplace he could find that wasn't blocked was in the attic, which he had already earmarked as his future apartment, so he made his camp there among the discarded old roof struts. Once the fire was lit and roaring, fearing for his teeth if he tried to bite into the solid, stale loaf in his food parcel, he ate half his lackluster stew instead until he could stand the bland, oily taste of it no more, then read the newspaper from cover to cover rather than mull over *her* some more, until his eyelids began to droop.

As he had all those years ago when he'd slept rough for almost two winters, he found himself a tight corner, wedged his body into it, and, much to his surprise after years of finer things, fell into a deep slumber.

He was still in it when a noise down below woke him with a start. It wasn't a loud noise, more the quiet protest of a rusty old hinge, but just like when he had slept under the stars, his body went instantly to full alert at the interruption.

Gal sat bolt upright. His candle had long extinguished and so had his fire, but instead of the pitch-black darkness he had expected to find in the middle of the night, the attic was filled with the shadows of the December dawn. Rather than alert the intruder, or intruders, to his presence, Gal stayed as still as a statue while he listened to the sound of boots entering the premises stealthily, then forgetting to creep once they had closed the door behind them.

Good.

They had no idea he was here. That gave him the advantage of the element of surprise, and he would be sure to surprise Venus's miscreants in the act. Catch them red-handed. Then march them back next door with matching fleas in their identical ears before he put some in hers, too, for either unwittingly or—more likely—wittingly putting the Claypoles up to it with her flagrant hostility toward him.

Somebody said something, but as it was three floors below, Gal couldn't make any of the conversation out. There was more movement. Doors opening and closing. Something being dragged. The sounds of exertion, as if whatever mischief the twin terrors were making took effort.

In case they gave him away, Gal gently toed off his boots, then unfolded himself from his corner slowly before creeping on stockinged feet toward the staircase door. With aching slowness, he turned the knob, cracked it open, and craned his ears.

"The higher the better, I reckon." Although the twins' voices were as identical as their faces, he knew that instruction had come from Tommy and not Sydney. Tommy ruled the Claypole roost and Sydney did as he was told. "If we shove 'em in the attic, they'll be harder to remove. They'll be even harder to get rid of if we nail the window frames shut, too."

The boys cackled at their own evil genius.

The clonking sounds of Mr. Evans's tools being disturbed were closely followed by footsteps on the stairs.

"We'll teach the blighter not to mess with us." The eager edge to this threat suggested that the loyal Sydney was keen to impress his brother. "We don't want no Sodom and Gomorrah bleedin' den of iniquity next door and we won't stand for it!"

"Too bloody right, Syd. We'll show him."

Something rustled as the brothers cleared the first staircase; it sounded like wicker. Or at least something moving against wicker. Wrestling against wicker? Squawking against wicker?

What the hell is that sound?

"Wish I could see their faces when they find this lot." Gal wasn't sure quite which twin said that, but both tittered at the brilliance of their latest childish plan to send him packing.

They did not pause at all on the second floor, and as the first foot landed on the final set of stairs leading to the attic, Gal pressed his body flat against the wall to lie in wait for them, hidden behind the door.

He held his breath as the boys reached the landing, his fingers flexing in readiness so that he could slam the door shut behind them the moment they foolishly entered his lair.

Then they'd be trapped. Like rats in a cage. Thwarted and neutered in one fell swoop. Inadvertently playing into his hands because he would be gracious when he personally delivered them back to Venus.

Merciful.

Because contrary to her current opinion, he *was* noble and honorable to his core, and it would do her good to remind her of that fact. After all, how many would be as forgiving of a gold watch being stolen as he had been when Billy Tubbs had lifted his? Hardly any, that was for certain. Even less would forgive a second transgression with quite so much magnanimity—but he would.

For her.

Still.

Despite her continued and unreasonable belligerence.

Despite all the sensible reasons why he was better off without her.

And despite her cruel jibe about Dorchester being better at kissing than him.

As if that pompous ass had the wherewithal to know or care how to please a woman. Or keep his flapping jaws shut long enough to even kiss one properly, for that matter. Venus had just meant to hurt him—and she had—but he would be gracious about that, too.

Because they were now neighbors.

And because that was the sort of man he was, goddamn it!

Gal held his breath as the twins reached his door. One of them pushed and he poised to pounce as the wood creaked open. The door and the shadows camouflaged him as the first boy entered carrying a large basket.

"Do I let 'em all go now, Tommy?" Sydney's fingers hovered over the leather strap securing a large basket, and whatever was within it moved with such determination the whole thing wobbled in the boy's grasp.

"Not yet, Syd. Not until I've sorted the windows." The dominant twin marched into Gal's attic as if he owned the place, wielding a hammer and jiggling the handful of nails necessary to do his own special renovations on the frames.

Gal let him get all the way to the first sash window before he lazily pushed the door shut.

"Mornin', boys."

As he expected, both tearaways screamed in alarm.

What he didn't expect was Tommy throwing the hammer at his head like the Norse god Thor unleashing his thunder.

The heavy tool whizzed, spinning through the air at such speed that Gal only just managed to sidestep it before it cracked his skull open, but not fast enough for it to miss him entirely. Pain exploded white behind his eyes as the hammer landed on his bootless foot and he screamed, too.

Then screamed some more when something wild and angry and definitely squawking burst from the basket in a hail of feathers and flew at his head faster than the hammer. With such fury he had to throw up his arms to shield against the birds flying into his face. Something that might not have been so catastrophic if Gal had been standing on two feet. But as he was hopping on one while his instep throbbed as if it were about to explode, the motion threw him off balance.

Before his backside hit the ground, it hit the half-empty earthenware bowl that still held the remnants of his lackluster stew. With an ominous crack, the bowl immediately shattered beneath his weight, sending a shard of dense pottery into the flesh of his left ass cheek like a dagger.

As fresh pain gripped him, and while Vee's terrible twins were attacked by what looked a lot like common street pigeons, the cold, congealed remnants of his dinner seeped into the seat of his breeches and made his dreadful first night in his new home complete.

Chapter Sixteen

I am not the only one convinced Diana and Giles were made for each other. Convincing my stubborn, cynical sister of that fact, however, is proving to be a challenge . . .

—from the diary of Miss Venus Merriwell, aged 18

"There has been an incident." Mrs. Witherspoon met her at the door of the orphanage the moment Vee walked through it at eight. "Unsurprisingly, it involves the Claypoles."

"Oh dear." Tommy had been doing so well of late, too. "Another silly prank?" If it involved spiders again, she wasn't sure she wouldn't strangle him.

"If you call breaking and entering and injuring a person silly." The older woman's expression was grave as she wrung her hands. "The reverend has had to summon the physician."

"What!" Because the matron had quickened her pace, Vee did, too. "Is the injury that bad?"

"One of them is bad enough to need stitches." Which rather suggested there were multiple injuries involved. "I pray the stitches are enough to stop an infection setting in." Which rather suggested the wound needing stitches was big.

Mrs. Witherspoon gestured toward the office where both Tommy and Sydney stood shamefaced like two sentries outside. The dried blood of several small nicks and cuts marred their freckled faces, but even wounded she had little sympathy for them and wagged her finger at them in outright disgust. "I shall deal with you two later!" The twins withered some more at her outrage as she marched past to slam her palm against the office door.

"I'm not sure that you should go in there yet!"

Mrs. Witherspoon's panicked warning came a second too late and Vee was confronted with the sight of Galahad Sinclair spread-eagled facedown over the reverend's desk, his naked backside practically staring her in the face.

"Oh my goodness!" Her hands flew to her mouth too late to prevent the high-pitched sound that came out. While they were too late for that, they were in time to clutch her suddenly beetroot-red cheeks. That it never occurred to her palms to cover her staring eyes when she couldn't find the strength to avert her gaze only made her face hotter. "Oh my goodness!"

The door swung shut behind her and still she stared. "What on earth has happened?"

Her wayward eyes were so fixed on the taut, firm bottom displayed to the world in all its glory, it took them at least half a minute to realize that the reverend and the physician were also in the room, and a goodly few seconds more to notice the inch-long wound on the exposed left buttock that the physician was in the midst of stitching.

After what must have been an eternity of gawping, Vee had to go into battle with her eyeballs to wrench them away from Galahad's pert posterior to focus on his pinched face.

"He was ravaged by pigeons by all accounts," said the reverend, enjoying the surreal spectacle more than a man of the cloth should.

"How on earth . . . ?" Vee internally had some stern words with her eyes to prevent them from wandering back to his backside. "Pigeons? *Pigeons?*" Apparently, she was so overcome by the splendid sight of some unexpected male nudity that now even full sentences eluded her.

"Funny story." The man himself managed to grunt this through gritted teeth as the physician's needle pierced his skin again. "Your most loyal *left*-tenant decided the best way to stop me putting my club next door was to sabotage the builders." He paused to wince again. Letting his breath out in a whoosh as another stitch was tied. "It turns out that he has been terrorizing my tradesmen for days. To begin with, he broke in and hid all their tools. After all the tools had been found, Tommy picked the lock again and removed them all to the yard where he left them to rust in the elements, and last night—"

He stiffened with another light grunt, his white-knuckled fingers grabbing the desk so tight she only just stopped hers from reaching out to grip them in support. "—or early this morning to be more precise—young Tommy decided it would be hilarious to fill the attic with four furious and feral pigeons to welcome Mr. Evans and his merry team of craftsmen as soon as they arrived. Trouble was, dear Master Claypole did not realize that, anticipating more skulduggery, I had spent the night in the building awaiting him and—" He growled in pain as another stitch got knotted. "—well, let's just say that we surprised each other and then the damn pigeons surprised us all."

"The pigeons did this?" She allowed her eyes to flick to his behind, where they couldn't help noticing how impressively tense his buttocks were rather than analyze the severity of the wound. *How on earth did they get that way when he prefers to walk everywhere rather than ride? Lord Argyll rode everywhere and his weren't so . . . developed.*

"Not directly." To his credit, much as it pained her to give the wretch any credit for anything, Galahad was bearing the ordeal with admirable stoicism. "After Tommy's hammer missed my head but nearly broke my foot, I was down a leg when the pigeons escaped and tried to peck my eyes out, so something had to give. Thankfully, before my butt hit the floor a handy stewpot kindly broke my fall." He squeezed his eyes shut as the needle jabbed again. "Now that the good doctor here has dug the bulk of that pot out from inside me, he's practicin' his embroidery while he closes the hole."

There was so much to take in from that summary, so many gaps in the story that her imagination tried and failed to fill, that Vee didn't quite know what to say.

Her muteness, and her overwhelming desire to feast her eyes on her new sworn enemy's delectable buttocks, made her blink dumbfounded at the reverend in the hope that he could shed some more light on the debacle. With a grin he did.

"Before you ask, as I know you will, Vee, and my apologies in advance, Mr. Sinclair, for the intentional pun, but I have yet to get to the *bottom* of precisely where the pigeons came from."

"Haha," said the injured party deadpan, not the least bit offended. "Very droll, Reverend. You should be on the stage."

"Out of tears come laughter." The Reverend Smythe chuckled, unrepentant. "And I suspect there is a whole separate and entertaining tale behind the procuring of the pigeons that has thus far been denied me. All I have managed to wheedle out of Tommy, in his brief and panicked confession, is that entrapping them somehow involved bread and Mrs. Witherspoon's old blanket basket."

"You have to admire the boy's industry, if nothing else." Again, Galahad's response to the crime against his person surprised her. "He'll go far, that boy, with those impressive problem-solving skills. Unless they send him to jail first, of course."

"At this stage, Mr. Sinclair, I fear it could go either way." The reverend shrugged before dismissing Tommy's eventual fate as part of life's rich tapestry that was out of his control. "But back to the summary, Vee." He smiled as if he were having a grand day out rather than watching a man's backside being stitched. "I have sworn testimony from Tommy that they decided to release said trapped pigeons into Mr. Sinclair's attic to frighten his tradesmen exactly as our patient has already stated, with the intention of preventing them from working on the building and thereby, after a sustained assault, eventually preventing Sodom and Gomorrah from ever opening."

Vee winced at the telling use of her exact phrase and realized she had to shoulder some of the blame for this. Spewing her pent-up hurt and anger in front of Tommy had undoubtedly influenced him, and she really should have admonished him rather than thanked him when he had declared that any enemy of hers was also his. Culpability she would explain to the reverend in private later when the punishments were divvied out.

If he noticed her guilt, the Reverend Smythe did not show it and continued retelling what he had learned of the story with a smile on his face and a twinkle in his eye. "The hammer throwing was, I am assured, nothing more than an involuntary reaction born out of self-defense after Mr. Sinclair surprised Tommy, and the lad has repeatedly reiterated how sorry he is for it. But of course, that does not condone what consequently happened to our injured neighbor's poor back paw."

"Why on earth did he have a hammer in the first place?" Of their own accord, Vee's eyes drifted to the distracting bottom again. There was something strangely hypnotic about it. A compelling allure that made her mouth go dry and her fingers itch to explore it.

"To nail my windows shut . . . so the tradesmen couldn't shoo those lunatic birds out . . . easily." Galahad's voice was a staccato series of grunts as the doctor tied the final stitch. "Obviously."

"Indeed." The reverend nodded as if this explanation concurred with the Claypoles' version of events. "But while the boys have confessed to bringing the pigeons into the building with the express intention of releasing the birds to *fowl* mischief." He chuckled again at his second inappropriate but intentional pun in as many minutes. "Sydney Claypole is quite adamant their release at the precise moment of the incident was an unfortunate accident, and that they had no clue that the pigeons they had procured were vicious attack pigeons, or that pigeons as a species were quite so vengeful after incarceration. It was, Tommy and Sydney both stressed when separately interrogated, *the pigeons* who were guilty of knocking Mr. Sinclair over. They have, however, acknowledged that he wouldn't have fallen over in the first place if they hadn't broken into his premises with the birds."

"Do we know where the birds are now?" In the grand scheme of things, it wasn't the most important question to be asking, but with the doctor now rubbing salve onto Galahad's skin, and the muscles in his mesmerizing behind squeezing in time with the motions in the most diverting manner, it was a miracle she could ask one at all.

"Still flapping around my attic, I reckon." The owner of the impressive backside shrugged matter-of-factly despite his prone position. "I managed to shut them in, in case those bloodthirsty birds decided to chase us and peck us to death, then delivered the boys back here for you to deal with. Because frankly, after the havoc they caused me this morning, I am over the moon that they are not my problem."

"That's exactly what he said when he delivered them." The Reverend Smythe seamlessly picked up the story. "He would have left it at that, too, Vee, and gone about his business if I hadn't noticed all the blood soaking through his already stew-stained breeches and insisted a physician attend him. He was most adamant it was nothing when it clearly isn't." The vicar's hand flapped over the doctor's handiwork, dragging her eyes there again. "When it is plain to see that Mr. Sinclair has sustained quite a wound."

For the first time, Galahad displayed some proper emotion, yet instead of the anger he was well within his rights to bellow from the rooftops, it was more embarrassment. "In my defense, it's not the sort of wound a man wants to admit to in polite company."

"No indeed." As if realizing for the first time that there was a lady present in that polite company, and an unmarried one at that, the Reverend Smythe suddenly colored. "Perhaps you should wait outside, Vee. Until the . . . um . . ."

"And deny her the joyous spectacle of me with my battered ass out?" Galahad waved that humiliation away with a wry smile as the doctor set about dressing his neat handiwork. "Aside from the inescapable fact that that ship has well and truly sailed, Reverend, I reckon she deserves to see me suffer a bit. I'll bet she's even enjoying it."

Her lips twitched. "Just a bit." She held her thumb and index finger a quarter of an inch apart while a rogue giggle escaped. "There is also no denying this will make an excellent story around Giles and Diana's dinner table tomorrow."

"Felled by pigeons and stew."

"And the gruesome twosome outside." As he was the aggrieved party, it seemed fair that Galahad be consulted on the punishment. "What would you like us to do about that?" She turned her back when the physician signaled he was done to at least give Galahad the privacy to return his breeches to their proper place without her gawping at what usually inhabited the front of them. Especially when the contents of the seat of those breeches had made her hot and bothered quite enough for one day despite all her lofty promises to herself that she was over him.

"Well, let's consider the list of charges first." His tone sounded strained—the only sign of the pain he had to be in as he righted his clothing. "There's at least three counts of breaking and entering that I have evidence of, some petty larceny albeit the goods weren't actually stolen but hidden, one count of attempted destruction of property because they left all Mr. Evans's tools out to rust in the snow. One failed assault with a hammer assuming my foot survives, and I'm not sure how to categorize what happened with the pigeons."

"And the stew?" Vee gingerly turned and was relieved to see all his distracting bits safely covered again.

"Wasn't really anything to do with them so let's pretend that part never happened."

"Not a chance." Aside from the magnificent story, she already knew the memory of his bare backside was one she would not forget anytime soon. Like his kisses, it was quite spectacular.

"In that case, I say we throw the book at them." He managed a smile. "Consign them to me for a month of servitude. Two hours a day doing whichever menial tasks I see fit as penance for their egregious crimes. Toss in Billy, too, while you're about it. If I'm going to be a taskmaster, I might as well deal with the whole triptych of evil in one go."

"Even though Billy hasn't done anything? This time at least." While Vee believed that bad behavior should always be punished, she was against doing it retroactively. Especially to a child as distrustful and still likely to run away as Billy.

"Call me a sentimentalist . . ." He offered her another wry smile as he tentatively wiggled his swollen foot into his boot. One that took her right back to another conversation, before everything between them had gone to hell in a handcart. "But I'm worried about the kid. It might do him good to put those clever hands of his to better use than picking pockets, and despite all the hell they've just put me through, I have a feeling that those pesky Claypoles might turn out to be a good influence on him." Part of her freshly hardened heart melted a little. "What time do they have their supper?"

"At five o'clock." It was hard hating him when he was behaving so . . . admirably. When he was being so kind and understanding. So magnanimous—yet again. Bighearted even when she wanted to believe he was heartless.

Drat him.

He smiled, and the gentle humor in his eyes reminded her too much of the Galahad she had met in Brighton, making her foolish heart yearn for more of him—until she remembered how catastrophically Brighton had ended. "On the dot." She would not be swayed or seduced by a pair of fine eyes, no matter how beguiling they were. Not when they said one thing while he did another. Like a chameleon, Galahad was an expert in camouflaging the real him behind whichever façade got him what he wanted.

"Have them report to me tomorrow at six sharp and hopefully by then I'll have figured out something they can do that will encourage them to reflect upon their actions. In the meantime—" He nodded his thanks toward the physician and the reverend in quick succession. "Thank you for your needlework skills and your hospitality, but I've got me some angry birds to catch before Mr. Evans arrives and holy hell breaks loose again."

He inclined his head politely and limped to the door.

"Galahad, wait—" She still might not like him, or ever forgive him, or be convinced that his true motives concerning her orphans were as noble as they seemed to be, but he had been wronged and he was in pain and some of that was her fault. "Those pigeons aren't yours to catch."

She marched past him, blaming his eyes and his bottom for creating an unwelcome new chink in her armor, and glared at the subdued twins still standing anxious sentry duty outside the office. "You two—follow me!"

They did, with their tails dangling between their legs, and so did an amused Galahad, who allowed her to take charge as he unlocked the door to his building with a giant, rusty key that had been hidden behind a loose brick. He stepped back while she ushered them inside.

Vee pointed to the stairs before she folded her arms. "Seeing as you are both expert poachers, I want those angry pigeons boxed and released into the wild within the hour." They both gulped at the prospect but nodded.

Sydney looked to Tommy, then Tommy looked to her. "We're going to need some bread and some buckets."

"Fortunately, I have both. There's bread upstairs wrapped in paper near that broken stewpot, and Mr. Evans has stored a pile of buckets in here . . ." As Galahad walked toward another door, the twins looked at each other in horror until Tommy found his voice.

"Er . . . Mr. Sinclair . . ." But it was too late.

As Galahad pushed open the door, a heavy drizzle of something gold and sticky oozed over his head from above, and a split second later one of the orphanage's pillows smacked him in the face. The pillow's casing had been cut and loosely retied, ensuring he was showered in downy feathers, which immediately stuck to the glue-like substance.

"Oh dear," said the more exasperating Claypole in a small, terrified voice, no doubt expecting Armageddon. "In all the excitement, we forgot to tell you about the honey."

Vee stared aghast at Galahad in all his ratty new plumage and didn't know whether to laugh or cry. In case she did either, she bit down on her bottom lip, but even that did not stop an unladylike snort from escaping.

"You know, I said I wanted a month of servitude in reparation—" Through his shroud of feathers, his unusual green eyes locked with hers, unyielding but amused, making her like him a little bit more. "Better make that six weeks."

Chapter Seventeen

It appears poor Giles is in some serious trouble, so for proprietys sake, and because the obvious frisson that they keep denying is so palpable it trails sparks, I am accompanying him and Diana on their clandestine dash to Shropshire to save his estate from the ghastly Gervais . . .

—from the diary of Miss Venus Merriwell, aged 18

"We've prepared you a special chair." Diana whacked a sniggering Giles as Gal hobbled into their dining room late the next evening. "Feel free to rearrange all the cushions for your own comfort."

His chair was one of two still vacant, and he couldn't help noticing that Venus was missing.

Maybe, despite the slight thaw in their war yesterday, she had boycotted this early festive dinner in protest at his invitation? He was tempted to ask where she was but didn't because Olivia was studying his reaction to her telling absence with interest.

"Vee is upstairs, Galahad. Reading all three of my darling grandchildren a bedtime story." Despite only two of the children upstairs being her actual blood relations—Theodore and David were Minerva and Hugh's boys—Olivia had claimed little Giselle as one of hers since before she was born, just as she'd declared Diana her daughter long ago, regardless of whether Diana liked it or not. She had also practically adopted Giles. There was no question she would do the same for Venus's husband and all of her children when the time came, as she was more mother hen to her than to any other of the Merriwell sisters.

Gal decided not to analyze why that prospect warmed him.

"But obviously she regaled us adults with all the details of your story before they stole her away." Olivia's wily blue eyes danced with amusement. "How is your poor posterior?" All six pairs of lips at the table twitched at the question.

"Not as wounded as my pride, Olivia. That took the biggest battering and will doubtless take the longest to heal." With the utmost care and trepidation, he sat down, making sure the stitches made absolutely no contact with the cushions or seat at all, and forced a smile at the others who were all staring and waiting for the wince. "I'm guessing you know all the gory details, so I won't bore you with them again."

"Spoilsport," said Hugh. "It all sounds hilarious. I am devastated to have missed it."

"Same." Giles genuinely did look devastated. "I'd have paid good money to watch you get tarred and feathered."

"It was honey—not tar—but I'll concur that the end result was much the same. I had to soap my head ten times to get all the sticky out of it." Gal chuckled himself, because even he could see the funny side of what had happened. "I'm still finding feathers in places feathers have no place being."

The door opened and he automatically gazed at it to watch her arrival, but instead of Venus it was Giles and Diana's butler-*cum*-valet-*cum*-journalist's-one-legged-assistant who clonked through.

"Sorry to hear about your bum, Mr. Sinclair." Dalton lacked social restraints as much as he lacked body parts, and to match his butler's livery his current eye patch was purple. "I took a musket ball in me hindquarters as a young seaman, so know it's no picnic. Felt like someone shoved a hot pike up my arse every time I sat down."

As there was no answer to that except agreement, Gal nodded. "How go things with you, Dalton?"

"Mustn't grumble, Mr. Sinclair." With a flick of his mangled hand, Dalton directed all the servants to load the sideboard with dishes. "As you can see, I am in fine fettle." About as fine a fettle as a man with one eye, one leg, and seven fingers could be.

"And Mrs. Dalton?"

The man beamed. "I just found out that my Dahlia is up the spout again, thanks for asking. We're hoping this one will be a girl."

Gal did a quick mental sum in his head. "So this will be number . . . *five*?" In just four years. Poor Dahlia seemed perennially pregnant.

"I've told him he needs another hobby." Giles rolled his eyes and pulled a face of disapproval. "Even with two jobs, and more additional young Daltons than this poor world could possibly ever need, he still has too much free time on his hands as he is disgustingly fecund."

At Gal's confused expression, Diana helped him out. "It means *fertile*, Gal."

"Ahh . . ."

"And I'll make no apologies for it. After four strapping sons, if my Dahlia wants a daughter, as a good husband it is my solemn duty to *give her one*." The reprobate winked unrepentantly at his coarse double entendre before he clonked back out again, using his peg leg to hold the door open for Venus.

"You might have told me you were starting dinner." Her eyes flicked briefly his way before she frowned at her middle sister. Against his better judgment, Gal took the opportunity to surreptitiously soak in the sight of her.

She was wearing a more daring gown than she usually risked in public. Plain. Undeniably simple enough for an intimate family dinner at home, but in a fabric luxurious enough to be as fancy as the occasion warranted. But while the heavy navy velvet had long sleeves in deference to the snow outside, the bodice was cut low enough to show an alluring amount of plump, alabaster cleavage and tight enough to make a man's mouth water. Gal certainly had to clamp his shut tight in case he drooled.

She glanced around, her movements uncharacteristically jerky. "Where is Lord Dorchester? Has he not arrived yet?"

Beside him Jeremiah shuffled while Minerva, who was on the opposite side of the table from Gal, inspected her cutlery as if her life depended on it.

"Well . . . um . . ." Diana looked to her pregnant belly for wisdom for a moment before she decided not to make any excuse for the pompous fool's absence and swiftly passed the buck. "I left Olivia in charge of all the arrangements." She tapped her stomach with insincerity. "What with the baby and all the packing still left to do before we all depart for Shropshire . . ."

Venus glared at Olivia, who smiled in response. "I must confess, I've been so busy organizing our own packing, dear, I completely forgot to extend the invitation. Probably because it has traditionally been only us eight for family dinners. I can only apologize for my absentmindedness, Vee."

"I see." Although like the rest of them, Venus knew that Olivia hadn't invited her pompous beau on purpose.

"To be honest, dear, I have probably done Lord Dorchester a favor, as he is bound to feel left out when we all inevitably meander down memory lane as this family are so prone to do at Christmastime. And once again, this is the only chance we have to celebrate the season of goodwill with dear Galahad here." She narrowed her eyes in mock chastisement. "Especially as he finds so many flimsy excuses to avoid spending the yuletide proper with us the way he so patently should."

"Hence I am here, Olivia, despite my embarrassing stitches, and quite resigned to my fate." The annual pre-Christmas dinner was one family occasion a year Gal could never get out of—not even for work—and the one he simultaneously appreciated the most and dreaded at the same time. He appreciated it because it was thrown specifically for him by his cousin to make up for Gal's perennial absence around the actual

Christmas dinner table. He dreaded it because it reminded him that it would soon be Christmas, and he hated Christmas. It dredged up too many painful memories, which were better avoided.

Thankfully, the family never celebrated theirs in town. They alternated between Giles's sprawling estate in Shropshire, where they were going this year, and Hugh's stately pile in Hampshire. Gal could always politely refuse, citing The Den as the reason.

"Tonight, in honor of Galahad, we are having roast goose with all the usual festive trimmings *and* plum pudding." Olivia wiggled her eyebrows at Giles, knowing his sweet tooth was his nemesis. "You have a whole pudding to yourself this evening, Giles darling."

The attempted deflection did little to placate Venus, who was clearly rankled at the distinct lack of her dull old windbag at the table. To her credit, rather than cause more of a scene, she bit her lip and took her allotted seat, not happy that she had been placed directly across from him as well as being denied the scintillating company of her pompous beau. She was also apparently suddenly uncomfortable to be wearing such a revealing dress; while the soup was ladled into bowls, she kept tugging the perfectly fitted bodice upward until she gave up and fiddled with her locket instead. A sure sign that she was rattled by something.

Much to his complete disgust, Gal's foolish heart hoped it was him.

"You'll be pleased to know that the Claypoles cleaned all of the feathers and bird droppings up without any trouble." That had been their allotted task today, the first day of their official punishment, because in the space of one short hour while they were being recaptured, those birds had completely redecorated his new attic. "The honey, on the other hand, proved more problematic." One of them had to break today's fresh ice, so he figured it might as well be him. "But Mrs. Witherspoon came to their rescue with some vinegar and two large scrubbing brushes and that did the trick, so everything's now back the depressing state it was in before the birds and the twins arrived."

"I am glad that those rascals sorted it." She snapped open her napkin rather than look at him. "I should probably thank you again for taking all their juvenile pranks like a good sport." Her fingers briefly grazed her locket again, dragging his eyes to where she toyed with the pendant against her distracting cleavage for a moment before he nailed them front and center on her face. "I cannot fathom what they could have possibly been thinking to do what they did."

"Can't you?" He couldn't let her off entirely scot-free. Especially as the others had already begun chattering among themselves and they had a brief and rare moment to converse without being scrutinized. "You must have realized by now that Tommy Claypole worships you and would do whatever he thought appropriate to avenge you. What did you tell him in the carriage that day to fire his blood?"

"I certainly did not tell him to release those filthy pigeons in your attic, if that is what you are suggesting." The apples of her pretty cheeks had reddened, and she still couldn't meet his eye. "Nor would I ever condone breaking and entering, no matter what the provocation."

"But you might have mentioned, in passing, that what I was opening next door to them was *Sodom and Gomorrah*?"

Her blush deepened, confirming it. "Tommy asked precisely what your line of business was, and that seemed the easiest way to describe it to a child."

"Interesting." He sipped his soup and shook his head. "You decided that I might as well be hung for a sheep as for a lamb, despite knowing The Mermaid is nothing like that and despite never having set a foot in my place in the docks."

"Ah yes—The Basket of Kittens." Two blue eyes locked with his. "I suppose I should also apologize for my incorrect assumptions regarding that. Because obviously there are no card or dice tables in that establishment. No drunken sailors and absolutely no reckless gambling is tolerated there."

"There's a card table here, Venus, and Dalton's a sailor. Or at least he was once upon a time before Napoleon blew his leg off. The presence of both things hardly makes this house a den of iniquity."

"We are supposed to be polite to each other here, Galahad—not pedantic." She smiled as she spoke, giving him hope that she had indeed passed the peak of her outrage and that they could finally move forward politely.

"I'm just stating facts, Venus."

"By comparing your bawdy tavern to my brother-in-law's town house. I am not certain that is a fair comparison. Or a particularly scientific one."

"Maybe I should give you a private tour of The Basket of Kittens so that you can see for yourself what goes on there before you leave? My cook does a mean roast on a Friday if you're free tomorrow evening?" That invitation to dinner slipped out before he thought better of it and, it was fair to say, stunned them both.

"Well . . . I . . . um . . ."

"What would it take to convince you to come with us all to Shropshire for the yuletide, cousin?" Giles's interruption saved her from declining and a panicked Gal from backtracking. "I hate to think of you all alone on Christmas Day. Again."

Truth be told, Gal wasn't particularly looking forward to it himself this year, any more than he had relished it the year before. Not even work did much to relieve the inevitable melancholy lately. "Sadly, Christmas is one of my busiest times. I suppose everyone on their own or far from home flocks to places like mine to avoid being alone over the festive season." Much like him. He had voluntarily worked every Christmas Day since his ma had passed simply to take his mind off the fact that she had. "It can be a miserable time if you have no one." Which he supposed was the crux of the reason he avoided these good people diligently year after year. Watching Giles with Diana, Hugh with Minerva, and Jeremiah with Olivia reminded him that he had no one of his own.

Of their own accord, his eyes drifted to Venus again, and he instantly mourned her loss even though she was less than three feet away and he was better off without her.

"Straight after, there are the renovations to oversee." He tore his errant gaze from her before it gave him away. "Work on that only stops for Christmas and Boxing Day." Not that he fully understood the concept of Boxing Day, even after years on this side of the Atlantic. "Then it'll be all hands to the mast till spring. I want to have staff employed and the place ready to open in time for the season to start." Before all his money ran out and bankruptcy loomed. Which, thanks to all the extra expenditure on the orphanage roof, would likely be sooner rather than later.

"You work too hard." This came from Minerva.

"What else do I have to do?" Gal hadn't meant to say that aloud, either, but the truth escaped before he could stop it. Now it was out there, he had no choice but to clarify. "I mean, it's not as if I have a nagging wife I *have* to go home to." Which sounded even sadder than having to work.

"*Yet.*" Olivia wiggled her eyebrows. "But I am convinced you will be snapped up soon, Galahad. A young, resourceful, and charming entrepreneur like you is too good a catch to languish in the oblivion of bachelorhood for long. Especially one as easy on the eyes as you are, isn't that right, ladies?" Her gaze moved from Diana's to Minerva's before settling on Venus's. "Galahad is such a handsome devil, isn't he?"

"He's certainly a devil," muttered Venus under her breath as she stirred her soup.

"I see all the ladies gazing after him whenever he is near," Olivia continued undaunted. "And I see him eyeing *certain* young ladies, too, when he thinks none of us are watching." She stared pointedly this time. "So I know there is at least one out there who has taken his fancy. How do you plead to that, Sir Galahad?"

"Gird your loins, Gal, my meddlesome wife has that matchmaking glint in her eyes again and it seems you're next on her list." Jeremiah nudged him and everyone tittered.

Everyone except him and Venus.

"He should be thrilled to be on that exclusive list, for am I not an excellent matchmaker?" Olivia asked this of the table while not expecting any response beyond unanimous agreement. "Did I not realize well in advance of everyone else here present that Minerva was perfect for Hugh, and that Giles was desperately in love with Diana?"

"I take issue with that," said Giles as he reached for his wife's hand. "This harridan fell hopelessly in love with me at first sight. And frankly who could blame her?"

"Everyone knows that was the other way around, idiot." Diana pretended to be peeved. "Like they know I only married you out of pity."

"You were not yet here to see it, Galahad, but it took me almost a year of throwing them together to *get* them together." Olivia's smile was smug. "But look at how happy the pair of them are now, so it was worth all my effort." That smile instantly became calculating. "You could do worse than having me assist you in securing your future bride, Galahad. You, too, Vee. I'd find exceptional mates for the both of you because I have the *eye*." She winked it to prove it. "I've always been able to detect a promising frisson at fifty paces." It was when she toasted them both with her glass that Gal realized Olivia had worked out there was more currently going on between him and Venus than their usual mutual dislike. "Say the word and my services are yours."

"Don't say it, and they will also be yours," mumbled Jeremiah unsubtly. "Once she's picked out her next victims, there's no escaping her *help*."

"Well, I certainly do not require your services, thank you." Venus smiled at their tormentor. "I have Marmaduke."

While Gal tried not to growl into his soup, Olivia shook her head, sighing. "There are suitors and *suitors*, Vee, and I shall not rest until I find the best one for you. Lord Dorchester isn't it."

Still blushing, Venus bristled, but did her best to cover it with nonchalant bravado. "That explains why my guest's invitation was purposefully forgotten, I suppose. Because you disapprove of him. Most likely because you had no hand in choosing him and I found Marmaduke all by myself." She smiled at Olivia, all innocence, when he knew she was purposefully rubbing his nose in it.

"Of course I disapprove of Marmaduke." The incorrigible self-appointed matriarch grinned at that as if Venus's admonishment had been framed as a compliment. "He matches none of the criteria I would like to see in your future husband."

"*Your* criteria?" Venus folded her arms and that did such magnificent things to her cleavage, Gal almost choked on his spoon. "When surely it is only mine that matter."

"Dearest—" Olivia reached over and squeezed her arm in pity. "—exactly like Diana was back in her embittered old spinster days, you are too close to the problem, so obviously cannot see the perfect solution to it as clearly as I can." She wafted her hand in Giles's direction as if his besotted cousin and his equally besotted wife would never have married without her guiding hand. "While I am sure Lord Dorchester has many admirable qualities as a person—" Her nose wrinkled in distaste as she made that concession, completely contradicting it. "—I fear he would make you a very disappointing husband, as the pair of you lack the frisson."

"I'll have you know—" Venus's beautiful blue eyes shimmered indignantly, then shimmered some more as Olivia interrupted with an imperious raised palm.

"A good marriage has a spark, Vee. A unique and special spark that sometimes blazes into a fire of passion, and sometimes makes you wish your other half burns painfully in the fiery pits of hell. Be honest, dear, does Dorchester really give your heart excited palpitations? Do your eyes wander to his person in lust and longing? For if they do, I have certainly never witnessed it."

"Some of us prefer to keep such things private." Venus clutched at her locket like an amulet to ward off the devil. "And can separate what is appropriate in polite company from *what is not*." If looks could kill, Olivia would be as dead as a doornail at her adopted daughter's milk-curdling, change-the-subject-right-this-second glare.

"That says it all!" Olivia threw up her hands as if her argument was proved. "For such things are as unconscious as they are unstoppable. You have eyes, girl, and those eyes must have seen the way Minerva looks at Hugh or Diana looks at Giles, and how even I frequently glance at the vexing Mr. Peabody in between bouts of wanting to strangle him." She smiled at Jeremiah and he smiled back. "A heart hopelessly in love cannot disguise such things. Nor can a body consumed with lust pretend it isn't. I want that for you, too, dear. More than anything."

"More than anything, I *want* to eat my soup in peace." Poor Venus's neck had gone all blotchy, but Gal studied his soup in case both he and his wayward looks got dragged into the conversation. Olivia, however, had the bit between her teeth, so she was typically relentless.

"You need a fellow who sets your pulse racing. One with vim and vigor. One who is gloriously vexatious but has a good heart that beats only for you." Olivia's eyes lifted with obvious calculation to Gal's, and the whole table saw it. "A man so obviously besotted that he simply cannot tear his eyes off you. One who might be right under your nose if you deign to look beneath it rather than down it for a change . . ."

As Venus's eyes widened in horror at the implication, Gal decided enough was enough.

For both their sakes.

"If that's aimed at me, Olivia, I can assure you that you are barking up the wrong tree. I don't have either the time or the inclination for any sort of courtship and—meaning no disrespect to Miss Venus—your *eye* is in dire need of some corrective lenses if it thinks that the pair of us are a match made in heaven." He choked out a chuckle. "What say you, Venus?"

She responded by taking off her spectacles, looking thoroughly bored by the topic, and passing them down the table. "Olivia can borrow mine."

Chapter Eighteen

I captured an intruder last night and would have beaten him to a bloody pulp if Diana hadn't forced me to release him. His name was Galahad Sinclair . . .

—from the diary of Miss Venus Merriwell, aged 18

While the gentlemen left them for a rare private glass of port after dinner, which was code for them all wishing to take a look at Galahad's wounded rear after he had been bullied into regaling the entire story again over dessert, Vee escaped to Diana's bedchamber on the excuse that she needed to borrow a shawl.

She wasn't cold, more self-conscious, and was kicking herself for wearing such a stupid gown. A revealing gown she had selected on purpose because she had assumed Lord Dorchester would be there, and a week ago when she thought she had invited him, she'd wanted to prove to Galahad that she was well and truly over him.

Or perhaps make him jealous.

She wasn't particularly proud of either motive now; thanks to Olivia, it had all backfired. Every glance, nuance, and comment she'd made all night had been scrutinized after all that matchmaking nonsense, and pretending she wasn't the least bit tempted by Galahad when he knew she had been pathetically easy to seduce was exhausting. Especially as his duplicity was still so raw and she still hadn't forgiven herself—or him—for falling for it.

There was a shawl hanging over the dressing table chair, exactly where her sister had said it was, but, feeling idiotic and exposed, she flung herself on the mattress instead to stare at the ceiling for as long as it took for the gentlemen to return. After Olivia's unsubtle machinations during the soup course, she wouldn't put it past her to reignite the topic while all the ladies were alone downstairs, and she couldn't face that onslaught again. Not with Galahad in the next room.

"Are you all right?" Minerva came through her door without knocking, then seeing her flat on her back on the bed sighed. "She means well, Vee." Her big sister did not need to clarify who the "she" was.

"By humiliating me?"

"It was meant as teasing—the usual family banter we've always tossed relentlessly at one another for time immemorial—but I'll concede that even for Olivia, tonight she went a bit too far."

"I'll say." If only she could turn back time and erase those painful few minutes, and then turn it back a few weeks more to remove their unfortunate kiss. While she was about it, she would turn the hands all the way back to last season and all the mistakes she'd made then with that other silver-tongued liar Lord Argyll and remove that indelible stain from her copybook, too. All those painful memories only served to remind Vee that she was a pathetic fool.

That she had always been a fool.

A stupid, gullible, and needy fool!

"She not only grievously insulted my absent suitor after purposefully excluding him, but also tried to pair me up with Galahad!" She wanted to weep in mortification, especially because he had looked thoroughly appalled at the unsubtle suggestion even if he had helped her escape the teasing. "Bloody Galahad Sinclair, of all people! When she knows I've always loathed him."

"Diana and I had no idea you were still expecting Dorchester tonight. That is the honest truth. However—and this is also the honest truth, Vee—neither of us could understand quite why you invited him in the first place when we were relieved the bloom appeared to have finally left that particular rose."

"By that, I take it you do not like him, either?" As her diplomatic eldest sibling had never vocalized her disapproval before, that stung.

"Whether or not I like him is by the by, but seeing as you have asked, I shall admit that I have always thought that you could do better. To be honest, I never viewed Lord Dorchester as a serious suitor from the outset. He always felt like a make-do, convenient, safe sort of acquaintance to me while your heart and your pride got over Lord Argyll." Vee had to turn away at the mention of his name because Minerva had always read her like a book, and that was a chapter that, frankly, deserved burning. "I never imagined for one moment you would develop real feelings for him despite all your valiant attempts to conjure some, and I knew you would soon tire of his pomposity given time—which you plainly have of late. Or am I wrong?"

"He is, I'll concede, perhaps more an acquaintance than a suitor."

"Then why, exactly, did you invite him when by your own admission you aren't that keen?"

"Well . . . I . . ." How to cover up for the pathetic fact that she had needed Dorchester for her pride's sake? The artful deception necessary to convince I-haven't-got-the-time-or-the-inclination-for-courtship Galahad that he hadn't thoroughly broken her heart in Brighton. "When we collided at Lady Belhus's the other day, he hinted most strongly that he felt aggrieved that he had not been invited to dine with us, so I panicked and mentioned an invitation was imminent." At best, it was a hollow lie.

"I see." The mattress shifted as her sister sat beside her. "I suppose in that respect, Olivia likely did you a favor in forgetting to send him an invitation."

"She did not forget. She did it on purpose. Olivia does *everything* on purpose—mostly for her own amusement—but tonight, frankly, the joke wasn't funny."

Her sister twisted to stroke her hair like she used to do when Vee was little. "Don't you remember how mercilessly she teased Diana over Giles? How we all did? We all enjoyed having fun at their expense, especially as Diana took it all so badly. You were as guilty of that as Olivia was. As I was. As we *all* were."

"That was different. It was obvious Giles and Diana were fighting the attraction that we could all see as plain as day shimmering between them."

Minerva was silent for a moment. "Is this any different?"

"Well of course it is!" Vee exploded from her prone position like a firework. "Galahad and I . . ."

"Seem to be behaving in much the same way as Diana and Giles did. At least to my eyes, Vee." At her sharp intake of outraged breath, Minerva caught her hand and tugged her back to sit before she stormed off. "I see the way that you look at him, Vee. The way he looks at you. When we last all dined together, I cannot deny that I noticed something different happening between you. A change I saw as a positive, because I have always liked Galahad."

"Of course you have! Because everyone, bar me, seems to be smitten with that charming devil. But I can assure you there is nothing whatsoever happening between us." He had killed whatever it might have been stone-dead. So ruthlessly, she feared she would never get over it.

"After he marched into Lady Brightlingsea's ballroom the other week, looking all windswept and wretched, determined to speak to you—after that passionate waltz you shared with him before that at the Rokebys'—I cannot help thinking that something . . . *else* happened in Brighton before he bought that contentious building from Lord Mallory."

"He bought that building *before* Brighton!" That flagrant duplicity seemed to have slipped everyone's mind. "That is why it is *so* contentious. He bought it and hid the sale from me, and then did everything in his power to butter me up before he confessed to it!"

Although now, with some distance, she realized that the real bone of contention was not so much that he had been the one to buy the building; it was more what that sale meant. It was yet another stark reminder of how stupid she was. How desperate she was for love and acceptance. That once again, she had fallen head over heels for a man who put his selfish needs first and foremost. He hadn't been honest, even when she had lowered her defenses and bared her soft heart to him, and that was unforgivable. More than anything, it cut her to the quick that that stupid building had meant more to him than her. That it obviously still did. When for a while—for a very short while—she had dared to think that Galahad might be different.

Minerva studied her expression and sighed. "Did something else happen in Brighton, Vee?"

"Of course not!" Her cheeks heated at the lie while her lips burned with the memory of his kiss.

"That would explain why you are so furious at him. Why you throw yourself at Lord Dorchester again whenever Galahad is around to witness it."

Vee scoffed at that despite knowing it was true. "Lord Dorchester is still my friend . . ."

"Lord Dorchester is a convenient decoy nowadays to convince Galahad that you aren't pining for him. Or are you going to deny the irritation that always crosses your expression whenever one of the viscount's ostentatious bouquets arrives? Deny that you haven't sent a single thank-you note to Dorchester or accepted his copious invitations to promenade with him on Rotten Row. Or why you have ceased attending his mother's reading salon, or that you have as good as ignored him at every entertainment we have been to since the Rokebys' apart from the one ball where Galahad turned up the day you got home from Brighton?" Minerva regarded her with pity but still squeezed her hand in support.

"We live in the same house, Vee, and I know you better than anyone, remember?" Although thankfully, not even the intuitive Minerva knew all of her shame. "When you requested Lord Dorchester's presence here last week, out of the blue, we all knew there had to be a reason you suddenly wanted a suitor—any suitor—in attendance that went beyond a sudden change of heart. It was obvious to all of us that the reason had something to do with Galahad." All truths she wanted to deny but couldn't. Not to the woman who had always been more mother to her than sister. "So what really happened between you and him in Brighton?"

"Nothing . . ."

"Absolutely nothing or nothing *serious*?"

"Absolutely nothing!" Except a kiss she couldn't stop thinking about and yet another male betrayal that made her shattered heart bleed and her soul wither in shame. "Because I am not that naive idiot any longer who stupidly believes the flowery nonsense that spouts from a man's mouth when he wants something."

Minerva's expression was instantly curious, but not particularly surprised. "He *did* declare his interest then?"

"Except his interest wasn't in me, Minerva. Not really. He pretended that it was, and he would have happily attempted to completely seduce me into believing it was if it meant he got to open his stupid club without any annoying obstacles or objections." She shrugged off that cutting detail as if it was no matter. "But since Papa showed his true colors, and thanks to every lecherous or socially ambitious gentleman who has disappointed me since—and most especially since I was made a fool of by Lord Argyll—" Just his name on her lips made her feel wretched. "—I have become quite adept at spotting charming liars." Although not that adept or she wouldn't have fallen for Galahad. She blamed her inappropriate body entirely for that. It enjoyed the touch of a man too much. Especially his. "Therefore, and thankfully, my heart is blissfully unaffected by Galahad's feeble and transparent attempts at wooing it." Perhaps if Vee kept telling herself that lie, her foolish, wounded heart would stop hurting.

"Which begs the question: Seeing as there are now no obstacles nor objections bar yours to prevent Galahad from opening that club, why does he keep looking at you with quite so much longing, Vee?"

Does he?

"The poor thing couldn't take his eyes off you over dinner, even when he tried his hardest." As if she knew that pathetic hope had made her heart leap, Vee's big sister wrapped an arm around her. "And for what it's worth, and all Olivia's clumsy matchmaking aside, he has always looked at you in a covetous way, but more so of late. Enough that I am increasingly convinced he is thoroughly besotted with you. He might even be a little bit in love with you—exactly as Olivia suspects."

Instantly, her foolish heart soared higher at that unlikely prospect—until she remembered how good he was at playing a role, and how eagerly she had allowed him to take advantage. Self-loathing descended like a fog.

For pity's sake, what is the matter with me!

Exactly how many times did she need to be made a fool of by this man for her to use some common sense? When common sense told her that a leopard never changed his spots.

"As I have no control over Galahad's eyes, nor care how he may or may not pretend to be feeling when he directs them my way, I refuse to be used as fodder for Olivia's incessant teasing when I most definitely do not feel the same way!" *Are my feelings that transparent? My heartbreak this obvious?* Did everyone downstairs now pity her for pining for a man who had only pretended to pine back when he wanted something?

"Are you sure, dearest? Only you appear disproportionately vexed for someone who is indifferent."

That brought her up short, because Minerva made a fair point.

In this family, any chink in the armor was used ruthlessly to tease, and the cracks in hers were clearly on display for all to see. Vee needed to rectify that if she wanted all the much-too-near-the-knuckle teasing to stop or be forever tormented like Diana had been until she and Giles succumbed to their passions. "I am positive." She grabbed the shawl she hadn't come upstairs for and pasted on a smile as she wrapped it around her shoulders. "I am genuinely angrier at Galahad's deceit than I am vexed by his presence, but your point is well made." She needed to keep reminding herself that he was still an opportunist and a liar, no matter how decent he could be sometimes with the orphans. And she needed to do whatever was necessary to ensure that both her family and Galahad knew that she was immune to his charms.

Perhaps if she was more matter-of-fact instead of mortified, all the teasing would be easier to bear? "It is done. The building is his and there is nothing I can do about it, so I suppose for the sake of family harmony, as well as to put a stop to all of Olivia's latest futile attempts at matchmaking, I should let bygones be bygones and suffer him with the same *enthusiasm* as I always have."

For the rest of this evening, she would muster every last ounce of her bravado to get through it with good humor. "Hopefully, after a month of distance in Shropshire and the arrival of her newest grandchild, Olivia will have found something else to amuse her by the time we get back other than my continued and depressing lack of love life."

Minerva stood and fussed over the shawl that Vee had unconsciously tied. "Poor Galahad. He looks so miserable. I cannot help feeling sorry for him."

"Whatever for?" Annoyance still leaked into her tone when she was trying so hard to sound unbothered. "He got exactly what he set out to get." While making a fool of her in the process.

"Did he?" Minerva fiddled with the knot Vee had tied tight across her bosom as she smiled a knowing smile. "He didn't get you."

"I told you, he doesn't *really* want me, Minerva."

"Oh, be in no doubt, he *wants* you, sister." In one swift move, she unknotted the shawl and held it open wide, then stared grinning at Vee's cleavage. "I've never seen a man so tortured by a gown as poor Galahad is by this one tonight."

Chapter Nineteen

Oh the horror! I caught Diana in bed with Giles this morning! Naked! Have given her a stern talking-to about the need for propriety and chastity. I have also made a note to visit her deflowerers extensive library here in Shropshire later to research all the possible reasons for my usually crotchety sisters uncharacteristic, yet undeniable, euphoria ever since her deflowering . . .

—from the diary of Miss Venus Merriwell, aged 18

"Who's up for a friendly game of cards?" As Jeremiah was already rubbing his hands together at the prospect by the time Vee and Minerva made it back downstairs, clearly he was. "After last time, now that I know that the witch isn't invincible, I'm feeling lucky."

"Oh, bless you." She couldn't resist stroking his arm as if he had said something stupid. "But if you think you finally have it in you to beat me after four years of solid defeat, Jeremiah, I am more than happy to remind you of my superior skills as a card player." It felt good to behave normally, despite Galahad's obvious presence by the fireplace. Not that she had looked his way, of course, but she could still feel the weight of his stare. Feel it everywhere. Even through the thick woolen shawl, which made her feel less exposed to his stormy green gaze.

"I have a better idea." Giles used the pack of cards in his hand like a conductor's baton. "Because I for one would like to see a rematch." The deck pointed first to Vee, then Galahad. "The exact same rules as before, only this time, I say we up the ante and open a proper book on the outcome. With folding money rather than the stuff that jingles."

"Ten pounds on Vee," said Hugh instantly as if the game was a fait accompli. "She'll have learned from her previous mistakes and is sure to trounce the upstart as revenge." He turned to Galahad, wincing. "No offense, Galahad—but I'll never hear the end of it if I effectively bet against my wife."

He waved it away with a lazy smile. "None taken."

"I'll match you but my money's on Gal." Jeremiah walked to the fireplace and slapped his countryman on the back as he glared at her. "He's the professional."

"Mother?" Hugh turned to Olivia, who appeared to be weighing up her options carefully. "Which gladiator is yours?"

After an age, she chose. "Vee. I see the light of battle in her eyes." At which point all eyes in the room swiveled to Giles, who was already enjoying himself immensely.

"Well, obviously it is my dear cousin Galahad, as blood is thicker than water. No offense, Vee dearest."

"Oh, none is taken, Giles, as I shall enjoy saying I told you so when I win." Vee looked Galahad up and down, telling herself that she would force herself to enjoy getting some revenge for Brighton and enduring all of Olivia's teasing, even if it was petty.

"My money is obviously on my sister." Diana smiled at Vee as if she realized she was feeling fragile. "I believe Galahad deserves a good thrashing." Further proof that the family suspected that her heart had been hurt again.

"Oh, you can't bet in *our* pot, harridan." Giles said this as he and Hugh carried the card table into the center of the drawing room.

"Whyever not?"

"Because you have to play. This is the rematch, remember, so everything must be the same as last time."

"But I don't want to play! I hate cards. Hate them with a vengeance!"

"And yet you are going to play because your beloved lord and master decrees it." Giles heaved his glaring wife out of her chair, which took some time as her sister had chosen quite a low chair and her protruding pregnant belly behaved like a wedge, preventing her from getting the purchase to rise. "I have ten pounds resting on you and Galahad."

"You have ten pounds resting on Galahad. My part in this game is redundant."

"Let us not split hairs, Diana." With the utmost care, Giles helped her into a chair at the card table. "You are hardly redundant. I am banking on you to be as useless at whist as you usually are so that my cousin can shine."

While Diana grumbled and massaged the side of her belly, Minerva took her seat. "I appreciate that nobody here rates my talent at whist, either, but I can assure you that I have also learned a great deal from my previous defeat and will not be so easily sidetracked again." In another show of support, her big sister glared at Galahad, who approached the table clutching the softest cushion from the sofa.

He arranged it carefully on his chair, but waited to sit, gesturing for Vee to do so first. "What are our stakes?"

"Hmmm . . ." Vee pretended to ponder it. "I suppose that depends. Knowing your penchant for wanting to win something that matters and something that would sting to lose, I think I should like to wager for the honor to name your precious club."

He nodded, impressed by her choice. "I'll agree to that so long as The Basket of Kittens is completely off the table."

"Spoilsport—but so long as that is the only caveat, I shall concur. What do you want?"

He didn't hesitate. "Another truce. Genuine politeness and neighborliness, at all times, no matter where we happen to collide."

"That would indeed sting." Vee held out her hand, regretting it instantly when he took it and shook it and reminded all her nerve endings how much they liked to rejoice at his touch.

At Jeremiah's instigation, they tossed a coin to decide who dealt. Galahad won, but this time as he shuffled the cards with the same showmanship he had displayed the last time, he did not pretend to be unfocused. Nor did he produce a lucky quarter to distract her with, almost as if he knew and respected that she wasn't daft enough to fall for that ploy twice. Once the hands were dealt, and the trump card turned, he scanned his quickly without sorting them, then snapped them closed while he awaited her first move.

The first rubber was a hard affair, with neither giving an inch, but in the end he won it by three tricks to her two. Vee snatched the second by a whisker in the last trick, bringing them level.

Everything rested on the last rubber, but as the room fell silent while Galahad began to shuffle the cards, an uncomfortable Diana groaned aloud.

"I need to move. This baby has given me indigestion and is currently kicking like a Morris dancer." She went to stand, and Giles rushed forward to help her.

"Dalton! Fetch my wife some peppermint tea!"

"If we are declaring a break, we might as well all have some tea." Olivia bustled off to chivy the Sinclair staff while the master of the house walked the mistress around the room as if she were made of glass.

"Tea?" As Hugh turned up his nose, so did Jeremiah, and they both simultaneously headed toward the decanters on the sideboard for something stronger.

"I suppose I am the one who is going to have to check on the children." Minerva rose, too, leaving Vee entirely alone with Galahad and with no earthly idea what to say to him after all Olivia's teasing and everyone unsubtly watching to see if there was indeed a frisson still between them despite his treachery in Brighton.

"I think I'm going to enjoy our neighborly truce." He folded his arms, smug, intent on riling her rather than them sitting in awkward silence after Olivia's dratted roasting.

"Not as much as I'm going to enjoy walking past The Fluffy Puppy every morning on my way to work."

"You wouldn't dare." His disarming green eyes narrowed. "That's worse sabotage than the Claypoles' pigeons."

"Are you scared, Galahad?" Mirroring his cocky stance, she folded her arms and was staggered to see his eyes flick briefly to the vicinity of her shawl-covered bosom. So fast that if she had blinked, she would have missed it. But she hadn't blinked. Hadn't missed it. And now, as she studied him, she noticed that his jaw was suddenly clenched.

Was Minerva right?

Chapter Twenty

When I started volunteering at the orphanage, I could not have foreseen how much it would affect me. But I have found my life's true calling. Those unfortunate, forgotten, downtrodden children have nobody to champion them—but as I already love each and every one of them as my own and know how it feels to be trampled on and abandoned, at least they shall always have me in their corner . . .

—from the diary of Miss Venus Merriwell, aged 18

"Is it me, or is it warm in here?" Much to Galahad's annoyance, Venus had been distracted throughout the first three tricks of the final round, and Diana wasn't behaving much better. Both women had been fidgeting like fidgeting was going out of fashion. Because all of Venus's shuffling kept sending puffs of her seductive fragrance his way while she continually adjusted and readjusted her shawl, she was also distracting the hell out of him. With all those brief flashes of cleavage combined with the seductive scent of jasmine, it was a miracle he'd won two tricks.

The second, he knew full well, had come more out of luck than judgment, because he had completely lost track of the cards for a good two minutes during the previous trick that she had stolen. Then lost track, again, during the next for a while, too.

During those missing moments, she had unknotted her shawl and it had slipped on one side, exposing the upper swell of her perfect left breast. He probably could have coped with that if she hadn't been idly twirling a finger in the stray curl that bounced above her left shoulder, too. Both things had made him hot under the collar, but the way she had bit her lip in the closing moments of the third trick, the way she had slowly drawn that plump, pink flesh through her teeth, had been the final nail in his coffin. Desperate for the torture to end, he'd squandered his highest trump, the ace of hearts, simply because he had no clue what she held anymore.

Consequently, he was now the most significant ace in the pack down and constantly backtracking in his mind to recount what had gone before. By his best guess—and thanks to the siren opposite him, it really was a guess—there weren't that many trumps left.

Minerva's brow kept furrowing, so it was fairly safe to assume she had only the five of hearts as all the lower trumps were now in the haphazard pile in the center of the table. With Diana's clumsy playing, so were the nine, the ten, and the king, and he recalled Venus had laid the queen. Or Minerva had. Either way, that was gone, too—but at least Gal still held the jack. And that jack was now unbeatable.

Or so he hoped.

He choked down some of the tea Olivia was force-feeding him to cover his anxiety, then, when he found his mouth filled with tea leaves, almost choked for real. Lord but he hated the stuff—even without the accidental bilge of leaves left because the hostess had forgotten to use the strainer.

"Well, of course you are warm." Also peeved at the erratic stop-start nature of the game, Minerva spoke in a snippy tone. "You are practically swaddled in a blanket, Vee, when the fire is roaring!"

"I suppose you make a valid point." Venus gazed at her tantalizing wool-covered chest. "I had quite forgotten I was wearing this." Her fingers went to the latest knot in the front of it and made short work of it. Then she inhaled deeply, fanning herself with her hand as she let the fabric slip from her shoulders to the back of the chair. "That *is* better."

It most definitely was, because perhaps now she would stop fiddling with the damn thing.

And it wasn't.

Because now he had to find a way to cope with all the slightly flushed, perfect skin back on full display when the perfume alone was killing him.

"More tea, Galahad?" Noticing his empty cup, Olivia brandished the teapot again. As a desperate distraction to all his inappropriate lust, Gal held his cup aloft. "There's one cup left in this pot."

Which would make it so stewed, the tannins would strip his teeth and make his lips stick to them. "That would be lovely." About as lovely as sucking up the stagnant puddle water from Piccadilly Circus. Before she poured, he forced a smile that he suspected was more a grimace. "Don't forget the strainer." He just didn't have it in him to choke down more sludge.

"Oh, of course! Silly me." Olivia grabbed it and leaned over him to top up his beverage, forcing him to lean closer to the Jasmine Enchantress who was suddenly much too close for comfort.

"Can the four of you get on with it as I'm losing the will to live." Jeremiah's constant complaining from the audience wasn't helping Gal's shredded nerves, either. "I swear I've never known a hand of cards to last as long as this one."

As Gal needed only one trick to win, and his body was rampant with lust and his molars were practically floating on tea, he was equally keen to get it over with. Frankly, the sooner he escaped Venus, the better. After Olivia's pointed observations of earlier, and all the talk of matchmaking, it would be prudent to put as much distance between them as possible.

Thank the Lord for Shropshire!

The day after tomorrow, she would leave and he'd have at least a month to get his goddamn urges under control. *Strict* control, because things couldn't go on like this! His preoccupation with her was like a sickness. His desire for her unbearable. The control she held over him terrifying.

"You'll be pleased to learn that I've changed my mind about The Fluffy Puppy, as I've come up with something much better." Venus had given up fanning herself with her hand in favor of patting the skin behind her neck with a handkerchief as she leaned his way. "I'm going to call your den of iniquity The Powder Puff." The folded square of linen made its way to the front of her neck, then caressed the silken skin of her collarbone before she flapped it in the vicinity of her chest like a fan.

"Over my dead body." He shot her a playful but warning look as his mouth dried while he tried resolutely to keep his eyes from wandering north. "What was I thinking, agreeing to such a stupid bet?"

Surely she didn't hate him that much?

If it came to it, he supposed he'd have to welch on the bet for the sake of the business, even though he had never welched on a bet in his life. His grandpa would be spinning in his grave if he did, of course, and the rest of the family would be up in arms. Then his relationship with all the good people around him would be as tarnished as his relationship with Venus was and she would be proved right about him by default. He could hear her victory speech already. Untrustworthy. Unreliable. Selfish. Dishonorable.

Despicable.

What a mess! And all mine!

What a jackass!

"It's not too late to change the stakes." Venus dabbed the handkerchief again on the skin just above her breasts. Breasts that were rising and falling above her straining bodice in time with her breathing in the most bewitching manner. "Care to up the ante?"

"What did you have in mind?" Frankly, anything would be better than being either the proprietor of The Powder Puff or the social pariah of the family.

"It really is very hot in here." Now Diana was apparently about to expire from the heat, although to be fair to her, unlike Venus, she was at least perspiring. Thanks to the impressive alabaster breasts directly across the table, so was Gal. His shirt had even started to stick to his back. Probably because all the tea he'd had forced upon him was now oozing from his pores. "Can somebody open a window?"

Hallelujah! "Giles—" Gal gestured to the big sash window closest to the card table. "I think we all need some air."

"Absolutely not!" Olivia stopped Giles in his tracks. "It's bitter outside and snowing! You'll let out all the heat! Why don't I ask Dalton to fetch Diana a cold compress to cool her down?" She bellowed in the general direction of the door. "*Dalton! Fetch a cold compress!*"

"I don't want a cold compress! I want some air."

As Diana was getting redder in the face by the second, Giles sidestepped Olivia and marched to the window. He flung the sash upward defiantly. "If my wife wants air, she gets air." He stomped toward Venus, yanked the shawl now dangling impotently over the back of her chair, and tossed it at the moaning matriarch. "You can ward off the arctic winter in this, Olivia."

Gal was supremely grateful for the frigid breeze that instantly blew across the card table—until he noticed the flurry of goose bumps blooming on Venus's exposed décolleté and almost combusted with need. Especially when she was now leaning forward again as if gazing into his undoubtedly filthy mind, looking all devious and sinful. And kissable.

Oh so kissable.

While everyone else was distracted by the arrival of Minerva, Venus touched his arm and dropped her voice to a breathy whisper. Both movements sent a fresh wave of unwelcome desire ricocheting around his system. "How about we play for buildings instead?"

"No."

She pouted, drawing his gaze to her lips again and reminding him of how good they had tasted. "How can you reject me when you haven't even heard me out, Galahad?"

"Go ahead. Say your piece. But it'll still be a no." With Diana still huffing and puffing as Giles fanned her, Gal made a show of checking his cards and trying to look blandly confident while he gave his needy body a stern talking-to.

What the hell is the matter with me? He wasn't usually so . . . rampant? Yes, she looked particularly beautiful tonight, and yes, the memory of their spectacular kiss in Brighton was still fresh in his mind, but still . . . Gal could usually control his emotions. Was a master at masking them. *What the hell is going on here that makes everything she does suddenly seem so . . . carnal?*

Perhaps somebody had spiked the tea? Or he'd drunk so much of it he was now hallucinating.

"I propose . . ." Her blues eyes smoldered as if she was proposing something sinful, her prim spectacles only serving to magnify the intense heat in them. ". . . that if I win, you sell the building next door to the orphanage to me." The fingers on his sleeve traced a sultry path to his wrist, which made his breeches tighten. "If you win, I sell the orphanage to you."

"A big fat no." *Heaven help me, she is scrambling my wits.*

"One cold compress." In clonked Dalton. "And more tea all around. I also brought some ice." He waved it all at nobody in particular until he saw that it was Diana who was in dire need of it and handed the compress to her alongside a dainty cup filled with peppermint tea. He left Olivia in charge of pouring all the regular tea and, for reasons best known to himself, decided the most appropriate place to deposit the bowl full of ice was in the center of the card table. Then he clonked away and Minerva finally retook her seat.

"Is the professional card sharp really that scared of a *drawing room amateur*?" Venus's earthy laughter trickled down his spine, causing havoc all the way, before it settled in his groin. "If that is the case, perhaps you should concede the game now, Galahad?"

"I only need one trick to win, whereas you need two, Venus, so there'll be no conceding." To the game or to his imprudent urges concerning her.

"But you'll at least concede that you are scared." As he went to remove the ice, she reached out and grabbed a shard then wrapped it in her handkerchief. "Scared that you might actually lose to me." She pressed the tiny cloth parcel to the back of her neck again as Olivia slipped a fresh cup of steaming tea under his nose. "I suppose I shall have to console myself with The Powder Puff—when I inevitably win."

"All right! I'll take your bet." His bark echoed in the silence of the room before everyone made a sharp intake of breath. He wasn't sure whether it was that awful name that made him agree, the unbeatable jack in his hand, or the melted droplet of water that slowly drizzled from the handkerchief down her warm skin to disappear in the bewitching valley in the center of her bodice. Whichever it was, he already regretted it. "May the best man win."

As if she had known he had dealt her a killer hand, Venus picked it up then used it quickly and ruthlessly to annihilate him. She laid the ten of hearts on his nine, smiling like the cat who had all the cream. "I make that two all." He had been sorely tempted to lay his jack then.

Sorely tempted.

Until common sense had prevailed, and he had remembered it would be tantamount to suicide to lay down the highest card now and leave himself without any insurance for the last trick. So she had won two? But so had he.

"Bravo, Venus. Well played." The game wasn't over till the last card was laid, and laying the jack would be his crowning glory. His triumph over the most torturous adversity. Hard-earned and harder-won—God help him.

"The *decider*," announced Hugh as all the spectators shuffled their seats closer. "Is it me, or can you feel the tension?" Gal sincerely hoped it was the tension of the game they could all feel rather than all his mounting sexual tension, which he was working his ass off to disguise.

Minerva threw him by laying the ten of hearts first, as Gal could have sworn blind that was already gone. But as he quietly panicked, Venus's fingers went unconsciously to her locket when Diana laid her card. His talentless partner tossed trash because she had nothing to beat it. But he did, and Venus knew it because she gripped the locket for all she was worth and clutched her remaining two cards closer.

"Scared, Venus?" He gestured with a nod to her fingers where they now toyed with the pendant above her erratically quivering, beautifully generous breasts, grateful that he had a valid excuse to be looking that way in the first place.

Two blue eyes locked with his, the rogue sparkle in them worrisome.

"Not in the slightest, Galahad."

There was something about the way she said it, a certainty that had him scrabbling back through every memory he had of the game so far. He had laid the jack of diamonds in that second trick he had bungled, and she had topped it with a queen.

A red queen.

He might have lost track of the cards for a moment or two, but his addled mind was sure that the queen had been a heart and not a diamond. Surely he wouldn't have missed such a high trump being played?

Of course he hadn't! The queen of hearts was long gone.

Long gone.

But was it sure enough to risk his building on?

Heck no!

Idiot!

JACKASS!

Gal's fearful heart hammered against his rib cage and his throat dried to dust. But the cat who had gotten the cream, opposite him, decided to toy with her prey, drawing out the moment for all it was worth.

"Put us out of our misery and lay the goddamn card, Vee!" Jeremiah bellowed exactly what Gal was thinking, only to be reprimanded instantly by his wife.

"There is no excuse to resort to coarse language!"

"*Ooooh!*" Diana's squeak made Gal jump because his frazzled nerves could take no more. "*Oh my goodness!*" Her white knuckles gripped the table while she gaped at them all. "*My waters just broke!*"

Then all hell broke loose.

"Get her upstairs!" Minerva jumped up with such force, she sent the card table toppling. Playing cards, counters, and hot tea flew everywhere.

"Summon the physician!" That came from Olivia, who started to bellow for Dalton again, while the sisters rushed to Diana's chair and Hugh and Jeremiah shuffled this way and that like headless chickens not sure which direction to go.

"Don't panic!" With impressive calm, Giles raised his hands in the middle of the room as if calming an unruly crowd about to riot. "Do. *Not*. Panic."

As his cousin sucked in a theatrical calming breath, everyone, including Gal, did the same. In unison, they all blew it out slowly.

But while that simple, single, measured breath apparently held magical powers to make all of them stop panicking, it had the opposite effect on the prospective father.

Because Giles started to panic with a vengeance.

"Summon the physician! Summon *all* the physicians! Get her upstairs! Oh my God! Oh my God! Dalton! *Dalton!* DALTON!" His breath sawed in and out at an alarming rate as he clutched at his wife, who was now trying to smooth his cheeks to calm him down despite being the one in labor. "This shouldn't be happening! The baby is too early! *It's too early!* Something's wrong! WRONG!"

It was Venus who took charge.

Somewhere amid all the commotion she had transformed from the overheated seductress to the cool-as-a-cucumber schoolmistress in the blink of an eye. She grabbed his cousin by the shoulders and shook him.

"Giles, breathe. Diana needs you." He nodded, his face ashen, and she smiled as she stared deep into his eyes. "Everything is going to be all right. I promise. Help Minerva get her upstairs."

That important task done, she turned to the others and started issuing instructions like a general. "Hugh—you fetch the physician." Hugh didn't need to be told twice, sprinting from the room calling for a horse like Richard III at Bosworth. "Jeremiah—Dalton . . ." Both men snapped to attention. "We are going to need plenty of hot water and as many fresh towels as you can muster. Keep them coming until I tell you to stop." They nodded and dashed out, too. "Olivia—ready the room." Because Giles and Minerva had already begun maneuvering Diana out of her chair, Venus snapped her fingers at Gal. "You—open the doors for them!"

As jobs went, Gal's was undoubtedly the least important and soonest done. Feeling like a spare wheel, he closed the bedchamber door on the ladies and his cousin the moment they got Diana to the bed. With nothing else to do, he went to the drawing room and decided to correct all the chaos that had been left there.

He picked up all the broken china first, then used Diana's discarded cold compress to mop up the spilled tea. Finally, he righted the card table and set about collecting up all the cards and counters. Next to his chair he found his jack of hearts in his discarded hand, and because it called to him like a beacon—because he had to know—he walked on leaden feet to Venus's chair and stared at the solitary card lying facedown in her abandoned hand on the floor.

If he had counted the cards right, this should be the eight of hearts. If he hadn't . . .

No. NO!

Best to leave it.

Forget about it.

Ignorance was bliss and Gal was certain he should thank his lucky stars that fate had intervened to save him from himself again. What he didn't know couldn't hurt him, and the game and bet were now as good as voided. Especially if *one of the servants* cleaned up all the evidence of it as unwitting but diligent servants were prone to do when a mess had been made.

But then *not* knowing would drive him insane.

Dreading it, he reached for the damning card and turned it over, and stared dumbfounded at the queen instead—a card he could not beat.

The witch had tricked him.

Acted for all she was worth.

Used his rampant desire for her against him to take control, and heaven help him, but he couldn't fail to be impressed by that despite the inescapable fact that he had been a goddamn fool for falling for it.

Bravo, Venus. Well played.

She really did wield the power to tie his head and body in knots. She really was that dangerous. That clever. He sighed at the queen of hearts, and because he had no clue what to do about it, he slipped it into his pocket to ponder.

Chapter Twenty-One

I learned two important lessons at my debut last night. The first was that simply because society deems a man to be a gentleman, it doesn't necessarily mean that he will feel obliged to behave like one. The second was that spectacles are, apparently, invisible to the male of the species if your bosoms err on the large side . . .

—from the diary of Miss Venus Merriwell, aged 19

Thanks to all the excitement of her new nephew and all the extra work that his arrival had entailed, it was the evening before Christmas Eve, a week later, when Vee finally had some spare time to visit the orphanage. Her sudden absence had left the reverend and Mrs. Witherspoon in the lurch, and although she had always intended to be away over Christmas and New Year's to visit Shropshire, she had left too many things undone thanks to the unexpected birth, and that wasn't fair.

A quiet evening tying up all the loose ends would be a more productive use of her time rather than trying to do them during the daytime.

At least that was what she had convinced herself and told Olivia to explain away coming here so late when she could have easily done so several hours earlier. That the lateness of the hour also helped her avoid a certain next-door neighbor she wasn't keen on seeing anytime soon wasn't entirely unintentional. The handsome cheat usually disappeared in a hackney to head to his hell in the docks well before seven o'clock so there was no chance of them colliding at five to the hour.

She'd seen neither hide nor hair of Galahad since the morning the baby had been born, thank goodness, as she still had no earthly idea what to say to him after her outrageous behavior at the dinner. At the time, she had justified it with: *What's good for the goose is good for the gander.* If he could take advantage of a person, seduce them to get what he wanted, and still sleep at night, so could she. Using that contentious building had seemed a fitting way to get some revenge.

Tit for tat, especially as that stupid building mattered to him more than she had. At least they now both had a good reason to feel embarrassed around the other. One that would go some way toward making her feel a bit better about her own pathetic enthusiasm to be seduced, even if it did nothing to fix her aching heart.

However, as she also firmly believed that two wrongs never made a right, no matter the circumstances or provocation, she didn't feel the slightest bit better about her outrageous behavior yet. There was no denying that some of it had been caused by her mortification at Olivia's matchmaking and Minerva's implication that Vee was wearing her heart on her sleeve—again—and they all knew it was broken.

Neither excused her using her wiles to distract him from the game quite as shamelessly as she had. Worse—if indeed her behavior could have been worse that night—she had wanted him to want her, and not just to teach him a lesson. The first moment she had witnessed his eyes darken with desire, she'd wanted to see how far she could push him. To see if she could push him far enough for him to be compelled to act upon it the second he got her alone. Wanted him to want her more than he wanted those buildings. Wanted to matter so much to him that he would get down on his knees and beg her forgiveness. Not because she wanted to laugh in his face or slap it when he tried to kiss her, but because she wanted him to kiss her! Throughout the entire game, her lips had tingled with anticipation as the need in his gaze had caressed her body until she could hardly stand the wanting herself.

If all that didn't bother her enough, the annoying, niggling voice in her head had joined her foolish heart and kept telling her that he hadn't deserved it. That there was more good in him than bad. That she should, perhaps, try giving him the benefit of the doubt for a change. Try to forgive and forget—at least partially. His casual regard for her tender emotions in Brighton aside, was she really going to hate him for all eternity because of a building?

If she had been counseling one of her students on a similar problem, she would tell them to turn the other cheek. To rise above it. To find a way to love thy neighbor, or at least to coexist peaceably with him, because hate was a destructive and malevolent emotion that festered. It wasn't worth the effort unless it was directed toward the most heinous individuals who threatened you or yours with real harm.

Galahad was a lot of things, most of them currently detestable, but he wasn't Genghis Khan. Nor was he as awful as her father had been, and she couldn't muster the effort to loathe that wastrel with every fiber of her being anymore because indifference seemed so much more fitting and comfortable. Indifference didn't make her heart ache or her innards tense constantly. It allowed her not to think about it. Nowadays, months could pass before she gave her worthless sire even a passing thought, and when she did it was more like an April shower than a thunderstorm. A passing annoyance that dissipated quickly rather than a cause to batten down the hatches. Indifference toward Galahad would certainly be an improvement on the way she felt about the thoughtless wretch now—exhausted, worthless, wronged.

Wounded.

In many ways it would be easier if he was a completely thoughtless wretch to his core. He had previously been such a good egg regarding the unfortunate incident with the pigeons as well as refusing to press charges at Billy's attempted theft of his watch. All evidence confirming her heart's forlorn hope that he wasn't quite as ruthless and selfish as her battered ego and bludgeoned heart wanted to believe.

Furthermore, to give credit where credit was due, Galahad's calm presence during Diana's labor had kept Giles's irrational panic in check—and unlike all the other gentlemen present, he had not needed to be told what to do or when to do it.

She supposed she had to thank his annoying business mind for that. His tendency to plan ahead and think on his feet.

Drat him for being a cool head in a crisis!

That morning, when they were all exhausted after the long night of labor, en route to her bedchamber to get some rest, Vee had accidentally caught sight of him visiting Diana before he left. Watching him, unaware of her presence, tenderly holding their new godson in wonder with unmistakable tears in his emotive green eyes showed her yet another side to his complex character she wished she wasn't now privy to. All those seemingly conflicting facets made him difficult to dislike even though she desperately wanted to, and irrespective of how much the less rational parts of her still wanted him.

Double-drat him.

Galahad Sinclair was more than a puzzle. He was a much-too-attractive and appealing enigma, and she had never been more confused about a man in her life. The only thing she wasn't confused about was her overwhelming desire not to have to face him anytime soon.

As she alighted from the carriage, she spied Tommy Claypole emerge from the darkness of Mercer Street carrying a large parcel.

"What are you doing out here in the dark?"

"'Ello, Miss Merriwell!" He offered her his best toothy grin. "You're here late."

"I have a mountain of paperwork and lessons to plan for the New Year." She pointed at the parcel, recognizing the distinctive robin's-egg-blue wrapping as coming from Fortnum. "What's in there?"

"Fancy sheets, though sadly not mine." He jerked the package upward toward Galahad's attic, where she was surprised to see candlelight illuminating the windows. "For Mr. Sinclair's new bed. He's adamant you can skimp on most things, but good sheets should never be compromised."

Fancy sheets? A new bed? "He's moving in? *Here?*" That was news to her. Unsettling news. "Why?"

"He says it makes no sense to pay rent to someone else when he owns his own roof nowadays, and apparently the Albany costs an arm and a leg and he's counting his pennies."

"Well, the Albany is in Mayfair." Where everything cost at least ten times what it did in Clerkenwell. "And Mayfair is expensive."

Tommy nodded. "And he don't exactly need to be in Mayfair anymore when his business is here now, does he?"

Vee supposed that made sense, although it added to her cringing sense of foreboding. "Surely he isn't moving into a building site?" That seemed a bit extreme, as well as awkward, but before Tommy could answer the man himself strode out.

"Is that the last of the delivery, Tom . . ." He stopped mid-stride. "Venus . . ." His handsome face was part surprised to see her and a greater part uncomfortable.

She sympathized because, thanks to her scandalous and wanton behavior, she was instantly discomforted, too. The flirtatious and seductive behavior that, according to her eldest sibling, had been the first time she'd truly lived up to her hideous name. Thankfully, in all the other excitement, only Minerva had noticed the lengths she had gone to in order to distract Galahad from the game.

"I heard Shropshire got canceled." There was no disguising the tinge of disappointment in his tone that that was the case.

She matched her peeved expression to his, determined to appear indifferent to his blatant lack of enthusiasm to see her even though she wanted to howl at the moon.

"Giles didn't want to risk it. He wants his wife within spitting distance of a Harley Street physician if complications arise. Never mind that my unstoppable sister was out of bed the day after little Gethin came into the world and has been in the finest of fettles ever since. But hence we are all now celebrating Christmas in Berkeley Square." Thank goodness it was dark and he couldn't see the hurt barricaded behind her eyes. "Olivia is livid that you refused her invitation, by the way." Vee, however, was relieved. She needed as much space between her and the confusing, befuddling man in front of her as possible until she was over him. "She is determined not to take no for an answer."

"I have to work. I tried to explain that to her when I called the other day, but you know Olivia." He had called upon Giles and Diana three days ago, managing to catch them in the only two hours that Vee hadn't been there, too. That avoidance was either sheer coincidence or entirely by his design. After the way she had tormented him with her cleavage, Vee could not help suspecting that it was the latter—that he wasn't any keener about seeing her on the back of her overtly come-hither performance as she was him. "My den of iniquity needs me."

"Not until at least ten o'clock it doesn't, Mr. Sinclair." Tommy's interruption earned him a glare spiked with daggers. "Muldoon will have everything so well in hand." Oblivious of the reluctance of his temporary master, the boy gestured toward Vee with a tilt of his ginger head. "Christmas is a time for families, Mr. Sinclair, and you should be with yours. The Den can spare you for one night."

Embarrassed to be caught in what appeared to be yet another lie, Galahad shuffled from foot to foot. "Muldoon wants the night off himself to be with *his* family." Another pointed look passed between the man and the boy, and this one Tommy caught.

Short.

Because it clearly surprised him. Or baffled him. She knew the boy well enough to know the innocent but rapidly blinking eyes were a sure sign Tommy knew more than he was letting on.

"Who is Muldoon?"

Vee asked the question to Tommy, but it was Galahad who answered. "He works for me. Behind the bar and the like."

She suspected the "and the like" was a line to fob her off to avoid any further explanations or talk of Christmas, so she filed it away to ask Tommy the moment they were alone. "How are the renovations going?" She gestured behind, pretending not to notice how the abrupt change of subject relieved Galahad. "I see the roof is all finished." Even under the hazy moonlight, the new slate shone.

"Indeed it is. No more leaks, for me or your orphanage." He rocked on his heels, clearly wishing he was anywhere else.

"Splendid . . . splendid." Good gracious. Thanks to her short stint as a temptress and the knife still lodged in her heart, this conversation was like pulling teeth.

As if he realized that, too, he blew out a breath and gestured awkwardly behind. "Care to see inside?"

No! I want to curl up into a blushing, humiliated, wretched ball and avoid you for all eternity. "All right."

"All righty . . ." His pained smile pinned in place, Galahad held the front door open for Tommy to pass with his parcel, then swept his arm toward it in wary welcome. "To set your expectations, it's still an unholy mess almost everywhere."

He wasn't lying.

The dim lamps that lit the stairwell revealed that the necessary destruction of the renovation was in full swing. Here on the bottom floor, several of the connecting walls that separated the three buildings were gone. Scaffolding supports currently held up the ceiling, but it was impressive how much those missing walls opened up the space.

Galahad picked up a lantern and wandered farther in, pointing to the now long back wall, using the building works to distract them both from their discomfort. "The bar is going to stretch all the way along here. All wood, but the wall will be covered in fancy mirrors to maximize the light. I'm having all the countertop brass for the same reason, with big crystal chandeliers above. Huge, ostentatious clusters of sparkles running all the way to the stage." He lifted the lantern toward the wall between their buildings to point out the location.

"A stage?"

His answering smile was faraway, as if he could see past all the piles of rubbish and debris to how it would all look. "For the musicians. Not an orchestra-sized stage but large enough to house four or five performers simultaneously to give the place a party atmosphere. Lively fiddlers and banjo players rather than those sedate string quartets the aristocracy favor that would only send everyone to sleep."

"Which I cannot help but notice puts all that lively fiddling directly next to my classroom." Vee hadn't meant to sound snippy, because she really was trying to be polite and indifferent to do her part to banish the awkwardness, but all that boisterousness mere feet away from the orphanage's dedicated place of study was a major cause for concern.

"I've thought about that, and believe it or not, I intend to be a considerate neighbor. Mr. Evans is going to reinforce all the walls between us, make them all a foot thick to muffle the sound. It'll be padded, too, in case all that additional brick doesn't stop everything. And there'll be absolutely no fiddling during lesson times. My business will open after yours closes for the day." He held up his palm solemnly, his unusual eyes dancing. "I swear your students won't even know that I'm there."

At her I'll-believe-that-when-I-see-it look, he grinned as he walked to the very center of the space and spread his arms wide, managing to look both boyish and sinfully handsome at the same time. "Right here will be the staircase. I've got an architect working on all the important structural details, but I can tell you it's going to swoop." His hand whooshed an arc in the air while his eyes danced with barely contained excitement. "It'll punch its way through all three floors and look impressive. Wider here at the bottom so everyone can get to the gaming tables on the floor above and getting narrower and narrower the higher it climbs to the third floor, because only my most prestigious clientele will be allowed up there." He rubbed his thumb and fingers together to let her know that "prestigious" meant the richest rather than the titled. "I want it to be seriously exclusive. By invitation only."

"A private club within a club. That's different. Sinclair's most definitely will be unique."

"I'm not calling it Sinclair's. I know it's my name and I know that's how you name clubs here, but it doesn't feel right."

"Then what are you going to call it?"

He shrugged. "I still have no idea. It can't have a tavern's name as it's going to be more than a tavern, and I don't want it to sound like a crusty, aristocratic gentleman's club because it won't be one of those, either."

"Especially if you come good on your promise to allow women." That, she had to concede, would be novel.

"Of course I'm going to allow women. I want this to be a place where all those stupid divisions in society don't matter. Where a duchess can rub shoulders with a docker and a marquess can lose his shirt to a modiste, where everyone is equal . . ." Conscious he was getting carried away again, he chuckled. "Or does that sound too American and revolutionary to your British ears?"

"It sounds positively Arthurian actually, as that was exactly how he ran Camelot." Out of nowhere, an idea popped into her head. "What about The Round Table? The original Galahad was one of King Arthur's knights, after all, so there's a tenuous link to you, too."

"The Round Table . . ." He pondered her suggestion with genuine interest. Or at least he did a good job of acting interested. "That might work. It's certainly a much better idea than The Powder Puff."

As that reminded Vee of her scandalous behavior over the card table, she changed the subject. "And the fourth floor?"

"Is all mine." Like an excited little boy, he dashed back to the narrow stairwell that Tommy had disappeared up. "With the roof in such a state it needed immediate replacing, it made sense to have Mr. Evans work from the top down, so most of the progress so far is in my apartment." The rickety old stairs creaked in protest under the weight of his boots as he hurried up them, expecting her to follow, which she did irrespective of the impropriety of an unaccompanied single lady technically visiting the home of a bachelor. Albeit a partially constructed home and her fitting only the loosest possible definition of a lady. It was difficult to see anything on the dark second and third floors beyond the piles of rubble ready to be removed, but the attic floor was a very different story. That had been gutted. All the old roof struts had been replaced and the high, angular eaves were already boarded awaiting plaster. The old plaster on the outside walls had been stripped back to the brick. As they had downstairs, the original walls between the three buildings had been taken down, but instead of leaving one huge open space, on this floor it had been partitioned with naked wooden batons marking out the new layout of the rooms.

Only one had been boarded toward the orphanage end. In the center of that new wall hung a door. The young oak was bare still, and unvarnished, furnished with a sedate but shiny brass doorknob so polished Vee could see her own face in it. As there was no sign of Galahad's new bed, she presumed beyond the solitary door was his bedchamber. Being so close to his sheets was unnerving.

"What do you think, Miss Merriwell?" A grinning Tommy moved to stand beside her while she took it all in. "It's going to be right smart, isn't it?"

"It certainly looks that way." She gave a smile to the boy and then to Galahad, forcing it not to falter. "But it's a bit spartan right now. When do you plan to move in?"

"I sort of already did. Two days ago, in fact. My tenancy at the Albany comes to an end on New Year's Eve, so I'm slowly migrating all my belongings over." He shrugged despite being obviously delighted by that. "For the first time in my life, I'm sleeping under my own roof and in my own bed and not somebody else's. As to it being spartan, I'm going to have to disagree with you. Look, Venus—" Amused, he pointed to a small cluster of furniture entirely lost in the middle of the cavernous space. "Aside from a bed and a huge new closet, I've also got this desk and a chair. What else does a man need?"

Both pieces were made of the same shade of oak as the door. The green leather top of the desk and on the seat pad of the chair were incongruous amid the still-drying pink plaster on the outer walls and the skeleton wooden frames dotted all around them. "Food? Water? Something to put them in?"

"If that's a hint you want tea, then I have to tell you this is going to be a coffee-only household because I hate the stuff." He even pulled a gagging face that made her laugh. "I have no clue why the British put so much stock in it. It's vile. Viler than vile. The worst drink ever invented."

She blinked, stunned. "Why, after four years of knowing you, is this the first I—or any other member of my family, for that matter—have heard about it?"

"Well . . . um . . ." The tips of his ears reddened, and she found that unintentional honest reaction rather . . . charming. Who knew that Galahad Sinclair—smooth, suave, sweet-talking, ruthless businessman Galahad Sinclair—had it in him to blush?

"You never turn down a cup, Galahad. *Never.*" Which struck her as ridiculous the more she thought about it. "I even know exactly how you take it. The merest drop of milk and two heaped sugars. Sometimes even three."

He winced, sheepish. "The more it tastes of sugar, the less it tastes of tea."

"Why on earth didn't you say something sooner?"

"I didn't want to seem impolite and . . . well, I'm the foreigner here and tea is your national drink, so I guess I always try my best to blend in."

She scoffed in surprise. "You drink it to blend in?" He had clearly not been built for blending. If you lined up a hundred silent gentlemen in a row, he would stick out like a sore thumb, and that would have everything to do with his golden good looks and broad shoulders and not with his accent. Although to be fair, that accent and the silky deep tone it was drawled in guaranteed he would always be noticed the second he opened his charming mouth. By the ladies at least, herself included, as it was rather alluring. Combined with his obvious physical attributes, it was deadly. "Even though you loathe it?"

He nodded, plainly embarrassed. "My ma always said it was bad manners to refuse hospitality if it was offered, and in my defense, none of the family has ever offered me coffee as an alternative else I'd have taken it. Grabbed it with both hands actually, while weeping tears of joy that I was spared the hideous ordeal of tea."

"Would you like a cup of coffee, Miss Merriwell?"

At Tommy's question she glanced again around the empty space. "You have a kitchen and a range, too?"

"Not yet." Tommy snorted as if she was daft. "Mrs. Witherspoon said that he can use the orphanage's, but she makes it for Mr. Sinclair whenever he fancies one."

"Does she indeed?"

As Mrs. Witherspoon had always had a soft spot for a charming man and had been quite beguiled by the one standing before her, she could well believe it. "Clearly more than this attic has changed in the days I have been absent. And talking about absent . . ." Vee searched around the space again. "Where is your brother? Isn't he supposed to be Mr. Sinclair's other indentured servant between the hours of six and eight? And Billy?"

"Oh, they'll be back soon. They're helping Muldoon with the beer delivery. Many hands make light work and all that, and without our help Muldoon has to keep going up and down like a bride's nightgown."

"I'm sorry?"

Galahad nudged the boy with his elbow. "That's not a phrase you say in front of a lady." For good measure he nudged Tommy again. "In and out like a fiddler's elbow would be a more appropriate choice of British colloquialism in front of Miss Merriwell."

"But it isn't in and out, is it?" Tommy flicked his finger left and right. "Because the cellar is downstairs, and we have to keep climbing up and down it to load the barrels in it." The finger flicked north and south this time. "So up and down like a . . ."

"It wasn't so much the turn of phrase I took issue with, gentlemen, more the location." Vee skewered Galahad with her stare, staggered that he had thought this appropriate. "Sydney and Billy are at the docks?"

Galahad shot Tommy another withering glance before he turned to her placating. "Before you hit my new roof, which I can already see you are on the cusp of doing, know that I cleared it with the reverend first."

"He gave permission for a trio of impressionable young boys to work in your den of iniquity?"

He nodded, folding his arms as if offended. "He *happily* granted his permission once he'd checked the place out, and the boys *like* working there."

Galahad might have been Tommy's sworn enemy a week ago, but tonight apparently he had switched his allegiance, because he moved to stand next to him in solidarity. "It's true, Miss Merriwell. We do. In fact . . ." He nudged his new best friend. "Perhaps now is a good time to ask her, Mr. Sinclair, seeing as the reverend says the final decision is hers?"

In response Galahad glared at the boy as if he couldn't quite believe what was coming out of his mouth. "You really need to learn to pick your moments, Master Claypole, as I can assure you this really isn't it."

Vee folded her own arms and glared at them both. "Ask me what?"

"Mr. Sinclair has offered the three of us apprenticeships!" Tommy could barely contain his joy at that. "And although we'll be splitting our time between here and The Den to begin with, we all get our own rooms downstairs." He pointed to the bare floorboards beneath his boots. "In the staff quarters, so I'll always be right next door to the orphanage in case you or the reverend or Mrs. Witherspoon need me. Isn't that brilliant?"

"Well . . . I . . . um . . ." It was Vee's turn to stutter noncommittally now. "I'm not sure that working in The Den would be . . ."

The muscles in Galahad's folded arms bunched tight. Enough to make her ponder them inappropriately. "She's going to say no, Tommy, so brace yourself. A flat-out no because she disapproves of me."

"Well, I . . ." She wanted to say no for precisely that reason, and would have said no to Galahad most vociferously if his bulging biceps hadn't disconcerted her and Tommy Claypole hadn't stared beseeching.

"Please, Miss Merriwell." The boy clasped his hands together ready to beg. "Mr. Sinclair thinks I have the potential to do well in the innkeeping trade and I genuinely do love the work . . ."

"Well, I . . ." Her gaze wandered to Galahad's distracting muscles again until she wrenched it away. "I need to think upon it." If the Reverend Smythe had gone, and he wasn't alarmed, perhaps . . . Or was that stretching the benefit of the doubt too far?

"You wouldn't need to think upon it if you saw it, Miss Merriwell." Tommy tugged at her sleeve. "At least come and see the place like the reverend did. You could come tonight . . ."

"Um . . . well . . . tonight I have to . . ." Vee was almost certain the absolute last person she wanted to spend any more time with was Galahad Sinclair, especially now that she knew his biceps were as potent as his kisses, but Tommy's pleading eyes combined with her burning curiosity to solve the puzzle that was Galahad overruled all her reservations and the words came out before she could stop them. "I suppose that I could come and check out the establishment now." *Good gracious, that sounded much too keen!* "If it means that much *to you*, Tommy, and isn't an inconvenience to Mr. Sinclair who likely has better things to be doing, of course."

Tommy's expectant eyes swiveled to Galahad's, which had instantly narrowed at that unexpected offer. "Can she, Mr. Sinclair? You don't have anything better to be doing, do you?"

"Now?" He seemed horrified at the prospect. "Well . . . er . . ."

"Unless now would present a problem and not give you enough time to hide the bulk of the debauchery?" Vee was pleased that the question made her sound less eager.

"We ain't got nothing to hide, have we?" Tommy tugged at Galahad's sleeve, forcing her gaze there again—heaven help her—and forcing him to see the hope etched upon the boy's freckled face. Hope that clearly got to him.

"We don't. Everything's all aboveboard." Two intensely peeved green eyes locked with hers in resignation. "So I guess I'll go hail us all a hackney."

Chapter Twenty-Two

Statistics from the final ball~

10 invitations to dance, 10 invitations to do improper things to my dance partners person on the terrace after the dance was concluded. Another 10 eligible bachelors struck off my list of potential husbands. I think it is fairly safe to say that my first season has been a disaster . . .

—from the diary of Miss Venus Merriwell, aged 19

Her mouth was drawn in a tight line of disapproval as the hackney wended its way into the docks, as if she genuinely expected to witness Sodom and Gomorrah as soon as they arrived at their destination. She kept a lid on her anger for Tommy's sake, but Gal could see it brewing behind the intense furrow of her brows and sense it in her distinct lack of conversation. He knew already this visit would be futile when she had made up her mind that he wasn't fit to have an apprentice.

"That's The Den—over there, Miss Merriwell." Tommy pointed to Gal's building by the waterfront, and while she scrutinized his establishment, he scrutinized her expression for the inevitable disdain he knew she'd display simply because he had the audacity to own it.

After an age, during which her face gave absolutely nothing away, she deigned to speak. "It's surprisingly well lit, considering the area."

"The lights attract the customers, don't they, Mr. Sinclair?" Tommy was doing his best to sell the place to her. "So does all the cheerful paintwork. Mr. Sinclair says you need to put up a good façade to get the good feet through the door."

"Mr. Sinclair is an expert when it comes to façades." She gazed at the building rather than at him while she shot her poison dart. "But it is always what's behind the façade that counts."

For Tommy's sake, he didn't take that bait. Instead, he bit his tongue until the hackney came to a stop and made sure he jumped out first, ensuring that she had no choice but to let him help her down so that she had to be gracious about something. "Do you want me to give you the tour or would you prefer to explore Hades by yourself?" He held her hand for too long on purpose to gauge her reaction to his touch, not caring that hers had such a profound effect on him. She knew already that he desired her.

That damn horse had already bolted.

She tugged her hand from his grasp the second her feet hit the road, plainly as disgusted to be here as it was physically and mentally possible to be. "Tommy can show me around while he explains to me exactly why he likes working here."

"Suit yourself." Gal stood back as he gestured inside. "I'll be in the bar awaiting your verdict." Not that he expected it to be anything other than guilty. There had never been any of her legendary benefit of the doubt for him, and she hated him more than ever since their kiss. There wasn't a hope in hell that she'd allow those boys to be apprenticed to him.

Even so, he held open the door politely while he waited for her to pass, then strapped on a mask of indifference as he left her in the hands of Tommy and made his way through the small crowd of early-evening patrons to the bar.

"Evenin', Muldoon."

"*Tráthnóna maith.*" He might not have seen the emerald isle of his birth for over a decade, but Muldoon was still more Irish than not. As usual, his manager towered above the bar top as he pulled a pint, his wily gaze watching everything and missing nothing. "Who's the bit o' raspberry?" He stared across the room at Venus in obvious masculine appreciation. "Yours?"

"*No.* Of course not." Gal tried to pull a face of distaste as he said that, which didn't feel convincing. "She's far *too* much trouble for my tastes." In case he was asked to elaborate, he did. "She's the woman from the orphanage. The one the boys rave about. The royal pain in the ass I told you about." Although he had censored most of what he had confided in Muldoon, sticking to her downright disgust at having him as a neighbor rather than all their other dealings. "Come to snoop around to see if we can be trusted to look after her precious orphans."

"That's the pious Miss Merriwell?" Muldoon stared at her some more, his eyes raking her pretty face and tempting figure with interest. "Well, she certainly isn't what I pictured. I had a plain, pinched, and pasty figure in me head—a scary, unapproachable, unappealing sort—not an absolute corker. You never mentioned your nemesis was a looker, Gal."

"Is she?" Gal checked the takings in the till with a casual air he was quite proud of. "I hadn't noticed."

"Of course ya haven't." Muldoon's bark of laughter called him a liar. "That'll be why you've got no clue how much money you just counted." One meaty paw slammed the till closed before Gal could recount it. "Prove me wrong, Yank."

"Ten pounds and some loose change." His guess was all bravado, but it was worth a shot.

"Fifteen pounds, seven shillings, and sixpence on the nose," said Muldoon with a grin so wide it displayed his three solid gold back teeth, "and you've noticed her. Ye'd have had to be blind not to."

As a pair of sailors had also noticed her, and were already prowling toward Venus with their tongues hanging out, Gal pulled rank before they pounced. "Go keep her subtly out of trouble until we can be rid of the witch."

Still laughing, Muldoon did the exact opposite, and sauntered past the sailors issuing an unsubtle warning before he went and introduced himself to Venus. Within minutes, and much to Gal's consternation, the reprobate had her laughing.

Put out, he busied himself behind the bar while he pretended not to watch her progress around his business, wishing he didn't crave her approval quite as much as he did. First Sydney Claypole, then Billy Tubbs climbed the steps from the cellar. As they were a welcome distraction, he decided to focus on them. "Good evening, fellas."

"Evenin', Mr. Sinclair." Sydney offered Gal a cheery grin whereas the other boy silently nodded a wary greeting.

In the few days Billy had been working for him, he'd managed to prise out some scant details about the boy's life. Most of the information he had so far came from Tommy, who had a knack for weaseling tidbits from people, and by any definition what poor Billy had been through was horrendous. He had been on his own since the age of eight, and the three and a half years he'd been surviving alone on the streets hadn't been kind. How Billy had come to be on the streets in the first place was still a mystery, but through the wiliest Claypole, Gal now knew that he had been scooped up by bad people almost immediately, who had used him to steal and had taken all of the profits until the then-ten-year-old pickpocket had broken free.

Billy still wasn't ready to trust anyone, and Gal appreciated that. As someone who had also been scooped up by what the English called *wrong 'uns,* he had had to learn the hard way how to avoid being exploited. His tenure as a pickpocket had been blessedly short, and with all the bartending and innkeeping skills his grandpa had equipped him with, it hadn't taken him a year to get himself off the sidewalk and working full-time at a tavern. But those terrifying, hopeless months had scarred him nevertheless, so he reckoned poor little Billy's wounds ran deeper. And consequently, they would take much longer to heal over.

"Sydney—there's a heap of glasses in the kitchen that need stacking behind the bar. Billy"—the lad typically jumped the moment his name was mentioned, because his brain had been trained to always think the worst—"there's around fifteen pounds in the till. Leave all the smallest change, count ten out, and put it in the safe in my office." He unhooked the key from his waistcoat and held it out, because his grandpa always said trust had to be given before it was earned, and Billy had nobody to teach him that.

The boy blinked at the thing, startled. "You want me to put your money in the safe? *Me?*"

"You can count to ten, can't you?"

"I can."

"Good." He thrust the key in the boy's still-limp hand. "Because it bothers me to have that much money in the till where nimble fingers can steal it. The cash boxes are in the bottom of the safe. The blue one is for coins and the red is for the folding stuff."

Billy swallowed, panicked by either the temptation or the test. "Are they both empty?"

"I hope not, else I won't be eating this week." Gal turned back to check all the bottles and his eyes instantly met Venus's in the mirror behind them. Only briefly, until she spun on her heel and disappeared into the growing crowd again with Tommy.

"I won! I *won*!" The burly docker leaped from the hazard table and danced a little jig of joy before his workmates as Gal maneuvered Venus out toward the waiting hackney.

As it was after nine and the place was filling up, it was sensible to send her home before things got too raucous. Especially when he had assumed she would leave an hour ago when his regular driver came to pick up the boys and take them back to the orphanage. But she hadn't, instead hanging around with Tommy as her chaperone and, to his complete surprise, whiling away a good hour chatting to his assorted patrons as they wandered past, tapping her foot to the music and sipping a drink.

The cynic in him couldn't help thinking she was toying with him again, and all those seemingly friendly conversations were a ruse to disguise the fact she was using the time to dig up as much dirt about this place as she could to reinforce her inevitable refusal.

"Thanks for kissing me dice, darlin'!" Before Gal could stop it, the docker grabbed her and spun her in a circle. "I knew you'd bring me good luck!"

"You are very welcome." Rather than being outraged at being manhandled by a stranger, Venus laughed at the fellow, not the least bit offended by his exuberance as Gal grabbed the upstart's arm. "I am glad I could be of service, Jonas."

As her feet returned to the floorboards and Gal gaped in shock, overfamiliar Jonas grabbed a handful of those winnings and offered them to her. "For your orphans, miss, and God bless ya. Merry Christmas."

"Merry Christmas to you, too." As if she talked to tipsy revelers in a tavern all the time, she dropped the coins in her silly little reticule then sailed toward the door with her arm around Tommy, leaving Gal to trail behind.

"Oi! Tommy!" Muldoon hollered from the doorway as Gal was about to help her into the carriage. "A word, if you please, young man." His manager waved the boy back inside and the door slowly closed behind him, leaving him all alone with Venus.

"So . . ." At least with Tommy out of earshot he could argue against her petty refusal to allow the boys to work here for him at the docks. It would be an argument that would fall on deaf ears, of course, but one he was determined to have regardless. "Did The Den fail the test?" He steeled his shoulders to prepare for the overprotective and still-aggrieved schoolmistress to return with a vengeance for the set-down.

"It didn't."

"Now look here, Venus, I know my place can get a bit rowdy but a den of iniquity it ain't and . . ." His voice trailed off when her words finally permeated his thick skull and she smiled—begrudgingly.

"Contrary to what you might think, and irrespective of our personal differences, I have never been either an unreasonable person or a prude, Galahad. I grew up in Clerkenwell, about as close to the gutter as I would like to ever venture, so I shall admit that my opinions about your rowdy tavern might have been influenced by my experiences there. I was expecting one of the base and debauched gin-soaked establishments my sisters and I frequently had to pour our inebriated father out of, but this . . ." She flicked her hand toward the building. ". . . is nothing like that. You do run a clean house, albeit a pleasantly rowdy one, but it's obvious your patrons respect the rules that you and Mr. Muldoon have set for them." She glanced back toward the door with a smile. "I am in no doubt your hefty but charming sidekick would have no trouble swiftly evicting those that fail to meet your standards."

"Muldoon used to box in the merchant navy."

"So he told me." Her smile this time was wistful. "The Claypoles will do well here. Tommy especially, I suspect, as he has the sort of mind that needs plenty to occupy it and has never excelled at the sort of quiet, contemplative repetition that a usual apprenticeship requires. Billy will, too—when he turns twelve next year—but in the meantime I think it would do him good to continue working a couple of hours for you every day to give him something to aspire to while he learns his letters with me." She fiddled with her gloves. "I noticed you have a way with him."

"He's a good kid . . . deep down. It's his hard life that's taught him to keep the truth about himself hidden."

She nodded, her expression thoughtful as she assessed him. "I suppose we are all shaped by our history, aren't we?" For a moment, it felt as though she were staring straight into his soul—his history—rather than contemplating Billy's.

A lonely snowflake fluttered between them. They watched its journey to the ground where it instantly melted, then as if joined by some invisible bond their chins lifted to scout the sky for more. It was the same exact shade of purple as it had been that fateful night in Brighton, dragging Gal straight back there. Even the full moon was identical, although it was the sound of Old Father Thames, rather than the waves of the English Channel, that lapped against the wharf side.

Another fat flake fell and caught in a stray curl poking out of her bonnet. Captivated by that as well as her, and thoroughly caught up in the odd but undoubtedly significant moment, Gal reached up to brush it away. Of its own accord his fingertip trailed along the perfect curve of her cheek. Her beautiful blue eyes locked with his, wide and uncertain; so much conflicting emotion swirled within them, he could barely stand it. "Venus, I . . ."

Gal snatched his errant hand away and fisted it behind his back as Tommy slammed out the door, thankfully before he said or did something reckless and stupid again like his heart wanted.

"If it settles, can we have another snowball match tomorrow, Miss Merriwell? We've got no lessons on Christmas Eve."

Her answering smile was brittle. Perhaps wavering?

Without thinking, she instinctively moved her fingers to her locket. "Yes. Of course. I don't see why not." And because she was flustered, she ushered the boy into the hackney. "Come on . . . it's late. Past your bedtime, and Mrs. Witherspoon will be worried."

Before she threw herself in behind him, Gal grabbed her hand and she stared at where their fingers joined as if she, too, felt the magnetic pull between them as he helped her up. He let go with reluctance but still couldn't tear his eyes away. "Good night, Venus."

"Good night, Galahad." Hers watched his, perplexed, until the carriage lurched away.

"Did your place pass muster?"

It startled Gal that Muldoon had stepped outside without him noticing. "It did . . . miraculously."

"And did you? Or are you and your troublesome *Venus* still doing the dainty dance of courtship?"

He chuckled at Muldoon's loaded look and suggestively wiggling eyebrows rather than deny it. "As if I have the time for any of that nonsense."

"A man cannot survive on bread alone, and—" Muldoon's bushy black eyebrows waggled some more. "—if I were you, I'd make the time as she looks like a tasty loaf. Too good for you, of course, but there's no accounting for taste, although what she sees in you is a mystery to be sure."

"Venus doesn't see anything in me . . ."

"For a woman who doesn't, she asked a lot of questions, and she certainly just looked at you like a woman who does." Muldoon winked while Gal's silly heart soared. "I know you too well not to recognize that you are equally as smitten."

Gal scoffed at that even though he knew it was true. "I don't have the time to be smitten. Or did you forget I'm opening a second, bigger, place in the city?" He wafted his hand downriver. "Or that I'm knee-deep in building works and plans for the foreseeable future. I'm finally building my dream, Muldoon, and nothing—and certainly no woman—is going to distract me . . ." Gal's second denial was cut short by a meaty Irish boxer's palm in front of his face.

"But who you doing all that for, ya eejit? Because if it's just for you and you alone, then that's the saddest thing I ever did hear."

Chapter Twenty-Three

Re-read Much Ado About Nothing yesterday to reignite my waned enthusiasm for romance and to remind myself that not all men put their own selfish needs and desires first. Benedick, where are you? I am in dire need of a good man who loves nothing in the world as well as me…

—from the diary of Miss Venus Merriwell, aged 19

Diana had turned up unexpectedly straight after breakfast the next morning, with little snoozing Gethin swaddled in a blanket, so Vee did not mind delaying her trip to the orphanage for an hour so that she could steal a cuddle. Now that both her sisters were married, it was rare that it was just the three of them anymore.

"I've warned Giles that unless I get two entirely uninterrupted hours of peace and freedom from his fussing today, I am going to divorce him." Diana took the cup of tea Minerva poured with a long-suffering sigh. "I am heartily sick and tired of being wrapped in cotton wool. I had a baby, not an aneurism."

"But in his poor, besotted head, you *might* have had an aneurism, and that is enough to panic him." Minerva could not hide her amusement at her middle sister's devoted husband. "Hugh was the same when both of our boys were born. It will pass."

"Well, it's not passing quickly enough." Diana had never had much in the way of patience. "I wouldn't mind betting he's still outside pacing the pavement, in case I take a turn."

"Would you rather an indifferent husband and father?" Minerva settled back on the sofa with her own tea. "I sincerely doubt ours would have curtailed his own entertainments for any of our births nor cared about how they affected our poor mother."

Diana huffed. "I suppose you make a valid point."

"He loves you." Vee couldn't help but be envious of that. "More than anything else in the world." As Diana huffed again, she rolled her eyes. "And you love him, so stop complaining."

Her middle sister smiled. The smug smile of a woman completely content with her lot. "I didn't come here for logic, Vee, I came here for sympathy. Where's Olivia? She would sympathize with my insufferable plight."

Minerva pulled a face. "Torturing poor Payne and the cook with all her plans for tomorrow's festive feast. Apparently, we are now having seven courses, and all the staff are currently on the cusp of mutinying. I couldn't be more delighted that you reached the end of your tether with all Giles's fussing, as otherwise I'd be roped into all the preparations, too."

"Do not worry, my dear, you soon will be." With her customary impeccable timing, Olivia sailed through the door taking absolutely no offense at her daughter-in-law's reluctance to be of service. "Just as soon as we've all finished our tea." With an unenthusiastic roll of her eyes Minerva poured her a cup, too, while the indomitable matriarch cooed over the baby in Vee's arms. "What gossip have I missed?"

"Diana was bemoaning Giles's over-attentiveness because she is apparently sick and tired of being utterly adored." Which was ironic when Vee had never had the good fortune to experience that joy.

She had only ever been desired on the most base and superficial of levels. Mostly for her bosoms. Bosoms that Galahad clearly also had a penchant for, likely more confirmation that he was just as superficial and selfish as all the other unworthy men she had a talent for attracting.

And likely further proof, if proof were needed, that her foolish, befuddled heart was barking up the wrong tree yet again.

His stormy eyes had unmistakably darkened with desire again last night. However, it was the rest of the storminess within those hypnotic green irises that she still couldn't decipher—or at least trust herself to read correctly. Had there really been longing and regret swirling amid the desire last night as he had bid her goodbye—as she had desperately wanted there to be—or had she, the world's worst judge of a man's character, imagined it? Imagined it because she had needed to see her own confused feelings mirrored in his gaze so very badly?

She didn't know and, worse, after going to The Den in search of some answers, had left managing to be more confused about him than she had been when she'd arrived.

That it hadn't been anywhere near as bad a place as she'd imagined had surprised her. How he had behaved there had surprised her more. She had barely recognized the Galahad Sinclair who'd stood like the king of the castle behind that bar. The Galahad of The Den had been charming still, exaggerating that beguiling accent of his every time he spoke, but was also undoubtedly in charge. There had been an air of gravitas surrounding him that she had never witnessed before, and he wielded that quiet power to keep everyone and everything in check.

To be confronted by yet another façade had been unsettling, making her wonder exactly how many he could conjure at will to hide behind, and which of the many versions of himself was the truth. Or were all of them in some way a piece of the puzzle? A part of the whole or just more showmanship?

What was undeniable was that everyone there, paid or paying, obviously respected him. His staff were positively gushing about him as an employer. While she knew talk was cheap, and those employees might not have dared say otherwise for fear of repercussions, the fact that most of them had worked for Galahad for years suggested that he was a decent master. People did not stay long in poorly paid jobs where they were ill treated. They sought greener grass the second they spied some. That was a fact.

But it was also a fact that he kept people at arm's length. Back in Brighton, Nelly had called him cryptic. Last night, when she had probed, Muldoon had said much the same. Galahad liked to keep himself to himself, he had explained when she'd tried to understand why he had lied to her face, and the rest of the family's, to get out of Christmas. The Irishman had concluded—after confessing that he had no family, that The Den was usually as silent as the grave on Christmas Day, so he had no clue why his employer had claimed otherwise—that Galahad was one of life's loners.

While that struck her as sad, it was the way he had been with Billy that disconcerted her the most. Entrusting the boy with money after all that he had done had touched her; witnessing Billy's stunned transformation from the unexpected responsibility given so generously had touched her more. The poor thing had carried that cash out of the taproom with total concentration and reverence, yet with a fresh spring in his usually world-weary step. As if he had been entrusted with guarding the holy grail rather than a few pounds. The pride on his little face when he had returned and handed Galahad back the key as if the man before him was suddenly his hero, and the way he had blossomed and instantly stood taller when that hero had casually patted him on the back . . . Well, that had been quite something.

But was it a glimpse of the real Galahad or yet another façade? An unconscious, genuine act of kindness or a calculated gesture used simply to win her around to his way of thinking because he had noticed she was watching?

She didn't know, and therefore wasn't yet ready to trust the voice in her head that was now recklessly cheering for Galahad all the way alongside the one in her heart that had been rooting for him all along. Leaving her still wounded and wary but so conflicted she could not stop thinking about it. Which of the many incarnations of Galahad was the real one? And was it possible that one of them felt more for her than just desire?

"Giles is a prince among men, and princes are always annoying." Olivia smiled at Diana in sympathy. "Probably because the admirable traits we cannot help but fall in love with are the same traits that also grate the most. For me it is Jeremiah's stubbornness. When that man digs his heels in, there is no moving him. He is intractable."

Vee couldn't help but laugh. "The phrase about people in glass houses springs to mind."

"Undoubtedly. We are alike on that score, and I never could have been happy with a man who allowed me to get away with murder." Olivia blew on her tea with a naughty glint in her eye, entirely comfortable with who she was. "Mr. Peabody is a constant, stubborn challenge who keeps me on my toes—but he is also stubbornly loyal. Stubbornly noble. Stubbornly kind. Stubbornly stubborn for stubbornness's sake because he knows that I am a better person for it. I knew he was *the one* the first time we locked horns, and we've never spent a night apart since."

"For me, it was Giles's intrinsic selflessness. In everything, but most especially when he stupidly put himself between me and a bullet." Now Diana was sighing wistfully, too. "All entirely unnecessary, of course, and a totally idiotic solution to a perfectly simple problem, but still . . . That was such a grand and thoughtful gesture, I couldn't ignore it—although I tried." She took a pensive sip of her tea. "It was important to be sure he was worth it."

After a lifetime of disappointment, that was a sentiment Vee now shared.

"There wasn't really one grand gesture with us that I can recall." Minerva's expression was reflective. "It was more gradual, but I suppose if I were to analyze exactly what it was that made me realize that Hugh was worth it, it was his compassion and kindness that convinced me that he was the one. He's a knight in tarnished armor to his core, no matter how hard he works to hide that side of himself from the world."

"Men are exasperating creatures, mostly because they are obsessed with behaving like men. Which inevitably means they get everything wrong, but it is always those unconscious and instinctive reactions and interactions that show a man's true mettle." Olivia's word felt prophetic. "The most fraught and charged moments when you see who they truly are." Like how you react when your watch is stolen, perhaps? Or when you've been pecked by pigeons? Or when you give an unloved child a chance to shine? Exactly what sort of proof did Vee need to trust that she was reading Galahad right most of the time? "The princes *never* run away from a crisis. And speaking of crises . . . Christmas isn't going to prepare itself." She pinned Vee with a narrowed glare. "If you are not back by five to help, too, young lady, I shall not be accountable for my actions."

The three sisters watched Olivia leave. When she was far enough away, Minerva groaned. "I love her to pieces, but when Olivia has a bee in her bonnet, she is impossible. If you hadn't arrived, Diana, I would have taken a leaf out of the rest of the family's book and disappeared for the day."

"I'm hardly skiving," said Vee, privately glad that she had an excuse. "Unlike Hugh and Jeremiah."

"The selfish wretches!" Minerva fumed. "As if we don't know that their *urgent business* involves reading a newspaper in the sanctuary of White's undisturbed while Christmas is prepared without them! Not that they would ever admit to it. Men do like to guard their little secrets."

Talking of men and their secrets . . .

"Diana . . ." In the absence of an alternate avenue to pursue, desperate times called for desperate measures. ". . . what do you know about Galahad's past?" The moment that burning question escaped, Vee bitterly regretted asking it because her sisters simultaneously gave each other a look over the rims of their teacups. One stating that she had somehow confirmed all their suspicions about her feelings for Galahad just by opening her big mouth.

But it was out now, and as she was at her wit's end trying to puzzle together that mystery, she decided to be brazen about it. "If anybody reads anything into that beyond polite curiosity while we are all lamenting the men in the family, or dares utter one syllable of teasing, I swear I shall never confide in either of you again!"

Two pairs of eyes widened behind their teacups rather than glance at each other, now more convinced than ever that something beyond lifelong dislike was afoot. As Minerva almost burned off her lips trying to sip her scalding tea rather than make a pithy comment about the question, Diana frowned, pondering. "I am not sure I know that much at all, now that you come to mention it. Galahad is . . . has always been . . . a very private person."

"But he must have told Giles something of his background, and Giles would have told you because he tells you everything."

It was clear her middle sister was searching through the vast archive of her mind, because her forehead and then her nose wrinkled as she considered it. "I know he hails from New York on the eastern seaboard."

"Don't we all know that?"

Diana nodded. "I also know that his grandfather owned an inn of some sort there and his mother died when he was young because it came up in conversation one day, briefly, before he changed the subject." Something he was so adept at, you barely noticed it. All by design and all beyond frustrating. "Perhaps he was not as young as you were, Vee, when ours passed, but I seem to recall it was somewhere around the age of thirteen."

Vee hadn't realized that.

She had assumed his mother had died shortly before he had come here with Gervais. That he had had to look after her before that because of her lung condition. Be the breadwinner after his grandfather was killed and his absent father was goodness knew where. "I presume he was stuck with Gervais for all of his formative years."

"Gervais abandoned his mother before Galahad was born." Vee's forehead was similarly wrinkled now as she pieced it all together. "He turned up again just before Galahad reached his majority. Galahad told me he was after his inheritance . . . but I have no idea what that inheritance was."

"I do remember that!" Diana seemed relieved to know something; being a journalist, she always prided herself on knowing everything. "He'd been left some share certificates! For some American shipping company, I believe. Galahad sold them and used the money to buy himself The Den."

"Jeremiah assisted." Minerva added another layer to the tale. "He used his business contacts back in Boston to broker the deal. They were sold in the end for five hundred pounds."

"I always assumed Giles lent him that money." Vee was suddenly annoyed that she hadn't inquired before today.

"Believe me, Giles wanted to. He wanted to set him up in an easier sort of business, but Gal wouldn't hear of it." Diana shrugged. "His grandpa had taught him the innkeeping trade and always instilled in him the importance of self-reliance. *Never a lender or a borrower be*, were Gal's exact words, and he's always stuck to those principles and never taken a penny."

"I think that's admirable. Thank goodness Galahad got all his good morals from his grandfather, rather than his odious father." Minerva scooped little Gethin from Vee's arms and rocked him, cooing, giving Vee nothing to distract her from contemplating those good morals. Would a man who was apparently so noble in every other aspect of his life really be so careless with a woman's feelings? Would he kiss her as if he meant it with every fiber of his being if he didn't? Glance at her with longing still if he didn't feel it? "Gervais abandoning him actually did him a favor on that score, didn't he, little man?" Minerva pulled a face. "Can you imagine what he could have turned out like if Gervais had brought him up during his formative years?"

While Diana shuddered at the prospect, it brought Vee up short.

"Except his grandpa also died at around the same time. He was killed during a bar fight when Galahad was twelve. Right in front of him." Suddenly Vee was sick to her stomach. Not just because of the senseless murder that he had been forced to witness, but because so many of the gaps he had omitted telling anyone were starting to fill. All the hardship the Merriwell sisters had had to face in their past seemed a mere drop in the ocean now compared with his.

The cogs of Diana's mind were turning, too. "But if his mother *and* his grandfather died while he was a boy and Gervais had absconded, yet again, from doing the right thing, then that means poor Gal was . . ."

"Basically an orphan from a very young age." Which explained why he had such a soft spot for all of hers. "He must have been on his own for almost a decade." Eking out a living doing whatever it took to survive, exactly like Billy Tubbs. That unpalatable fact choked her. Horrified her. Forced her to reevaluate him yet again.

Now it made sense why he was so forgiving of that boy's thievery and suspicious nature! Why he hadn't wanted the boy punished by the law. Why he held his cards so close to his chest. Why he was so ambitious and driven and determined to succeed. Why he kept the world, including his adopted family, at arm's length and never confided anything to anyone.

Ever.

It was his hard life that had taught him to keep the truth about himself hidden. Which begged the question as to why he had chosen to share some of that truth with her.

And more important, what did that mean?

Chapter Twenty-Four

I am officially noting, for the record, that my second season was more disappointing than my first. I am increasingly convinced that balls are not the best place to find my soulmate and I should also like it noted again that I hate my stupid name. I swear it does nothing but give libidinous men ideas . . .

—from the diary of Miss Venus Merriwell, aged 20

"Line up in an orderly fashion or you will be left behind!" For some reason, the Reverend Smythe was bellowing on the street below, so loudly that even the thick pillow over Gal's head did little to drown out the sound.

With Mr. Evans and his boys constantly hammering away downstairs, and sleep being a necessity he couldn't live without, he had trained himself to sleep through all sorts of morning noise in the last few weeks. But there was noise and then there was *noise*, and there was no blocking out what was going on outside his window this morning. Especially as he had spent most of last night's designated hours of sleep pondering Venus and what he was going to do about her after Muldoon had put an unwelcome flea in his ear.

An annoying, nipping, persistent little critter that had forced him to stop and think exactly where the path he had stuck to so diligently was actually going. And more important, whether he wanted to continue on it alone.

"Tommy Claypole! I am warning you . . ." As the reverend's anger rose in volume, Gal gave up trying to either sleep through it or make any sense of his conflicting feelings regarding Venus, shrugged on his discarded shirt, and padded barefoot to the window to see what the hell all the hullabaloo was about.

In the midst of a crowd of children in varying stages of maturity were the reverend and his wife. Lined up behind them were at least six hackneys, one already holding a fraught Mrs. Witherspoon and a coach full of the littlest orphans. Standing in the road waving another carriage down with her latest silly little reticule was Venus.

As if she sensed him watching she went from waving at the coachman to waving at him before she scurried his way, flapping her hands to encourage him to slide up his window.

"Can you skate?"

As that was the absolute last thing he expected to hear after the odd way things had ended between them last night, he frowned. "Skate? As in *ice*-skate?" She beamed nodding and suddenly he did not mind in the slightest being so rudely awoken. "I haven't done it in years."

"But you *can* skate?"

"In the loosest possible sense, yes . . ."

"Good. We could do with another adult. Get dressed and I'll wait for you." Before he could argue, she spun around to help the vicar and his wife wrangle the children.

Ten minutes later, and still not entirely sure which way was up, he reported for duty. "I thought the British stopped press-ganging unwitting recruits after Napoleon."

She scoffed at that while still loading the second-from-last hackney with excited orphans. "You have to take the shilling to be officially press-ganged, Galahad, and you're doing this gratis, out of the goodness of your heart."

"I am?"

"Of course you are." She grabbed his arm and yanked him toward the carriage and all the expectant faces inside, one of whose was Billy's. "Because it is Christmas Eve, a time for goodwill to all, and because for the first time in what feels like months the sun is finally shining and the Serpentine is frozen. Because that makes it the perfect day to go skating." With one subtle flick of her finger, all six of the tightly packed occupants inside shuffled over and Venus pushed all six feet of him into that six-inch space then slammed the door shut. "And because you clearly had nothing else pressing going on this morning." She slapped the side of the conveyance, and off he went.

For all of thirty seconds, every child except Billy eyed him in silent appraisal, then—after assessing him correctly as someone who was out of his depth and doubtless smelling his fear—they all began to misbehave.

It started with just one boy, who licked his index finger thoroughly before shoving it into the ear of the girl next to him.

Obviously, and he really couldn't blame her, that violated little girl took umbrage and thumped the boy. While Gal attempted to calm her down and chastise the owner of the offending spittle-covered digit, two of the other boys squashed beside him began to wrestle.

He tried to tell them off, wagging his finger with calm authority exactly as Venus had done so effectively. But where her pointed finger held the magical power to make children comply, his didn't.

One of the girls, the one without the wet ear, decided to ignore his finger to join in the wrestling, and from the outset she fought dirty, using her teeth as well as her nails to give the boys what for.

"Stop that now!" Gal tried to prise the knot of wrestlers apart. "If you don't stop this instant, I'm going to have this carriage turn around and take you all back to the orphanage!"

As if they all knew that this was the empty threat of a man who'd never had to deal with a child in his life, the wrestling continued unhindered. Worse, the biter stepped up her game, sinking her teeth into one of the boys' arms until she drew blood. The kid screamed and kicked her to free it, then managed to kick Gal in the shin, too.

He was on the cusp of hollering at them all red-faced, like the good reverend, or throwing himself out onto the road to escape them like a coward when the hitherto silent Billy produced a pack of cards and held it out.

"Can you teach me that fancy shuffle that you do, Mr. Sinclair?"

Gal gave him his best death glare as he tried to separate the wrestlers again. "Now's *really* not the time, Billy."

The boy grabbed his hand and slapped the cards into them. "Trust me, Mr. Sinclair, now is the perfect time." He gave him the look. The look that told him in no uncertain terms that with nothing else in his arsenal to control these little monsters, that fancy shuffle was likely all he had to prevent anarchy. His gaze flicked toward the original miscreant, who was again slathering his index finger in spit with his tongue ready to poke uninvited into another orifice. "Only Miss Merriwell always says that the devil always finds work for idle hands . . ."

Panicked, Gal cut the cards one-handed, his eyes focused on Billy—who was, bizarrely, the only child in here that he *could* trust—and prayed that the scamp was right. "Shall we start with the basics to begin with, Billy Boy?" Although as he knew already nothing basic would work with this tough crowd, he began to perform every complicated trick he knew with all the exaggerated flair of a street entertainer.

Within moments—and to his complete but grateful surprise—one by one the children stopped attacking one another and focused on the flying cards, mesmerized. So entranced, he never heard another squeak out of them beyond shocked *oohs* and *ahs* until they pulled up in Hyde Park.

"Collect your skates over . . ." Because this was clearly his lucky day, it was Venus who opened the hackney's door. Instantly her eyes widened in outrage as he flicked the pack together in a final flourish.

"You are teaching them to gamble?"

"Of course I'm not teaching them to gamble." He did his best to convey with his eyes that he had just avoided all-out war, hoping that she, of all people, would understand how unpredictable and uncivilized these orphans were. "I was occupying them with a few tricks to keep them quiet for the duration of the journey, that's all."

"With cards, Galahad! *Cards*, for goodness' sake?" She managed to make the word *cards* sound as dangerous to their welfare as knife juggling. "These are impressionable young minds!"

The offending cards were snatched from his hand and swiftly deposited inside her ridiculous little reticule, filling it completely. Staring at him in exasperation, she used nothing but her magical index finger to shepherd all her suddenly obedient flock in the direction of Mrs. Witherspoon, who was handing out a huge mountain of hired skates as if her life depended on it. "Once you have your skates, put them on and sit quietly until I tell you otherwise."

Feeling inadequate and still bewildered as to why he had been dragged along, Gal followed suit, strapping on some skates and sitting dutifully with all the rest of the orphans while he awaited the all-powerful finger's next instructions.

"I suppose it's all showmanship." At Galahad's unconvinced expression, Vee laughed as they slowly skated side by side along the top edge of the perimeter she had set for the older children they were supervising. "My finger does not possess magical powers. I simply act as if I am the one in charge and they believe it." She swept her arm to encompass the twenty grinning orphans skating close by. "Children need clear rules and are always much happier when they know exactly what those rules are. In hindsight, it was remiss of me not to set them for you in the carriage."

"I'll say it was. You fed me to the lions. On purpose, too."

She smiled, guilty as charged, but would never admit that she had done that to test his mettle, or that he had passed that test with flying colors. "In my defense, I assumed a man of your many talents would manage well enough on his own."

"What made you think my specific talents would stretch to controlling a carriage full of over-excited children?" Despite the crease of concentration on his forehead, Galahad still wobbled on the ice, proving that he was able to skate in the loosest possible sense, exactly as he had claimed. But what he lacked in ability he made up for in tenacity and good humor. "I know innkeeping, cards, and business—in that order. None of those things involve humans below the age of twenty."

"You manage to control a bar full of rowdy drinkers and gamblers night after night with no problem, and surely that is harder than a few children?"

"If a drinker or a gambler gets too rowdy, I can punch him and throw him out. I can imagine how well me punching one of your unruly orphans and then tossing them out of a moving carriage would have gone down with you and the reverend and your liberal policies against violence."

"You are not a violent man, Galahad." Vee felt that in her bones. "I'd bet good money that you've never used your fists once to ensure compliance at The Den."

"I haven't—but I could if I had to. That's the difference." His confidence building, he lengthened his stride. "It's the threat that matters. It's implied. My customers know that I could pummel them, or I could unleash Muldoon's meaty fists upon them with a click of my fingers . . ." He clicked his. ". . . and so they behave. Besides, my customers are all adults, and in the main, adults don't lick then stick fingers in each other's ears." He pulled an outraged face. "In *my* defense, that's not a situation I've ever had to deal with before. Any more than supervising a bunch of children on ice when I can barely keep myself upright is something I've had to deal with before." He stared at her in feigned annoyance. "Something you should have thought about before you kidnapped me and made me your minion. We both know I'm as good as useless out here."

Vee did not believe that for a second but wasn't ready to give him a compliment when she still wasn't sure what to feel about him. "You have two working eyes."

"And you have a schoolteacher's extra pair hidden in the back of your head, which make mine redundant, so why did you really drag me out here, Venus?" He twisted to face her as he stopped on the ice.

"Because I have questions." So many, that were so important, they made her brain hurt.

"About The Den? About letting the boys work there?"

"About you actually." Seeing as he had brought it up, there was no point beating around the bush. "Who *are* you, Galahad?"

His bemusement was instant. "Who am I? What sort of question is that when you've known me for years?" That he started skating again was telling.

"But do I? Does anyone?" As she was better on the ice than him it was no trouble catching up to him, and in case he did all he could to maneuver out of her way both physically and conversationally, she threaded her arm through his to anchor him by her side. "You seem to be so many conflicting things, Galahad Sinclair—you play so many different characters—I have no clue which version of you is real."

"I am exactly what you see." His expression tried to shrug her observation off as nonsense, but the muscles in his arm bunched beneath her fingers. "A fish out of water trying to make a go of things in a strange land."

"What I see—what I've seen—is a man who can adapt to whichever environment he happens to be in, with such ease and swiftness it is confusing. Occasionally, when he wants to disarm, he pretends to be the lackadaisical foreigner filled with lazy charm. That character is at odds with the ruthless, ambitious businessman who is always scouting the horizon for opportunities to seize and circumstances to adapt to. Sometimes, like last night, he is the eyes-everywhere king of The Den. Adored by all his loyal but lowly subjects in the docks. Yet that same man can rub shoulders with the aristocrats of Mayfair and not seem out of place. In crowds, he can be the life and soul, but among his family he is the shy, reluctant dinner companion who quietly reads Shakespeare in his spare time. Other times he is a dreamer who sees nothing but the infinite potential of an idea. Someone who is harmlessly flirtatious and, occasionally, dangerously seductive." There was no point lying about her overwhelming attraction to him, as that was the crux of the matter.

The flirt arrived with a vengeance to disguise the brief flash of something that looked a lot like hope that skittered across his handsome face. "You find me seductive?"

Vee rolled her eyes rather than answer that, not ready to bare her hand entirely just yet. "I see a man who is often carried away by enthusiasm and allows his future to be guided by dreams. However, that same man often seems haunted by his past and uses it like a barricade to hide behind. A shield to keep out the world and guard his heart." He blinked at that. Only once but enough to tell her that he wasn't comfortable that she had seen that. Or particularly comfortable with her canny assessment of him at all.

"A man who is universally liked by everyone, yet who keeps everyone at arm's length. A man who forgives unconditionally yet refuses to bend an inch elsewhere. A determined, patient, stubborn, generous, single-minded, vexing, kindhearted, unyielding, unreadable, untrusting, resourceful, selfish, passionate, and compassionate man." He was all those things and more, but it was the more that she wanted now.

"In short, I see a man of wild contradictions, Galahad." Because he had stopped looking at her to stare across the ice instead, Vee slowed and tugged him to face her. "A man that I do not know at all. Does anyone?"

He was silent, turning his head and shielding his brows from the glare of the midday sun to study all the people littering the frozen Serpentine rather than allowing her to see the truth in his eyes.

But she could feel the tension in his body. Sense the turmoil in his soul. After an age he blew out a misty breath and watched it evaporate before he answered. "Probably not."

"Why?"

"Habit." He shrugged, still staring at nothing. "Self-preservation. Self-defense."

"What people do not know, they cannot use against you?"

"Something like that." His eyes slanted begrudgingly to hers then focused outward again. That was when she noticed he was watching a ragged boy slipping over the melted puddles on the ice a few yards away. He was swaddled in so many filthy old coats that his body resembled a barrel balanced on two skinny little legs. Without skates, the unyielding wooden soles of his too-big boots slid here and there with every determined step as he hawked a tray of hot chestnuts to warm the revelers. For several moments Galahad watched the lad struggle but doggedly refuse to give up selling his wares and earning those next few pennies, which were probably the difference between eating and not. "He's probably more of the real me than all those others you just described. At least inside . . ." His gloved hand splayed across his chest as if he could still feel that lost boy within. "And that's not someone I want the world to see anymore."

She had suspected it, but her heart still bled. "How long were you on your own for?"

"Eight long years."

"Oh, Galahad . . ." She hugged his arm, wishing she could make it all better and devastated that she couldn't. "I'm so sorry . . ."

"It's the past, Venus." Typically, he withdrew, stiffening as he tried to shrug it off. "And undoubtedly best left there. It was what it was—I survived—so I choose not to dwell on it."

"Don't you?" As he clearly wanted to skate again—preferably as far away from this conversation as was possible—she took the lead and refused to allow him to lose her. "Mine wasn't anywhere near as bad as yours and yet I still do." Perhaps some of her own truths might loosen some of his? "I don't dwell exactly, I just know that it influences my decisions and impacts my judgments. Like last night. I fully expected The Den to be the sort of depraved place where my father lost all our rent money while he drank himself into oblivion. I do not mind admitting that it unsettled me when it wasn't."

The Claypoles whizzed past laughing and waving and dragging several others in their wake, so Vee paused long enough to do the same, before she trusted Galahad with something as important as he had Billy with his takings. Hoping that her honesty might coax out a confidence in return to help clear a path between them, because she was all done with the barricades—both his and hers. All done with fighting against that invisible pull between them. So done with trying to hate him and denying what both her heart and her head clearly wanted. "Similarly, and entirely because I was deprived of the secure, traditional sort of family that I read about in fairy tales and I craved growing up, I've set my cap to all manner of unworthy men in the vain hope that one of them would be *the one* to make my own fairy tale with. It's a pathetic trait that has caused nothing but humiliation and heartache, but one I have been working hard to correct. Especially since Lord Argyll."

He didn't seem at all surprised by the substance of that confession, more that she had made it so openly. "How do you explain Lord Dorchester?"

"Habit." As his previous words fit perfectly, she used them. "Self-preservation. Self-defense. Thanks to my stupid name, my lack of blue blood, and some inconvenient and exuberant meddling from Mother Nature—" She briefly touched her own chest. "—I have always been the sort of woman men desire but do not *want*. At least not in the forever sort of way, so I decided to listen to my seemingly sensible, bookish head for a change and not my foolish, needy, gullible heart. Lord Dorchester was—is—a very different kettle of fish from every other gentleman of my acquaintance as he is the only one who has never shown the slightest bit of desire for me as a woman."

He regarded her without outright bewilderment. "That *appealed*?"

"After Lord Argyll, yes. Very much so."

"Yet I still caught you re-reading *Much Ado*—a story about unrequited love and longing coming good."

"Clearly, I'd convinced my head, but not my foolish, romantic heart." She laughed bitterly at the ridiculousness of it. Of the ludicrousness of her own warped logic and contradictions. Contradictions that she hadn't even realized until he had pointed them out. The overwhelming urge to read about her favorite fictional couple to fill the void left by her lack of feelings for Dorchester should have told her that he was wrong long before she had been forced to acknowledge it. "What can I say, Galahad? I have always been a dreamer and the worst judge of a man's character, and as a result I've always ended up with my stupid heart disappointed or broken in some way." Nerves at laying herself so bare made her tummy flutter and constricted her throat, and yet, bizarrely, she wanted to entrust him with her whole self. Needed him—just him—to be the one to know the real her completely. "That in turn has made me cynical, and that also taints my judgment. I no longer trust myself to see things clearly. I hear alarm bells everywhere nowadays and always think the worst. Second-guess myself at every juncture and yet still take it all to heart. Further proof that we all dwell on the past in some shape or form and allow it to hold us back—even from what our hearts most want." She let go of his arm to stare at him levelly, daring him to be as honest with her as she had been with him. Daring him to trust her with his truth, too. Willing him to take that leap. That gamble. "Or do you disagree?"

He skated around her as he pondered it. Or pondered what to say.

Or more likely pondered how to avoid answering at all.

The silence stretched and she felt foolish. So self-conscious, her eyes dropped to her toes and would have stayed there had his finger not tipped up her chin. He withdrew it immediately the second her wary gaze met his equally wary one, yet the potency of that brief touch lingered on her flesh even when he put several feet of distance between them.

"You do know that it is possible to desire a woman and want her at the same time, don't you?" His smile was cautious as his eyes raked her up and down, so thoroughly she felt it everywhere. First from the front, then behind her back as he continued to glide around her, assessing her, like a fighter in the boxing ring sizing up a feared opponent.

"What has that to do with the past influencing our futures?" She was going to get a straight answer out of him if it killed her. Or completely humiliated her. Or she died of utter mortification. Or her heart made a total fool out of her yet again because she'd got it all wrong. *Please, God, I hope I haven't.* "For once in your wretched life, be honest with me."

"Well, if I'm being honest . . ." He shrugged but held her gaze. "I'm sorry for every idiot who ever broke your heart. I'm sorry about your name and all the problems it has caused you over the years, but I have to confess that I like it. It suits you. And I, for one, shall be forever grateful to Mother Nature for her exuberant meddling, as she did a fine job on you, Venus. A mighty fine job." The emotive green eyes darkened as he dropped his voice to a silky, private murmur and skated much too close. "So fine that if I'm being brutally honest, I find myself desiring you more than I've ever desired any woman in my life—and you know already that I want you. I've never been any good at hiding that."

Her irritation was instinctive, because he was using her confession and his own lust as an excuse to deflect again. To avoid having a meaningful conversation about himself. About them. To hide, yet again, behind his beloved deceptive showmanship.

Or so the jaded cynic in her thought, until the molten heat in his unusual green eyes morphed into something else.

Something more honest and vulnerable than she had ever seen there, but more enticing somehow as a result.

"But what you might not know . . ." His feet slowed and his body drifted toward hers braced, as if heading into battle. "What I've never let you see before now . . . never even dared admit properly to myself before now because it scares the hell out of me . . ." His index finger found hers and reverently grazed it as he swallowed. ". . . is that I've honestly always wanted you in the forever sort of way, Venus." His reluctant smile was one of resignation. Of fear and uncertainty. Of surrender. "And it turns out I'm just not strong enough to fight that anymore."

Was that a declaration?

It felt like one, but she needed clarity. Needed all the answers. All the secrets. Needed to know him properly before she listened to her foolish, needy heart again. Knew somehow that this man, this complex and frustrating man, didn't so much have the power to break her heart as to possess it completely.

"Galahad, I . . ."

"*Get off the ice!*" The bloodcurdling shout from beyond caused immediate panic to erupt all around them. "*It's breaking up!*"

Chapter Twenty-Five

I am officially <u>*in love*</u>*! I have finally found my prince! Lord Anthony Argyll is perfect in every way. Hes handsome and charming, and while he isn't rich and will never inherit anything, he is so eager to do good in the world he is determined to work for the government...*

—from the diary of Miss Venus Merriwell, aged 21

". . . fifteen, sixteen, seventeen . . ." Vee counted all the heads in a blind panic as each orphan raced off of the ice amid what had to be half of London. "*Three are still missing!*" She shouted this to Galahad who was still out on the ice looking for her charges. A quick scan of all the frightened faces lining the bank revealed exactly which three weren't there that should have been. "*Tommy, Sydney, and Billy!*"

Galahad nodded and searched the chaos for them, cupping his hands as he called out their names.

The reverend dashed toward her. "Are we all present and correct?"

She shook her head. "We are still waiting for Mr. Tubbs and the Claypoles. The little ones?"

"Are all mustered over there out of harm's way with my wife and Mrs. Witherspoon." He pointed farther up the path, and she allowed her gaze to leave the ice for a moment to check that it was so.

That few seconds was all it took to lose Galahad in the melee. "Take the others to safety while I . . ."

The reverend's fingers gripped her arm and yanked her back from the edge. "It's too dangerous, Vee!" She knew that but could not stand by impotent when he was on the ice for her. "You must stay here."

"Get the others to safety!" She tugged her sleeve away, shaking her head in apology as she plunged into the fray. "Galahad! Tommy!" She was shouting into the wind, her urgent calls swallowed by all the others. Mothers. Fathers. Husbands. Wives. Brothers. Sisters. All frantic. All carrying or dragging loved ones to safety. It was a fight getting through them, but all at once she did, only to be confronted by a different kind of chaos in the middle of the lake where the ice had fractured.

Only the brave ventured there. The selfless or the desperate. Dotted like statues and frozen in fear; their focus all converged on one precise spot. One sported a ginger mop of hair, so she raced toward that like a woman possessed.

"Sydney! Oh my God, Sydney!" One down, only three to go. "Get back to the shore *now*!"

His body static, his eyes as wide as saucers, he shook his head. "Not without my bruvver!" He pointed to an enormous patch where the shimmering arctic blue-and-white ice had been eaten by the familiar murky turquoise of the Serpentine. Crouched upon a floating shard the size of a rowing boat were the other two boys. Tommy first. Billy tucked right behind him. Six feet away and flat on his belly on the jagged edge of the hole was Galahad.

"No sudden movements . . ." His voice was calm and reassuring in the strange eerie silence that now cloaked them. "We'll do this as many times as we need until you catch my sleeve." Up until that moment, Vee hadn't noticed he was coatless. "Don't panic if you miss the first time and if you don't, don't yank it, ya hear?"

Tommy nodded, his freckled face more serious than she had ever seen it.

"I'll count to three and then I'll throw." Tommy nodded again, sucking in air as Galahad counted. "One . . . Two . . . Three . . ." He whipped his coat out across the channel and the boy whimpered as he missed it. "Never mind . . . That was just a practice run . . . If Billy holds you tight around the waist, you can reach a bit farther."

Billy didn't waste a second doing as he was told, and the coat was gathered up again by Galahad, wrung out, and rolled into a corded spiral. "One . . . Two . . . Three . . ." Out it snapped again and this time Tommy caught it, the precarious ice boat rocking back and forth in protest. "Stay still . . . Let it settle . . ."

Like the boys, and everyone around them, Vee held her breath until the chunk of ice calmed and Galahad made them all wait until the water beneath it was still, too, before he began to pull them in. Slowly.

Inch by painful inch.

The second he grabbed Tommy's fingers, she rushed forward to help, only to be stayed by several pairs of hands—including Galahad's—when the surface beneath her skates creaked menacingly.

Vee stopped dead, and for the first time looked to her feet. The ice, which had been so opaque and robust nearer the shore, was as translucent as glass out here in the middle where the afternoon sun had melted it.

"We need to keep the weight to a minimum." Another man ushered her back. "We need to keep it spread out." He pointed to the human chain waiting patiently to assist in the rescue.

She nodded, petrified, barely daring to breathe as she edged backward until there was no sign of the ominous bubbles of water visible through the reassuringly thicker ice beneath her feet. Then watched, impotent, as Galahad alone carefully eased first one boy, then the other from one dangerous piece of the ice to another. Only when Billy was safe and painstakingly being passed from hand to hand toward her did she sag in relief.

She hugged both boys close, shivering more from the fear of what might have been than the cold. "Go back to the bank slowly. One at a time."

"Y-yes, Miss M-Merriwell." Poor Tommy's teeth were chattering, and his brother quickly stripped off his coat to wrap it around him. As the much thinner Billy was practically blue with cold, she gave him hers, then turned to where she assumed Galahad would also now be heading toward her.

Except he wasn't.

He was still perched on his knees at the thinnest edge of the ice issuing calm instructions again.

That was when she realized that her boys weren't the only ones left stranded by the failing ice. The little, ragged chestnut seller was, too, and to her complete horror, the much farther-away and smaller shard of ice that he was clinging to for grim death was sinking.

"Try to keep still, little fella." How Galahad could sound so controlled when the situation was so perilous was a mystery, but he was as cool as the ice around him. "Give us a minute to make a line long enough." The few men who remained were frantically tying together coats, cravats, and scarves to span the thirty feet between the boy and the man, but by her best guess it was still several feet too short. "At worst, you'll have to swim for a little bit—but we've got you."

"I can't swim, mister!" The boy's breath sawed in and out as his grubby face crumpled with terror. "I can't swim!"

"It's a good job that I can, isn't it?" That he had the wherewithal to smile at the lad in reassurance suddenly told her everything she needed to know about Galahad Sinclair.

Whatever façade he hid behind genuinely did mask a prince among men with a heart of pure gold.

Her prince.

Who had always been right under her stupid nose.

"In case I have to, I'm going to get ready—all right?" Galahad shifted, never once breaking eye contact with the boy, so that he could carefully remove his boots. Boots that still had his hired skates attached. "You just hold still a few moments more . . ."

Needing to do something to prevent Galahad from plunging into the frigid water and potentially killing himself from the shock of it, Vee wiggled out of her petticoat and set about ripping the soft linen into strips. She knotted them quickly, then picked her way tentatively toward the others so that it could be joined to the whole.

Beneath their feet, the ice creaked ominously as a fresh crack began to form within its surface. Everyone stilled, paralyzed by the filigree of dainty fingers that sprung like twigs on a branch from it. A spider's web of death ready to fail.

"We've not got long," said one of the men quite unnecessarily, the whites of his eyes filled with terror. "It's going to go any second."

That was all it took to make the boy panic, and as he scrambled to grip the shard tighter, it listed.

"You have to keep still!" But Galahad's stark warning came too late, and the shard tilted some more, then flipped over, taking the boy with it.

Without a moment's thought for himself, Galahad sank into the water. Gasping at the impossible cold, but undaunted, he swam toward the flailing boy. Without mercy, the Serpentine inhaled the child, the weight of his many coats sucking him down more effectively than any deadweight could. Before he could be reached, he disappeared without a trace, but that didn't stop Galahad from searching.

Twice he sucked in a lungful of air and dived under, and twice he came up empty-handed.

"Leave it! He's gone!" One of the men beside her tossed their makeshift lifeline out toward him. "This ice is about to fail! You have to save yourself!"

Galahad shook his head and dived deep into the dingy depths once more and then . . .

Nothing.

Nothing but the stillness and silence of the water.

He was gone for five seconds . . . ten . . . fifteen . . . until Vee could stand it no more. She rushed to the edge, ready to jump in herself to save the man she loved, until he emerged like a volcano. Coughing and spluttering but clutching the limp child as he groped for the end of the rope of sodden clothes.

Everything that happened next occurred in a blur.

The pair were dragged from the water, then hauled to safer ground. Two men worked on the boy, pumping the water from his chest while Vee hugged Galahad tight, trying to use the warmth of her body to stop his shaking when he refused to leave the scene.

Anonymous hands draped them all in coats as they watched trickles of water seep from the boy's lifeless blue lips and over his ghostly gray cheeks, while shouts from the shore signaled others had now taken charge.

"Make way for the physician!"

She recognized the reverend's voice.

Recognized the prayer he began to mutter as he knelt beside the prone child and the doctor rolled the boy onto his side.

". . . *Look down from heaven, we humbly beseech thee, with the eyes of mercy upon this child* . . ."

"Come on, kid! Fight!" Galahad's voice was choked now, laced with panic. "Don't give up! Don't you dare give up!"

". . . *save his soul for thy mercy's sake* . . ."

The water ceased spewing from the boy's mouth but still the doctor persisted.

Still the reverend prayed.

After an eternity, the boy coughed and wretched, and while she clung to Galahad crying, he clung to her right back.

Chapter Twenty-Six

Anthony proposed last night, and I said yes!

We are keeping it a secret from everyone until he returns from Scotland with his grandmothers engagement ring . . .

—from the diary of Miss Venus Merriwell, aged 21

Gal couldn't stop shaking.

Whether from the cold or the fear or the ordeal—or an amalgamation of all three—he couldn't say. In all honesty, he was so goddamn cold he was barely capable of speech anyway, so he didn't suppose it mattered.

All that mattered was he was still here, and she was right beside him.

He had a vague recollection of Venus bundling him in a hackney. Of her holding him tight as she rubbed heat into his muscles. Then being draped around her as she hoisted him up the four flights of stairs to his sparse apartment.

"We need to get you out of these wet clothes." She peeled the shirt from his skin and swaddled his top half in the blanket she had stripped from his bed before she set to work on his breeches. "We need to get you warm."

"Where's the boy?" Gal had lost track of him somewhere on the ice. "Did he make it?"

"He's next door. With the reverend and the physician."

"Will he make it?"

"The doctor is coming to see you next, so we can ask him." She grunted as she wrestled the tight kerseymere down his legs, then steadied his quaking hands as he stepped out of it. He heard the sodden fabric slap against his bare floorboards as she tossed the last of his clothing to one side and supposed he should be embarrassed that he now stood as naked as a jaybird before her. But he didn't have the energy. Every last ounce he possessed was being used to keep his body upright. Because for some reason it kept curling as if his muscles had all shrunk or shriveled. Muscles that now burned—except bizarrely with cold rather than heat.

She set to work drying him with a towel while he shivered on the mattress, and then she tucked him into bed while she lit a fire.

"Hot tea!" Mrs. Witherspoon dashed through his bedchamber door with a steaming mug and for the first time in his life he was grateful for it. As he cradled it in his hands, she apologized. "Doctor's orders, I'm afraid, Gal, so it has to be tea not coffee, but it's loaded with honey."

"How's the boy?"

"Doc says he's better than he expected but not out of the woods completely. The cold has sent his body into a bad shock, most definitely, but so long as the plucky Johnny keeps rallying, he thinks the boy might beat it. All thanks to you."

"Johnny? Is that his name?"

"Short for Jonathan, he said." Mrs. Witherspoon smiled. "Jonathan Hicks."

"If he can say his name, that's gotta be a good sign, hasn't it?" He searched Venus's face for confirmation. "Means he's conscious and compos mentis."

"It does indeed." She stroked his cheek, and he leaned into it.

"Mrs. Witherspoon will keep us posted of any change, won't you? And she'll bring more blankets."

She held him tight as soon as the matron left and Gal must have drifted off, because he woke with a start and Mrs. Witherspoon was back. There was a bed warmer near his feet and he was now swaddled in so many blankets and eiderdowns he could barely move. But at least he wasn't shivering anymore.

On the other side of the room, the older woman and Venus were talking in hushed tones. "Doctor won't be long, Vee, but says it's imperative neither patient is left alone. At least overnight, as anything nasty will show itself in the first few hours."

"You watch the boy and I'll stay with Galahad."

"The reverend says that for propriety's sake he'll . . ."

"I said that *I'll* stay with Galahad." Venus's lovely blue eyes and tone brooked no argument. "He's family. And hardly in any fit state to . . . you know . . ."

Unfortunately, Galahad couldn't argue with that because he likely wasn't in any fit state. He suspected his privates had shriveled and shrunk like all his damn muscles had.

Good grief! Had she seen that?

Concerned that she might judge him on it, he was sorely tempted to take a peek beneath the blanket to see how bad that shrinkage was, and if it was bad, to see if he could surreptitiously tease his frozen friend out of hiding. Although to what purpose he had no clue, as he could hardly whip it out to prove he wasn't usually such a disappointment.

"Frostbite in the extremities might be a problem, too." As if she had read his mind, Mrs. Witherspoon gave him something else to worry about. Noticing he was awake, she smiled.

"Do you have any numbness of the nose, fingers, or toes, Galahad?" He touched his nose and wiggled all ten toes to check if he could feel them and shook his head when he did. But his recently oh-so-rampant manhood was another matter entirely. He couldn't immediately feel any sensation in his nether regions, and he could hardly wiggle that to check with ladies present. "Any pins and needles or blisters?" He shook his head again, quietly dying inside at the thought of blisters *there*. "Because if you develop blisters, those blisters could turn gangrenous and we would need to have all of that dead flesh chopped off."

Chopped off!

Oh dear Lord!

Even Vee appeared concerned at that. "I shall check him every half hour, Mrs. Witherspoon." Then she gave her a look. One that told her to shut up and stop scaring him. "There will be no gangrene on my watch."

"No doubt the doctor will want to do a thorough examination to be sure. I'll go chivy him now. I've also got a pot of soup on the stove. I'll bring some over once it's ready as the doctor said we need to warm our hero's insides, too." The matron smiled kindly as she squeezed his arm. "God bless you, Sir Galahad. You saved the day." A compliment that did not cheer him in the slightest now that the prospect of being a eunuch loomed on the horizon.

After Mrs. Witherspoon left, Venus went to stoke the fire. While she did, Gal did a quick, precautionary fumble around what Muldoon called his wedding vegetables to check that they were blister-free and sighed aloud when he realized his groin still possessed some feeling.

Instantly, Venus's head snapped around. "Are you all right?"

"As ninepence," he said as he guiltily let go of his chilled genitals beneath the covers. "Isn't that what you British say?"

"It is." She smiled in obvious relief as she turned back to the fire. "Although I have no idea why."

Venus had left the room while the doctor examined him an hour later, but Gal could sense her hovering behind the door listening. Even so, once the doctor let her back in, she still asked a million questions until she was satisfied he wasn't about to die and followed him downstairs so she could probe some more out of earshot.

He hoped it was all evidence that she cared.

While she was gone, he took the opportunity to leave the bed, which was to be his prison until the morning, to stretch his thawing limbs and grab a shirt from his new wardrobe. He much preferred to sleep naked, but to be naked and shriveled with her sitting by his bed watching him like a hawk had made him self-conscious. He'd feel less vulnerable covered, especially if she intended to keep vigil all night as she had threatened.

Checking first that the coast was clear, he padded quickly across the room and began to rifle in his closet. His fingers found the shirt as the door reopened, and in the absence of anything else to cover his modesty, he used that as she walked through it.

"It seems, miraculously, that despite everything you are indeed as right as nine . . ." He wasn't sure which of them was more surprised by her swift and silent return. Her eyes raked the length of him before they rested, transfixed, on the strategically placed bunched linen in his fists covering his unmentionables. "You are *not* supposed to be out of bed!"

"I know but—"

"You need to stay warm!" From nowhere, the schoolmistress had returned, and for some reason she was furious. "What is the matter with you!" She came at him, magic finger wagging. "What are you thinking?" She gripped his upper arms and shook. "What *were* you thinking! What were you thinking, Galahad, to jump into that water!"

All at once she was crying as she admonished him. Ugly, noisy crying that came from somewhere deep inside.

"You could have died, you idiot!" She pushed him, her face contorted. Wretched. "You could have died, Galahad! *Died!*" A tortured, feral sound came out. Part snort. Part growl. Part scream. She raised her fist as if she was going to hit him with it then pressed it to her mouth fighting for calm. But even that didn't prevent the noisy outpouring of emotion that he had absolutely no clue how to deal with. "You scared the hell out of me!" She lunged and pushed him back against the wardrobe with two splayed hands. "You could have died!"

"I know . . . I'm sorry . . . I . . ." Gal hadn't seen her look this terrifying since the night they had met, when she had flown out of nowhere and pinned him to the ground ready to kill him. Her rage was that visceral again.

Yet this wasn't just rage.

He understood that, despite not knowing what to do about it beyond blink dumbfounded and keep apologizing. "But I'm not dead . . . I'm all right . . . You heard the doctor . . . I'm all right, Venus . . ."

"More by luck than *judgment*!" She screamed that, her hands fisting against his chest. When she drew them away, she stared at them for an age, then up at him shaking them. "But if you ever do something like that again, you will be! Because I'll kill you myself!"

Her eyes were wild with fear and relief. "I almost lost you . . . I've only just realized that I love you and I almost lost you!"

His head spun as his heart rejoiced. "You . . . love me?"

In answer, she threw herself at him, wrapping her arms around his head as she kissed him. It was a hard, brutal, and angry kiss, and yet it was utterly perfect just the same.

Because she loved him and that was everything.

While he kissed her back, her hands checked him everywhere—face, neck, shoulders—clawing at him as she pressed her body against his with animalistic fervor.

Gal's desire was instant.

Hot and all-consuming. The need to have her, all of her, suddenly as necessary as the air in his lungs.

In a tangle of limbs, lips, and longing, they staggered toward the bed as one. When she stumbled, he lifted her rather than delay their journey. Hauling her upward so she could wrap her legs around his waist and plunge her hands in his hair.

He practically threw her on the mattress and then fell on her while they both wrestled with her skirts. When he hesitated, when the significance of the moment finally hit him, she filled her hands with his backside and dragged him close. "Take me . . . Have me . . ."

He almost did.

Almost allowed his desire free rein, but the plaintive cry of his damn conscience was too loud.

"I can't . . ." Gal pulled back, and it was the hardest thing he ever had to do. "Not like this, Venus . . . It isn't proper when . . ."

"There's no need for propriety." She yanked him back, fusing her mouth to his. "I'm not a virgin."

Chapter Twenty-Seven

Anthony did not go to Scotland to fetch my engagement ring. The despicable liar eloped to Gretna Green with the chancellor of the Exchequer's daughter instead! My foolish heart is broken...

—from the diary of Miss Venus Merriwell, aged 21

He withdrew from the bed and, rather than be disappointed or disgusted by her confession, stared perplexed for the longest time. Seemingly oblivious of either his nudity or the impressive jut of his obvious desire. Desire that showed no signs of deflating despite his reluctance to make good use of it.

After an age, he huffed and shrugged. "Neither am I, so I guess we have something else in common, apart from our talent for counting cards and a soft spot for orphans." Then he smiled—sheepishly. "But that wasn't why I stopped." He sat on the mattress beside her with a heavy sigh. "I have a conscience issue."

"A *conscience* issue?"

"I know . . ." He was chuckling—*chuckling!*—when she had just told him her most shameful secret. As if he genuinely didn't give two figs that she hadn't saved herself for marriage as a prim and proper good girl should. ". . . it probably comes as quite a shock to learn that I actually possess a conscience, Venus, but I do, and it won't let me have you till we've squared off what's plaguing it."

He reached for the drawer in his nightstand and retrieved something, his handsome face suddenly serious. "I've been trying to pretend it doesn't matter, that it didn't happen, but this has been bothering me all week. After making the mistake of not telling you about this place when I should have . . ." He gestured around him. "And if what is happening between us is what I hope it is, I want no more mistakes. We can't start our life together with secrets that'll fester. This—us—has to begin with a completely bared hand." He passed her a playing card and waited for her to look at it.

"The queen of hearts?" A very battered queen that had obviously been used a lot.

"*Your* queen of hearts, Venus. The one you still had left in your hand to play when we wagered for buildings." His shoulders slumped in defeat. "The queen that would have trumped my lousy jack if Diana hadn't gone into labor."

Armed with that knowledge, it sat like lead in her hand. "I assumed Dalton had cleared it away."

Galahad shook his head. "I did, and I'll admit I hoped you'd all think that the servants tidied it up and that the outcome of the game would always remain one big mystery." He wiggled his hands by his face. "The rematch that never was. With neither of us truly knowing which of us was the better player." His palms landed heavy on his thighs. "Except I knew. I knew you'd had me before that game ended . . ."

"I shouldn't have distracted you as I did. Seducing you so overtly wasn't fair." Vee winced as she was forced to recall all the lengths she had gone to in order to keep his eyes anchored on her cleavage. "It was tantamount to cheating, and I'm sorry."

He reached for her hand and laced his fingers through hers. "You didn't cheat. You used deflection and artful deception, the same as I did when I took your book. You worked out my Achilles' heel and you exploited that."

"But your Achilles' heel was *me* . . ." Except it hadn't been just his desire for her she had been exploiting. It had been his feelings, she now realized, which she supposed made her no better than Lord Argyll, who had exploited hers so ruthlessly. Used all the flowery words and empty promises it had taken to get her into bed.

He watched the war waging on her expression and smiled. "You did nothing that any professional card player wouldn't have done in a heartbeat, so don't feel bad about it. In a funny sort of way, it's done us a favor. Because now that I am honor-bound to sell you my building, there'll be nothing whatsoever standing in the way of us being together."

Vee didn't know what to say. Didn't know what to think. To do. The hope and longing in his eyes overwhelmed her. The sacrifice he was prepared to make choked her. "But it is your dream, Galahad . . ."

He shook his head. "You're my dream, Venus. Anything else is a bonus." He kissed their entwined fingers, then leaned in to kiss her. Soft, long, and lazy until he smiled against her lips, using just the pressure of his mouth to push her backward. "Now, where were we before my conscience got in the way . . . ?"

Vee had no clue beyond being a melted but confused puddle on the floor. But his sacrifice felt wrong. Unfair. Unfair enough that she tore her lips from his. "I am not sure if that's what I want."

He pulled back, hurt. "You don't want me? *Us?*"

His expression was so tragic, she looped her arms around his neck and kissed him. "I don't care about the stupid building. I only want you—despite all your masks and closely guarded secrets."

"I'm not wearing one now." That was plain as day in his eyes. For the first time she could see everything in them. For the first time in her life, she also saw love. It shone through his desire and burned through the last remnants of her defenses. "I'm not even wearing any clothes, so what you see is what you get. As for the secrets . . ."

Delightfully awkward in his vulnerability, he pulled the covers over his lap. "They're not so much secrets as things I prefer not to talk about. I'm not accustomed to sharing confidences—" He glanced down, as if even admitting that much scared him. "When you're left to fend for yourself, you never show others any weaknesses to exploit."

"You think that I would exploit them?" Seeing as her fingers itched to touch his beautiful body, she allowed them to trace the defined shape of the distracting muscles in his arms. Muscles she knew came from a lifetime of hard work and struggle.

His gaze followed their progress, heating again until the gold flecks in his green irises turned molten. "You've already exploited my desire for you, witch. You already know that I want you so much, I can barely think straight half the time."

"That's not a bad thing." The pads of her fingers learned the contours of his chest, whispering over his nipples to follow the dusting of dark-blond hair that arrowed down his abdomen. She kissed his neck, below his ear, and smiled when his heartbeat quickened beneath her flattened palm. "I rather like witnessing the effect I have on you."

He growled softly as her teeth nibbled the lobe, gripped her hands and shifted position so he could do exactly the same back to her. "And I'm not entirely comfortable relinquishing all control. Or any of it, if I'm honest." By the deep furrow between his brows, it was obvious that admitting this cost him.

She kissed it to smooth it. "Then how am I going to prise out all those deep, dark secrets that you've never told a soul? The sort of secrets a true soulmate should know."

"I like the idea of us being soulmates . . ." His mouth found hers. Did wonderfully sinful things to it. "So how about I play you for them?"

"You want to play cards? Now?"

"It's something I've thought about often." Those golden brows wiggled mischievously. "It's a fantasy that keeps me awake at night. I'd be happy to share some secrets to turn that dream into a reality." His fingertip toyed with the trim on her bodice. "So what do you say? Play me for them and each time you win, I'll answer a question."

"Thoroughly and honestly?"

"There's your proof that I'm honest." He pointed to the discarded queen on the mattress and then took his sweet time raking her body with his eyes. "And I promise I'll be thorough." Yanking the blanket out from under her, he stood, wrapped it around him, and padded to where she'd left her outside clothes. He held her beaded velvet reticule aloft, then shook his head at it as if it was the most ridiculous of fripperies before he removed the deck of cards she had confiscated. "You in?"

"Of course. It suits me to play for deep, dark secrets because I only had the one left, and I've just told it to you." Shame at that secret made her intended bravado fall flat. "If it's any consolation, there was only one man and I've bitterly regretted my stupidity with Argyll ever since, but I thought we were getting married and . . ." He pressed a finger to her lips.

"You grew up in Clerkenwell and I survived the mean streets of Five Points, so we both know that life can be ugly and some people uglier. We all make mistakes while navigating the gutter, Venus. All have regrets, and we all get hoodwinked at some time or another by someone whose motives aren't good." He traced the shape of her mouth then kissed it reverently. "I'm glad he was a no-good, worthless fool—because now I get to be the one you choose to spend forever with."

"Sometimes, Galahad Sinclair, you say the loveliest things."

"I'm feeling all sentimental after all your soulmate talk." He cut the cards and dovetailed the pack together again without his adoring gaze once leaving hers. "But don't let my romantic notions and blatant affection for you fool you into thinking I'm going to let you beat me at cards again, missy, for I can assure you that I intend to be ruthless." Instead of dealing them, he laid the cards out facedown in neat rows on the mattress. "Let's see exactly how good that big ol' brain of yours is at remembering cards once and for all. I take it you know the complicated rules of pairs?"

"*Pairs?* As in the children's parlor game?"

His serious nod made her giggle. "It only needs two players and frankly, it wouldn't be proper for anyone else to witness you losing."

Once all the cards were laid out, he sat back and folded his arms tightly across his delicious bare chest.

"For each pair that you find, Venus, you get one deep, dark secret, and because, apparently, you don't have any secrets worth winning and I've been planning this game for a while in my dreams, for each I find, *you* remove an item of clothing. The overall winner gets to be the one in complete control when we have our wicked way with each other afterward." A fresh bolt of arousal ricocheted through her body at the prospect. "Are those terms acceptable to you?"

"More than acceptable." Any more and she would combust.

"Good. Ladies first."

Chapter Twenty-Eight

After a period of reflection in the wallflower chairs, I have concluded that an older gentleman might make a more suitable mate for me. Not someone so decrepit as to require a knee blanket, pipe, and slippers, but one who is mature enough that he is naturally calmer around the opposite sex. In the way in which a gelded horse is calmer than a hot, young stallion who is prone to foam uncontrollably whenever a fertile mare is close by. And most important, someone who does not hold any power whatsoever to break my foolish heart again . . .

—from the diary of Miss Venus Merriwell, aged 22

It was the third time his fingers had flipped the three of spades. "You should probably know that I've been dreaming incessantly about this since our waltz. You losin' then slowly stripping has caused me to wake up achin' more mornings than I care to count." Galahad had been undressing her with his eyes for the last five minutes, seductively distracting her as they took turns flipping the cards while they memorized them. As the wretch had clearly worked out that his accent had a profound effect on her body, he was exaggerating it in a velvety whisper almost as potent as his touch.

"You haven't won a single pair yet, so . . ."

He smiled cockily as he flipped another three and waved. "Bye-bye, dress."

"I am a stickler for rules, and I think you'll find that as there was no initial caveat in the agreed parameters for this game that you got to choose the item of clothing, the dress remains." But to tease him, she inched up her skirt to reveal her silk-clad leg and slowly peeled her stocking off. She dropped it in front of him, enjoying the way his eyes darkened. "One item of clothing. As agreed."

"And thank you for being the prim schoolteacher, too. I've always enjoyed that . . ." His fingers caressed the exposed skin from her ankle to her thigh while his expression made no attempt to disguise how much he liked what he saw. "Surely, seeing as stockings come in pairs, they both should come off?"

She flicked his hand from her thigh, enjoying herself immensely even though she was torturing them both. "I would refer you again to the aforementioned lack of specific caveats." She turned a new card—the five of hearts—and grinned in triumph as they both simultaneously remembered where the five of spades was. "What secret to prise first?" She tapped her lip. "What happened to The Four Leafed Clover?"

"*Ouch!*" He winced. "Go for the jugular first, why don't you?"

She shrugged. "You failed to stipulate at the start that I should ease you in gently."

"I told you already. It got demolished."

Vee folded her arms, obviously unimpressed with that answer. "You promised to be thorough, so start at the beginning." In case he was in any doubt where the beginning was, she helped him. "Your grandfather died when you were twelve, and . . ."

He blew out a resigned breath. "And within a few weeks of his funeral, Gervais turned up again. I say again with regard to my mother's life, as I'd not yet had the pleasure of meeting him. I suspect he knew that we were both floundering without Grandpa. I was too young to take over the business and my ma didn't have the first clue about how to run it, so when Gervais returned, seemingly oblivious of our recent tragedy and so keen to convince us all he was a changed man, we believed him. He stepped into the breach—or so we thought—and for a while things were better. My ma needed the help and I . . . well . . ." He glanced down to pick at some imaginary lint on his blanket. "I guess I really needed a father."

"But instead, you got Gervais." She knew already that would have been disastrous.

"Yep. We got Gervais all right, and the bastard wasted no time turning a profitable business into one so deep in debt the bailiffs came knocking."

"He lost it."

Galahad nodded. "He mortgaged it up to the hilt behind our backs to release all the capital."

"He could do that?"

"He was still legally married to my mother, so the law was on his side. So in true Gervais Sinclair fashion, once he'd gotten what he came for, he hightailed it out of town and left us to deal with his mess." He flipped a ten and then another, abruptly ending the sorry tale, but she had an inkling it was barely the start.

Rather than take off her second stocking, she lifted her skirt and proffered her leg so he could do the honors. She purposefully missed finding the next pair to give him some time to regroup and find his sinful smile again. Which he did quickly with a pair of aces.

"Bravo, Galahad. Well played." Exactly as she had during their last, fateful card game, Vee ran her fingers along the edge of her bodice as if she was about to undo it to draw his eyes to her breasts, then withdrew them to take off her spectacles instead.

The second they hit the mattress he picked them up, scowling. "If I could make two points of order, Miss I'm-a-Stickler-for-the-Rules. First, these are eyeglasses and not clothing. A necessary medical device like Dalton's false leg. Second, if you're not wearing them, you can't see anything close up . . ." His gaze positively smoldered as he replaced them on her nose. "And I want you to witness absolutely everything I intend to do to you until you are so blinded by pleasure, nothing, not even these prim and seductive corrective lenses, will help you see straight."

"Fair enough . . ." Good gracious, that excited her. So much that her fingers immediately went to the laces of her gown so that he could get cracking on that threat sooner rather than later. Nervous anticipation made her fumble, so he twisted her so her back faced him, and set about removing every pin in her hair first. Once that was unbound, he ran his fingers through it, sighing at the texture before he brushed it to lie over one shoulder.

He kissed her neck as he undid her gown and eased it from her shoulders as if he were unwrapping the most precious gift that he had ever received. Vee was so lost in the moment and the sublime sensations just the gentle press of his lips could elicit, she did not notice that his nimble fingers had also made short work of her stays until they, too, were gone.

"That's cheating."

"Maybe—but I'm oddly at peace with it."

As his lips continued their thorough exploration of her nape, the hands that rested gently on her hips snaked around her middle and slid upward to cup her breasts. She arched against them, her body desperate for his. So ready for his that it hurt. "You are deliberately trying to distract me."

"Again . . ." He punctuated his answer by nuzzling her ear. ". . . guilty as charged."

She shuffled away to prolong the sweet torture, and as he tried to follow her, she held up her finger. "Not until you've paid your penance and given me a secret in return. You did say you wanted none between us . . ."

"Hoisted by my own damn petard." He groaned, rolling his eyes to cover how uncomfortable that prospect made him. "Ask your damn question, woman."

"What happened in between Gervais leaving for a second time and you sleeping rough on the streets?"

"I think that's technically more than one question. In fact, I'd say that's actually several questions all rolled into one, so now who's the cheat?"

"Perhaps—but you can either answer it all in one go, or I shall use my big ol' brain to ensure that you do not win a single pair to remove this last vestige of my clothing . . ." She ran her hands over her flimsy chemise to draw his eyes to her body. "Instead, I shall ask question after question until I know everything your soulmate should."

He stared at the heavens. "Why did I have to fall for the cleverest woman in the world?"

"The longer you deflect, the longer I will make you wait." Vee settled back on her heels. "Which would be a shame when we've got all night . . ."

He grabbed a couple of pillows and punched them into a suitable shape before he settled back against the headboard. "It turned out that Gervais hadn't only mortgaged the business, he'd mortgaged the house, too. With him and all of the capital gone, the banks wanted their money back in a hurry. We got no stay of execution and less than a week after he disappeared, they evicted us. Both the house and the tavern were sold out from under us, and we didn't receive a single cent from the sale."

Vee wrapped her hand around his, wishing she was surprised that Gervais would do such a dreadful thing to his wife and child.

"I knew I'd been left something in Grandpa's will, and I knew that included some cash, but the lawyer refused to release it to either of us as the will stipulated I had to be of age. In desperation, my ma sold all the jewelry Gervais hadn't taken with him, and we used that to rent some cheap rooms on Magazine Street. I got a job in the brewery hauling grain, and for a while we managed to make ends meet."

"I sense a *but*."

"*But* it didn't take long for the damp and cold to affect her health. By the winter of 1818 she wasn't well at all. She had this persistent cough." Unconsciously, he moved his fingers to his collarbone. "No medicine would shift it. By Christmas, it had developed into pneumonia and . . . that was that."

"She died at Christmas?" That explained why he wasn't keen to celebrate it. Why he avoided it like the plague.

"She managed to hang on for most of Christmas Day but . . ." His expression was bleak as he shrugged, the pain swirling in his irises so intense it broke Vee's heart. "I'd spent all the rent money on medicines, and the brewery had fired me for taking so much time off to look after her, so I ended up getting evicted again. Only this time, I had nothing but the clothes on my back and nobody left, so that's how I ended up sleeping beneath the stars alone. Like Billy, I got found quickly by some bad people and learned how to pick pockets, and I did that for two years until I almost got myself killed for picking the wrong one. That's when I realized something had to change or that would be the sum total of my life. Short, pointless, and always at the mercy of someone else."

He fiddled with her fingers. "As I was sixteen on the outside, but nearer sixty on the inside, I blagged my way into another job behind the bar in a tavern in the Bowery. That's pretty much where I stayed, biding my time and saving until I hit twenty-one and could finally claim the bequest from Grandpa's will. Because Gervais knew about it, too, he was there waiting for me. All contrite and convincingly sorry for everything that happened."

"You didn't believe him?"

"Do I look like an idiot, Venus?" He pulled a face of outrage that she could even ask such a thing. "But he always thought I was, so when he told me his harebrained plan to cheat someone else out of what was rightfully theirs, I went along with it. Not because I intended to reap any financial rewards, but because I wanted to make sure that he got what was coming to him. For my mother."

"Revenge is sweet, or so they say."

He shrugged, unrepentant. "He deserved it, and it helped me turn a page. Until I came here, I assumed I'd take the first ship back to New York once I'd delivered him to the authorities. I hadn't factored in a second chance with a family or meeting you . . ." His eyes rose to meet hers, bemused. "Do you remember flattening me that night in Giles's garden?"

"It wasn't a meeting easily forgotten."

"You scared the hell out of me that night, Venus. Not because you seemed capable of killing me . . . but because something about you felt significant. You've always felt significant, and I guess that's why I've always kept you at a longer arm's length than I've kept everyone else. I knew, somewhere deep down, that if I didn't, you'd be my undoing." He lifted her hand to kiss her fingers. "I was right. You are. I adore you." His gaze heated again. "By my reckoning, that's all my secrets told, my soul bared, and yet you *still* seem to be wearing too many clothes. Say adios to that chemise, Venus, and be a gracious loser."

She hadn't lost, she had won, and so much more than a silly game of cards. Even so, Vee stuck out her chin in defiance, making sure she stuck out her bosoms to torment him in the process. "You need to earn it with a pair."

"Oh, I have a pair. The definitive pair, in fact. A pair that cannot be beaten . . ." He eased the fabric from her shoulders, then gently jabbed the newly exposed flesh with his index finger. "You." His other finger touched his own chest. "And me."

"Bravo, Galahad." Emotion made her voice catch. "Well played. I concede."

"So do I." He twirled a finger. "Now put me out of my misery and take that damn thing off." He sat back as if waiting for a show to start.

Emboldened by his obvious desire for her, she stood before she unlaced the front of the chemise, then took her time easing it from her shoulders. The fabric naturally caught above her breasts, and she left it there for a few moments before she shimmied out of it.

Galahad's breath hitched as it puddled at her feet, then came out in one big whoosh. "You're the most beautiful thing I ever saw." Every nuance of his expression told her that he meant that; the intensity of his gaze so visceral she felt it as it skimmed over her curves.

He stood, too, his need for her as apparent below the waist as it was on his face, allowing his palms to explore everything his eyes admired. The gentleness of his caress set her nerve endings aflame. Her nipples puckered, almost painfully, as they awaited their turn to be worshipped. Her earthy moan was involuntary as he grazed them with his thumbs, arching against him as his lips found her neck, then her ear, and finally plundered her mouth.

Neither held back as they kissed this time. Vee didn't have the capacity to stop and certainly did not want to. His skin felt wonderful against hers. Hers felt alive beneath his hands. So sensitive that every brush of his fingertips made her body crave more.

He filled his hands with her bottom to anchor her hips flush against his erection, and when that wasn't enough for either of them, he lifted her again so that she could wrap her legs around his waist before they tumbled back on the mattress in a frenzy of teeth and tongues. Of mutual need and desire.

Of total trust.

Of its own accord, her impatient body shifted position to open in welcome and his instinctively knew the way. Her hips tilted and he stilled. "Do you want children?"

"A house full."

He smiled and reached for her hand. "I'm glad—because so do I. I'm all done with being lonely." That smile turned seductive and wicked. "But I'm gladder that I don't have to keep enough wits about me to be responsible."

He swallowed her surprised giggle with another kiss, lacing his fingers tight through hers as he slid all the way into her, filling Vee so completely, so perfectly that she gasped. Then sighed in utter bliss as he began to gently move inside her.

She smiled up in wonder, instantly losing herself in the intensity of his eyes.

"I've wanted you since the first moment I saw you, Venus." They fit together like a glove. His hardness gliding slowly along the walls of her softness as if he had been designed specifically for her.

He withdrew then slid deeper and she thought she'd died and gone to heaven.

Whatever she thought she knew about the physical joining was not at all what she experienced with Galahad. Her first time had been awkward. Impersonal, bizarrely, and in hindsight not at all right. It had been all about another's needs, another's passion, whereas this was a union of two hearts that wanted to beat as one.

Galahad moved again, his kiss as deep as his body was buried in hers, and she arched against him wanting more. And he gave it to her, until the tiny bead of nerve endings at the apex of her sex sang against the sublime press of his skin. She moaned her appreciation and he swallowed it in a kiss, groaning against her ear as her fingers raked his back and his delightfully pert bottom.

Within moments, there was so much passion, so much need, that it consumed them. Controlled them—yet still he loved her with all that he was. He came undone in her arms as he adored her with his body, denying himself his release until she was writhing beneath him and begging for mercy.

Even then he made them both wait. Both suffer. So that when it happened, and the walls of her body pulsed around his in surrender, Vee was so blinded by pleasure that she couldn't see anything but him as they tumbled, holding hands, into oblivion together.

Chapter Twenty-Nine

Galahad kissed me tonight on Brighton seafront, so thoroughly and so magnificently, I quite forgot how much I've always loathed him . . .

—from the diary of Miss Venus Merriwell, aged 22

"I know we urgently need to expand, and that your solution is simple and has merit, but the more I ponder it, the more I see the benefits of moving the orphanage away from all the temptations and cruel depravity of the city. Besides . . ." She winced. "In hindsight, the only reason I wanted that building so badly was because you chose it over me."

"And the only reason I wanted it so badly was because I got my dream all wrong, so at least consider it as a short-term arrangement?" After the most spectacular few hours of his life, he and Venus were now snuggled up together beneath his fancy new sheets.

"But what about all your meticulous plans for all three buildings? Your stage and the giant, swooping staircase?" Gal had just reiterated his offer to sell her the building for the same bargain price that he had paid for it, had explained that he wasn't the least bit bothered about doing it, and even confessed that thanks to all the unforeseen costs of renovating three buildings to his exacting specifications instead of two, the money would come in handy. Despite all that, for reasons best known to her stubborn and unfathomable self, she was now the one reluctant to be convinced this was the right thing to do. An irony that wasn't lost on him when he considered how much consternation his owning the building had caused in the first place.

"How many times do I have to tell you that my grandpa taught me that the best-laid plans are always adaptable? So I'm adaptable and gladly so. Circumstances change, Venus, and in this case for the better." He could tell she didn't believe him, so he guessed he would have to spend a lifetime convincing her that she was, without a doubt, the best opportunity fate had ever gifted him. "Have it for a couple of years and then sell it back to me when you find a better place to put it." As she rolled her eyes, he came up with another solution. "At least borrow some of my space for a little while."

"Absolutely not. Never a lender or borrower be—wasn't that what your grandpa also taught you?"

Lord, but she was maddening. "Rent it from me then. Mr. Evans hasn't even started knocking down walls on the second and third floors, so it would be just as easy to add a little bit of my building into yours while you look for a pretty new home for your orphanage. Trust me—it takes time to find the right property, and then more time to make it fit for purpose."

"We could borrow a room or two . . . as a temporary solution."

"Hallelujah! We've finally found a compromise on something." He snuggled closer. "And I like the idea of a little bit of me jutting into a little bit of you."

She nudged him for that unsubtle innuendo, then frowned again. "But moving it out of the city also still concerns me." She twisted within his arms to face him, her hair a riot of mussed curls thanks to the exuberance of their lovemaking. His Venus had been as passionate and wanton as her name suggested, and the reality of her in the throes of pleasure had far surpassed all his wildest fantasies.

Within minutes of her first orgasm, she had been ready and quite determined to have another, so Gal had been only too happy to let her take charge in order to achieve it, then had watched in uncharacteristically passive wonder as she had ridden him. Head thrown back in abandon, magnificent breasts jutting proudly, until she came noisily, dragging him right with her. Her enthusiasm had piqued his imagination and given him a few more fantasies about how he could have his wicked way with her. And next time he'd be the one in charge.

Already his body was twitching at the prospect, when by rights it should be exhausted.

"The orphanage relies on donations for survival." She propped herself on one elbow. "Those donations could very well dry up if we move to where the wealthy cannot see us. Here we remind them that we exist. Our location shames them into supporting us."

Gal put aside his lustful thoughts to ponder that. "It's never wise to rely on charity. In business it's always better to be self-sufficient and generate your own revenue."

She gave him one of her schoolteacher's looks. "In case it has escaped your notice, the Covent Garden Asylum for Orphans isn't a business, Galahad."

"It could be."

"Are you proposing we hawk out the children for money? Sell them as indentured servants for profit? Or should we simply scrap all lessons and have them sew sacks or make matches instead?"

"I do so adore your British sarcasm." He dropped a kiss on her outraged nose. "How many times do I need to tell you that you need to stop thinking so small, Venus. Sometimes you need to speculate to accumulate, to scan the horizon for possibilities and adapt to the circumstances." He waved his hand in the air. "Somewhere out there is the perfect solution to your problem. All we need to do is find it."

"Just what I need, another puzzle to solve." She sat up, irritated, and to his delight clean forgot that she was naked.

"I'll find the solution for you, Venus, I promise. I've a knack for making money and I like the challenge of thinking up new ways to make it."

"You'd do that for me?" Her softened gaze did odd things to his heart—but he liked it. Didn't feel threatened in the slightest that she now held that power.

"I'd do anything for you." Because the sight of her bare breasts had tipped his body from just twitching to downright desperate, he jumped out of bed and held out his hand. "But while I ponder how to make your orphanage pay for itself, follow me."

"Where?"

"You'll see." He grabbed the single candle he had lit the second the sun had gone down and tugged her to follow.

"Don't I need clothes?" She pointed to the tangled pile on the floor and quirked one eyebrow when he shook his head.

"I need you just as you are." He led her out into the cavernous expanse of his unfinished apartment. "Because now that we've christened the bed, we need to christen my desk."

"You want to . . ."

"Yes."

"Again?"

"Yes."

"On the desk?"

"Most definitely yes." He turned her by the shoulders until she faced it, then set to work kissing her neck while caressing her delightfully oversensitive breasts. "Might I remind you that I could have died today . . ." But his earthy Venus didn't need much coaxing to be ravaged. Within seconds, she was all for it, and within a minute she was bent over his desk thoroughly enjoying herself while he congratulated himself for being the luckiest man in the world. His future suddenly rosier than he could have ever planned it.

Things were just getting interesting when they heard the commotion from the street outside.

"*Venus! Galahad!*"

He stilled inside her as she stiffened.

"*Vee! Is Galahad alive!*"

"Oh my goodness! That sounds like Olivia!" In a blind panic,

Venus edged him back as she scrambled upright, her hands clutching her bare breasts, her lovely eyes wide as she darted hither and thither, looking for somewhere to hide. “I forgot that I promised I’d be home by five!”

“Relax . . .” His passion deflating, he edged to the window. “The front door’s locked.”

That calmed her, and she joined him, then began to panic all over again as they watched the entire family tumble out of the carriage onto the curb. Jeremiah, Hugh, Minerva. Then Giles and Diana clutching little Gethin. All looking distraught but thankfully all heading up the steps to the orphanage.

Gal sighed in relief as they all disappeared inside it.

“Don’t panic. We’ve got a few minutes to make things look proper.” And heaven help him, Venus would need every one of them. Thanks to his rampant twitching, she looked like she’d been ridden hard and put away wet. Her hair was a wild bird’s nest, and the texture of the leather desktop was imprinted in her flushed cheek. “Let’s get you dressed.”

They dashed back to his bedchamber, but despite all his efforts to instill some calm, she was whirling around like a dervish with a maniacal expression on her face. “They cannot find me like this!” She wrestled with her dress tangled among all the extra blankets Mrs. Witherspoon had brought and that they’d kicked to the floor.

When she finally freed it, the sleeve had become hopelessly knotted in the laces of her stays, but the more she frantically tugged them, the tighter they went.

“Let me do that!” Gal grabbed it, but she slapped his hand away.

“Put your own clothes on!”

That was when the worst happened, and they heard the Reverend Smythe’s booming voice below. “The doctor has reassured us that Galahad will make a complete recovery.” Gal ran to the window, cracked it so that he could hear, and no sooner had he done so than there they all were again. “He’s displaying none of the signs of serious shock, and so long as he doesn't develop a chill in the coming days, there is nothing to worry about."

"Oh my goodness! They are about to knock on the door!" Venus burrowed into her tangled dress. "Don't you dare open it till I'm decent!" Her matted head appeared through the neckhole and her eyes widened some more in horror. "And don't you dare open it until you're decent!" From somewhere beneath all the folds of fabric her schoolteacher's finger emerged to wave at his nudity. "Put that away!"

"The key's behind this brick here." They both panicked at the sound of Tommy Claypole's voice, because that was the precise moment when it became apparent that there would be no knock on the door. The amassed Sinclairs, Standishes, and Peabodys were already coming in and there was nothing either of them could do to stop them.

Figuring that it would be quicker to source a new shirt than the one discarded in the chaos, Gal rushed to his wardrobe and grabbed one as several pairs of hurried feet hit the first staircase.

Venus was mewling now, clearly in a state, and one glance told Gal the jig was up.

They were doomed.

Because her arm had worked its way into her twisted sleeve wrong and was trapped upright, yet still she was futilely trying to do up the laces like some sideshow contortionist.

"Make the bed!"

He threw up his palms at that stupid instruction, because frankly, with his wedding vegetables still in full view and her stays swinging from her elbow, a neat bed wasn't going to convince her family that nothing untoward had gone on in it.

He did, however, yank the bottom sheet from the mattress to wrap around his exposed nethers a split second before everyone arrived in his attic. Then they all, to a man and woman and boy, stopped dead to gape.

Typically, it was Giles who spoke first, already enjoying himself immensely. "I'm glad to see that you are in fine fettle, cousin, and that you found your dip in the Serpentine so *invigorating*."

"This isn't what it looks like." Her trapped arm still at a right angle to her neck and her stays swinging and calling her a liar, Venus tried to explain their state. "You see . . ." She looked to him, hoping he could think of something, and when he shrugged, useless, she tried some more. "Our clothes were drying and . . . um . . . when we heard you outside we . . . um . . ."

Gal exhaled loudly. "This is exactly what it looks like." As eight pairs of stunned eyes suddenly swiveled to him—one additional pair gaped mortified at his perceived betrayal—he smiled. "But it's all right—we're getting married."

"Are we?" Instead of agreeing, Venus gave him a stern look. "Only I do not remember saying yes to your proposal, Galahad Sinclair, or even there being a proposal at all for that matter."

The eight pairs of eyes instantly swiveled back to him, expectant. "Well . . . I . . ."

"You goddamn well better propose, young man, or you'll have me to answer to!" Jeremiah stepped forward aggrieved and all paternal.

"He will." Olivia dragged him back. "And you will desist from using coarse language at such a pivotal moment in Galahad and Vee's long and much-too-protracted romance."

Gal supposed it was pivotal and had been a long time coming.

"Venus Merriwell . . ." He shuffled toward her in his blanket, then dropped to one knee before her. ". . . you have always been the fly in my ointment and the itch I couldn't scratch . . ."

"Didn't I tell you that they were destined for each other," Olivia interrupted, nudging first Minerva and then Diana. "I have *the eye*."

"Shut up, woman," said Jeremiah in a stage whisper out of the corner of his mouth. "This is Vee's moment, not yours!"

Venus sniggered and he did, too, because this was about as unconventional a proposal as their first meeting had been.

". . . from the moment you first flattened me, you've bothered me . . ." He took her hand, and in the absence of a ring kissed her ring finger. ". . . but it turns out that I do love nothing in the world so well as you—isn't that strange?"

"What a lovely thing to say." Minerva sighed.

"It's not his—he stole it from Shakespeare." Giles had always loved the theater. "From *Much Ado* if I'm not mistaken." That earned him a jab in the ribs from Diana.

"It's her favorite," sighed Olivia.

"Don't mind us," said Hugh by way of an apology as he scowled at his mother. "Please continue."

"You'll have to say it quick to get a word in edgewise in this family." Venus stroked his cheek with her free hand, tears in her eyes.

But as he couldn't ask her with her arm in the air, he stood and helped her fix the sleeve. He tossed the mangled stays to one side and righted her distracting spectacles. Then he tugged her into his arms. "So what say you to marrying me, Venus? Not because you have to—but because you want to."

"I want to." She kissed him. "I want you." The next kiss was deeper. "I suspect I always have."

"We are too late for a Christmas wedding, but with some finagling we could have them up the aisle by New Year's. At St. George's, seeing as we are all in town. Madame Devy can make the dress and . . ."

As everyone groaned at Olivia divvying up the errands she suddenly needed run to get them hitched fast, Gal kissed the woman of his dreams. As usual, she ended it before he was ready, and stared into his eyes.

Into his heart.

Into his soul.

"What profound and wise words would your grandpa have to say about all this, Galahad?"

"Oh, I know exactly what he'd say." He tugged her back, laughing. "He'd tell me to go put some goddamn clothes on."

Epilogue

While I am sad to be leaving our cozy little apartment above the club, and all the happy memories we made there, I am beyond excited about the new house and cannot wait to move in. That is, if my vexing husband ever finishes planning where he wants Mr. Evans to put the dratted staircase . . .

—from the diary of Mrs. Venus Sinclair, aged 27

"It's so much smaller than I remember." Vee stood in the center of the dilapidated room, taking it all in while the memories assaulted her. Some were good, most were bad, but they were all part of who she was regardless, so she embraced them all.

Minerva frowned at the thick layer of dust covering the tatty windows. "It's so much more dingy than I remember. But I see the stain is still there." She pointed to the big, brown smudge on the cracked ceiling. "You'd have thought after ten years the landlord would have had the roof patched."

It had been a decade since they'd left these depressing rooms in Clerkenwell, and it felt like a lifetime. For nostalgia's sake, they had come to visit it one last time together before it was all torn down.

"It's every bit as dreadful as I remember, so good riddance to it."

Diana had always been the least sentimental of the three of them. "If somebody wants to fetch me a hammer, I'd happily knock the place down myself right now. Better still, I'm going to do some digging on our old landlord as he deserves shooting for charging desperate people rent for this!" Her middle sister still worked at *The London Tribune* and still crusaded against all the wrongs in the world. A happy marriage, two children, and a thriving Shropshire estate hadn't dampened that passion. Only nowadays, two other anonymous crusaders helped her write the Sentinel's feared column while the one-legged reprobate Dalton did the legwork.

"I think what you are doing with the place is so fitting, Vee." Like her, Minerva had let it all go. It was such a blessing to see her older sister so happy after all the years she had struggled to keep the family afloat and raise Vee at the same time. It had taken a few years, but she had finally picked up her art again, and instead of carving woodcuts for a pittance, Minerva now painted landscapes in between raising her own three boys. She'd even sold a few—or rather Payne, the Standishes' loyal but disobedient butler, had sold them behind her back when she refused to believe her efforts were good enough. "A school is exactly what the poor children around here need."

"The three of us would never have escaped here if we couldn't read." Which was sort of the truth. Reading had always been her escape and she was still passionate about passing on her first love, as well as opportunities, to those who had so little.

But altruism wasn't the only reason that Vee had purchased this building the second she had learned that it was on the market. She had done it to close the door on that part of her life once and for all. Turn all her lingering and resentful memories of her father into something positive.

A better final memory to replace the one he had left her with.

They never did find out what had happened to Alfred Merriwell. For all the sisters knew he could be either dead or alive, but whichever it was, they didn't care. They had all thrived despite him and to spite him, so in that respect, with hindsight, he had done at least one thing properly.

"Can we go now? Only this place gives me the shivers." To prove that, Diana shuddered.

They left together arm in arm, all quiet and lost in their own thoughts as they descended the stairs. Outside, waiting patiently for them, were all the people who mattered.

Hugh and Giles stood chatting, still the best of friends that they'd always been, except nowadays they weren't outdoors being scandals, but indoors discussing crop yields and newfangled farming methods. Jeremiah and Olivia, the matriarch and patriarch of their oddly blended untraditional family, were bickering, seemingly ageless. The only clue that any time had passed was a few more distinguished silver streaks in Jeremiah's black hair and some discreet wrinkles on Olivia's wily face.

The Reverend Smythe now leaned on a walking stick, though his jolly, naughty smile was as vibrant as ever. Vee saw him less nowadays. Since his wife had convinced him to retire, he only visited the orphanage once a week, but everything she and Mrs. Witherspoon did was still very much based upon his original vision, even in its spacious new premises in the leafy village of Hanwell just outside the city.

Galahad had found that new oasis for them, exactly as he had promised, and thanks to his brilliant solution to all their financial woes, the orphanage now funded itself. As much as it pained her to admit it, it had made perfect business sense not to sell her building to him, but to use it as collateral to buy the orphanage a 25 percent share in The Round Table. Which meant that a quarter of his club's lucrative profits winged their way to Hanwell every month and saved unloved little boys and girls like he had been from the depravity of the streets. Those profits had been so good, she had also been able to buy up this building on the back of it.

Her husband, of course, was busy working. Issuing instructions to the crew he had hired to demolish this old building ready for their new school to rise from the ashes. Galahad being Galahad, he had no end of plans for the place and was still thinking up more on the hoof while his devoted assistant Billy Tubbs jotted them down beside him.

As if Galahad sensed her, he looked up, and as always Vee lost herself in his emotive green eyes for a moment. "And where, pray tell, are our twins?" Because of course she would be cursed with twins. Without thinking, she moved her hand to her distended belly, and she sighed, wondering if the enormous size of it so early in her pregnancy already confirmed that a second set was nestled inside. Her own fault, she supposed, for always wanting a house full of children to love. When she wished that, she forgot to stipulate to fate that she hadn't intended to have them all at once, but such was life.

Nobody could plan for every eventuality. Not even Galahad.

"In the carriage. Playing cards with all their cousins and the Claypoles."

"And you thought that was wise? Leaving impressionable minds with *them*?"

He shrugged, chuckling, the silky sound of it still giving her wayward body ideas after five years of marriage. "I think you're overestimating our darling daughters' abilities to cause mayhem in a confined space and under-estimating Tommy Claypole's abilities to outwit them."

"I wouldn't trust our two troublesome little girls as far as I could throw them. But then again I wouldn't trust the Claypoles, either." Not that she could throw a Claypole nowadays. The pair had grown like beanstalks, and after years of working at The Den and The Round Table, they had ceased being gangly and were now both built like brick walls.

"Are you ready to go?"

Vee took his arm and stared at the exciting horizon ahead rather than back at her past. But she couldn't resist one last peek at where the Merriwell sisters had come from. One last look at the shabby streets and all the flotsam and jetsam they were once a part of. As a tear pricked her eye, she swiped it away, proud of how far they had come. Of all that they had overcome to get to where they were now.

"I'm ready, Galahad." She smiled at Minerva and Diana, not only her sisters, but the two women in the world who she most admired. "It's time to turn this page and say goodbye."

Acknowledgments

Now that my Merriwell Sisters series is finally finished, it seems fitting to thank everyone who played a part in its journey. First and foremost, those thanks go to my little family of five, who make it all worthwhile. However, a special mention has to go to my husband, Greg—the long-suffering Mr. H—who never fails to believe in me even when I frequently don't believe in myself. He spurs me on when the imposter syndrome strikes and makes me tea when I'm banging my head against the table because I don't know what to write next—things that are almost weekly occurrences! I appreciate his unswerving support—despite the fact that he has annoyingly categorized and numbered all the different phases I go through whilst writing a book and I frequently want to throw something at him when he nods sagely and says irritating things like "You're in classic Phase 4!"

I'd also like to thank my wise and wonderful agent, Kevan Lyon, who has championed this series from the outset and has advanced my career exponentially as a result. Thanks also go to St. Martin's Publishing Group, who have been a dream to work for and who have given all three of my Merriwell books the most gorgeous, standout covers. And while I will always be grateful to my former editor, Jennie Conway, for acquiring the series, I am especially grateful to my new editor, Sallie Lotz, who picked up the baton seamlessly and has been an absolute joy to work with. I am so looking forward to collaborating with you on the next series, Sallie!

I have been blown away by all the love my Merriwell Sisters have received on social media and from all the bookstores who have their stories displayed upon their shelves. I am so grateful to every single reader who has bought or borrowed one of my books over the years. Writing is such a solitary profession that every little like, comment, or photo lets me know that all the hours I spend thrashing out a story behind my desk are hours well spent. You all remind me that I am not only living my dream but that I also have the best job in the world.

Finally, I would like to thank the Romantic Novelists' Association here at home in the UK. I stumbled across this wonderfully supportive organization at the start of my writing journey in 2015, and I cannot say enough good things about it. Thanks to its eclectic membership it is the font of all knowledge, a mentor and a counselor and a safe space to commiserate and celebrate the crazy roller-coaster ride that is writing romance. It has given me a community to belong to, filled with people like me who have characters' voices in their heads screaming to get out. It has also blessed me with some of my very best friends in the world—they all know who they are—and that is worth its weight in gold. The RNA also proudly champions a genre that is beloved by millions of readers across the globe and yet is consistently dismissed by those who ignorantly believe that if a story involves love and human relationships and ends happily then it cannot possibly be "worthy" literature at all. This proud author in the genre begs to differ and solemnly promises to be a faithful and shameless purveyor of happily ever afters for the rest of her life!

About the Author

Nicholls Photography

When VIRGINIA HEATH was a little girl, it took her ages to fall asleep, so she made up stories in her head to help pass the time while she was staring at the ceiling. As she got older, the stories became more complicated, sometimes taking weeks to get to the happy ending. Then one day, she decided to embrace the insomnia and start writing the stories down. Twenty-seven books and three Romantic Novel of the Year Award nominations later, and it still takes her forever to fall asleep.

Virginia lives in London with her long-suffering husband. When she isn't furiously writing rom-coms fueled on too much English tea, she likes to travel to far-off places, shop for things she doesn't need, and be dragged around the streets by her devoted Labrador, Trevor.

If you want to find out more, check out her website, www.virginiaheathromance.com, join Virginia Heath's Headstrong Hellions Facebook group, or follow @virginiaheathwrites on Instagram.